Tears of the Violin

by

Alexandria May Ausman

Book cover illustration by Alexandria May Ausman
Editor: Jon M. Ausman

Library of Congress Control Number: 2024908863

ISBN: 978-1-963335-11-8 (ebook)
ISBN: 978-1-963335-10-1 (paperback)

Published By:
Ausman & Cousins LLC
1700 North Monroe Street
Suite 11, Box 284
Tallahassee, Florida 32303-0501

For author interviews: ausman@embarqmail.com

Das Kaiser Haus Series

The Collar King Series

The Psycho Series

Metallic Burden (Chapters 75 to 83)

27 Masters Series

Book 3 Characters: Tears of the Violin

Aara: a silver collar turned black collar
Altergott, Dr. Reese: a clinical psychiatrist
Annette: a Haus black collar
Ben: a deceased silver trainee
Bladrick: a deceased Elder of the Haus
Byron: a Haus Dominant
Cary: a black collar door guard
Chenowith: a deceased child molester
Christian: the anger and lust shard
Christian Axel: a Haus Dominant, the Priceless
Claus: an Elder of the Haus
Cora: a FemDom of the Haus, the Fur Queen
Debbie: Meine Liebe's sexual psychopathic and sadistic mother
Der Goldene Hund: the Voice or the Boss shard; the Conscious shard
Der Makellos: German Shepherd named "The Unblemished"
Dieter: a black collar stable hand
Edger: killed in arson fire at Straußenfarm
Egon: Haus seduction Master and trainer
Eric: co-leader of FBL Club
Felicity: a lamb
Felix: a decease black collar
Friedrick: a Haus Dominant, friend of Byron
Fritz: a young Haus Dominant

Geraldine: a hard working lamb that cooks for Maxximillian

Geraldine: a deceased silver trainee

Gerard: a deceased sadistic stepfather to Christian Axel

Ghazi: a silver collar turned black collar

Gretta: a Haus FemDom, the Silk Queen

Grisham: a deceased Haus Dominant

Hermann: a friend of Peter

Jakob: a Haus Dominant

Jonas: an Elder of the Haus

Julius: a deceased Haus Dominant

Justus: a High-born Dominant, brother of Xavier

Karsten: a Haus FemDom

Kay: co-leader of the FBL Club

Kilian: an Elder, psychiatric rehabilitation counselor

Kloe: Marc's big sister, the name of Marc's lamb

Lambs: Abelard, Annette, Geraldine, Milo, Ryker

Leif: a painter of portraits

Leighherz, Dr.: the Haus dentist

Leo: an Elder of the Haus

Lucus: a Haus Dominant, a royal

Mad Max: the sadistic shard of Maximillian, aka the Heart and Judgment

Mad Maxx: husband of Meine Liebe; a Haus Dominant

Mad Maxx: the masochistic shard, aka the Brain and Guilt

Magnus: a first floor Haus Dominant

Malfred: a Haus Elder

Marc: a Haus black collar

Matz: a first floor Haus Dominant, a loan shark

Max: the Soul shard

Maximillian: the submissive name given to Christian by Peter

Maximillian: the seductive shard, aka the Libido

Maxximillian: the submissive adopted by the Elders

Meine Liebe: submissive and spouse of Mad Maxx

Oswin: a first floor Dominant

Peter: a Dominant of Der Kaiser Haus; best trainer of submissives

Rolf: a Haus Dominant

Roland: a first floor Haus Dominant, a violinist

Rudolph: black collar Master of stables

Russell: a switch and sadist, spouse of Debbie

Ryker: a deceased Haus trainee

Vagnar, Dr.: a clinical psychiatrist

Valitin: a first-floor Haus Dominant

Prologue

Book three of the Collar King series finds that Mad Maxx's flock of lambs are growing larger by the minute. It seems that everyone has the Maxx Madness. All around the first and fourth floor hearts that once were cold beat with fresh fervor. The young Priceless Dominant seems to be leading everyone he touches right to their dreams.

For only the price of giving a name, and of course shouldering the responsibility of caring for the one that will give you all they have; anyone high or low born can find the green fields of happiness. Except for the poor cursed shepherd himself.

Everyone knows that Mad Maxx has been diagnosed with schizophrenia. No one doubts he has come by the illness honestly. He has a long history of abject subjugation, torture, and abuses of the most disgusting kinds.

Yet, despite the chaos inside his head, his twisted perceptions are starting to make sense to some of the residents of the Das Kaiser Haus. They are starting to question the world they have always assumed to be just and righteous.

Some are even asking themselves if what they do is not 'immoral, criminal and cruel.' Others are working hard to prevent a revolution. Is it all this turbulence real or just the delusions of a severely mentally ill young man?

Mad Maxx demonstrates that sometimes, madness is more reliable than sanity in a world where nothing is ever what it appears to be.

Language in italics is a conversation between the adult male Master Mad Maxx and his female submissive Meine Liebe.

Chapter 15:   The Lost Little Lambs

Matz's expression became one of panic. "Wait, Maxx, I need more time. You didn't give me fair warning damn it."

I glared at him. "Sixty seconds, Matz. Make up your mind motherfucker. Take it or leave it. I am not putting up with this arguing anymore."

He sat there as if frozen in the spot as his clock ran out. I let out my breath. I was more than a little grateful than when push came to shove, the man was all mouth and no action. That tension of worrying that he intended to become nothing more to me than the regular customer was most concerning. I wanted to believe Matz, despite his stupidly sexually assaulting me while drunk, was deep down better than all the others I had ever been cursed to know.

I reached out my hand palm up with a bitter smile. "Hand over that three hundred, brother. You forfeit the money. You were offered the service but refused. There will not be another chance. That you can be assured."

Matz snorted while staring at the bottle of lube on his lap. "Get on all fours on the couch. I will take you from behind. If you treat me like the dog, I return the favor of it."

I was startled at that. "Huh? What did you say Matz? I surely hallucinated just now. I swear I heard you say to take the submission stance and endure you advances."

He raised his eyes to glare at me with fury in his expression. "You heard me just fine Maxx. You can say it fancy as you like. I said I am going to fuck you. You won't give me any kindness then I don't desire to treat you as anything more than the sperm pocket in return. You can have the money when I get my service completed."

I frowned at that then shrugged, "Fine. Hurry up though. I need a shower after then I have another appointment before attending the customer tonight." I began to remove my jacket and undo my breeches as Matz stood up to clear a spot for me to take the position he requested.

Matz growled, "You really are a worthless whore. To think I was in love with you. Ha. Who the fuck could desire one without any more respect for themselves than to take any cock without any care."

I stopped my preparation and shot him a hateful look. "I will have to ask you to shut your mouth at this point, Matz."

He smiled with evil in his expression. "Why is that Maxx? Did I hurt your feelings by telling the truth of it?"

I grinned back with wickedness. "Nein Matz. The sperm pocket has no heart. Isn't that what you said? In any case, you didn't pay the fee I demand for speaking derogatorily to me during intercourse. You paid for penetration only. You want to feel better about yourself for the cruelty you show me, then you will pay me for it like everyone else. After all, I don't have any respect for myself, and take any cock without care, ja?" I got on the couch as he requested.

Matz scoffed but kept his mouth shut as he took his place of mount behind me. I waited patiently as possible for him to gain his erection. I admit it took all I had not to turn around and punch him in the mouth during Those minutes. I confess I was more than a little pissed at him. It was not because he was taking the service but over his immature attempts to make me feel less for doing the job he talked me into doing in the first place.

Matz appeared to have difficulty getting himself to the point of penetration. I realized his anger had gotten the best of him too. It's obvious that stupid sonofabitch had managed to convince himself, as a few others had in the past, that despite me being the straight man he was the exception to my truthful preference in lovers.

He acted as if somehow he was above all the others that had and would pay for the privilege of taking their pleasures from my flesh. Well, the reality he had managed to avoid had come to him at last.

I nearly got up assuming this wasn't going to happen when after another five minutes Matz still had not started his intercourse service.

He yelped out, "I am almost there. Don't you move Maxx. I want what I paid for."

I groaned in frustration. "Then get to it Matz. I am not going to sit here on my hands and knees all night motherfucker. You are wasting time again. This is starting to really piss me off. Hey, you better not forget that lube either. I mean it cocksucker."

Matz bellowed, "This time I tell you to shut up. You are making it harder for me to find my interest God dammit. I got the fucking lube right here. Stop nagging. You sound like my mother with your constant reminding me of what I already know. That is a real killjoy. I won't forget it if I ever get to where I can use the shit. If you would be a little decent and help me out this would go faster you know."

I shot a furious look over my shoulder. "Pay me for it, then I aid you. Otherwise, it is your problem asshole."

He blew out his breath. "Fine, I pay you first thing in the morning when I collect from Fritz. Now get me the fuck up Maxx. This is never going to happen without a little extra thrill."

I scoffed, "Nein. Money up front, brother. You said I am not to ever work on credit. You pay me tonight or the only thing I put up with from you is the intercourse."

Matz yelled out as he grabbed my waist and ripped down my undone breeches, "You are such a cold hearted dick, Maxx. Have it your way then. You won't be decent, then neither will Matz. I let out a loud vail of agony as he rapidly prepped, then slammed into me with a single violent thrust.

I grabbed one of the fancy pillows from the arm of the couch and gagged my mouth quickly. I was going to be damned if Matz would get the pleasure of knowing that his brutal mount was painful to me. He threw the power to his prodding my backside making that pillow a truthful dignity saver.

I gritted the nubs that used to be my teeth and did my best to think of other things. Matz moaned and panted in ecstasy appearing to take forever in his obtaining my favor. I had to assume he was purposely avoiding reaching orgasm in an effort to "get the most bang for his buck." *Master Maxx laughed bitterly, and I joined him, at that most dark humored statement.*

That said when a good ten minutes had passed, he took a rest without breaking his couple with me. That caused me to pull the boy's face out of my pillow gag full of the fury.

Understand Meine Liebe, there is nothing we can do about a customer taking a bit to reach their apex. Everyone is different in how long they can hold out naturally. Not to mention, enjoyment of what they paid for is their right.

However, what Matz did by resting his thrust was, without a doubt, a flagrant abuse of his privilege to my intercourse service. He knew I needed time to prepare for another appointment (that dinner and tryst with Leo that was none of his business). He was trying to punish me for standing up for myself and not allowing him to take more than his fair share.

I turned my head over my shoulder and shouted out angrily, "Matz, you finish this indignity or so help me when you are sleeping tonight I will sneak home and cut off your balls. That would solve the arguing between us driven by your so called sex drive when you no longer have one."

Matz reached out and grabbed my shoulders draping himself over the boys back as he whispered in my ear, "Thank you for demanding that I cum. It was not the sexy way I hoped to hear it from you, but it will do for my fantasy." He kissed my ear causing me to shout out angrily and buck to knock him off.

My struggling to end his nasty affections caused the man to become enthralled. Before I could get away, just as before when he took without paying when he raped me, he lifted off my back rapidly and grabbed the boy's waist digging in. His resumed his harsh thrust, holding on so tightly I couldn't break free. Within only moments after that horror scene, he wailed out that he was about to orgasm at last, damn him.

I buried my face into the pillow as he yipped and yelled out, spasming with vigor in his apex. I swear to God I wanted to kill that bastard so bad, I was almost certain I wouldn't be able to resist letting Christian take the wheel.

Mad Maxx padded my shoulder with an expression of pity. "You will be able to rest soon Brother Maximillian. Stay calm. Mad Max will take over in a moment. This nightmare is almost over. You do us proud."

I sighed, "As you say Mad Maxx. It will be over for a bit. This cocksucker will return and next time he will pay more money. Once they get the taste they never stay satisfied. Too much thrill in their ability to subjugate one they believe stronger than themselves. Like Peter and Kilian, ja?"

Mad Maxx smiled. "Der Hund says I am the intelligent shard, but Maximillian you rival me with that bit of insight. I agree with you that Matz is now a genuine problem. The man is useful to our continued survival so we must endure him. That said, he is not the truthful black heart. Merely misguided, low esteemed and lonely. That can be fixed. I will work on a plan to end this situation before it gets further out of hand."

Mad Max growled out in irritation, "I can end it right away. When that fucker gets off the boy, I will go to the closet and get that cane. A quick flash of that blade and no more issue with Matz. I could use the practice with surgery, and he needs to have his lust culled."

Christian chuckled with evil, "Ah. Now that sounds like a party. Sign me up for that."

Mad Maxx shook his head. "De-sexing Matz is not the answer Mad Max. We will remove him from our list of customers peacefully or not at all. I demand all you keep your hands off that idiot. If he turns on us then all is lost for the lambs. Mad Max you better remember what I say. Der Hund made you Father of the flock you know. If

Maximillian cannot make the money, the children pay with their flesh and lives."

Mad Max looked at his boots. "Shit. This sucks. I want you to know I hate you and you too Maximillian. Max, I think I hate you the most. Christian, uhm, I don't hate you, but I do strongly dislike you."

Christian grinned with his fiery eyes lighting up. "Aw, how sweet. The true schwuler among us has affection for me. I am truly touched brother. Why don't you come over here and let me give you a nice hug, around your fucking throat."

Mad Max snapped up his gaze, his expression full of disgust. "You touch me, and I will shatter your ass, motherfucker. Go ahead and try it. If you think you are man enough, cocksucker." The sadistic shard started to make a run at the anger shard.

Max, who is usually calm and happy, suddenly grew so big he nearly took up the entire wheel room with his size. "Stand down, you bastards. There shall not be arguments among the Brothers. Der Hund gave strict orders to work together or find yourselves shattered," his voice vibrated in the boy's causing him to reach up and cover them with a loud groaning.

Matz assumed I was trying to block out his sounds of excitement. That made him laugh with much bitter humor. He teased that I would need to "get over" my disliking to hear him cuming since he intended to do it loudly and often. I winced as he reared back and slapped my bare ass just as his ability shrank away breaking his couple.

He plopped down on the couch behind me blowing out his breath loudly as he pulled up his pants to cover his shrinking cock. "Damn, I feel like a new man already. Nothing like cleaning out the pipes to put a hitch in my step and smile on my face."

I got off the couch and pulled up my breeches without bothering to button them. I didn't hesitate. I rushed for my bathroom in silence and with my head down. I was doing my best to keep him from viewing my look of disgust. I would be damned if he would have evidence that his using me for his sexual thrill had bothered me even though it did. I was hell bent for him to believe that his intercourse was not any different than any other I had to endure in my job as the prostitute. He paid me, and his money was as good as anyone else's, right? Ja, that is what I told myself.

Too bad even this idiot didn't buy that lie. I really thought he was different, but Matz turned out to be human. It was my childhood's fantasy that he was helping me survive for completely honorable reasons. I should have known better than that. No one does anything for another unless there is something in it for them. Matz was aiding me because he wanted a lover, not a brother.

That reality was never going to change. I would have to accept it and take his lustful interests or lose everything that I hoped to obtain, like the freedom for the little silvers for starters.

I admit it was most difficult to hide my disappointment in him from him, but impossible to keep that secret from me. I barely got into the shower to wash away his foul seed when I broke down into tears of despair, shame and hopelessness. Life was just so fucking cruel. There never seemed to be an end to the limits of indignity I had to face with any and every one I ever encountered.

I emptied out my inner pain through my eyes then got out of that tub feeling less depressed than when I first entered. Nothing like a good cry to clear out the bullshit that collects in one's soul. ja? Thankfully, I had my Leo to help balance out the scales of inequality of my life. Thinking of his loving embrace helped get me over that dark moment in my early life as the Haus prostitute.

I dressed quickly moaning in frustration when I realized that the single outfit I had that fit was starting to get rather smelly. I made a mental note that in the morning I would pack up all the clothing the Vampire gave me and mind his orders to return them with correct sizes pinned on each.

Like it or not I needed fresh material to cover the boy's flesh. The creepy long jackets, waist coats and lacy black breeches Jonas insisted I wear were better than walking around in clothing that had become the germ factory of foul odors. I gave Felicity a kiss and tucked her into bed just before I left my bedroom to head for the arms of my lover Leo.

I quietly closed the door and headed with speed for the exit. I didn't wish to speak to Matz any more than I had to for the rest of the night at the very least. He was sitting on the couch writing in his notebook as I flew past him nearly in a run.

He cleared his throat and spoke loudly but didn't look up from his notes, "You need to be back by eight thirty, Maxx. Osvin's final night this week requires we remind him of his next rotation, and he needs to get a good look at that menu for the future. Also, tomorrow after you finish with Peter's lesson, you need to report to the Haus dentist. You have the appointment for assessment. I need you to bring the man's estimate of what fixing that nightmare you call a mouth will cost us. Do not attempt to shirk the dentist. He has already been paid for the service. You miss then we lose the money. I don't think you desire to toss away that which took so much from your soul, ja?" he shot a look of seriousness at me.

I stopped my rapid retreat and stared at the floor avoiding his gaze. "I told you I neither desire to see the dentist nor throw away money on such a trivial thing as the caps and bridges."

Matz snorted then stated in the sternest of voice tones, "You have no choice in this case, Maxx. I am your business partner. It is my job to find the clients and keep the protection in line. You will mind me or be sorry for it. Those ugly choppers lower you value to the customer. You are going to submit to the dentist and allow him to fix them and there will be no further arguments about it. The

13

prostitute must appear the fantasy, Maxx. You will care for your teeth, hair, and skin with as rigorous a regiment as you do the hygiene of shaving, and cleanliness. That pretty face, beautiful physique, tight ass and an attractive mouth are your bread and butter. You must take care of the product with the finest of care or you will end up sucking cock for pennies instead of thousands in an abbreviated time. I will set up a schedule to get your maw fixed and time for the workouts to maintain those sexy muscles of yours. Again, no debate will be allowed. I have decided you are not eating enough either. I have contacted Geraldine. She has agreed to cook three full meals a day. I demand you come home to take your medication and grant that lamb the respect of enjoying her hard labors for a scheduled breakfast, lunch and dinner. There will be no excuses. Furthermore, after tonight, you will report to this apartment for naps throughout the day. That lack of sleeping is taking its toll on you. You look like shit. That will not bode well for future sales, and I will not stand for it any longer. Now, if you desire to argue that I am being unfair, then be ready to find yourself reported to Peter and Jonas for it. I am not playing around with you anymore Maxx. You obviously do not give a damn about you, so I will assume the slack of that most important job." He crossed his arms appearing to be ready to fight if I dared to complain about anything he said.

I dropped my head and nodded. "As you say Matz. I see you at eight-thirty." With that I took off out the door feeling like less of a free Dominant and more like Matz's collared submissive.

I hurried down the hallway for the stairwell. I felt insecure and frightened. All of us shards were in counsel trying to figure out why we had been incapable of standing up for the boy when Matz bullied us like that. I had never been afraid of Jonas or Peter since breaking my collar, well other than getting sent to Heslach. Why the hell is he invoking their names in his reading me the riot act that sent my heart to beat with terror? It was confusing to me.

As I hit the steps, I realized it was over that bullshit Byron told me about Gretta and Kilian looking to recollar me. If my father or the Vampire turned on me, then that bitch would invoke the law of incompetence which would ban me from breaking the metal.

The fear of becoming the Priceless pleasure submissive once more made the blood in my veins turn to ice. I couldn't allow such a horror to occur. I decided, like it or not, it was best to mind those with power over me until I could finally get out the front door to medical school. Then I would run like hell and never look back.

I was about to turn the wheel over to my brother Mad Max when I spotted Lucus leaned up against the wall on the fifth floor of the stairwell. He was writing in his book named after me, but I could tell he was watching my approach using his peripheral vision.

I stopped my climb, scoffing loudly. "Do you ever stop hounding me? Perhaps you are expecting I will jump from the banister, and you will miss out hearing my screams on the way down?"

Lucus looked up with a startle. "Huh? Oh, my Gott. You are not suicidal again, are you?"

I rolled my eyes at that. "Oh, fuck off Lucus. I was being sarcastic idiot. What the hell do you mean again? I never have been suicidal in my life, fool. I am trying to survive, not die. If that is what I wanted, there are plenty around here willing to make that dream come to truth for me, ja?"

He narrowed his eyes. "Okay, if you say so Christian. I suppose drinking bleach or being caught midair by your leash when Felix still wanted you alive was merely a cry for help. I could list a few other incidents where I wonder if you had decided to give up the fight, but I don't think you need to be told of your own mind. You are more than aware that you are telling a lie."

That made me angry. "You think you know everything don't you, Lucus? Well motherfucker, if you are so fucking sure of my actions and future, tell me something about me that I don't know. There is a rumor that Gretta will see me re-collared. What is your bet on that motherfucker? How are the odds stacked, for or against me?" I crossed my arms with fury in my eyes.

He rubbed his forehead and groaned. "I don't think you wish to know what I forecast on that possibility Christian. I don't desire to see you taking another chance that a black collar guard will catch you mid-air. Besides, you have beaten many of my predictions in the past, maybe you will outfox the powers that be on this one too. Nothing is written until it is."

I snorted at that. "You know Lucus I am really starting to hate you. I think the odds of your seeing the summer this year are shrinking fast. Do you believe it wise to go poking at the desperate like you do? Perhaps it is you with the death wish here."

Lucus glared at me, "Are you threatening me Christian?"

I smiled with wickedness as I nodded and Mad Max took the wheel. "Ja, which is exactly what I am doing. You need me to be clearer? I apologize for rudely being so vague then. I thought you said you were the learned man. Let me rectify that error by stating it in terms that even the baby could understand. You stop following me or I will be forced to put out your eyes. Is that better? You getting me this time?"

Lucus dropped his gaze to the floor with suddenness. "You cannot tell me what to do Christian. I have the right to sit in the hallways and stairwells without fear of another injuring me for it. Who do you think you are to dare to say such a thing to me? Are you aware I could see you put to the yard with only a single word?"

I pretended to tremble and behave as if afraid with much drama. "Oh, my Gott. Please Master Lucus. I beg your mercy. I didn't realize your powers. Allow me to apologize for my insolence toward your most superior person." I pretended that I was going to drop to my knees but instead I bowed as I flipped him the bird with an evil smile on my lips.

Lucus growled out, "You are a vulgar cad. I must wonder why I have bothered with you all this time. Whatever happens to you, there is no doubt you deserve it."

I chuckled as I pushed my way past him. "I don't know why you bother me either. I am glad we are in agreement that you need to stop it immediately. I would bid you good day, but I wouldn't wish you to call me the liar once more. I really don't care what kind of day you have. In fact, I hope the ones you have left are limited in number." I resumed my climbing the staircase.

Lucus yelled out behind me, "Kiss my ass, Christian."

That made me giggle all the way to Leo's apartment. That man called me the crude one. Yikes, I thought he was the gentleman but screaming that out for all the Haus to hear was most low brow and rude, you know? *Master Maxx laughed loudly. The more I thought of that fancy, king guy Lucus yelling out that insult like a common trucker, the more I laughed too. So much for cultured manners.*

I walked to Leo's door watching the Vampire's apartment and Kilian's door with much fear. Had a mouse broken wind at that moment, your Master likely would have jumped right out of his skin. I had enough of the drama in one day to do me several lifetimes. I hadn't slept a single night in days and my stomach was aching with hunger.

18

You can say I was beyond miserable and a tad more than irritated. A big dose of affection from my lover was just the thing I was certain would make that hellish day worth surviving. If something didn't give, then I was truly unsure that I was willing to live to fight through another.

I barely knocked when he answered. His face demonstrated he had been crying. My chest immediately ached for him. I knew that Jakob bragging about that favor I owed him was the cause of his cold tears of deep heart break. He motioned me inside but caste his eyes to the floor.

I rushed inside and pushed the door closed as I pulled him into a loving embrace. Leo broke down into a crying jag the second his face was in my chest. I rubbed his back attempting to hush him, but he continued to shudder and weep.

His despair set off my need to protect him from such agony. "Leo, please love. You shouldn't believe everything Jakob says. I merely promised him a date in return for his aid to help me oust Kilian from the Vampire's bed. I didn't realize he would go telling the world our confidential business. I swear to you, no matter what happens, I will never love anyone else but you. You mean everything to me."

Leo sniffed loudly and put his arms around my waist as he said, "Nein Christian Axel, you are the one that misunderstands. I am not upset about that little Queen's bragging. I know you better than that. You don't give your heart away with ease. I don't fear that Jakob could ever hope to earn your rare treasure. There is something else that causes my tears."

His saying that both made me feel better and worse at the same time. "If not that bullshit scene then what is it Leo? Tell me how to grant you comfort, my love. I cannot stand to see you cry."

Leo pulled out of my embrace and walked to his couch in a slump then sat down. I watched him full of confusion and fear. I had never seen him this depressed before. Whatever was bothering him appeared to be quite serious. I followed sitting down next to him on his couch. He reached out and pulled my head into his lap. He ran his fingers through my hair and took several deep breaths.

I suddenly realized that my buddy Der Makellos wasn't there to greet me. I felt terror grip my spine as I assumed that something horrible had happened to him. That must be why Leo was so distraught. I felt my own tears start to well and my breath became shallow.

I closed my eyes. "Leo, is this sadness over Der Makellos? Where is our baby? Has he been injured or worse?"

Leo gasped and held me tightly. "Nein, Christian, our pup is healthy and well. I sent him to the vet to have him fixed today is all. He will live longer if we curb his need to mate and wander. I am so sorry to scare you by not saying that the second you entered."

I let out my breath in relief but still couldn't understand why he was so upset. "Then please tell me Leo. What has happened?"

He nodded then did his best to quell his tears. "I was informed today that the Straußenfarm has burned to the ground. It was arson committed by some locals from the town. They claimed that they were attempting to rid the community of evil homosexuals."

This made me gasp in horror. "That is terrible Leo. I am sorry to hear it. I know you enjoyed many fine memories of that club. Surely the owner will rebuild, ja?"

Leo shook his head. "He may Christian Axel, but it is not the building nor even the reason it is gone that causes me grief. There were many black collars hanging out in the club when they set it alight. Most got out uninjured, but a handful were unable to escape."

I frowned at hearing that sad news. "Oh, those poor fellows. I have to assume at this moment you knew one of the unlucky victims of that savage and ignorant attack?"

Leo nodded. "Ja, I did indeed and so did you. Rudolf from the stables had taken his young handsome lover Edger to visit for his first time. The ceiling caved in killing poor little Edger immediately. Rudolf tried to pull him from the inferno and was seriously injured in his attempts. The doctors say he will live, but his heart has been broken. I went by and saw him just before you arrived. I sat there looking into the eyes of that sad man that lost his love. Bad enough I have to mourn that beautiful lost boy. Today I was reminded how fragile life is, my bunny. I could see that grieving man could be you or me weeping for the other. Our years are so far apart and your future in so much peril. It was a wakeup call to Leo." He wiped his eyes.

I sat there in a stun. I knew Edger from that day on the basketball court. I had shown him mercy during my thudding test when he came to be punished. Rudolf had been the fair and kindly caregiver of my lamb family.

In one afternoon, two lives were shattered by a criminal act driven by hate and intolerance. No matter how much cruelty I had ever known in my life, the brutality one human can demonstrate to a total stranger still takes my breath away. Edger had been killed and Rudolf maimed over nothing but a belief that their preference for a lover was a wicked thing. You know it seemed to me that what those boys did behind closed doors never would affect a single one of their attackers on any level.

The entire thing was simply incomprehensible to me. Leo said the arsonists claimed their bible said it was against God's law to have same gendered sexual congress. I found that strange. I seemed to recall that same book said killing a person and judging another's actions was also against that same God's law. I have to say I was grateful I never believed in any of that fantastic bullshit. That is insane to believe there is a supreme being sitting around in the clouds watching everyone below.

Seemed to me if such a fellow existed, he could send down his own wrath without relying on his creations to do his dirty work, ja? Well, regardless Edger died, and Rudolf was severely burned. All thanks to insanity of a handful of idiots that hid behind the religious words of a book that was written by humans many centuries ago. I held Leo as he emptied his tears of empathetic sorrow for his old friend and the youngster he watched grow into a promising young man only to end up the corpse far too soon.

Sadly, I was unable to speak with Leo regarding my own pain thanks to the most heinous tragedy. I dared not cause him any further despair with such a tough blow delivered to him only a few hours before.

I was grateful that he was not worried about anything that may or may not occur between Jakob and I. I was, however, blocked from confessing that I had my own serious troubles, with Kilian and Reece being the biggest, but I was also concerned about Lucus. I kept my mouth shut and listen to his woes attentively. Without quarrel I granted him much affectionate non-sexual holding.

I spend that precious hour and a half comforting my grieving lover rather than finding myself in his arms. It was alright not engaging in a wild romp in his bed. That was not necessarily the thing I had been seeking, mind you.

However, being the young man myself, and after enduring that domination of Matz's brutal intercourse, the mercy of finding my own thrill with Leo maybe would have helped me feel less, well, powerless.

Needless to say, I didn't enjoy a release of pent-up urges nor a meal. The hour grew late fast. I informed my

Leo that I had to regrettably leave his side to attend to my studies. He wanted to argue, but he could see my mind was made up. I reminded him that the next night I would be with him from darkness till dawn.

I finally got him to smile when I offered to grant him bedtime service like I had back in the old days. He chuckled as I pulled him along his hallway to his bedroom, but he didn't offer to resist the gift I offered.

I quickly undressed him, got him into his night clothing and tucked him in for the night. I leaned down and gave him a long, loving kiss and then reached over to turn out his light. I spotted his romance novel sitting there on the nightstand. I smiled as I realized this was exactly the research material I was in desperate need to possess.

I thought Leo would die of joy when I asked if I could borrow that book. Of course, he was most happy to loan it to me. I snatched it up and placed it in my jacket pocket. I hoped to read a bit of it during the night when and if I could keep Osvin's sticky fingers off me for any length of time.

I thanked Leo for his kindness and turned out his lamp. I quietly slipped out of his room the way I had been trained all my life, on my toes to keep down the racket of my footsteps. I rushed from his apartment barely checking the hallway for the enemy Kilian or frightening Jonas.

As luck would have it I made it all the way to the fourth floor without a single incident from either of them. I noticed Lucus was also scarce. That made me chuckle with happiness. I thought he finally got the message that I was not in any mood to tolerate others' nosing into my private affairs. For that moment, things were starting to look up again.

I hoped everything had finally settled down. It had to or I was not going to make it much longer. That stress was killing me. It had not even been two weeks since my return to the Haus and already I was sure a shattering was bound to happen if my life didn't calm and soon.

It was eight-thirty exact when I came thru the front door. Matz grabbed me by the arm and dragged me to the couch the second I got there. I let out a yelp of fear as he manhandled me appearing furious.

I had no idea what the hell was going on this time, but his ambush set off the inner terror that lead to full paralysis. I allowed him to pull me where he desired to go unable to find the will to fight him off. I flashed a look of distress at my brother Maximillian that was preparing to take the wheel. He stared back at me with a blank expression as he shrugged.

Mad Maxx spoke up, "Allow this Mad Max. Let's see what the asshole wants."

I glared at him. "That is bullshit. I will not allow this nothing to tell us what to do. He has no right."

Maximillian padded me on the back. "I am taking the wheel brother. You stand down. I can handle this idiot. It is nearly my turn anyway with Osvin's appointment time approaching."

I backed off and let that schwuler shard take over. "You know Matz owes you big time brother. Another order to me comes out of his mouth I am going to hit him till he is in that dentist chair next to the boy tomorrow."

Maximillian nodded "That could still be a possibility. Mad Maxx, get your shard ready to fight. I wonder if maybe Christian may not be the one needed to remind Matz of why even our worst enemy is careful how they behave around us."

Christian smiled with much joy. "I am ready anytime you call brother. Just say the word."

Mad Maxx blocked the anger shard and used his cane to keep him pinned to the wheel room wall. "Stand down Christian. There will be no attacking Matz. I already told all you, like it or not, we need this man to save the silvers and survive in this Haus. You be still. Maximillian you smile and pretend to be the subdued. We see what is on his mind, then work out a plan to free ourselves of his presence in our existence the second it is feasible."

Maximillian nodded. "As you say Mad Maxx. Though for the record, I am with Mad Max. I do hate you a great deal. Just so you know it."

Mad Maxx glared at me and Mad Max. "Well, for your information, the feeling is mutual, fuckers. If it were not for Der Hund, I would destroy the two of you and laugh while I did it."

Max thundered out, "I am not going to tell you boys again. Enough of the bickering. This inner fighting weakens our position of power. Cut the shit and do your jobs. Mad Maxx is correct. Matz is necessary for now. Mind him and allow the shard of intelligence to find a solution that will keep us on track for the mission but ends this sonofabitch's hold over our good welfare."

Despite the collective bad feelings about the sudden bossiness of Matz, no Max boy nor Christian dared to anger the Soul. Such a foolish endeavor would only land that unruly shard in the garbage of the boy's brain busted into a million pieces.

By now we were all very aware that Max had a direct connection to our lost inner self, Der Hund. To get crosswise with him was to deny the wishes of our Master shard himself. Max's stern warning calmed the barely contained irritation each of us felt toward our brothers, at least for that moment anyway.

Matz was standing there staring at us with his mouth open in what appeared to be shock. He had forced us to sit down on the couch where only a little more than an hour before he had taken his paid service from us. I kept the boy's eyes to the floor in silence while the five of us had been arguing with each other over destruction of this idiot.

He licked his lips as if nervous then said, "Maxx? Who the hell are you speaking to?"

I looked up at him in a startle. "What? I said nothing Matz. You must be hearing voices. I have medication for that you know. Crazy motherfucker."

Matz shook his head appearing completely in shock. "Holy hell, you are worse tonight than this morning. I never realized how fast the madness could come over someone. Damn. Okay, this will be fine. You need to take your medication better is all. Malfred told me that you can get unstable rapidly without it. I suppose I should have listen to his wise advice."

I glared at him in open hatred at his saying that. "Well, you going to continue to insult me? What the hell is this all about cocksucker? I have work to get to don't I? Or maybe you want to fuck me again? We still have another twenty minutes. Shit, you could do it twice, ja?" I sneered at him.

Matz narrowed his eyes at me suddenly shifting from concerned to pissed. "Enough out of you Maxx. As it is I did go see Fritz while you were off doing whatever it is that you do at night. Here, this is the three hundred from my cut of the take and the other three hundred I owed you for earlier." He threw the money on the table in front of me.

I stared at that six hundred dollars. "Okay, so what do I do with it. Wait, why are you giving me your cut of that take from Fritz und where the fuck is my part of it." I shot an angered look at him as he crossed his arms with a frown.

"Your part goes to the dentist, I told you. You can do whatever you want with that six hundred. Three I owed and three you now owe back to me in services." He smiled with smugness.

I rolled my eyes. "Seriously Matz? I just attended your needs, motherfucker. I don't have the time nor interest in serving you again tonight. I have that lusty Osvin waiting to tear me apart downstairs idiot. Give me a fucking break will you?"

He snorted. "Damn you are the crybaby, Maxx. I pay you now for the blow job tomorrow whenever I can fit me into your busy schedule. I want that whole service with number one this time."

I groaned. "The whole service cost more than six hundred Matz and you don't get a discount no matter who the fuck you think you are."

Matz covered his eyes and took a deep breath, "I meant I want the full blow job, not just head or the hummer fool. I didn't mean number one, blow job and intercourse. Shit. You are making me feel like I am the one going nuts here. Shut the fuck up and listen to me for a minute. No more noise or complaints out of you until I am finished speaking. I mean it."

I crossed my arms and sat back in on the sofa. "Oh, do please tell me all about it King Matz. I am dying to hear what you have to say. Be careful though. You may be the one that finds the grave if you insist on angering me any further with this bullshit bullying. I don't care for it. If I were you I would reconsider how small you are compared to the one you appear to think is obligated to mind your words."

Matz took on an expression of incredible fury and leaned down to stare into my face. "You threaten me one more time Maxx, I swear to God you better do what you promise. If you don't, then you will find yourself trapped on your knees before a Vampire, my friend. You are clearly unwell. Neither your so-called guardian nor your trainer seems to give two shits that your slipping off the deck into the stormy waters of madness. If your mind continues to faulter then in short order you may not need worry about another silver collar. That rat fuck Kilian will get you wrapped up tight in his straight jacket and haul you away again. The way I see it, Matz is the only one that cares what happens to you. I confess I thought the rumors of your insanity were hype. That is my cross to bear since I realize finally that if anything the gossip has done the truth no justice. You are indeed mad as the hatter."

I scoffed. "I already told you to stop insulting me Matz. It is not necessary. Get to the point of your reason for hijacking me from my duties downstairs. I tire of this conversation."

Matz nodded his head wildly. "Oh, I bet you are sick to death of hearing it. Too bad you never bothered to listen. Maxx, I notice you haven't eaten a thing since those pancakes earlier. I was told by the Voters you been vomiting. You shall not leave this fucking apartment until you eat and take your meds. I also need to discuss with you the scheduling for tomorrow. You have that fucking favor you owe Jakob tomorrow night. Then you have the training with Peter at eleven and somewhere in the mix, you have the service to Roland. Fritz tried to move in on the night, but I held him off for another two days as you requested. I need to know your plans and movements until the last nine full nights of services are completed with Fritz, Justus then Osvin to pay back for Kloe's collar." He reached over and picked up a plate with plastic over it and tossed it at me.

I caught the thing and noticed the signature work of Geraldine. "My lamb sent this. When did she have the time to cook?" My eyes were wide in shock. *That damned lamb is amazing, I told you.*

Matz nodded with a bitter smile. "Remember I said I spoke to her about fixing more meals and she agreed? Well, there it is. You eat all of it and tell me where you hide your pills. I will go get them and make sure you take them properly. Do not argue with me. I mean it."

I glared at him as I angrily opened the plastic to start on the pancakes on that plate. "They are in my overnight bag in the closet. I don't have to take them though. Jonas told me that Malfred is wrong. Kilian cannot order any blood testing. No one will know if I don't take them."

Matz snorted "You couldn't be more wrong there Maxx. No wonder you are losing it. God dammit. You must take your medication, or you are finished. That illness will get a foothold and take you right to hell brother." He stormed off into my room as I choked down the meal Geraldine sent me.

Matz returned in a few moments with several bottles of that nasty shit that Doctor Vagner sent home with me. He got a glass of water and stood there tapping his foot on the floor. That noise was getting to me. He noticed my irritation at it, so he increased his fidgeting until I took the fucking pills to get him to stop that infernal annoyance.

He stood there barking out orders that I come back to the apartment immediately after sending Osvin off in the morning. He reminded me that the second I was finished with Peter I was to see the dentist, bring him the estimate sheet, then prepare for the service to Roland. He assumed that would take an hour and a half, leaving the rest of the afternoon to attend to Jakob.

I told him that I was leaving to stay the night with my Mann the second I was finished with the Queen. Matz had some choice words to say about my spending yet another night in a bed other than my own. He bitched that I was not leaving myself any time for rest, studying, nor working out.

I rolled my eyes at his nagging and assured him I would find a way to work all three of those things into my daily schedule. At that point all I could think is that I wanted Matz out of my life as far as I could get him. That bastard was acting like he thought himself my father instead of flat mate and business partner. It was getting on my last nerve.

Yet, oddly, I found myself unable to do a fucking thing other than privately fume over his overbearing behavior. That strange overwhelming terror was starting to rise within the boy. Each time I went to open my mouth to voice discontent at his ordering me around. That inner fear froze my tongue.

I felt so fucking helpless, and useless that thoughts of ending my life flooded the wheel room.

I looked at my brother shards. To my surprise I noticed they all seemed subdued, pale and kept their eyes to the floor.

Something was wrong here, but I couldn't figure it out. It was as if Matz was stealing our will to stop his interference with our status as the freeman. I decided it was time to call Der Hund in for advice. I feared if we didn't stand up for ourselves soon, then in a week Matz would have us kneeling and calling him Master.

Matz looked to the clock and snorted with irritation. "You heard what I had to say. It is time for you to get downstairs to work. You don't let that pig Osvin get away with more than he paid for Maxx. You remember what I told you. Just because he paid doesn't mean you have no right to say nein. I need you to try to get some rest. He surely cannot expect you to fuck all night long."

I grumbled out, "That bastard does. Can I go now or are you desiring to criticize me about the way I breath the air or blink my eyes?"

Matz motioned me to stand and follow him. "Stop being the histrionic, Maxx. I am not being critical. I am trying to help you stay well. You think managing your busy life is fun for me?"

I got up and walked out while he closed and locked the door behind us. "Seems to be the thrill for you. You were quite loud about your enjoyment of managing me earlier," I spit out the words keeping my sight to the floor.

He chuckled with sudden mirth. "You asked for that Maxx. There was no reason for you to be so callus. I don't desire to be your enemy any more than you desire to be my lover. I know you may hate me for stepping up and taking responsibility for your short falls. That doesn't really matter anymore. I have no choice. If I don't do it, no one else will. You will fail or worse and then you will not be the only one finding yourself in dire straits. I promised to look after you and I am doing what I must to see you get to where you want to be. Taking a little thrill from the tough situation wherever I can get it is not such a crime when you realize that Maxx. It also is more than fair service return. Bellyache all you like. Call me names if it makes you feel better. I refuse to take it personally. In the end, you will do as you are told, and old Matz will keep his buddy from being snatched by those that are calling for Priceless blood."

I snapped up my head to look at him when he said that. "You have a plan to keep Gretta from re-collaring me? Is that what all this bullying is about?"

He nodded appearing a bit startled by that question. "Uhm…ja…sure. If that is what you want to believe then

34

who am I to argue it? You follow the schedule I lay out for you, mind my orders and be honest with me, then I can promise Gretta won't get the chance to send you to your knees. Deal?"

I smiled suddenly feeling much less stressed that Matz had a plan to foil that horrible bitch. "Why the hell didn't you say this in the first place, Matz? I thought you were being the dick to piss me off. Of course you have a deal, but how can you be sure it will work? Do you have inside information on what that woman is looking to use against me from the undercover agents? Oh, I know. You managed to decode that secret messages from that tapping in the walls. Well don't listen to that fucking DJ on the radio whatever you do. He is the gossip and I swear if he keeps telling everyone my thoughts I am going to send him over the banister."

Matz gasped then whispered, "Ja, uhm, you figured me out. I broke those, uhm, codes. Plus, there are lots of spies in the Haus you know. If you grease the right palms, uhm, that is all I want to say about this. You need not know my methods to realize they work. Uhm, Maxx, you did take that medication, ja? All of it?"

I snorted. "You know I did, Matz. You were standing there watching me. Why?"

He shrugged. "No reason, just wondering. Do you think Jonas or Peter can call that Doctor Vagner in to see you?"

I flinched. "Now why the fuck would they want to do that? Dr. Vagner is the quack, Matz. The whole lot of them work for the KGB you know. They run illegal experiments and Kilian's brother Reece is the worst of them. He tried to put a fucking radar in my back teeth. Ha. You can imagine how stupid he felt when he realized I didn't have any. I suppose he will use the radioactive fleas the next time. I wonder if the emissions can be tracked by seismographic signature or if there are some litmus testing strips?"

Matz grabbed my arm. "Maxx? Brother, do you hear yourself? What is going on? I better tell Roland and the boys you need to cancel. I think maybe you are too tired to deal with Osvin tonight. Sleep will make this go away, I hope." He glanced off down the hallway toward his old apartment.

I chuckled. "What are you talking about Matz? Is this a yoke? I feel fine. Geraldine is the finest cook. You were right I was having the stomach problems but that lamb's dinner fixed Maxx up to vigor once more. Ha, I race you, ja? Catch up if you can old man." I took off running for the first-floor apartment with a sudden surge of euphoria pushing my legs faster with every step.

I reached his place with speed leaving Matz in my dust. I laughed loudly as I pushed through the door and entered. I found a somber looking wolfpack sitting around the living room with Osvin in the ratty recliner appearing sourer than the rest of them. I approached the group with a frown wondering why the long faces.

Roland spoke up, "Osvin has a problem Maxx."

I shrugged. "Osvin has more than one, that I can assure you. What is the issue that matters to me?"

Osvin dropped his head then grumbled out, "Fiona told me that if I don't come home tonight at a reasonable hour she is demanding a divorce."

Matz came plowing through the door the minute Osvin confessed to that. "Maxx, you fool. God damn you are fast for the damned cripple. What the fuck is going on in here? Did someone die?" He walked over and stood next to me glaring at the pouting Osvin.

I giggled then said, "His Frau says that he cannot stay out late playing with the boys or she will leave him. Doesn't matter though. Osvin couldn't do a thing with any lover tonight anyway. Fiona let him leave but kept his balls back at their apartment as collateral in case he decided to try to have a good time without her." That caused the wolfpack to snicker loudly as Osvin dropped his head even lower in shame.

Matz groaned at my open insult. "Don't mind him brother Osvin. Maxx hasn't been sleeping well lately. He told me your quite the handful stud. That said, I cannot grant you a refund Osvin. You know the rules. If you must leave tonight you forfeit the money."

Osvin shot a look of shock at Matz "That is not fair. I paid three thousand for the night. I can only stay two hours or face the courts when she sues me for divorce. Cut me some slack Matz. This is not my fault."

Matz shrugged. "Not my or Maxx's either. I cannot just reschedule you easily brother. You are welcome to do the two hours, but if you leave that is the end of it. There will be no money returned. Two hours or the twelve you booked this night and that prevented another from taking it. That is the way it works. If Maxx couldn't stay but two hours you would get some back but as you see he is here and ready to fill your needs with honor."

Osvin nodded then blew out his breath. "Ja, okay you have a point Matz. That God damned woman has me in a bind. Is there not some kind of compensation you can offer for my loss?"

Matz pursed his lips then smiled as he pulled the menu from his jacket. "Roland, you and the boys go guard the door. Give me a minute or two to see if Osvin and I cannot come to a reasonable agreement that will keep everyone happy, ja?" He walked over and knelt next to Osvin in the chair.

Roland whistled and motioned Valitin and Magnas to follow.

They began walking out the door, but I reached out and grabbed Roland by the arm. "I need to speak with you a minute."

He stared at me in a surprised startle. "Uhm okay, Maxx. Boys, you heard Matz. Take a powder. I be out in a

38

moment." Valitin and Magnas went out as directed and Roland followed me to the bedroom for our discussion.

I closed the door watching Matz shooting me a look of caution. He appeared anxious for some reason. "Roland, Matz told me that you purchased a full service for tomorrow afternoon."

Roland smiled with glee. "He is telling you the truth. I am excited beyond words. This is the event that only happens once in a lifetime. I thought I would be up all night guarding the door but now it appears I will get sent home for a good night's rest. Though I doubt I will sleep a wink."

I shook my head. "Roland, I warned you not to do this to yourself. I beg you to reconsider. I am happy to provide oral or any other service that will keep you satisfied. That intercourse business though, you should wait for the right lover. No one should lose their virginity to the cold whore. You will be disappointed. Is this really the cruel memory you desire? To know you paid to have your first experience. I have heard such a thing is something that is the most beautiful thing when granted by truthful lover."

He frowned then rubbed his hair back. "Maxx, I already told you once, it doesn't bother me that you are the prostitute. Even if I could find someone that cared for me in the loving way, believe me nothing in this life is free. I would pay for this experience no matter who grants it. The only difference is you tell me up front what is owed and that is the end of it. The money is forgotten and the thrill of it remembered for all time. With one that claims affection there is no telling how much it would cost me in tears and pain when one day that man tires of our love and leaves. Then I will always be stuck with the sour thoughts and feelings of loss tied to the special first time we shared. with you though, that will never happen. You are the lover that will always be smiling and happy to see me. Matters not that I paid you to demonstrate that behavior. Thanks to that, I can have more protection of the glorious memory than possible otherwise and best of all, you can never break my heart Maxx. You are the fantasy lover of my dreams that for a moment will become the reality for Roland. What a glorious thing to hold for my own till they lay me low. I do thank you for the mercy of it brother. I will never forget this kindness you will give me tomorrow nor that you kept your word of silence in the matter."

I felt my air leaving my lungs as I barely breathed out, "You are not who the others think you to be, Roland."

He shook his head with a silly grin then dropped his eyes to the floor. "You got me, Maxx. I am the hopeless romantic at heart. I can confess that I never slept with anyone before this because I am the picky bastard. I wanted a lover of quality and skill. It was my dream to be with the artist or poet, maybe even the classical musician. Well, I am neither the looker nor with any money as I said. The years passed and until you, I was unsuccessful at acquiring the man that could meet my requirements. I thought if I couldn't have what I truthfully wanted then I would rather go without."

I scoffed at that. "I am not a poet, musician nor true artist Roland. You are settling I take it."

Roland chuckled and shot me a coy look. "You are funning me, ja? You are better at all the things tied to romance than I could have imagined. For starters you dance beautifully. I have seen it. I can also lay claim to have witnessed your incredible intelligence and skillful word smithing. You are rumored to be the escape, sexual and seductive artist of the highest caliber. You enslaved the entire sixth floor and half the fifth before your fifteen birthday Maxx. As for being the poet, ah brother, the children hold little stuffed lambs that lead them to their dreams. If that is not living poetry then there is no such a thing as beauty. The idea of uniting with such a harbinger of all things that make life worth living brings me to near tears. I am so unworthy of such a blessing. Please tell me you are not denying my honest and honorable request to your favors."

I stared at him with my mouth open unable to believe what this man, I thought to be a common thug, had said to me. "Nein, I will not turn you down. You argue your case better than the college educated attorney."

He grinned. "Well, glad that my schooling did some good, what little of it I got. Thankfully, they have a large library in the Haus, and a lovely bookstore in town. I read a lot. Mostly poetry and music but sometimes I confess I read the great romances of history. I do miss playing music though a lot."

I was startled by that admission. "You play an instrument? Guitar or drums right?"

He wrinkled his nose at that. "Nein Maxx. I play the only instrument that can cry, the violin. It has always been my passion. I used to play it for loose change on the streets before Malfred came to us and saved us from starvation or prison. I sold it to pay the rent for our apartment the first year. I have never been able to get another. I saved my money for it, but I gave that to Matz for this glorious baptism into manhood you will give me tomorrow."

I winced at that. "You used your savings for such the fleeting thrill of sex? Roland, the violin could grant you a lifetime of joy long after you have forgotten your tryst with me."

Roland slapped my back hard as he laughed. "I can save up for my dream violin in the years to come, but you Maxx are here today for sure only. There is no doubt a man of your talents will wake up very soon and realize you are better than this dark business you are ensnared into with us. I hear rumors that you study to be the doctor. I can believe it. You are smart enough and finer hands I never have seen. You should play the piano. What beautiful music we could play together."

I smiled at him with sadness in my expression. "Ja, indeed. I guess we will find out if that is truth tomorrow afternoon." He laughed loudly as he realized I was making a thinly veiled sexual reference.

Matz entered the room to inform me that Osvin was ready to begin his two hours' worth of service. Roland left quickly and my pimp informed me that I was to return to the apartment, escorted by the wolfpack to the door, the second Osvin was done with me.

Later I found out that Matz had worked with the hen pecked Osvin to assure he received what he believed to be fair service from me. Matz was careful to assure the money he had already contracted to pay was equalized. Osvin had chosen many services from the Menu.

Matz had arranged that he would receive over a period of the next three weeks at convenient times twelve thousand dollars' worth of my favors. He had to give at least twenty-four hours' notice in advance of time and service he desired.

I was grateful to know that I would not have to endure another three full nights in the octopus grips of that man. I was, however, unhappy to realize there would be more nooners and rapid fire intercourse trysts with him than would have occurred. I think, at that time, I would have preferred to just deal with him over that four-night period.

Like him or not, in time I would discover that Osvin was a customer that paid without quarrel, wasn't into fetishes, didn't like to hit me, and was wanton enough to keep the money rolling in on a regular basis. All and all I was lucky to have him hooked on my false affections. If only that bastard had been seduced into a "pay for love" situation long before he met me, then Fiona wouldn't have ever met, and then married him. That twist of fate would have made both his and my life better by miles, but we get ahead of ourselves.

I got through the two hours of constant aggressive sexual attack from a most agitated Osvin by focusing on that fact that I had yet to crack a single textbook. I knew Peter would tawse the fuck out of me if I showed up to my lesson without having completed his assignments. I endured Osvin's clumsy intercourse feeling a bit of anxiety overcoming me that I needed to get back to Felicity and study or find my ass in worse shape than Osvin was trying to make it. Yikes!

There was a moment that I thought I would lose my dinner when that greedy bastard forced his kissing on me during his goodbye. I managed to barely keep the pancakes down and the fake smile on the boy's face until the second that door shut with him on the other side.

The moment it did I nearly fell face first onto the floor in my rush to that bathroom. I thought a return to using the sandpaper was not such a bad idea. I didn't have any, but I sure could have used some. I scoured till the flesh was raw. I jumped from the tub and rushed my dressing.

The wolves nearly had to run to keep up with my wild pace to get back to my bedroom and sweet lamb. Matz attempted to scold me for trying to outrun the boy's like I had. Fucking Magnas told on me, that stool pigeon. I ignored his bitching and took off for my books. He came to the door demanding I get some rest.

I of course nodded and said I would only study for a bit then hit the sheets. He left me be, but I could tell he was unsatisfied I was listening to his good advice. I spent several hours attending to the lesson plan Peter had included with the books.

Then around dawn the fatigue was starting to become unbearable. I had mostly finished his list but was worried the tawsing was inevitable. There simply wasn't enough time to do all he listed. I thought he must be insane to expect so much. I took my little Felicity that had worked as my "study buddy" (she is smart as the whip you know, and talented in acrobatics.) to the bed with me. I planned on getting a few hours shut eye before my appointment at eleven.

I was nearly asleep when I recalled that "deflowering" I had scheduled with Roland later that day. I groaned as I got back up and dug in the pocket of my jacket. I retrieved that romance novel of Leo's and took it back to the bed. I began to read of the ways of the lovers just as the first rays of the sun peeked over the horizon.

I was beyond fatigued but I knew deep inside that book would come in handy. I needed to be prepared for maybe the strangest, most stressful, and oddly beautiful days that I would ever encounter in my young life. I had barely gotten to the fifth chapter when I heard the knocking. Matz cursed to himself as he passed my room to answer the door. The apartment suddenly erupted with the sounds of a familiar high pitched voice. It was that of my lover for the day. Jakob had arrived.

Chapter 16: The Tears of the Violin

I crawled out of the bed keeping my ears open to hear the mumblings of Matz to Jakob in the other room. I gave my beloved Felicity a quick kiss then rushed to the bathroom and covered my nakedness with a towel. I rifled through the pockets of my jacket and grabbed the six hundred dollars that Matz gave me the night before. I looked at that money before I placed it in the bed next to Felicity. She and I took a moment to make sure I was positive I wanted to carry on with this plan of mine.

For a change all the shards were in agreement, and Felicity granted her approval as well. I, the Mad Maxx shard, had determined a way to end the mistake I had made by granting a favor to Jakob that surely would hurt Leo's heart no matter what he told me. I had also come up with a way to undo the obvious mistake Roland was making by choosing to lose his penetration virginity to a whore.

It should not have mattered to me about Roland's future memories, nor Jakob's silliness at wishing that I fuck him. I was of no real consequence to either man. What I had determined was that it was not their heart I desired to protect at all, it was my own.

In the dark world of brutality, I had not been given the choice in losing my own virginities, none of them. Even Annette had taken a bit of advantage of a dumb boy that was halfway through the act of intercourse before he had any idea, he was having it. Peter raped away my innocence.

I had received that most horrible lesson of adulthood while I was helplessly bonded in his bed. Even worse I was ignorant of what was occurring till the deed was cruelly (und painfully) done.

Then the Vampire Jonas took yet another liberty with me when he gave me a lesson in hidden penetration ability. The long history of being the victim of sexual assaults had lowered my value of myself to rock bottom. Humiliation, helplessness, and loss were all I ever experienced when in the embrace of another. Not even my Leo could aid me in reclaiming the manhood that had been stolen from me.

I didn't desire to do that same thing to Roland. Nothing more than a false lover that steals away the innocence of childhood and forces the person into the brutal realities of becoming an adult. For Jakob, I didn't wish to be just another liar that would let him down, and further lower his self-worth. I could see both men viewed themselves no better than I did the Mad Maxximillian. They shared the same illness of believing their only value in life was the masks they wore that hid their inner pain from everyone around them.

The stress of becoming the thing I hated the most, an abuser of another for self-gain, pushed me to the limits of my ability to endure. I had been a loser, submissive, killer, whore, liar, and if you look closely a rapist. Annette had told me to stop at least three times and I ignored her pleas, then there is you my Liebe, ja? I was going to be damned if I would be the abusive psychopath too.

Meine soul Max depended on the actions I would take with Jakob and Roland that day. If I failed to undo all the harm caused by my desperations, my need for money from Roland and need for aid from Jakob, I knew I could mortally injure that most important shard for all time. I took a deep breath then walked out the bedroom door ready to spend the day fixing all that I had broken once and for all.

Matz gasped and Jakob nearly fainted when I appeared in nothing but a towel. The two of them stared at me in disbelief as I rapidly approached the Queen with a loving smile on the boy's face. Jakob could not tear his eyes from my bare chest and stomach, appearing as if in a trance.

I reached out and took the dumbfounded Jakob into a tight embrace and placed my mouth near his ear, "Good morning beautiful. What a glorious sight to see first thing in the day? I swear the sun himself is jealous that he can only warm the skin when Jakob can make the heart glow." I kissed his cheek then let him go.

I watched as Jakob nearly choked and turned bright red with a silliness coming over him. He reached up and covered his mouth then padded his hair appearing unsure how to react or behave. Matz stood there with his eyes wide and mouth dragging on the floor as if he witnessed something so incredible he was frozen to the spot.

Jakob spoke without a single signature overdramatic movement and his voice was not typically overly girlish. "Uhm, good morning to you Maxx. I, oh hell, I cannot remember what I was going to say. Matz here says, uhm, Matz? What were you saying again? I seem to have had a stroke or something, maybe," he stammered out.

Matz shook his head still appearing in shock. "I said that Maxx will be free for that favor by six Jakob. You can leave now and return at that time. He has other tasks to attend until then."

I smiled at that. "Ah ja, Matz is correct my beauty. I sadly have many work tasks and studies to attend, but you fear not. I await our date with much eagerness. What a lucky man I am to get such an honor as to call you my very own for this single magical afternoon? Though I am most unworthy of it, I am most grateful that you are momentarily struck with such generosity. I intend to make the most of what until this day I could only dream of."

That statement made Matz cough and sputter. "Holy hell. What the fuck? Jakob, I must ask you to relent your bid to get this favor Maxx owes you out of the way today. He apparently is too psychotic to be of any use to you."

I turned with sudden irritation and growled out, "You be still Matz. Jealousy is most unattractive on you. I will not stand here and allow you to bad mouth this amazing man in my presence by chalking up my truthful statements about his value to psychosis. The only crazy thing about me this morning is that I don't have the ability to rush him into a blood bonding to make him my own for all time."

Jakob swooned with a loud moan when I shouted at Matz. To my horror he began to fall backward. I barely caught him before he hit the floor in his faint. I had thought it was his usual dramatics but nein. He actually passed out.

Matz ran to the kitchenette while I gently laid the unconscious Jakob on the floor. He returned with a damp rag. The two of us spent a few moments wiping his face and speaking to him calmly until he regained his alertness. He opened his eyes initially confused.

Then he smiled with much pleasantness and said, "You swept me off my feet, Maxx. What a lucky girl I am to have experienced something until this moment I only ever read about. Thank you for that."

Matz snorted. "I think I maybe am in a dream state and never woke this morning. I cannot believe you just thanked Maxx for causing you to pass out nor that his silly words to you made that happen in the first place. This cannot be real. Can it?"

I laughed at that then offered my hand to Jakob to aid him standing. "Matz, you are the cad. If you want to believe you sleep still, then who are we to stop you in that delusion. Go back to bed and mind your business."

Jakob took my offered paw and regained his footing. "Ja, I am with Maxx. Go back to your room and leave me alone with this hunk. I pray I am dreaming. I wish to never wake up." He ran his hand down my chest as he said that.

I reached out and grabbed his hand then kissed his knuckles making him groan and shudder. "This is no dream, my heart. It is I that wishes to enjoy the beautiful vision that is you and never find reality again." I let his hand go and he grabbed his chest threatening to faint yet again. Damn, he was the over sensitive one, ja?

Matz scoffed. "Stop that Jakob. You hit the floor this time I am leaving you as the doormat for the apartment. You surely know that Maxx is lying. He is the trained pleasure submissive, fool. He knows how to speaking pretty to you. He says only what you desire to hear. It is all illusion and false. Maxx cares nothing for anyone."

Jakob's face, which had been gazing at me completely enthralled, suddenly twisted into one of fury as he yelled back at Matz, "You shut up, Matz. I wouldn't care if everything Maxx says were a lie, false, or manipulation of the worst kind. It makes me feel special and I never would have believed myself more adored, wanted, and beautiful than this moment. I will ask you kindly to stay the fuck out of my fantasy. You interrupt it again, I will forget that I am a lady and kick your grouchy ass."

Matz backed up as if Jakob threw punches rather than harsh words. "Okay, okay. Damn Jakob, you are a moody bitch. What the hell do I care if you get hurt by this fakery anyway? I was only trying to help. Don't come crying to me tomorrow when you awaken to find yourself the used creature you surely are."

I turned around and punched Matz right in the gut sending him to his knees gasping for air. "That is enough, Matz. You will not call this beautiful soul a creature again in my presence. You can call me names, abuse and bully me all you like, but Jakob you will only discuss in the most honorable of terms. There is not a soul in this fucking Haus that is more loving, giving, or generous than this man. I owe him my life. I can think of nothing sweeter than being the indebted man to this angel on Earth. I would never lie, use, injure nor hurt him. You have no right to judge what you are of completely ignorant about. Say another cruel thing and he will not have to lower himself. Maxx will do it for him."

Jakob gasped then tears welled up in his eyes as he watched Matz glare at me with anger from his place on the floor. "Oh, my Gott. I need to get out of here. You are making me ruin my makeup Maxx. I never thought, this cannot be, I need to go. I see you at six." He fled for the door just as the first trickle of water began to run down his cheeks.

I yelled after him. "I will pick you up at your apartment at six. Not the other way around. Matz was in error, love. I see you then. I will think of you all day." Jakob let out a loud sob then rushed out closing the door behind him.

Matz slowly stood never taking his furious gaze from me. "You are a fucking demon. I never would have believed it had I not seen it. You play with Jakob's heart and hit your brother in the stomach. You are right, I had no business judging you because I certainly missed the mark. You are cruel, hateful and ungrateful to your rotten core. It is one thing to whore when you have no choice but to do it or starve. This brutality I see you pull this morning, that Maxx I cannot ignore or give you an excuse for."

I glared back at him with my own anger rising. "You know nothing, Matz. You claim you love me, then rape me. I forgave you for it and that was not enough. You demand my services then try to crush me beneath your feet for doing what you paid me to do. Now, you dare to speak with a bitter tongue about my heart and intentions. You better look in the mirror, brother. I think you project. While I am on the subject of misunderstandings, I want that money that Roland gave to you. Give it to me this minute. I am giving it back to him. I will not accept his offer for the full services." I held out my hand palm up.

Matz stared at my hand. "Nein, you cannot turn him down. He will leave I told you. We cannot afford not to have him and the wolves help."

I growled out. "I will take my chances. You again do not know everything, Matz. That money Roland gave you cannot be accepted. You sell my soul for thirteen hundred dollars without my approval. I would hope to think I am worth more than that. Give it to me or I will finish what I started and beat you to the floor over it."

Matz shot a look of shock at me. "You wouldn't dare. If you tried, I will go get Jonas, Peter and Gretta."

I smiled with evil. "Fine by me. You will go with broken limbs and a busted face. In this life Matz there are some things worth fighting for. I only lay down my arms when there is hope of a better day if I survive and the chance of winning at that moment is zero. You take Roland's money on this, I am lost for all time. There will be no second chances. You threaten my soul, and that brother is worth whatever I must pay to protect. You still going to deny me that money I ask for? I warn you, I mean what I say."

Matz shook his head but began to tremble. "Maxx, this is insane. The wolfpack is going to purchase your services, eventually even the right to intercourse with you. You cannot deny them if they offer their cash. They will feel slighted and that will cause ill will. You need their help. I do too."

I nodded. "Ja, this I know. I only deny Roland this service this one time. I will never deny the others nor you. Roland will understand what you cannot. I assure you he will not leave nor will the wolfpack turn on us brother. Give me that money and trust my judgement."

Matz sniffed as if about to cry. "All right if you feel that strongly about this, I will do as you ask. I maybe am the fool I claim Jakob to be." He reached into his pocket and counted out thirteen hundred dollars in cash then put it into my outstretched hand.

I smiled at him relaxing at last. "Thank you for the mercy of it Matz. I will not apologize for hitting you though. You had that coming for insulting someone that has been hurt all his life. You of all people should be empathetic to that. Kilian spent a decade tearing that beautiful heart of Jakob's to shit. You brother, and Roland, all the volves think nothing of yourselves thanks to the cruel opinions and words of others. I would remind you to think before you ever spread the very poison that keeps you forever doubting your value to yourself and the world around you. Matz. You fall in love with me because you think I have the answers to find the way out of the nightmare. You see my scars and pain that blind you to the truth. I am not the strength that you think you lack. That is the illusion you have taken as the reality. The honesty is you are the strong one and Mad Maxx the lost. I follow you Matz because I have no choice. You know the way, not me." I turned and left Matz standing there with a stunned look on his face.

Without hesitation I return to my bedroom and gathered up the wrong sized vampire outfits. I grabbed my pen from the study notes I had taken and quickly marked them all with correct numbers. I then dressed and grabbed my overnight bag.

I placed the six hundred dollars from Matz, the thirteen hundred from Roland and all my books with the assignments I completed inside. I picked up the bundle of clothing and kissed Felicity good day. I was off to clean up the mess that I called my life. I had a lot to do and almost no time to complete it.

I was almost out of the apartment when Matz came out of his room bellowing, "Where the fuck do you think you are going Maxx? I do believe you are trying to skip out on Geraldine's hard work and your medications. You come back here, sit down and eat first."

I blew out my breath in frustration. "Matz, will I come back later and eat breakfast. I told you Those medications are not necessary. It was a quack that claimed that diagnosis. You try to poison me with that crap."

He pointed at the couch. "Shut up, Maxx. Sit down and eat. I mean it. I will not interfere with your giving Roland back his cash, nor that sham date with Jakob, but this I will not bend on. I let you get away with shirking once, then it will be twice, then every time."

I grumbled but put the bag and clothing on the love seat and took a place on the couch. Matz went to the kitchenette and returned with Geraldine's signature plate of food. He also had my pills and a juice he said came with that lamb's meal. I was marveling how that lamb could even make the juice like that, but I knew that lamb. She was pretty amazing as I have said. I bet there was nothing she couldn't manage when it came to the food and drink.

Without quarrel I ate her breakfast and tried to get away without taking that medication. Matz watched my every move. The second I tried to slip off without them he chased me down and demanded I take them or else.

I did as he told me while enduring his thousandth reminder to stop by the dentist after my lesson with Peter. I didn't say anything as he nagged me. I wanted to punch him again over it, but I kept my temper. Max was watching and to incite further fights with Matz would only assure he would betray me further than he already had. I was aware I couldn't vin a battle with Jonas or Peter. There was no reason to encourage Matz to call them in merely to get his way.

I left my pimp/flat mate with fury rising in my heart. I really needed to figure out a way to get him out of my apartment and life for good. The guy was driving me nuts. I was headed up to the sixth floor when I spied my stalker doing his best to stay out of my detection.

I stopped my climb up the steps and yelled out, "I can hear you, Lucus. Why are you still bothering me? What the hell, man? Are you stupid? I told you if you persist in this silly game I am going to end your life."

Lucus stepped out of the shadows from behind me with his notebook in hand. "Good morning to you too, Maxx. Fine day for moving out?" He was staring at the bundle of outfits that I was balancing in my arms.

I scoffed. "You are the nosey bastard indeed. You know last night I forgot to brush my teeth and had a wet dream about your mother. Go ahead and write that down in your book, asshole."

Lucus rolled his eyes. "Well, I might, Maxx. However, if you ever saw my mother you would not have been dreaming of her. She was the ample girl without any qualities of beauty unless you compared her to an old man."

I nearly fell down the stairs. "Huh? You dare to insult your mother like that, Lucus? I must assume you didn't care for the woman much."

Lucus chuckled. "You are wrong there, Maxx. I loved her very much. Near killed me when she passed away last year. I merely state an honesty. All her beauty was in her soul, but her flesh didn't share in that glory. Poor thing was ugly as they come, and she knew it. Didn't matter though. The woman focused on her less fleeting attributes and all the world is a better place for it."

I frown at that. "Well then, aren't you the lucky one Lucus. Stop following me weirdo or you will be hanging out with your ugly mother with the gorgeous soul shortly. I will not warn you again." I began heading back up the stairs.

Lucus yelled out after me. "You better be ready to put action behind that threat, Maxx. I am not going to stop studying you."

I snorted but didn't respond to his stupid statement. For the moment, Lucus could wait. I knew that shortly I would have to send the bastard over the railing. I wished he wouldn't test me, but I was already painfully aware none in that Haus gave a fig what I wanted. They always did whatever they wished at my expense. Lucus wouldn't be any different so there was no choice as usual. I had resigned myself that I would have to kill him.

I hurried to Jonas's door and knocked sort of hoping he would not answer it. My luck has always been of the shitty kind. The Vampire opened it with a huge smile on his face by my third hailing pound on that wooden entry.

I stood there with my eyes to the floor. "I apologize for bothering you so early this morning, Jonas. I was on my way to another appointment and thought I would drop these off with you as you requested."

Jonas practically purred out. "Ah, of course my love. Come in. You're a sight for these poor old eyes. You can put the outfits on the chair by the door. I will have the sixth-floor black collar attendant get the corrected items to you by this afternoon. You will have no excuse to come home tomorrow looking less than gorgeous in the new clothes your Mann gives you, ja?"

I nodded as I stepped inside and followed his orders. "I will not fail you, Jonas. I thank you for the mercy of it. I must beg your pardon, but I am due somewhere in ten minutes. I only came by to get this out of the way and find out if tomorrow after I finish my services to the Honorable Claus, will be okay to return for my night with you?" I caste a nervous eye about wondering if Kilian had spent the night or if the Vampire's desire to have him out held true.

Jonas smiled even larger. "Ja, which will be perfect Christian Axel. You will be finished with him by three, ja?"

I groaned. "Hopefully sooner but three by the latest. Can I expect I return to my Mann alone or will there be company," I hazarded asking about Kilian.

The Vampire's smile melted immediately. "If you are asking if Kilian will be gone by then the answer is ja. I threw him the fuck out yesterday. He will be by later to pick up his things. I let him go live in Bladrick's old apartment. I have no use for snakes in my life."

I looked up with the relief obvious in my expression. "You do me great honor, Jonas. I appreciate your taking me back exclusively. I won't mess up this second chance to keep your affections."

He reached out and stroked my face causing me to close my eyes, to hid the disgust in it. "Ah, you are the dream come true for this old Vampire. I look forward to holding you in my arms tomorrow. Can you stay for only a bit and attend me?" That caused alarm bells within the boy to go off loudly.

I opened my eyes doing my best to appear disappointed. "You tease me, Jonas. Not fair. You heard me when I arrived that I am due at an appointment. I cannot stay much to my despair I assure you."

The Vampire smiled and grabbed a handful of my hair on the side of the boy's head. "An appointment that can wait, I am sure. Come with me and take me to the world of pleasures." He began to pull me along after him by my locks.

Panic filled my chest as I gasped out, "Nein, Jonas please. Leaving you is hard enough without your promise that I am missing thrills with you. I must be at the dentist in only a few minutes. I beg of you, let me go in peace."

He stopped his march and let go of my hair. "The dentist? What? Why? Your teeth are fine. I find no quarrel with most of them gone or incapable of injuring my soft parts anymore. I knocked most of them out for that reason Christian Axel. You know that."

I nodded. "Uhm, ja I do, Jonas. I must apologize for that woeful issue of biting you there when I was under your collar. I was not well. I swear I wouldn't ever do that again. I learned my lesson well." I dropped my gaze to the floor and trembling as the memory of his hammer came rushing through the wheel room.

Jonas scoffed. "You cannot be sure to keep that oath, Christian Axel. Your brain goes daft at regular intervals. You will forget, then I will have to break all your teeth out again. That screaming and crying you did during and after was most annoying. I don't desire to have to endure that shit again, not ever."

I winced. "Nein, Jonas. The dentist will only be able to give me the false ones. If you fear my bite then take them away and lock them up. There won't be a need for you to fear my lack of gratitude for your mercy at not breaking my jaws this time."

He chuckled as he nodded. "Well, that may be truth. I suppose the dentist cannot grow them back. They were the adult teeth I destroyed I do seem to recall. Okay, maybe you would be even prettier with a full set of the pearly whites. As long as I can take them away if you get out of hand in the future I will permit this silliness. However, I must ask where the fuck you going to get the money for dentures, boy? Matz surely cannot afford such frivolity."

I kept my gaze down. "Uhm, ja, he got a large payment from his tables. He desired to give me this gift of the fake teeth. I told him you would not like him undoing your work, but he thought maybe if you saw them you may change your mind since they are not permanent, ja?"

Jonas shrugged. "It's that pissant's money. If he desires to throw it away then who am I to say nein? I want them out of your mouth whenever you provide me the special services though. I still bear the scars from your little fit awhile back. There was no reason to act the fool. Malfred had the right to be there and when I say I want a blow job I don't care what the fuck is going on otherwise, you do it without quarrel or biting me."

I sniffed back my tears at the most horrifying memory of how and why my teeth got broken, not that they were not already in shambles from chronic beatings even the day he bashed them with that hammer and file. "I understand, Jonas. There will be no quarrel nor biting."

Jonas snorted. "Okay, then give me a kiss and be on your way love. I am looking forward to seeing you home tomorrow." He pulled me into a deep kiss and as usual I endured it masking my disgust at it.

The second he closed his door I rushed to Leo's apartment keeping my eyes open for Lucus and Kilian. I knocked softly and my beautiful lover came quickly to answer.

He pulled me inside with an expression of surprise on his face. "My bunny? What are you doing up here so early? Something wrong, honey?"

I pulled him into a loving embrace and breathed in his scent deeply with a satisfying smile. "Nein, Leo. I just needed to see you. Sometimes I need to be reminded the entire world is not horrible."

Leo hugged me back and sighed loudly. "Thank you for saying that my bunny. You are my reason for being too. I cannot wait to see you tonight. I will have Geraldine send your supper up and Der Makellos will be home from his adventure. Tonight, we can hold each other and pretend all is perfect and there is no tomorrow."

I chuckled as I let him out of my arms. "You are always the romantic, Leo. I must be going now. I have a few things to do before my lesson with Peter. Then Matz insists I see his dentist. I want you to ignore anything you hear from Jakob about this favor. I must pay him back for aiding me in getting Kilian out of Jonas's bed. I see him at six but expect that to be done within a couple hours. I pray you can understand it is nothing personal. I owe the man this pleasure for all he has done. Once the debt is paid, I can move on."

Leo frowned then looked at his shoes. "Ja, I understand my bunny. You do what you must. Try to remember it was your Leo that taught you there is a difference between sex and love. I know you love only me. No matter what you must do with Jonas, Peter, or even Jakob, I never fear you will leave me nor forget our heart are one."

I pulled him into a long, deep, passion filled kiss. "My love, till the day we are no longer together in this life, I will hold you tightly as I do this moment. I would rather die than hurt or lose you. That is my promise, and I am a man of my word.

Leo smiled as he ran his fingers across my lips. "The dentist, ja? Ah, long overdue. That cruelty shall be hidden from the world by the porcelain mask, but I will never be able to forget you, cannot forget why you wear it. When you get the appraisal you bring it to me. I will not allow Jonas to pay for the lies that hide his sins."

I smiled at him with much affection in my expression. "Leo, you are too kind. Jonas doesn't pay for this silliness. Matz does."

That made Leo break out in laughter. "Does he now? I guess then neither of you realize how much this is going to cost you. My bunny, your mouth is destroyed. I will not allow a pair of cheap ass dentures to be your reward for suffering such horrors. You tell Matz I want that bill and tell that dentist only the best for my bunny. Do not deny me this chance to help you find a bit of peace. It would break my heart. You know I have the funds for anything you may need. This is no hardship for me, but it would nearly kill Matz."

I dropped my gaze in true shame. "Leo I need to tell you something, I, uhm, love you." I almost confessed to my disgraceful lifestyle but at the last minute, Maximillian covered my mouth and spoke for me as he forced the boy into another deep kiss with Leo.

Mad Maxx glared at me as did Christian and Max. "Brother, don't you dare. Leo can never know. It would kill him, and no doubt put the black collar flock in danger." I nodded and dropped the subject.

It took all I had to pull myself away from the only person on Earth at that time that made me feel calm and happy. I rushed down the hallway with the reminder that come nine I would be back in his arms, safe, and cozy where I desired to be more than anything.

I was practically flying down the steps to the fifth floor for my next assignment. Mad Maxx took the wheel from me and warned the rest to stay back until called. He glared at me with suspiciousness. I suppose they were all a bit miffed I almost spilled the beans.

I shrugged. "I hate lying to him is all Mad Maxx. We can afford those stupid dentures. Why should he pay for it?"

Mad Maxx scoffed at me. "Mad Max, you are a fool. If Leo pays for the teeth that Matz insists we get. Then that money he would have used can go towards the flock's care or lodgings. You never think. Lies are okay when they protect the ones you love from pain. Telling him that we are the prostitute will kill him and likely get Marc, Kloe, Ghazi and Aara, sent back to the silver. Keep this shit to yourself or everyone will be sorry for it."

I heard a sudden gasp that pulled me out of my lecturing Mad Max. The boy's head swiveled around a seek out where this human noise came from. I spotted Lucus not more the a few feet away watching from the shadows as he had earlier. I groaned and ignored that idiot. I took off down the fifth-floor hall head straight for Rolf's apartment.

I kept a baleful eye on Lucus that was still following from a distance as the Voter answered my knocking I was beginning to think I may have to move up that stalker's execution date if he persisted to interfere and listen in on things that were not his business.

Rolf smiled with thrill. "Mad Maxx. Ah, you come to join me for breakfast?"

I nodded. "Well, ja, I was going to but just as I arrived something came up. I wonder could I ask you to do me a favor? I do not expect you to put yourself out for free. I have some money I can pay you to go back to the store where you buy the Felicity sheep."

Rolf nodded with a look of much humor. "You need not pay me for every fucking favor I do for you Maxx. You know sometimes friends do things for each other without expectation of return. I am happy to go get you more lambs anytime. I would like to ask though, what the hell are you doing with them?"

I smiled with pride. "I am collecting a flock, Rolf. I thank you for the mercy of doing this for me since Peter makes sure I cannot leave to do this myself. I have the money and a note of just what I need from town. I must

66

insist you take what you think is owed for all this I ask, and I need them delivered to my apartment no later than one if you could? If I am not back home by that time push Matz out of your way and place them in my room. In fact, if you need to hit him to get this done, I won't argue with you over it." I chuckled as I handed him the six hundred dollars and written instructions.

Rolf laughed hard as he took the list without looking at it or the money. "You are an evil cuss, Maxx. Sure, I will hit him if he interferes."

I nodded and started off down the hallway to my next destination when Rolf led out a loud wail. "Maxx, holy fuck. Are you kidding me? What the hell. Are you sure?" I turned to see him holding up the huge wad of cash and gazing at the note with his eyes wide in shock.

I laughed with much humor at his silly face. "Is that not enough for all that I desire?"

He flashed his stunned eyes at me. "There is more than enough. Maxx, what are you going to do with all this?"

I shrugged. "I already told you, Rolf. I am collecting a flock. I see you tomorrow morning for breakfast, ja?" He nodded still looking at that money in surprise.

I started down the steps and noticed the Lucus was gaining with each floor. I quickened my pace and so did he. I was nearly beyond angry by the time I made it down to the first floor. I could not have him following me to Karsten's apartment.

Bad enough he already knew so much about my movements. I dared not allow him to gain information on my little black collar family. I took off down that dead end hallway I had caught him in the few days before. Like an idiot, he came after me just as he did the first time. As he rushed past my place of holding up the wall I jumped out behind him blocking his exit.

I growled out. "Lucus, I don't want to kill you but apparently you are insisting that I do. Forgive me. It is nothing personal, okay ja it is. I am going to inform you after I have strangled the life from your flesh, I will break into your apartment and burn your notebooks. I have had enough of your useless studies." I began to walk toward the man.

He stood there trembling but didn't back away. "Christian, please. This is not how you work. I am never going to use the information I have against you. If I had wanted to do that I would have long ago. Think for a minute will you."

I kept coming with an evil grin as I got ready to let Christian take the wheel. "You haven't used it yet, that is true. Eventually, you will though. No one goes through this much trouble collecting the dirty laundry without interest to send it to the washer at some point. I don't believe your crazy story that you are merely watching me for personal thrill of making predictions in a game that doesn't exit. I am not willing to wait till you can injure me, and everyone around me with your nosey observations."

Lucus dropped his eyes to the floor looking at his boots as he shivered in fear but didn't move. "Okay, you are right. I have been lying about my reasons for following you all these years, but not to you, to me."

I stopped in my tracks suddenly confused by that weird statement. "What? How can you lie to yourself but not to me? Christ you are fucking nuts. I almost feel bad killing the insane. I realize you cannot help yourself, but damn it Lucus, I have to do this, or you will do far worse to me in the end."

He nodded. "I suppose I already have Christian. I saw Julius and Grisham snatching you from the halls. I was there when Ben pulled you into that closet. I watched you rushing from the Haus door to your most certain death the day Geraldine and Felix died. I watched you being restrained outside of Peter's apartment in tears when they hauled that friend of your Ryker to his doom, and so many other horrors. I stood there and watched it happen but did nothing. I do deserve your wrath, and any death you grant me is too kind."

I stood there completely flabbergasted by that shit. "Why are you telling me all this now, Lucus? I tell you I have come to kill you and you are blabbering out damned good reasons to do it. Are you wishing for death? Is there someone going to jump out and haul me away the second I try? What is going on?" I felt the terror within rising as I flashed looks all around me wondering if the Guard was on its way.

Lucus frowned "Nein, I tell you this because it is truth. There is no other reason. I have done wrong by you all these years and last night on the stairs for the first time I realized it. You are not some actor that doesn't feel the pain I have never warned you was coming. You could have been killed and many others were when I had the power to stop it. I understand when I never did that I am as bad if not worse than those I thought myself better than. So, you go ahead and end my pain. I swear I cannot live with this remorse I feel for never being there to help anyone, especially you."

That made me shrug. "Why should you care what happened to a stupid silver collar? That is what the Dominants of this Haus do. They use the weak to feel strong. You need not throw yourself into the jaws of death over no more or less than any in this place deserve. I merely want you to stop following me. That is all I ask. If you swear to leave me in peace, I forget all that you did by doing nothing. I told you this already."

He shook his head. "I cannot stop following you Maxx. Go ahead and end me. If I am not close to you, I think I may die anyway."

I scoffed. "You are fucking weirder than anyone I ever met, and I know Jonas far too well, brother. So that is saying something. How the hell will you die if you stop stalking me? Is Gretta going to kill you? You have a deal with her to collect things to use against me no doubt, or Kilian maybe?"

He looked up and stared right into my eyes. "Nein, I told you I work for no one. I need you Christian to feel alive. I realized last night I am in love with you and likely always have been."

That made me near faint away in pure shock and terror. "Holy hell. Okay, psycho, I have had enough of this conversation. One more God damned schwuler tells me he is in love with me I swear I jump from the banister. I am leaving now. I will kill you later." I turned and ran, not walked, from that hallway nearly ready to piss my pants at the latest nightmare unfolding.

Once I got to Karsten's apartment and made damned sure I hadn't been followed by Lucus, I turned the wheel over at Mad Maxx.

I was most irritated at that weirdo's confession to me as I knocked on her door with vigor. Marc answered as usual. His innocent, loving smile as always melted my stony heart. I allowed him to wrap his little arms around my waist and happily accepted his invitation inside. All the little lambs had just returned from there stable duties and were sitting around playing with their stuffed toys.

I sat down on the couch next to Karsten. She gave me an update on the health and good welfare of the children. I understood all of them needed to have the physical done by the Haus doctor. She wrote down the cost for the four to hand over to Matz. He needed to work it into the expenses list. I smiled with much humor as Ghazi proudly announced that he possessed the strongest lungs and toughest heart on earth.

Marc and Arca giggled while I could see the look of love in Kloe's eyes. My oldest lamb was falling head over heels for her youngest brother. I watched as the proud little Ghazi demonstrated his muscles, then he slipped a look back to the smitten fair-haired beauty.

Ah, the feelings were mutual. That budding of first love between the two was both beautiful and refreshing to watch. I briefly imagined that one day Annette and I would have Kloe and her Mann Ghazi bring their flock to play among our own.

That said, as their father I needed to be assured that no funny business happened between them until the day Ghazi was ready to make Kloe his own for life. I called Karsten to the kitchenette pretending to need her aid for gaining a glass of water. I pointed out the situation and that clever woman nodded indicating she was aware of our little pair.

I was relieved to hear that Karsten had enforced a strict policy with regard to sleeping arrangements. She would make sure that Kloe would be wearing white to her wedding day with the little boy that had the big dreams of a huge flock of sheep.

Karsten frowned when after our brief discussion of the love birds I informed her that it was time for me to go. "Maxx? You look very tired. I and the children worry that you work too hard. Is Matz giving you no time off? Honey, you cannot keep going at this pace. Please, I beg of you, take a rest. If you need a place to hide, my home is always your own. You have granted me the joy of raising your children. You take care of our family better than any truthful man could dare to try. I am eternally grateful to you for it. If you will not take my favors then I would ask you to never turn away my offer of sanctuary." She pulled me into her warm embrace looking deep into my eyes with a bit of sadness in her expression.

Before I could stop myself I leaned down and kissed that beautiful woman on her lips. I found it incredibly hard to keep it to just that kiss, as my interest in her began to, uhm, grow. "Thank you for all you do, Karsten. You can see the honest affection in the children's eyes for their adopted mother, but not one of them can rival that of her Maxx's true love for her. I must go now before I never can leave you again."

She groaned as if in pain as I pulled from her embrace. Without another word I quickly retreated to the living area while keeping my hands strategically over the front of my breeches. That woman drove me to madness with her incredible mouth.

I kissed them all good day on the forehead and reminded them to mind their mother. Each waved and swore to be the good kid. I found much pride in those glorious little boys and girls that the Haus would have seen as nothing more than the disposable sex toys.

I left the apartment with the gratitude the each would have the choice in their lover and timing of it. It seemed so wrong that what all humans should be permitted was only theirs thanks to the color they wore on their necks. I wandered down that hallway toward the dungeon stairwell trying to block out the memories of humiliation, loss and despair that seemed to greet me in every corner of that hellish place.

The silvers and black knelt all around me in reverence as I traveled. I wanted so badly to save them all, but I didn't have the power nor the money. I made it to the thudding room to find Peter sitting on a table with his head down appearing asleep. I silently entered and stood there waiting for him to awaken.

After ten minutes of my doing nothing, he opened his eyes suddenly and glared at me. "You didn't bother to alert me to your lesson time?"

I shook my head. "You were asleep Peter. That is not my place."

He growled out in anger. "You are the dumbass, Maximillian. Only a fucking submissive would treat his equal as the Master. When that clock says eleven you are to begin the lesson with me whether I am asleep, or the fucking Haus is on fire. You hear me?"

I shrugged. "As you say Peter." He reached out and slapped me hard.

I backed up and looked around for the tawse and he noticed that fear in my searching eyes. "What is the matter, Maximillian? Worried I will get that thudder out on you?"

I nodded. "Ja. I don't desire another thrashing, Peter. You want me to awaken you next time then I do it. You need not hit me over that, uhm, over dat."

Peter scoffed. "You mean that directive? You were going to say the word. Say it."

Meine head dropped and began to hurt. "Peter, I don't understand this shit you do. If you desire I do something than say so. I am not trying to anger you. Why does the Dominance training seem like the same thing as the submissive one?"

He stopped his approach and sighed loudly. "Fuck. This is not working at all. You are not getting any of it. You are supposed to stand your ground, Maximillian. I tell you what to do and you tell me fuck off."

I winced. "Then you beat me for it. No thanks. I am tired of broken bones and busted lips. Sucking a cock is painful with a swollen mouth. You still expect me to do that, ja? Well, then I will not get crosswise with you. I learned that lesson long ago. You say do something, then I fucking do it. No quarrels. I want to be the doctor and have the Frau. You will see that neither happens if I make you angry."

Peter groaned. "This is going to be way harder than I ever imagined. Shit. Okay forget this for now. I want to see your lessons. Bring them out and hurry up about it."

I put my bag on the table then pulled each book out with the work I had finished. I trembled slightly as I handed it all to him. I expected he would beat me for not getting the list completed. I stood there awaiting my fate. I sincerely hoped he would keep his thudding to the safety zones this time. Otherwise, I was in for a long night or two.

Peter gasped with his eyes wide as he went through each list and checked my work. I flinched with each noise of surprise he made. I thought for sure I was a goner. That expression he wore was unlike any I had ever seen. I assumed the worst and braced for it.

To my surprise he put all it on the table then gazed at me appearing shocked. "You almost did the entire list, Maximillian."

I nodded keeping my eyes down. "I apologize Peter. I will do better tonight I swear it. There is no excuse for not completing the work. I accept the punishment for the failure."

He shook his head in disbelief. "I cannot believe you. Maxx, that list was for the whole month. You did a month's worth of work in one night. I have not checked it closely, but when I spot checked it, it was all correct. How the fuck did you do this?"

I looked up in my own startle. "The whole month? I thought you meant me to do all that in one day. I misunderstood."

He smiled with glee. "Ja, you did, but then again you didn't Doctor Weiss. Holy hell. You are smarter than I ever imagined. That brain of yours is amazing. At this rate you will be done with four years in less than two. Ah we must start moving you faster. I will get the next list prepared tonight. You finish the few lessons you have left on this one. We take the first tests on Monday instead of two weeks from now. You think you can be ready that fast?"

I smiled, as what he was saying sunk in at last. "Ja, I can be ready. I want to finish as quickly as possible. I thank you for the mercy of it."

Peter chuckled. "If only you could learn to be the Dominant as fast as you comprehend the human biology and mathematics the we could say goodbye to Mad Maxximillian and hello to Master Maxx."

I frowned. "I will try harder to understand your Dominance lessons, Peter. If maybe you explain it more completely then I can grasp it?"

He shook his head. "There is no way to do that. You either find the strength to stand up or you stay on your knees Maxx. For now, I believe you owe me services. I cannot continue the lesson I wanted to do, and you need no instructions on your studies. I have forty-five minutes to kill. Each time you fail the lesson in Dominance I will punish you not by the tawse as I always have. Nein. If you insist on behaving like the pleasure submissive. I treat you like one. Hurry up, go lock the door and then get back here and do the job I trained you to do."

I grumbled at that most unfair punishment for the failure that I didn't understand but did as I was told. He, as usual, made me wish I had taken the thudding instead. I never have learned to get over the disgust that sex with Peter causes me. I suppose if I ever did, it would be time to put your Master Maxx to the yard as a true mad dog.

I finished that nasty task and was released early. I took my books and put them back in the bag. I rushed from that room mainly because I feared he would want seconds. Yuck. I headed right to the dentist. The entire way I kept my eyes open for Lucus. This time he was nowhere to be found.

I arrived at that small room and took a seat. The Haus dentist only came to visit once a month and often this room was packed wall to wall. That day, I was the only customer waiting on him. The man came out into this makeshift waiting area and called me back. I got into his fancy laying down chair trying to recall if I had ever seen a dentist before this one. If I had, my memory was too young to remember it.

He told me to open my mouth and he stuck fancy devices inside it that looked torturous. He swore to me that it wouldn't hurt but I didn't believe him. I closed my eyes and braced for the pain as he pushed on the broken shards and nubs that used to be my teeth. He gasped and groaned for several minutes then pulled his tools out and looked at me with seriousness.

This man called Dr. Leighherz said, "Maximillian, in all my years as the dentist I have never seen such a mess in one so damned young. Did you go through the windshield of a car or some other severe accident? This damage I see is not from poor care or disease. I see blunt force trauma. What the hell happened to your teeth?"

I shrugged assuming he seriously wanted to know based on the way he acted. "Well, the Vampire Jonas and Malfred back when they were my Masters, they wanted me to do that London Bridge business. Malfred he is the young man, and he became too eager in his thrust. I couldn't hold myself against the force of it and I was pushed forward without warning. Jonas was pushing his cock into my mouth at that moment, and I accidently gasped from the pain. That caused my mouth to close slightly too much, and the teeth scraped down on Jonas's manhood scratching him up a bit. The Vampire thought I bit him on purpose. He pulled me off that bed out of Malfred's couple to punish me for it. He got his hammer and busted the front ones out with it one by one. Then he got the metal file and used it to grind what was left down to the gum line. He completely filed the back ones when he couldn't reach them easy with the hammer. He said I couldn't bite him anymore that way and that I didn't need them. Blow jobs are smoother without such frivolity. Anyway, the nubs started to rot fast in the hospital. The nurses told me that medication of Doctor Altergott's was eating away at what was left of my teeth. So, then Matz said I need to get new ones. I wish you would leave my mouth be, mister. I don't desire any more trouble. It seems everyone is concerned about my teeth."

That Doctor Leighherz sat there with his mouth open appearing horrified, then finally he cleared his throat. "Uhm, okay then I will get an estimate done for you Mr. Weiss. I will need to pull all your teeth but four that I

79

believe I can cap, save and use to attach full upper and bottom teeth. Partials, holy hell, are you funning me? A hammer? Really? Oh Christ, I am going to have nightmares."

I winced at that. "You think you will? I see that fucking hammer almost every night. You got to pull all of them? Will that hurt much?"

The dentist frowned. "Maxx, I will make damned sure you feel nothing. I think you have suffered enough, don't you? You go sit in the waiting area while I write down some numbers and cry like a fucking baby at that horror story. I will bring this out to you and give you an appointment to begin the work in one week. When we are done you will have beautiful teeth once again. This time, no one can take that away from you." He patted me on the arm.

I frowned at that "You mean I cannot take them out when I need to. The Vampire won't like that, sir."

The dentist shuddered. "Please Maxx, go sit in the other room. I don't desire to hear any more of this. I am sorry for the abuse you suffer but I am not able to do a fucking thing about it. I would rather not know what dark horrors lurk behind the eyes of the foul people that inhabit this Haus. I don't think I could work here anymore if I did."

I nodded. "You are smarter than I realized then. You should have gone the extra years and become a real doctor." I got up and did as he told me.

He came out within ten minutes with an envelope that contained the estimate, several appointments for the work, and detailed descriptions of what he planned to do to fix everything. He bid me good day and I stuffed that envelop in my pocket and headed back for the fourth floor. Once again, I was without my stalker in tow. I wondered if he had taken my advice to stop following or if he did himself in before I had to. Either way, Lucus appeared to no longer be my problem. I cannot lie and say I was not glad of it.

I arrived back home just fifteen minutes before one. Matz was out for a change. I happily let Rolf into the Haus when he knocked exactly on time. I smiled as he brought in the boxes full of the stuff I requested. He smiled as I marveled at each thing he showed me.

Then to my surprise he handed me back ten dollars. "I don't want this that was left over by your purchases. I know you will want to argue but do not Maxx. I had so much fun seeking all the things on your list, and I got a date with a gorgeous Frau that worked at one of the stores. She was aiding me and if not for your list, tonight I would not be stepping out with that amazing woman. We are even, ja?"

I took the money. "As you wish Rolf. Thank you again for the help."

He started to leave then turned around. "Adagio for Strings? That is a beautiful sound. Must be a special lady you are courting. Good luck, tiger." He giggled then left the Haus with a quickness to his step.

Another knocking came almost immediately as he left. I answered to find a handful of black collars there holding fancy Vampire outfits still in there plastic garment wrappers. I led them to the closet, and they put all the clothing Jonas had promised to replace inside. I was finally ready to deal with the hardest part of my chores for the day. I needed to inform Roland I would not be the whore that deflowered him.

I hit the shower cleaning up Peter's mess and preparing for a night with my lovers Jakob and Leo. I got out and chose the fanciest of the Vampire outfits and didn't skimp on the makeup. I had to hid all the fucking bruises on my face from the beatings over the days before you know.

I packed up one of the boxes that Rolf left me and kissed Felicity goodbye. I headed out back to the first floor to break the news to Roland.

Matz passed me on his way to the apartment and tried to get me to return. I stood my ground informing him I was headed down to give Roland back his money. Matz was pissed off, but he realized this time I was not going to listen to him. I swore I would eat and take his medication the second I got home. That caused him to relent, and he let me go.

He stopped just as I was almost out of earshot and yelled out, "You look gorgeous, Maxx. Roland is going to throw a fit when he sees what he is missing. You shouldn't be so cruel to tease him like you will do."

I yelled back, "I told you to trust me, Matz. You cannot know everything can you? I didn't get this far being the complete idiot. I will see you shortly." I rushed down the stairs before he could retort back to that.

I arrived at the first-floor apartment and let myself inside. I knew that Roland was due in less than thirty minutes. He was likely going to be upset that I would not take his money, but I hoped he would understand.

While I waited, I unloaded the things that I knew would make my job as the whore easier. Matz had not spent much money on his home, and it was barebones furniture without any comforts of worth. I smiled as I pulled out the small radio with the capacity to play a cassette tape. I had never seen such an amazing technology before.

I sat there several minutes marveling at both these items, then after a bit of work placed that tape inside the radio hole for it. I pushed the buttons until I learned the crude ability to work the gadgets. I admit I had a great deal of fun with it. I heard Roland come into the apartment just as I finished placing aside the last item that I purchased that day.

I came out into the living room to find Roland wearing his finest clothing and smelling to high heaven of some cheap perfume. In his hands he carried a dozen red roses and on his face he wore a shy smile as he held them out to me.

I smiled back and took the flowers. "Roland before you get the wrong idea. I must tell you I cannot accept your money for this service. I apologize but it simply is the wrong thing to do, no matter what you say."

Rolands smile melted and his face fell. "Maxx, I, uhm, please I beg of you to reconsider. This is what I want. I swear I am at peace with it and don't see you as a whore. I wish for you to be the one I lose my virginity to. I don't know what else I can say to get you to see it through my eyes."

I nodded as I reached into the bag and took out the thirteen hundred dollars. "I do want to see this through your eyes Roland. I do believe you misunderstand me. I am giving back your money, but I am not turning you away. I agree to give you the fantasy, but I cannot do it as your whore. I must do it as your truthful lover."

Roland gasped as he stared at me dumbfounded. "I don't understand. You are going to sleep with me for free?"

I chuckled bitterly at that. "Nein, I do nothing for free Roland. Today I had the Voter Rolf put a deposit on a precious violin of the finest quality in your name. There is thirteen hundred dollars still owed on it due by this afternoon. You can have me this moment for the price of hearing you play that instrument in serenade for the honorable Jakob at our table in the Great Hall at six-thirty tonight. I wish to hear you make it cry over the beauty of that most magnificent man and for the grace of the one that strokes its strings. You agree to pay that price and I will take you as my lover and bring you enlightenment from your innocence."

Roland's eyes began to flood with tears as he shuddered, appearing almost unable to speak. "You have my word Maxx, but I cannot accept such an unbelievable gift."

I interrupted him. "You ask me to accept one from you far more precious than what I grant in return, don't you? There is only a fleeting moment in time when all is simple Roland. You are untouched and pure but the second you lay with me you will become a slave to your drives. I didn't have the choice, but you do. Allow me to see what it would have been like through your eyes. I want my vision to be as clear as your own for this. You pretend that I love you and I will pretend I choose you. No money, no force, only a moment in time where both are the honest lovers that have but a short time to live an entire life together. There is no yesterday and there is no tomorrow, only now."

Roland wept but came forward and pulled me into a deep, slow, kiss that tasted of tears of gratitude. I allowed him to drag me along in his embrace that grew more fevered with each step closer to the bedroom.

Once inside he pulled out of our kissing and gazed at me with adoration in his expression. "I accept your price Maxx and your mercy. I am forever honored by it." He then turned to look at the bed and gasped almost coming apart in tears again.

I smiled as I walked over and hit the button that was marked play. The slow, mournful sounds of the violins echoed in the room. I had picked Samuel Barber's Adagio for Strings as the serenade for the fantasy lovers. One untouched by the flesh and one untouched by the heart came together, called by the rich music to unite.

Roland took me in his arm and swayed to the music doing his best to quell his tears as we slow danced for a few moments. "You did all this for me? Rose pedals on the bed, the music, my dream violin, and you become the romantic lover of my fantasies. Why Maxx? I am nothing."

I stroked his cheek. "You are not nothing Roland. You are the poet, the musician, the artist that you thought me to be. I see a man that thinks with his mind but feels everything with his heart. The world is a cold brutal place without those like you to add color to the grimness of reality. I thought it funny that you say you are still the virgin because you could not find a lover that fit your ideal of everything you think you are not. Well, Maxx is the one that is getting your fantasy. I am the lucky one here. I can boast that my lover is pure, beautiful and talented. You my love can only pretend the same is true of the one in your arms."

Roland stopped dancing and grabbed my chin staring into my eyes. "You are so wrong there. You may not be the virgin Maxx, but I will damned if you are not the purest soul I have ever known." He pulled me into his kiss once more.

Slowly he undressed me, and I did the same for him as we touched like wanton lovers do. I made no excuses when my interests didn't rise but his did. He was aware that I am the straight man, and even in the romantic fantasy, I can only lie to myself to a point. I gently employed the full oral services until he begged me to grant him release of my charms.

I returned to his passionate kissing. Carefully, I rolled to my back pulling him to take his place above me in the position of the lovers. I did my best to instruct him on how to prepare for this act without appearing crude or cold about it. He was trembling but kept his nerve and erection despite the realities of same gendered sex comfort necessities. *You know Meine Liebe, lubrication. A must when there is no female involved.*

The second we were properly situated and both prepped, I nodded that I was ready.

He leaned down and kissed me deeply once more and whispered out, "I will treasure this moment and you for all my days Maxx. I can never say I felt more loved or special than I do this moment." He rose back up and began his penetration with surprising gentleness and much shaking in fear.

He asked me several times if he was hurting me. I smiled bitterly and assured him he was not. *Though that was not entirely truthful, now was it my Frau? Master Maxx winked at me, and I glared at him. He screwed up his face as if he had stepped into a bee's nest and patted my head. Ja, you get it. Yikes!* Roland than began his thrust dropping to my chest to kiss and embrace me as he took his steps into full manhood. It took less than five minutes for him to moan out he was about to find his climax.

I held him tightly as he bucked with the thrill of spilling his seed into his fantasy lover in one single perfect moment. His virginity was lost at long last to the sounds of the crying violins playing in the background just as he had always envisioned it would be.

Roland was overtaken by the emotional upheaval of it all. I allowed his cuddle as he broke into tears of joy thanking me repeatedly for setting him free and opening his eyes to the beauty that was himself.

I finally got him to calm down. With some convincing I talked him into the bath service. In the tub he received the final surprise I had rushed to the apartment to set up for his romantic deflowering. A candle lit bubble bath with the rose pedals and perfumed salts. Roland pulled me into the water with him before I got halfway done with the service. You could hear me laughing at his silliness for miles.

I allowed this 'newly minted man' to clumsily try to wash me in that crowded tub as I thought of Jakob and wondered could my plan for him to see the gorgeous soul he truly was work for him as well as it did for Roland. I certainly hope so. I only had a few hours left to prepare for the most unusual love affair I can ever boast to have had so far.

Chapter 17: The Queen of the Knight

It took a bit to get Roland talked into the bath service, but it took longer to get him out of that tub. He was enjoying his single moment of fantasy to the hilt, trying hard to never let it go. I couldn't help but laugh at his groaning when I told him his time was nearly up. I could see that desperation to stay in the dream, until dragged out kicking and screaming back to the cold, lonely reality in his eyes.

He stepped out and I dried him off then gently pulled him back into the bedroom. Roland sat down on the bed in silence as I redressed him in completion of his full-service request. He watched me pick up my own clothing and start to cover my nakedness.

I nearly screamed and ran away when he slipped up on me. He grabbed my blouse from my hands. Then aided me in his own version of dressing service. I chuckled at his clumsiness when trying to button me back up, but I was careful to give him many kind compliments. *Though between you and me Meine Liebe, Roland was terrible at this most simple of pleasure sub tasks.*

He was helping me put on my jacket when I noticed the sadness in his expression. "Maxx, I cannot thank you enough for the magnificent things you have done for me. I feel ashamed that you give me the dream, and my passion in the violin back. I give you nothing but a dozen red roses, a song for Jakob, and a mess to clean up. It doesn't seem fair to me somehow."

I smiled as I stroked his cheek. "Ah, you are so wrong to think that is all you give me this afternoon, Roland. I can see the change in your eyes. You are no longer afraid to be the beauty that is you. In time, you will understand how much of a gift that truthfully is, my love."

He shook his head as if confused. "That doesn't make any sense, Maxx. How is my realizing that I have been asleep and hiding from the world matter to you?"

I kissed his cheek and he shuddered. "I told you Roland, the world is a dark, grim place. Brutality causes a man to hate. Pure kindness is the only cure for it. That music I can now hear truthfully playing in your soul sooths my beast. You must understand I want to find my way home. I will never be able to do it alone. When the glorious heart around me is shining, then it helps to light my way. You, Roland, took me one more step to my own fantasy come to reality. I thank you for it and shall treasure it for all my days."

Roland nodded. "I think I am beginning to understand, Maxx. I suppose I must hurry to pick up my violin. I do believe I owe you a kindness return." A peaceful smile broke across his lips.

I laughed. "That you do Roland. Be sure to never tell Matz nor the boys that I let you have the service before the payment, ja? Don't want anyone to get the wrong idea and think I am in love with you. You are ready to hit the scene and break a million heart with your newly acquired skills. I am far too sensitive to endure the pain of it. Oh well, that is my punishment for fooling around with the musician. You know my mother warned me about you fellows. Love them and leave them she said." I winked as he chuckled, turning red with his bashfulness at that statement.

He leaned in and kissed me once last time with passion then said, "You can be assured this musician will be back a million times. You warned me and I realize too late your wisdom. I am now a slave to my drives. I cannot wait to hold you in my arms again. I already feel that I may cry that I must leave you."

I playfully swatted his shoulder. "Stop toying with my heart, Roland. You damned artists are all the same, seducers. Now go get your violin and let her do the crying for you at six-thirty. Don't be late. Play something worthy of royalty for Jakob, nein, good enough for a Queen."

Roland nodded. "I have something I composed many years ago that I am sure he will love. I never let anyone else hear it because I swore I wouldn't play it for less than the finest of ears."

I smiled as I watched him begin his rush to get a car to take him to town. "Go see Rolf. Better hurry or that kitty hound will be off to chase the girls. He knows where your soul is waiting. Also, if it wouldn't be too much, can you give the roses you brought for me to Jakob instead?"

He stopped with suddenness at the door. "Maxx, those are for you, my love."

I nodded. "They are beautiful Roland. Yet you gave me something of yours that make them seem trivial in comparison. Jakob on the other hand could use the love. I ask you to take them and you give them to him in your own name. Make him feel desired Roland, the way I did for you."

Roland's face broke out in adoration. "Ah, you are something else Maxx. If only my fantasy were real. I could die in your arms a happy old man with or without fortune or future."

I chuckled bitterly. "If you don't hurry and get that violin you are going to die in my arms, Roland, when I kill you for being late and losing what took me great pains to acquire. Go, damn it." I pointed at the door, he laughed as he grabbed the roses on his way out never looking back.

I sat down in that ratty recliner of Matz for a moment. I looked around that empty apartment feeling utterly lost. I wondered what Annette was fixing for supper. The thought that she never missed me at all took hold of my heart and threatened to send me into the crying jag.

I couldn't remember the green fields nor the sound of her voice anymore. Too many years had passed and far too much pain. I closed my eyes. No matter how hard I tried I couldn't see my lambs nor feel their soft coats. All that came to my consciousness was the ashes of the nothing.

I shivered as the fear overtook me that my dreams of the perfect world were not real. For a few moments I was paralyzed with the reoccurring idea that there wasn't anything outside that Haus for me. I felt like the walls had reached out and pulled me into them. I had become a part of that place for all time. I was no longer the prisoner but the fixture. Escape was always a lie I told myself, but the truth had started to rear its ugly head at last.

I gasped and opened my lids looking around wildly with tears beginning to well. That couldn't be fact dammit. I was getting out. I would see the world outside the dark halls and carpet covered rooms one day soon, right?

I left the mess in the bathroom for the black collar maid. I usually would never be so rude, but I had to get out of there. Something was wrong. I needed to get back to the apartment. Felicity would remind me that all was not lost. I needed to hear her voice and feel her soft fur. She always knew how the calm the boy.

I fled down the hallway in a blind panic nearly knocking over the silvers and blacks in my way. *You'd think as often as I ran wildly around like I did those people would have learned better than to get in my way by then, ja?* I was speeding up the steps when suddenly Lucus appeared at the level just above me. He stood there, his head down, right in the way of where I wanted to go.

I halted and almost turned around to run back the way I came. The terror was rising within. I really didn't need a showdown with this creepy guy at that moment. I didn't go forward, but I also didn't desire to head away. All I could do is stand there staring at him. I suppose I was waiting for him to make the first move.

He looked up flashing a look of despair. "Christian. I apologize for upsetting you earlier. I beg your forgiveness for it."

I could barely breath from the anxiety coming over me. "Okay, ja. Apology accepted. You can go now. Thank you Lucus. Be on your way. No harm done." I couldn't believe that I said those words, but I really didn't want to fight with him until I could calm a bit.

Lucus smiled. "You mean it? I have not frightened you away?"

I groaned. "Uhm, can we discuss this another time Lucus? I am in a hurry right now. Please let me pass."

Lucus nodded. "Of course, Christian. I will be happy to speak to you at length when it is convenient for you. Maybe tomorrow morning? I can take you to breakfast at the Great Hall?"

I craned my neck around looking for any other way around this weirdo. "Sure, ja, whatever. I need to go Lucus. See you later. I thank you for the mercy of it." I was so panicked at this point I would have agreed to let him paint my toes pink if he would have just fucking moved out of the way.

He clapped his hands in glee. "Wonderful, I see you at nine ten. I will pick you up." He took off back down the hallway leaving my path open at last.

I waited a few moments after Lucus disappeared to continue my flight. I don't really think his words or invitation really sunk into my stressed out brain. Well till later that night anyway. I was so freaked out by the odd sensation that the Haus was eating me alive I barely registered anything other than the need to get back to Felicity.

Once I arrived at the apartment I didn't hesitate nearly kicking the door in due to my terror. Matz was sitting on the couch, pouting as usual, when I ran past him right for my room. He yelled out causing me to panic even more. I nearly fell as I attempted to cower and keep hauling ass at the same time.

I crashed through the bedroom entry. To my relief Felicity was still sitting on my mattress waiting with patience for my return. I snatched her up and headed right for the closet. Matz came rushing in behind me just in time to see me flee into that enclosed space. I slammed the door behind me.

Matz began pounding on it as I curled up with my lamb to hide. "Maxx, what the fuck are you doing? Did something happen? Come out of there and talk to me, dammit."

I covered my head with the boy's arms. "Go away Matz. I am tired. I need some sleep."

He growled in anger. "In the fucking closet? Geraldine called here crying when she heard you refused her lunch. You expect her to work like she does, then go disrespecting her food so rudely."

I groaned out. "I haven't seen her in a long time. Maybe it is time for a visit. I go later and explain the situation. You ask too much of her, Matz. That lamb cannot hold up at this pace."

Matz yelled out sounding even more upset, "Maxx, get out here this minute. I mean it. I hate to break the door in since they are so expensive, but I will. Don't test me. You want maybe I go get Peter or Jonas? I bet you come out for them."

I wailed, "Please Matz, I need to be in the dark for a little while. Don't call them. I thought you loved me. Why ae you torturing me like this?"

He snorted. "You don't even know torture, Maxx. Come out. Eat your fucking lunch and tell me what Roland said when you gave him back his money? Are we without protection? Is that why you are hiding? Afraid of my wrath? I told you he would be pissed."

I pulled the boy's arms down and scoffed. "Shows what you know Matz. Roland left the apartment with a smile on his face. He was many things but pissed was not one of them."

Matz paused then blew out his breath. "You relented and granted the service request, didn't you? That is why you took over an hour to get home. Fine. That is great. You did the right thing. Come out and give me my cut. Your lunch is getting cold."

That made me cover my head again. "I don't have your cut, Matz. I gave his money back like I told you I would. I traded him a service for the service instead."

Matz sounded furious. "You did what? Holy hell, Maxx. What the hell are we running here? Unless Roland was paying Karsten's fucking rent what the fuck could he possibly train you worth thirteen hundred dollars?"

I sniffed back my tears. "A violin, Matz."

The pimp grew silent then shouted out, "You traded the full service for a violin? Can you even play the fucking thing? Where is it?"

That made me really moan in pain. "Nein, I traded him for his playing the violin at that date with Jakob tonight."

Matz started really pounding on the door full of anger. "You are fucking insane. I am going to get Peter or Jonas, whichever one I can find the fastest. This has to stop. You won't take care of yourself. You won't let me help you do it. Now you sell yourself out for a fucking song that is geared to the seduction of one you had already laid low with your charms. I cannot believe I am yelling this to you while you hide in a closet like a fucking kid. Christ Maxx, this has gotten out of control." I heard him back off the door.

My heart started racing thinking he would go alert Peter or the Vampire to come punish me, "Matz, nein. Wait, I will come out. I eat and take the meds. Please, mercy." I scrambled to get out of the closet to stop him from telling on me.

Matz was standing next to the bed with his arms crossed when I practically fell out of that storage space. He glared at me tapping his foot as I stood up and clutched Felicity to my chest panting in fear. I kept my eyes to the floor and trembled uncontrollably.

He blew out his breath. "Well? You going to tell me what the hell you were thinking trading that service for nothing?"

I shrugged keeping my head down. "I wanted Jakob to feel special is all. I thought Roland could use the boost too. Please Matz don't be angry with me. I can make up your cut the next customer."

Matz rolled his eyes at that. "Oh? So, you will not take my credit but expect me to take yours? Hypocrite. You don't even have the decency to ask me if I was alright with such a selfish decision."

I stole a look at him then dropped my head again. "You were not there to ask, I seem to recall. It was not your ass the man wanted to use for his pleasure. I didn't think you had the right to any say in the bargain."

That made him furious again. "You didn't think I had any say, huh? Well for your information I do have it. I don't care if you are merely stripping down for the fucking doctor. I am to be consulted. You are not well. At this moment anyone can take advantage of you like Roland has,

Maxx. I am sickened that my brother would stoop so low. He knows you are mentally ill. God damn him. Of course, he agreed to such a one sided deal. What a clever bastard he must think he is. What do you think is going to happen when the other wolves hear him bragging about how he outfoxed the daft Maxx? Shit, they will expect you to suck them off for marbles and toys from the cracker-jacks boxes. Oh, this is a nightmare. I am calling that cocksucker out. I swear to God I don't give a fuck if he is my oldest friend. This is going too far with his criminality."

I sniffed as the tears began at his harsh words. "I am not daft Matz nor mentally ill. Why are you always saying that? You treat me like a kid. I am the grown fucking man and a Dominant. You cannot keep telling me what to do."

Matz groaned and covered his eyes. "You are the adult are you? Hmm, and the Dominant too? Funny thing is that usually grownups don't hide in closets cuddling a stuffed toy. They also don't let thugs fuck them for nothing more than a stupid song."

I snuggled Felicity tighter and wept openly. "Leave me be, Matz. You are not my Master, damn you. If you are angry about that money I owe you then fine. Take it out in service. You use me like the sex toy without any care. Not even fucking Osvin is so cold."

He dropped his hand from his face and glared at me. "You think I'm cold? I worry about you constantly. I pick up your food from that lamb and count your pills. I even pay the bills and keep up with the black collar kinder. My whole life is all about Maxx. You dare to say I don't care? Oh, fuck you. I accept your service offer. Get over here on your knees and give me what is owed right this minute. I show you what cold is."

I shook my head "Not in here Matz. I told you never to be in my room. Anywhere else you want what I owe is fine. But not here, not ever." He growled out in irritation as he rushed over and snatched my upper arm. I didn't fight him as he dragged me into the living room.

I stood there still weeping as he plopped down on the sofa undoing his pants. "This good enough for you Maxx? I will put off the other service you already owe till tomorrow. At this rate, I will be entitled to fuck you every day. I am waiting. Get to your job and give me my cut of that take from Roland."

What he said made me cry even harder. "I don't want you fucking me Matz. Mercy please. I need rest. I have this thing with Jakob in only a few hours."

He interrupted me with a snarl, "You should have thought of that before you discounted asking me if I was okay with that service agreement Maxx. I am sick to death of hearing about the poor long suffering straight Priceless. You had no problem letting Roland fuck you. In a few hours you are off to screw around with Jakob. Then off to see your Mann. Did Peter cut you any slack earlier? I bet he got his services attended, didn't he. Matz asks for what is owed him, suddenly you are full of tears over it. You hurt my feelings without any qualms but spare everyone else. I don't see them here watching out for you. Nein, they use you and you seem to like it that way. Well guess what? I can do that too if that is what it will take to earn your respect. I will not repeat myself Maxx. This cock isn't going to suck itself. Get to it. Pay me back now."

I nodded as I wiped my tears and hid Felicity under the pillow on the loveseat. *So, she didn't have to see that shameful scene you know. She is the innocent and going to stay that way too..* I approached Matz and dropped to my knees. Without further quarrel I endured his service demands to pay back his cut of the lost income I gave back to Roland.

I would like to say he showed a little mercy. That would be a lie. He demanded I begin with the oral services. After he was nearly ready to finish the service he pulled me off him and demanded I submit to his penetration.

I tried to argue that he was taking more than owed but he was not going to hear of it. The man was beyond angry full of jealous rage over his misguided belief that I was giving Roland and Jakob the affection he was being denied.

Without further quarrel I put up with him taking his mount from behind. Once again, I used the couch pillows to hide my yells of agony. This time he started the horror forgetting to use the lube. I will never know for sure if that was purposeful or in his fury it slipped his mind. Either way I had to beg him to stop and fix that error. He did thankfully show at least the much decency.

I was quite sure it couldn't get any worse when after an alarming ten minutes of his doing all he could to drag out the act. He told me that he was not satisfied with climaxing the way he already had twice before.

The man uncoupled and rushed to the boy's head. I busted into fresh tears when he demanded I finish this humiliating sexual tryst with my "fucked up mouth." Of course, I did as he wanted, just to end that horror. I was grateful, that thanks to his orgasming this way, I wouldn't have to clean up another mess before seeing Jakob. *Hey, you got to find the silver lining remember.*

He finally reached his apex, rather quickly, thank Gott. He redid his pants while pushing me back away from him. I retreated without further aggression as he sat down on the couch glaring at me still appearing angered.

I dropped my gaze from his and pulled up my breeches feeling about as low as one can get. There wasn't even enough self-worth in me to push the boy's legs to go save Felicity from her pillow tomb.

Matz scoffed. "Tell me Maxx, did you even bother to see that fucking dentist? That Mann of yours is the idiot. Your blow jobs are perfect and smooth, but it is not from lack of teeth. You are quite talented in all areas I have noticed. I would think you were born to do nothing but fuck. I suppose I get what I deserve falling in love with a common whore. To think once I thought you the greatest thing on Earth. You are not. You are over experienced is all. That means used if you missed that insult."

I nodded as I wiped my eyes. "Ja, you are right in that assessment. You love a nothing. I did see the dentist. He says I will have to have all my teeth pulled out and dentures put in."

That made Matz gasp out. "What? Dentures at sixteen. You have to be funning me. That rat bastard is being lazy. You will go back and tell him that we can pay top dollar. There is no reason for you to lose all your teeth."

I stared at the floor. I was sitting at Matz's feet unable to find the will to get out of there for some reason, no matter how nasty he was being to me. "He said that the file Jonas used killed the nerves. There is no repair possible. They are all dying anyway."

Matz sat forward with his eyes narrowed. "What is this you say? Jonas used a file to try to fix your teeth. What a fucking idiot. Of course, that killed the nerves."

I shook my head. "He wasn't trying to fix them, Matz. He was trying to get rid of them. The hammer wouldn't knock them all out. I wouldn't hold still because it hurt so bad. I shouldn't have acted the fool when Malfred took his services. Then I wouldn't have slipped up and bitten the Vampire. I would still have my teeth. Now I won't have any for good. It was my fault. He told me if I ever used my teeth on him he would do it. I fucked up like today." I sighed and wished I could just die and be done with it all.

Matz startled me when he reached out and hugged me tightly. I began to struggle thinking he was trying to attack me. He held on despite my bucking and begging him to let me be.

I grew silent when I realized he was sobbing. "Maxx, oh my Gott. Forgive me. I am the fucking asshole. I thought you are being cruel to me on purpose. You aren't mean at all. Everything you do is, oh Christ. What can I do. How can I help you and not lose my own fucking mind. I am nothing but an uneducated idiot. This is more than I expected. You are not like everyone else, and I keep trying to treat you that way."

Matz's weird behavior frightened me so badly I just sat there as he soaked my jacket with his tears. I couldn't understand this moody fellow. First, he was angry, then he was lustful and suddenly remorseful. It occurred to me he had been telling me repeatedly he was going crazy. I suppose I thought that it was only an expression. That afternoon I realized he was indeed the nutjob. Yikes!

Matz held on to me for several minutes weeping like the kid before I hazarded asking to be released. "Uhm, Matz? Can I have Geraldine's food now? I need to get Felicity tucked in before I go see Jakob in a couple hours too. I apologize for disrupting this, uhm, not attending your emotions? You said the food was getting cold, ja?" I wasn't hungry but I wanted him the fuck off me.

Matz lifted and nodded still crying a bit. "Oh ja. You need to eat Maxx and take your pills. I shouldn't have broken down like that. You don't need more drama I am sure. Okay, I cannot undo the mistakes I have made.

Instead, I will have to buck up and try harder to keep my stupid feelings under control. Poor baby, you wouldn't understand love if it bit you in the ass would you? Here I was acting like the jealous fool, and you are only trying to survive to see the next day. I am really going to beat the stuffing out of Roland for using you like he has."

I started at that. "Nein, Matz. Roland didn't do any such a thing. He argued my deal and was initially unhappy to accept it. He relented when I told him it was my way, or he could go without the service. I have his word that he will never repeat the arrangement made today. He also is aware it will never happen again. The next time he wants services, he must pay like everyone else. If you don't believe me, you can ask him."

Matz glowered. "You can bet your sweet ass I will. That boy's story better match yours or he will be wishing he never met me. No one has the right to take without giving you something of the same value in return Maxx."

I nodded. "Then you will understand I owe you no further services until you pay me again. You used up that three hundred and the money from Roland today. You speaking derogatory during sex, you took full oral services, intercourse and came in area one. That is equal to what you paid, and what I owed."

Matz chuckled with bitterness. "Damn you are good at math Maxx, which is for sure. Ja, you are right. I used up all that I paid in. I better get more money soon or old Matz will be the lone ranger with his hand like always. You forgive me for being the ass to you then?"

I shrugged. "I don't understand what you mean. You paid to speak ugly to me and treat me as the whore. A service is a service."

He sighed. "Ah, ja, I should have seen that coming. You were trained to see it that way. Those feelings of yours are injured but you don't have the will to recognize it. I see your tears but your so used to crying it is second nature to you, isn't it? Well, I am many things Maxx, but I heard what you said this morning. I don't want to be just another bully and abuser in your life. I still don't know how to fix my weakness nor how to reach you without threats, but I am going to keep trying, that I can promise. For now, I suppose that something is better than what you are accustomed to which is nothing."

I kept my eyes down as the confusion came over me. "Can I have the Geraldine plate? I need to fix my makeup and pack the overnight bag. You waste time, Jonas."

Matz gasped. "Maxx, I am Matz not Jonas."

I shot a look of terror at him. "Huh? Nein. Why are you calling the Vampire? I did what you told me to do. Are you displeased with the service? I can try harder if you give me another chance."

Matz backed up and returned to the couch. "Uh oh, okay. I am happy with the service. I am not going to call your Mann I swear it. Be assured you always please me.

Tell you what though. Maxx go get that food in the kitchenette. I will get your pills ready. If you are still tired in a bit, I am sure Jakob will understand if you need to cancel the date."

I stood and began wringing my hands. "There is no reason to put this off. I am tired but that is not unusual. I have been that way for a long time." I took off with speed to get that lamb's food.

Matz sat there watching me eat and I kept a baleful eye on him as well. I didn't desire to have any more troubles out of him. I wanted to seek a way to get him out of my life for good, and fast too. I couldn't handle all that moodiness of his, nor did I care for his constant bullying. If I wanted to live with such difficulty, I could have moved back in with Jonas.

When I finished the meal, he demanded I take the stupid medication as well. That made me more than a little angered. I groused about it expecting him to threaten me as he always did. To my surprise he merely dropped the pills on the coffee table in front of me.

He took a deep breath then said, "Look Maxx. I cannot force you to take them and I am not going to keep being cruel about it either. I confess I have no idea if they are even helping you. That said, I must beg you to keep with the prescription. If you continue to get sick, then soon Kilian will get his way and they will come take you to Heslach. I know you think that man won't know you are skipping them, but he will. This is not my wish for you, believe me. I am like you in this matter, without a choice. If these things don't help, then we both are doomed. Yet we will never know if you don't try."

I looked at him feeling nervous about his words. "What if that Doctor Vagner is trying to poison me? Maybe these things are rotting my brain. Did you ever consider that?"

Matz nodded. "Sure, I did. Maxx I don't want to injure or harm you. I checked with someone that is the expert in the pills and he said they are correct for keeping down the disease you have. I suppose you don't have any trust in me, and why should you. I can only say that I know this medication is not tainted."

I stared at the pills on the table. "But I don't need any medicine. There is nothing wrong with me, Matz."

He sat down next to me and sighed. "You are lying to me or yourself Maxx? Surely, even you can tell something is not right with you. You don't sleep or eat unless I threaten you. Half the time you are shaking in nervousness, and the other half screaming in anger. This doesn't seem unusual to you. Tell me honestly, there is for truth nothing going wrong inside that head of yours and I will relent begging you to take the pills."

I groaned. "I am just needing more sleep is all. You have to stop bullying me and I need more time to study."

Matz nodded. "I agree with all of that. Yet, I think you are fooling yourself if you think a nap is going to solve this hiding in closets and forgetting where you are, Maxx. Please, take the pills. I beg of you." He picked them up and handed them to me.

I winced. "As you say. I don't want to fight with you anymore, or anyone for that matter. If I take them, then you leave me in peace, ja?"

Matz smiled. "You bet brother. I won't threaten or be cruel to you ever again. You have my word. Now I realize my stupidity. I will work hard to make up for the damage I have done."

I popped the pills into my mouth and washed them down. "You leave me alone and there will be no quarrel between us. I don't like you working Geraldine so hard. Stop telling me what to do all the time. I can take care of myself. You are neither my mother nor Master."

Matz nodded. "Nein, I am neither. I am, however, your faithful friend Maxx. I am human and make mistakes, but I am man enough to admit to my shortfalls. I am not going to relent on insisting you eat, sleep, and take the medicine though. I simply must find a less hateful way of getting that done."

I growled at him. "Insist all you like but do it from a distance. I am going to speak to Geraldine tomorrow. She should not be used so badly as you have done. These pills I will flush them down the toilet the second I get half a chance. Then you can shut the fuck up about all of it." I got up and stormed off to my room before I ended up punching him like I had earlier that day.

I'd had enough of Matz's bullshit for a lifetime. If this was what it meant to have a friend you could count Mad Maxx the fuck out of it. I didn't need any.

I cleaned up my face and reapplied fresh makeup. That bath service for Roland and all that crying ruined the first application. Then I made sure that I smelled alright and was in my best look given the situation. I spent the last hours before heading off to see Jakob finding anything to keep me busy in my room. I was avoiding going out to face that flat mate of meine, that I confess.

I swear it took an eternity for that clock to reach six. I really was ready to get the fuck on with that favor for Jakob and end that weird day in the arms of my Leo. It had occurred to me that Rolf was the smart one to forbid the Voters from committing any sexual acts in my apartment before I broke my collar.

If only Matz had followed that rule, then perhaps I would have continued to see my apartment as the sanctuary Rolf intended it to be. As it was, all I could think of was being out of there the second I could escape. The fear that Matz would demand more service from me had managed to set me on edge with anxiety to the point of near madness.

I kissed my Felicity and dropped her in her hiding spot inside my long jacket. I grabbed the items I purchased for this date with Jakob and made sure to put my packed overnight bag, for two nights as Jonas was after Leo, where I could quickly grab it later.

I didn't intend to return to that fucking place for at least the next two days. If I were lucky then maybe I could find another place to live, besides Jonas's home, before I had to come back. Matz could have it. I no longer wanted to live there. Yikes!

I rushed out the door ignoring Matz's wishes of good luck. I knew he didn't mean that a bit. He hated Jakob or anyone he viewed as the rival despite the fact that I was not interested in him nor any of them, well except for Leo.

I was moving with speed down the hallway to Jakob's place when I saw Lucus sitting in his chair watching me. I groaned at this most annoying re-occurring theme in my life lately. I decided to pretend he was not there. I really needed to focus on the heart of Jakob and as usual as of late both Matz and Lucus were doing their best to shake me up. At least that is how I saw it.

Lucus shouted out to me when I moved past him without even looking at him. "Where you headed Christian? You look amazing. What is in the box?"

I snorted but didn't take the bait and respond. I kept my eyes forward and the boy's feet hauling ass. If Lucus wanted to know so bad, let him work for it. I thought of what Peter said about standing up for myself. I thought it was maybe time I attempted that very thing. Though I was in no mood for anymore beatings, that was for damned sure.

I arrived at Jakob's door hoping that Lucus took the hint that I wasn't interested in his commentary or involvement. I nearly fainted when I saw him come around the corner. He took a place leaning against the wall and started writing in his Mad Maxx book.

I wanted to yell at him to leave me be, but I could hear Jakob coming to answer. I dared not ruin this night for him. If there was anyone on earth I desired to see have a beautiful memory it was this generous man.

Jakob opened the door and immediately the smell of expensive perfume lofted into the air. I smiled as I noticed he was wearing his signature pink blouse, white jeans and a fancy brown fur coat. I almost messed up and giggled when I saw he also sported a pair of white chunky heels like the frau's wear. It was not that I was humored at this mild cross dressing. It was just so damned, well Jakob.

Jakob saw my looking him over and he blushed. "Ah, you like what you see my sexy hunk?" He posed dramatically.

I grinned with a wicked look in my eyes. "Very much, my beauty. You are as always the vision of perfection. I fear if you do not hurry and come out here than I will be tempted to skip dinner, ja?" I winked at him.

He grabbed the door jab wildly as if trying to catch himself from falling. "Christ, Maxx you keep teasing me like that and you will get desert before the main course."

I chuckled then reached into my small box and pulled out a single long-stemmed rose. "I brought this for you. I thought it was surely the most gorgeous thing I had ever seen, but now it pales in comparison, I fear."

Jakob swooned as he took the flower. "You are one hell of a sweet talker, Maxx. I fear I am going to have to insist you ravage me at least twice tonight. Let's get this silliness of eating out of the way so I can at least pretend I am the lady, ja?"

I laughed even harder. "You are more than the lady, Jakob. I believe if you insist on everything being done twice tonight then allow me to repeat my attempt to woo you." I reached into the box and pulled out another long-stemmed rose.

He let out a loud yelp as he took it. "Two? Oh my God, Maxx. What else do you have in that box you carry?" His eyes were glassy with adoration as he stared at it panting ever so slightly in anticipation.

I handed it to him. "Only the minor things one could expect when being seduced. I fear they are all far too common for one of your exquisite value. Yet, it was the best I could do."

Jakob squealed as he dug into the box and found a box of chocolates, bath salts, and a new romance novel. "Oh, this is more than I expected Maxx, and I thought this night was going to be special already. I love all this. You wait here. Don't you go anywhere, or I will die." He grabbed the back of my head and planted a quick kiss on my lips before rushing off into his apartment to store his treasures for later examination.

I giggled as I heard him knocking things down and swearing in his haste to get back to me. I stole a look down the hall and saw Lucus staring back his eyes wide and mouth open.

I waved with a mischievous smile crossing my face. He looked back at his book quickly trying to pretend he didn't see me do that. Ha, what an idiot.

Jakob came back within only minutes. I waited for him to close and lock his door then allowed him to take my arm. I smiled brightly as I led him down the hallway headed to the Great Hall.

At first we traveled in silence. The silvers and black all knelt as we crossed their paths and that always made Jakob giggle.

He looked at me appearing curious,. "Does this thing they all do bother you? I once thought it would be pretty cool if they knelt for me, but then I decided maybe it would be annoying."

I nodded. "It can be. Especially when you are running from an enemy or trying to sneak off to enjoy a little privacy with a beautiful man on your arm. They all give away my position, ja?"

Jakob laughed out loud and swatted my shoulder playfully. "Maxx, you are so bad. I am happy to hear you call me such a thing, but you shouldn't lie. It causes wrinkles, you know."

I frowned. "I never lie to you, Jakob. You are beautiful both inside and out. I cannot even begin to tell you how honored I feel that you look my direction and notice me. I have no idea why you have, but there is not a day that goes by that I am not thankful for it."

He gasped. "Honey, you need not lower yourself to try to impress the likes of me. I wish you would keep that pleasure submissive training in check when Matz or Leo isn't around to make jealous with it. It is just the two of us. You can be Maxx without the bullshit."

I stopped immediately, halting Jakob in his stride by the suddenness of it. "You stop that right now, Jakob. Unless insulting me is a way to bring you a smile, then just don't. It is beneath you."

Jakob craned his neck around wildly to see if we were being eaves dropped on then said in seriousness, "Look Maxx, I know you only take me out to pay off a favor I was most happy to do for you. You are doing me a mercy and I will never forget the kindness of it. That said, you didn't really have to go all out. If you wanted to fuck me, then skip the fancy meal and we can go back to my apartment. I will get the beautiful memory, and you will be out of whatever debt you seem to think you owe."

I reached out and grabbed Jakob's face making his eyes go wide in terror. "Enough, Jacob. I will not use you like a sex toy. I know that is all you think you are worth to me. You couldn't be more wrong. I also use no tricks, nor do I lie to you because I was trained to do it. I love you, for truth, dammit. I will always love you in fact. Why can you not see that? You are so precious to me, I couldn't even fathom being so blessed to sleep with you. You are a treasure that I am lucky to hold this night even if only for a moment. You are allowed to be ugly to me all you like, but I will not stand here and listen to you be cruel to the man I adore. I mean it. Do recall what happen to Matz for such a dishonor?"

He stood there trembling and blinking as if he couldn't remember something as he stammered out, "Okay, Maxx. I apologize for, I didn't know you really love me?"

I nodded as I let go of his face and stroked his cheek softly. "Always have, my Liebling, and always will. Since that first day you pulled me into a closet and showed me mercy. A more gorgeous person I have never met. Even Leo has difficulty keeping pace with your place in my heart. You have always been there for me and never once asked for a thing in return. Until tonight, I thank you for this chance to show you the Jakob I see through my eyes."

He nodded with his eyes welling up threatening tears. "Uhm, I, okay. I didn't expect this, that you, I assumed, oh I don't know what I thought."

I leaned down and kissed his lips briefly. "Don't think, Jakob. Watch and listen. Let my heart speak to you. It will tell you all the truths you have forgotten. Now come, we are going to be late, ja?"

Jakob had closed his eyes when I kissed him. Without opening them he nodded appearing unable to breathe. I smiled at that as I gently pulled on his arm to guide him the rest of the way to the Great Hall. I heard him sniff and I reminded him not to cry or he would muss up his makeup.

Master Maxx laughed hard then said, "Did you know he carries a purse? Ja. When I told him that he grabbed it and took out a compact mirror to check his face. Ha. I swear that man is the funniest person I have ever known and the most good hearted too."

He winked at me causing me to chuckle that a man walked around with a lady's purse on his shoulder. Hey, I was nine. Cut me some slack.

The black collar attendant took us to a table almost the moment we arrived. Jakob walked in my arm flashing looks of pride around as we passed each table. The Dominants were all staring and wagging their tongues at the sight of the infamous Priceless and his date the Queen Jakob.

I could tell he was enjoying the drama such a thing was causing everyone. Without Leo there to offer them an alternative explanation for this odd pairing, no one could deny we were 'the couple.' I giggled when he made a lot of noise and flounced as I pulled out his chair for him to sit down.

I took my seat next to him and leaned over to whisper in his ear. "You are the apple of everyone's eyes tonight my beauty. Look at them watching what they can only wish they could be."

He giggled loudly and swatted at me as if I said something dirty into his ear. "Oh Maxx. You bad thing, again." I pulled away acting as if I had been caught misbehaving.

Jakob shot a cat smile and sideways glance. "You are simply too good at this love. You know exactly how to start a juicy rumor."

I nodded. "I should. There are enough of them floating out there about me, ja? Been doing it since I could barely walk."

He laughed then popped his tongue. "Shit if that ain't truth. Where the hell is the wine list? I intend to get drunk."

I chuckled. "Good. It will make it easier for me to take advantage of you later."

He yelped out and grabbed his chest dramatically. "Oh hell. Then I will order everything off that list and start on the hard stuff immediately. Where is the waiter. I need alcohol now."

Jakob was prattling on about his dislike of the color of his living area wall when I spotted Roland enter the hall. I nearly choked on my glass of water when I saw he was followed by Valitin, Magnas and fucking Matz. I glared at the wolfpack as they all were lead to a table not far from Jakob and me.

I had no idea why Roland brought his brothers, but I was mildly calmed by the sight of him carrying a violin case in one hand and the roses from earlier in the other.

I also noticed he was still dressed in his finest. I expected him to come alone. It was beyond infuriating to see that jealous Matz sitting there ready to watch the show that had nearly cost me my soul.

Roland saw me glaring at them and he flashed a smile. I nodded at him then looked at the clock on the wall. It was ten minutes to showtime. I took a deep breath and prayed he really could play that fucking violin like he'd sold his soul to the devil to learn. If he flopped at this task then I was sure it would ruin the perfect date.

I had worked so hard to plan for the one man I desired more than anything to aid him to reclaim his self-worth. I was shaking from the anxiety that failure was inevitable. I told you I have the most terrible luck. I didn't think this elaborate plan would be any different. All I could do is cross my fingers and wait.

I leaned over and kissed Jakob's cheek quickly when I saw Roland stand up and begin his approach. Jakob smiled and petted my face keeping his attention on me so closely he missed the coming wolf that held roses and a violin.

Roland came up behind the fawning Jakob and lightly tapped him on the shoulder. "Excuse me honorable Jakob. Pardon me, brother Maxx, but I couldn't help but wonder if I may give your gorgeous date a gift?" I noticed the wolf was sweating bullets, he was beyond nervous.

I nodded as Jakob sat there staring at Roland stunned into silence. "By all means brother, do worship my beautiful date, Roland. You are intelligent to pay homage to such a glorious soul. I dare not be the greedy one to keep this Goddess all for myself, ja?"

He nodded with an anxious smile. "You are most generous brother. I thank you for the mercy of it. Here Jakob, for you." He handed Jakob the roses.

Jakob shot a look of confusion at me. "Maxx? What is this all about? Oh, thank you Roland for these beautiful flowers but I am not fooled. My most clever date is behind this."

I shrugged. "I do not know what you are speaking about Jakob. Roland, tell my suspicious lover that he is in error."

Roland giggled. "Jakob you are indeed wrong. The violin I am about to play for you, that is from your man Maxx. The flowers, those I brought for you on my own. When he came to me and ask I do this for you. I rushed out to get them praying that you would bless me with your smile." He reached out and took up Jakob's hand and kissed his knuckles making the man yelp in shock.

I feigned irritation best I could. "You upset my date, Roland. I told you a gift is fine, but you cross the line trying to obtain a taste of what is mine. You desire to be in my seat best be prepared to fight. I will not allow you to steal Jakob's heart from me."

Roland gasped appearing afraid. "Oh, my goodness. I do apologize brother Maxx. I was swept away by the gorgeous Jakob and forgot myself."

I nodded still appearing angered. "That is apparent. You keep your hands off my prize and do what you were contracted to do. Play something fit for my beloved and be quick about it. If you dare to paw him again, I will thrash you for it."

Roland dropped his head trying to appear shamed. "I wonder if such a beating would not be worth it. That said, I will do as you asked me, and later we can see if this beauty doesn't rethink his choice of date." He dropped his violin case on the table and pulled out that amazing instrument.

Jakob sat there with his mouth open holding his chest. He looked around the room to see all eyes were on him. Not a single Dominant in that place didn't hear the mock battle for Jakob's adorations that had occurred between Roland and me. He was without a doubt blown away that not one, but two suitors were vying for his adorations.

You got it. Jakob didn't realize nor did anyone else that Roland and I were acting. Somehow the wolf realized I was doing my best to make Jakob feel wanted. He played along perfectly despite his not being told of the plan ahead of time.

I shot him a grateful smile as he prepared for his task of serenading the amazing Jakob. He stole a look at Jakob to make sure he was not watching then winked back at me with a cat smile on his face.

Jakob leaned over and barely breathed out, "What is happening, Maxx?"

I took his hand into my and leaned into his ear kissing it then said, "I am proving my love for you, my Liebling. I know you have been abused, neglected and treated poorly. That has given you the false belief that you are only useful as a piece of flesh for another's pleasures. That is not the truth Jakob. I choose the violin's music to be my hands, my tongue, my words of affection that I wish to lavish upon you. I beg of you to do me the honor of allowing me to couple with your soul this way. If you grant this wish to this unworthy man, you can be assured you will forever possess my respect, purest adoration and awe for all your days. You my beloved are my Goddess on Earth."

Jakob face flooded with tears as he sat there staring at me with pain in his eyes. "Maxx, I don't know what to say to this. I am swept away by the beauty of it."

I smiled and kissed his lips with a slow passion then pulled back with a smile. "Then I will hold your hand to keep you from becoming lost in the waves, my love. I am with you and will never let you go."

He broke into weeping and leaned his head onto my shoulder. I felt Jakob's grip on my hand tighten as we watched Roland placed his beautiful new violin under his chin and lift his bow. His back was straight and his eyes full of the passion only the greatest of musicians can boast.

Roland cleared his throat and looked at Jakob. "I composed this song one morning long ago as I watched the beauty of a sunrise. Until today, I have never seen such splendor worthy of playing it again. Maxx reawakened the warmth of that daybreak. I had been lost in the darkness, but no longer. I came here tonight to do him a favor and find that he sits with a vision that rivals the one that moved my hands to write it. This song is for you Jakob, I will call it the "Queen of the Knight" in your honor, and that of the man that loves you so." Jakob grabbed his chest and sniffed loudly as Roland ran the bow across the violin bringing life to that silent work of art.

The chatter in the Great Hall halted and all eyes fell upon Roland and his violin. The melancholy, mournful sound rose to the ceiling and spread across it. It seemed to grow larger with each perfect note. I was in awe of Roland's talent as the sound hung in the air then fell to the earth filling that room. The music he played was something I can only describe as breath taking.

Not a single eye in that Hall was dry within only a few moments as that violin wept so completely one felt the need to join in the grieving of it. Roland appeared to have a faraway expression on his face. I wondered if he was somewhere warm, happy in another world of peace. I knew that he known such a place before all the sorrow had sent him to hide behind a mask of the criminal thug.

Jakob sobbed openly and held my hand tightly through the entire tune. I could feel his heartbeat as he snuggled his head into my shoulder. It quickened each time Roland's composition reached a high spot and it slowed with every drop of the sound.

I could not see his face, but I knew he was feeling the truthful love I could not provide to him any other way. I was not lying. I do love Jakob. The purest lover I had ever known. It is not physical, and it is far more than that of a brother. Jakob is part of my soul. You see it is to him I owe my happiness tonight Meine Liebe.

He stepped up and took a beating so that I could be free to choose. No one had ever shown me as much kindness nor mercy to me as that man. I am forever in debt to him for it.

Meine Frau, our children, our love, that my Demonseed is all I ever wanted. Jakob gave me the chance to make my dreams come to truth. I follow Felicity to find the place that Annette told me about, but Jakob was the Shepard that led me to my flock.

When at last Roland's perfect melody was finished he dropped his bow and violin to his sides and bowed to Jakob. You could have heard a pin drop in that room. No one dared to move or speak for several minutes. Then Jakob turned to me, his face vet with tears.

He mouthed silently, "I love you too Maxx. Thank you for this."

I smiled and wiped his eyes as every Dominant and FemDom in the Hall stood up and began clapping loudly. Roland stood there his eyes scanning the room in total shock.

They all whistled and begged "Encore."

He looked at me with his own tears beginning to spill down his face. Roland couldn't believe that he was being appreciated and adored at last for the artist he truly is.

I stole a look at the wolfpack table and saw they too were on their feet. Even Matz. I saw a look of awe focused on Roland in my flat mate's eyes. His cheeks, like everyone else, were wet with rain. He had known the man all his life but until that night, with that song, he had never genuinely appreciated him.

When the Hall finally quieted, after Roland finally relented and promised to play more for them, he approached us and leaned in. "The others wish for me to play Maxx. Is this okay with you? Are you and Jakob well satisfied I have adored this beauty the way he deserves?"

I smiled with gratitude as I glanced at Jakob. "What do you say, my love? Are you adored enough, or shall I demand this artist try harder to thrill my Goddess?"

Jakob sniffed and wiped his eyes with a napkin. "You play beautifully, Roland. That song is the most wonderful thing I ever have heard in my life. If you ever record it, I beg of you, I want a copy. I would pay anything to have it."

Roland chuckled. "Jakob don't be silly. If I ever did such a magnificent thing you get yours free. The Queen never pays for the things she owns. I thank you for your kind words and grace. If ever you are free of that most unworthy cad you fawn over tonight then come see me. I will show you the proper way a lady should be treated. One afternoon listening to me play and you will forget about Maxx and think only of Roland," he boasted.

I chuckled. "Jakob, don't you listen to him. The musician only loves their instruments. He will steal his inspiration from your gorgeous eyes then elope with his violin leaving you lost without any vision."

Jakob laughed. "Boys, now you stop that. There is plenty of Jakob to go around. Roland when Maxx tires of my nagging and seeks his glory elsewhere. I will come by, and you can write another song for me. Perhaps I can give you plenty of inspiration."

Roland blushed. "I think I am ready to write this very night. Ah if only I could be the lucky one. I would run away with you now if you would have me."

I wrapped my arm around Jakob's waist tightly causing him to yelp in shock. "He will not. I already told you this beauty belongs to me. Jakob, forget him. Roland will be old and grey before I let you go. Maybe he can hold up that violin with his walker, ja?"

Roland snickered. "Alright, I see I have stepped too far into Priceless territory. I know better than to anger him further. I leave you two love birds to your romancing. I have an audience to attend to."

I yelled out, "See, told you Jakob. The musician always leaves with his instrument in hand with empty words of love in his wake." Roland laughed loudly and waved to me headed out to appease his eager fans with many more songs.

Jakob smiled as several of the dining Dominants got up to dance to the crying of Roland's violin. "What do we do now? You have knocked me off my feet and made me feel like the most beautiful thing to ever walk the planet. Perhaps you are ready to go back to my apartment and show me the physical adoration. Now that you have stroked my heart to apex?"

I grinned with wickedness. "You are teasing me again, Jakob. Not yet. First dance with me lover. Let me feel you in my arms. There is no better way to learn your rhythms, ja?"

He shuddered then snapped with a smile, "Damn you are too good at this. I am going to have so many wet spots in my jeans not even the strongest bleach will get out the stains."

I chuckled as I stood and held out my hand. "Then give them to me. I will frame them and hang them next to my bed for the lonely nights."

He took my outstretched arm and giggled covering his mouth. "You stick with Jakob and there will be no more of those. I am more than happy to keep your bed warm, and sleep well earned."

I took him around the waist spinning him till he swooned. "You are making me wanton, Jakob, with your promises. Keep that up and you will never be able to be free. My love is not the kind that ends. You will be my prisoner and I will be yours till the earth claims our bones."

Jakob pulled me into a passion filled kiss. "Then arrest me this night and throw the book at this bitch. I am the criminal that deserves to never be paroled." We danced and swayed with many romantic words said between us as Roland played on.

I noticed many known schwuler eyes were focusing on that gentle beauty as I paraded him around in my graceful grip. Jakob wore confidence well and he is a gorgeous man (and would make an amazing Frau too.). I was not surprised that his magnificent smile and perfect moves on the dance floor earned him many admirers.

I suspected that his schedule would no longer be empty, and he would soon have his pick of the suitors. I believe the only reason no one approached to start the bidding var for his affections that night was their fear of the one that brought him to the dance.

Jonas, Peter, Matz and Kilian may not have been hesitant to tango with me, but most other Dominants in that Haus were not too keen in finding out why they had leveled me Priceless.

After the song, dinner and dancing, I merely sipped water and watched Jakob eat. Geraldine handled all my culinary needs, you know. Jakob was finally ready to head back home. The moment of truth had arrived at last. He would expect me to make love to him or the other way around.

I was unsure exactly what he was thinking. We both play the bottom role in the sexual situation, and I am straight. That would surely cause him distress if he thought I could penetrate him and couldn't. I feared he would take offense to it. There was no way I could gain erection with a man, other than Leo, not even my precious Jakob.

That worry kept me full of anxiety as I walked him back to his apartment. Jakob happily chattered on about how wonderful Roland could play the violin and the thrills of this most perfect date.

I smiled and said, "I promised you the date of your dreams, my Liebling. I am most grateful you are satisfied I have kept that oath."

Jakob smiled even wider as we approached his door. "Ah but the date is not over yet, Maxx. You have given me a most spectacular memory that will keep me smiling for years every time I go to the Great Hall. However, when we get inside and to my bed, I am going to give you one that you will never forget." He clicked his tongue and snapped with a flounce.

I chuckled at that. "Well, perhaps I am not done with you yet love. You assume that I have shown you all there is to see of Mad Maxx. If you did than you'd be wrong."

He dug into his purse and retrieved the keys with an expression of curiosity as he stole a glance at my groin. "I confess I have been dying to see all there is to see of you. I only remember a frightened little boy in a cock cage. I have never fully seen the man that matured from that strong kid that I admired more than he ever knew." He opened the door and pulled me in after him.

I took him into my arms. "You are wrong again, Jakob. I knew or you and I would not be here now. I never can thank you enough for being you. I hope that the trivial things I have done tonight have brought you the joy you deserve." He kissed me deeply with much trembling.

He nodded as his breathing went shallow. "I have never been happier than I am tonight. It is the best day of my life."

I smiled as I pulled back and began to unbutton his blouse sending him into loud gasping sounds. "The best day thus far, my Liebling. You are a young princess yet. There will be many more hot, thrilling hours ahead of you. However, I have heard it said, the first is always the one you remember the most." I removed his shirt and unbuttoned his pants.

He could barely breath from his panting. "You are sure about this, Maxx? I mean, I want you to be with me but what about Leo? I would feel so horrible to betray a friend." He licked his lips as I dropped his breeches to his ankles.

I chuckled. "Leo knows I am with you Jakob. I never would dare to betray either of your heart. Come lay down on the sofa. I wish to admire my prize ja?" He nodded as he allowed me to gently pull him to the couch and push him down.

I laid him to his back with a kiss then pulled back his legs out straight. Jakob was like puddy trembling and excited to the point of obvious interest in my gentle touching. I shot him a coy look as he giggled and shrugged as if embarrassed that his manhood was making his underwear work to hold all that Queen inside it.

I grabbed a blue blanket that was draped across that couch and laid it across his bare feet. "Can you lean up on your arm, my beauty. I wish to pose you and glory at the fabulousness of the gorgeous treasure I have found this night."

He covered his face with his palm as he did as I asked. I noticed two large fans made of ostrich feathers hanging on the wall. After standing back and looking him over I thought maybe they would add something to this work of art before my eyes. With his permission I took them down and handed both to him. He posed until I was sure it was perfect.

I smiled. "Ah, you are the artists dream come true Jakob. Tell me, do you feel beautiful?"

He nodded with a big grin. "I am beautiful, Maxx."

I approached him. "Never forget that truth again, my Liebling. You know what? I think the only way to be assured you will not is to preserve this memory for all time, ja?" A knocking began at the door.

Jakob started to sit up with an expression of irritation on his face. "Who the fuck could that be? Hold on my love.

Let me tell this asshole, whoever it is, to fuck off. I am busy. Shit. I haven't had a date in more than twelve years and the minute I get lucky I get a visitor. You have to be funning me."

I put up my hand to still him. "Nein, Jakob. Don't move. I will get this. I know who this is."

He narrowed his eyes as I rushed for the door. "Maxx? What is going on?"

I opened the door and let the handsome painter, who happened to be the single schwuler of Jakob's age, into the apartment with his easel and canvas in tow. "Come in Leif. I am grateful you could make it. Did the door guards give you any troubles?"

Leif shook his head as he held out his hand to shake. "Nein. Rolf took care of it all as he said he would. It is a pleasure to meet you Maxx and this must be my subject. Jakob, it is a real pleasure to meet you. Ah, Maxx said you were worthy of a masterpiece. I see he was not exaggerating." Je took Jakob's fan filled hand and kissed his knuckles.

Jakob swooned as he eyed the gorgeous blond painter. "The pleasure is all my I am sure. Maxx? What is this?"

I walked over and knelt next to Jakob and stroked his cheek. "I told you they say your first is the one to remember. I desire that you have something to hold this moment in your heart for all time. I paid Leif to do your portrait, my love. I wanted you to have a memento of your glorious birthday. It is the final gift I grant you for our perfect date."

He frowned. "Maxx, honey, today is not my birthday."

I leaned in and kissed him deeply. "You are wrong again, Jakob. I see you re-born this very night. You grow so fast, you have moved far beyond my reach already. Accept my offer and be the unspoiled work of art you truly are. You owe it to yourself and to the heart that already beats for you."

He looked at the pretty artist setting up his tools then back to me. "You devil. Couldn't you at least have gotten an ugly painter? How the hell am I supposed to hold still for hours with that hunk of man standing there staring at me."

I chuckled and shot Leif a glace. "Well Jakob, Leif here is single, and already thinks you are a fox. Maybe when you both tire of the work, you can get to know him better? Just be careful and remember what I told you about the artist types. He will likely get caught up with being with an incredible beauty and realize too late you are far too good for him. You will most certainly break this man's heart."

Jakob snorted but cut his eyes at that man again with eagerness in them. "You don't say. Well, maybe I am in the mood for a little sacrifice in the name of art, ja? But what about you Maxx? I thought you would expect to, you know, want to make love to me."

I leaned in and whispered into his ear. "I already am Jakob. You are inside me and I am within you. I owe you my soul and that is what I give you. I must go now but try not to do anything I wouldn't do lover. Which leaves open every possibility, ja?" I winked at him as began to exit and let Leif to do his work and Jakob to enjoy his romantic fantasy come to life.

As I was about to step outside to leave the thrilled Jakob yelled out, "You are going to just leave me alone with this gorgeous total stranger, Maxx? What if he is the sex fiend."

I chuckled and shot the blushing artist a glance. "Then you can thank me in the morning. You two have fun. Love you Jakob. See you soon." I went out closing the door behind me.

I was heading back to my apartment with speed to grab my overnight bag. I prayed that Matz was still in the Great Hall with Roland and the wolves. If I hurried maybe I could avoid him for the next few days. I really hoped so.

I came around the corner and nearly ran into Lucus standing there in my path. I led out a gasp of terror as he reached into his jacket, his eyes lit up with flames. I began to step back as the terror rose within me. He seemed furious and I could smell the liquor on his breath. Even from my spot of striking distance. I should have kept myself alert. I suppose despite all I had endured I will never learn.

Chapter 18: Dirty Deals

I gasped and backed away never taken my eyes off that man's hand reaching into his jacket. The smell of heavy liquor made the boy's stomach lurch from that memory of my own dance with the demon alcohol not that many days before.

Lucus staggard a bit as he took a step toward me. "You stop right there Christian. Make another move and I will throw you from the banister. Ha, how about that? I threaten you for a change, ja?" He hiccupped.

I shook my head and did the best I could to look defiant though I admit I was scared to death. "Lucus, you are drunk. Go home and stop bothering me. Say nothing else or be sorry for it in the morning if there is a morning for you."

Lucus slurred out angrily, "What? My, my you are arrogant for a whore. For your information. I have something for you right here. Here, he pulled out a huge wad of cash and threw it at my feet. I don't know what you charge but I bet this is more than enough. I am now the customer of the Priceless. I didn't realize that all I had to do is pay you and I could have anything I want. Makes sense why you were so nasty to me with my honest admission to affections for you. You listen only to what you are paid to hear. So, now Lucus has your ear, ja? You take my money and get a violinist to serenade me, and you can bring me flowers too. I want all that Jakob got and that includes what happened behind those closed doors."

I glared at him filled with sudden fury. "Lucus, go home. You are mistaken. That alcohol makes you daft. I am not a whore. I see you nothing. Get out of my sight before I forget you are not yourself and end this conversation for good."

He nearly fell and tried crossing his arms clumsily as he snorted, "You are a whore. I was unable to figure out what you were doing with Matz every night down in his old apartment. I watched that fucking Osvin go inside. I assumed like everyone that he was gaming on Matz's tables, but then I would see Matz leave, and the wolves take the door. You, however, never come out and neither did Osvin till much later. I admit that had me more than a little confused. Then I heard you speaking to yourself and admit to the prostitution business. Tonight, I watched what you did with that fucking drama Queen Jakob. He must have paid far more than that slovenly Osvin to gain so much attention from the cold hearted Priceless Mad Maxx." I come forward and punched him right in the face. Lucus fell to the floor onto his back, groaning loudly while holding his nose.

I approached and stood over the writhing Dominant glaring at him full of hatred. "I am real sick of everyone thinking they are the experts at my private business, Lucus. Call me the whore if it makes you feel better about the evil you have done and will do. However, you will hold your tongue when speaking of Jakob or will I finish you and damn the consequences. I will not take your money nor your most rude offer that goes along with it. Sober up idiot. When you wake in the morning be grateful for the mercy I give you tonight. Do not expect me to show it to you again. Good night Lucus." I kicked him in the ribs causing him to yell out in agony.

Then I stepped over his struggling flesh and continued my journey to the fourth floor apartment. I was furious at this nosey bastard. His figuring out my situation was not good and allowing him to live with such information even worse. I didn't actually know what the hell to do about it. Killing the powerful Lucus could endanger my bid for medical school, but if he told anyone what he had figured out and that I had beaten his ass for it, I was finished.

I nearly kicked in my own door for the second time that day. I ran thru the apartment nearly ready to jump out of the boy's flesh in terror that Matz would return before I could get out of there. That weird sensation that the Haus was devouring me returned as it had earlier after my tryst with Roland. I was panting and sweating worse than I had been earlier with that last attack.

The overnight bag was waiting on me right where I left it. I snatched it up and turned to flee from that room that once had been my only sanctuary. I was almost through the living area when the front door burst open. Matz and Roland came inside hauling the sobbing and bloody nosed Lucus.

I screamed in pure panic. "What the fuck are you idiots doing? Why are you bringing that horror show into my apartment. Matz, you motherfucker, and you Roland, you backstabbing dog. Get him out of here immediately. You have no idea what you do."

Matz glared at me while Roland nearly fainted from fear. "Maxx, calm down. Lucus says he was struck in a surprise attack. We found him near choking on his own blood. He didn't see who this did, but you cannot expect me to allow a Dominant of his level to lay out in the hallway in trouble like that." Roland and he aided the groaning Lucus to the couch and gently laid him out.

I stood there feeling the walls closing in on me. That sonofabitch had managed to get himself into my home. I didn't know why he kept the fact I was the one that injured him from Matz, but to be truthful I didn't care either. I wanted all of these assholes out of my apartment and life.

Matz yelled out as he knelt next to Lucus laying there in obvious pain. "Maxx, stop standing there acting useless. Go get a damp rag from the bathroom. We need to clean up the blood and make sure he is not severely hurt."

I shook my head. "Nein, let him bleed. I am due on the sixth floor. Looks to me that he got what he had coming. That is what happens to snoopers. They get their nose punched for sticking it where it doesn't belong, ja? I bet he will be less likely to slink about in the hallways observing other people's business now. You want to comfort that useless bitch then do it yourself. I will not aid you." I tore off for the door ready to leave and throw a lit match behind me to end this nightmare once and for all.

Matz gasped as I speed past him. "Maxx, did you do this? Holy hell. Oh, my Gott. You are in so much trouble. You cannot hit Dominants of his status the way you can Roland or me."

I chuckled full of evil as I opened the door. "Nein, I cannot you say? Hmm, then why is that rat bastard laying there bleeding? Seems I sure as shit can. I bid you good night, Judas." I took off slamming it shut behind me.

I ran down that hallway fast as my shitty legs could go. I practically flew up the stairwell in a mad dash to get to my Leo. The terror was rising faster than spring flood waters within the boy. Mad Max took the wheel driving the flesh ever faster, fueled by his growing paranoia.

I looked at Maximillian wondering if he was demonstrating any signs yet of the onsetting disease. It was well known to me, Mad Maxx, by now that Mad Max was always the first of us to show signs of illness. He will become suspicious, paranoid and often keeps the boy from sleeping and eating over it.

The next of us to take on the symptoms is sadly yours truly. I am the one that does all the planning and thinking. Lately I have had moments of confusion, loss of memory access, and even tended to misunderstand the simplest things. The weakness of my abilities to be sure of accuracy in understanding meant the boy could be misled, frightened easily, and even become catatonic when it was overwhelming.

Maximillian was the real canary in the well despite all that early warning from the two Max brothers. When the usually gentle, kind and depressed shard grew full of the delusions of grandiosity it would be time to call in Der Hund to take the wheel. If I didn't call him the second the seductive shard began to show the stress, then Maximillian would turn into a more deadly killer than even Christian could boast.

I turned and flashed a glance at Christian the anger shard. His eyes burned with the fires that could go a lifetime using the fuel of years of tormenting of the flesh. He smiled at me showing all his pointed teeth. I shivered despite myself. I was getting weaker by the day. Soon, that monster would overpower me and join with Maximillian in their misguided delusions and fucked up belief that everyone was the enemy.

I wondered who was going to find their grave due to this cycle. I secretly hoped to awaken in another two years to find the Vampire, Peter and Kilian (among a few others) long inhabiting the pine box. It is truly too bad that it was not that easy to allow Maximillian and Christian to clear the path by taking out the proper hurtles. Those boys were just as likely to end Leo, Jakob or even our precious black collar children thanks to their Mad Dog thirst for blood.

What is the matter, my Liebe? You didn't realize that the real Killer in us is the sweet appearing Maximillian and

140

not Christian? Ah, well you didn't pay attention did you? Maximillian is the shard of lies, my Frau. He is not the schwuler nor does he really mean anything he says. That is why all the rest of us keep our distance, and why he wears no collar.

Even Der Hund dares not try to submit that manipulator. Nothing you see in the Maximillian is true. He is trained to fool you, make you love him, make you want him, but beware, the only thing he wants is revenge. He is the most dangerous shard of us all. That sexually abused and tortured boy cannot love, nor does he desire to.

All he knows is pain without any pleasure. He wants to be free. Maximillian cares not what lies he must tell, nor who must die for him to get it. I know it can be confusing to realized that our sadist shard is the true lover/romantic that has empathy, and our seductive shard is the eternally cold hearted killer but if you look you can see why that is my Demonseed Frau.

I turned around and looked at Master Maxx. "It makes sense Master. Maximillian cannot have any feeling, or Der Hund is finished. You can't either, or you will be driven crazy by the understanding of the pain. Mad Max, the mean one, is the only one that can handle it without letting it get to him too much."

Master Maxx smiled with jo., "Ja. You get it my Frau. Ah, you are a smart little demon. Though I think maybe you have another reason for appearing the brilliant in this most *unusual psychology. I wonder if you have something of an experience with it?" He looked at me appearing curious.*

I glared at him. "I thank you to not to ask, Master. I don't want to talk about it. I say that with respect."

He nodded., "I that so? You don't want to or cannot? You think I am not aware of what the core can do to you for disobeying their rules? I have done such stupidity in my youth too. That did not end well. Whatever Der Hund wants he gets or there will not be a Mad Maxx for long."

I nodded. "I think maybe you should continue with the story and leave me out of this conversation, Master."

Master Maxx chuckled and ruffled my hair. "You wish, my Liebe. This whole fucking story includes you like it or not. One day you will understand that we are the same creature, and there is no separating our souls. It was not what we choose, since such a thing as choice was never ours to possess. You and I were engineered to be the lovers by more than Malfred and Bladrick. It is the way the stars aligned. Our fates are one, and for us there will be no escaping it."

I snorted. "One of us or both of us could die, Master. That is one choice we can make."

He grinned from ear to ear with a faraway look in his eyes. "Is that so, my Liebe? Then you must understand it is also our choice to live. The way I see it, sure there are a lot of bad people in our way to happiness. Maybe we never even find it in this life. Yet, dying will not end those bad hearts, will it? Nein. Debbie, Russell, Peter, Jonas and Kilian to name a few will live on harming others that fill the void we left behind. You and I possess the intelligence and strength to lay there and take it when others would give up. We cannot stop them from the evil they do, but we can hinder their path to happiness as much as they do our own. If you cannot get out the door to escaping, then make fucking sure the sonofabitches that trapped you there never get out either. Be the hurtle they cannot clear. Equal service, my Liebe."

I gasped in sudden surprise with a smile breaking out on my face. "Ah, I understand, Master. Yes, to live when Debbie wants me to die is the best revenge."

Master Maxx kissed my cheek. "That is the right answer. Live and seeking the green fields. Matters not if we find them. Our very existence darkens the ones that try to use us to get to their own. Though they cannot see that. They are as much a prisoner to you as you are to them. The lust that you bring out in them holds their black souls' hostage to it. They can never replicate the thrill they acquire from the disgrace they think they bring upon you. Each encounter squeezes more and more of the pleasure they can take from anything. We are like heroin my Frau. That first few hits addict the user to the extreme taboo ecstasy they get. However, as each dose is injected more and more of the pleasure centers in the brain are destroyed by the overstimulation of them. Pretty soon the druggie cannot get anything from that hit like the first few and worse they cannot feel good even when they stop taking it. They are condemned for all their lives to remember that mind blowing experience but unable to even obtain the simple joys any longer. They took everything from us. Our lives are stolen, our passions are ash. You return that favor my Liebling. In time, you will understand this is our only outlet to feel anything of worth. This pseudo-life we live is useless to us. We are lost for all time. Yet, we can overdose the evil and aid the innocents that are not as far gone as we are. You will join me one day in leading our flock of the cursed away from that soul sucking hole that we were sacrificed to. You already are ruining the lives of those that killed you though you cannot see it."

I groaned. "No, I can't Master. Debbie and Russell don't seem miserable to me."

He giggled. "You say that because you never have been a slave to a drug addiction. One day those two will rue the day you were born. I suspect if you don't kill them out right you will do something that they will never be able to forget."

I shrugged. "I could do that tonight if you would help me get out of this basement, Master. You can just leave the door open and slip away to your apartment. I won't tell anyone about you and when I am older you can come back and find me."

Master Maxx frowned at that. "Nein, Meine Liebe. If I leave and return to Germany for more than a few months without you, they will recollar me. Then I can never come back. You killing your parents and going to the juvenile hall will end the mission I was sent to complete as a failure.

144

The Haus and Jonas will refuse to wait that long on you. Worse still, I will be implicated. I have no other home anymore in the USA but this basement with you."

I nearly choked. "Huh? What happened to your apartment, Master?"

He looked at the floor and loudly sighed. "I cannot afford it anymore. Debbie has taken all I can make to assure I can keep seeing you. Peter won't allow me to live with him, not that I would wish such a horror anyway. I got caught sleeping in one of the rooms at the hospital. If I try that again they will fire me. It is this basement or the ditch outside. Those are my choices."

I felt a chill run up my spine. "Master, did you call Jonas and ask him to help you with money?"

Master Maxx nodded. "Ja, he refused. Living here with you was his idea."

That really made me tremble as I glanced around at the dark walls. "Master, I wonder, what if the Masters like Malfred are plotting again."

He looked up at me appearing afraid. "What? Tell me why you would think that?"

I shrugged as I tried to figure out what was bothering me about his being told to live in the basement by Jonas., "Something feels wrong with the whole thing, Master. I don't know. I just wonder if maybe you either haven't told me everything and I deserve to be caned for jumping the gun again or if there is a plan here. What you just told me scares me, but I cannot figure out why yet."

Master Maxx sat there a moment appearing to be frightened too. Then he shook it off and reach out to grab me in a tight hug.

"Aw, Meine Liebe. You are getting paranoid like Mad Max. I am here with you. This is where I wish to be. I cannot stand to be without you anyway. It wouldn't matter if you were kept at the bottom of the sea. Your Mann Maxx would come and drown to be with you." He kissed me deeply.

I pulled away and took on a serious expression. "Yeah, I know that Master. So, do they. I think that is what is scaring me about all this. What if they are using me as bait?"

That made him howl in laughter. "Bait? Meine Liebe why would day bother to capture what was never free in the first place. I cannot go anywhere. That is silly."

I shivered again. "Is it Master? I know it sounds stupid, but I think there is something wrong here."

He nodded. "Okay then we will have at agree to disagree my Frau. Now you turn around and we get back to this story. I think you are starting to let things that happened in my past bother you too much. I am here to train you, then you break my metal. We make a child and the second we prove ourselves the fertile ones our contracts are done for all time. Once that is done, we can decide to *leave and never come back or join the Haus and take over. Up to you. That is the agreement with Jonas, Peter, and Gretta. There is no reason to doubt the truth of it. I have that in writing, you know."*

I nodded as I turned around still trembling. "I believe you Master. I don't believe in them though. I hope you are right, and I am wrong. They have lied to you the entire time. Not sure I would be so willing to buy into anything they told me if I were you, piece of paper or not."

He scoffed. "Well, you don't have to buy anything. It is up to me to do the thinking for both of us. You are only the child. You listen to what I tell you and you'll see this time we will be free."

I shrugged. "As you say Master. Not like I have any choice in the matter."

Master Maxx chuckled. "That is correct Meine Liebe. Be still, and we get back to it."

*QUICK NOTE HERE: Hey, Christian Axel. Bet you wish now that you had listen to the wise fears of that nine-year-old kid that night, huh? Things may have been a lot different, ja? Told you not to believe anything those ruthless assholes told you, blood signature or not. Hate to say I told you so, but hey man, I DID TELL YOU SO. Okay, enough of that, on with the story.

"Maximillian saw me stealing glances at me and that caused him to frown. "You like what you see there brother? What the fuck?"

147

I shrugged. "I wasn't looking at you."

Christian growled out. "Aw, too bad there Maximillian. For a moment I bet you got hot. You been fucked by everyone else but still haven't bagged a single one of us. That must be just eating away at your ego, ja?"

Maximillian flipped Christian off. "Dream on low life. I wouldn't be with any of you scum if I was paid a fucking fortune and promised all the women in the world for life."

Mad Max chuckled at that. "Well, of course you wouldn't. You don't like the girls, schwuler freak."

Maximillian rolled his eyes at that. "Ah, spoken by the Leo lover himself. Hey, brother, tell me something. When Leo fucks you do you really need him to stroke the boy's cock too? I mean maybe if you just stare into his eyes you will reach that orgasm just thinking about how great it is to have him inside you, ja?"

Mad Max frowned. "You shut up about Leo. You are just jealous that I get the release that you are denied."

Maximillian shot a wicked smile at Christian. "You bet I am jealous brother. I only wish I were the real thing like you are, schwuler freak."

Mad Max led go of the wheel rushing to hit Maximillian, but Max held him tightly as he yelled out, "I am calling Der Hund. This is the last straw. All you mongrels are getting out of hand. Mad Max, get back on the wheel. Maximillian shut up. Christian, you stay back. Mad Maxx, get that boy of yours under control."

148

Christian shouted back at Max, "Someone needs to get this motherfucker out of here. Mad Max, kill him damn you. It is fucking bullshit his being around to spoil all our fun."

Before any of us could stop it, the anger shard raced past me to attack our Soul. I was pulled along behind him helplessly trapped by my leash that he holds. Mad Max also was pulled along the prisoner as Max took the stance of aggression and flew back at Christian. The two of them began to grow to amazing size. It was more than a little scary to witness.

The flesh responded as he pounded on Leo's door. The Elder opened it to find the boy full of fury, irrational and spouting obscenities so foul I rather not repeat them to you even with your history. Leo backed away with fear in his eyes as the three of us Max brothers watched the war break out of the Anger that went right to our Soul.

The boy rushed inside Leo's apartment. I was terrified that without any of us at the wheel the flesh would go zombie and injure Mad Max's lover without care.

I yelled to Maximillian that was standing there with his eyes wide in shock at the inner battle taking place. "Brother, grab the wheel. Shit, where the hell is Der Hund? This is out of control. Take the boy somewhere dark and quiet fast. Do not allow him to injure Leo."

Mad Max shot a frightened look back at Maximillian. "Do as Mad Maxx says Maximillian. Hurry, I cannot hold Max back." He was dragging his feet pulling back on

Max's chain with the veins popping out on his forehead with little effect.

I too was straining to pull Christian the Mad Dog out of that fray. Nothing I tried worked. The Anger shard was beyond furious. He had grown so powerful only Max could pull him back. I noticed Mad Max had come to the same conclusion as me. The Sadistic shard let go of the chain and stopped trying to slow the Soul's clashing with Christian.

I let go and allowed the enraged Christian to do what he wanted. The two met in the center of that wheel room with a loud crashing sound. It was so loud that Maximillian, that had taken the wheel, covered the boys ears to keep him from blowing out his eardrums.

Christian growled like the lion with flames shooting out of his eye sockets. Max had become the giant. His usual silly smile was replaced with a fang filled grimace of malice. I trembled in fear at the sight of those two monstrous shards ripping at each other like wildcats. Christian was clawing at Max and Max was striking back with a vicious bite.

Both began to wail in there torment. I hit the wheel room floor covering my head, and Mad Max did the same from the other side. That war raged on out of control while Maximillian did his best to seek shelter from this horrific turn of events.

On the outside, Leo witnessed the boy throw his overnight bag across the living area. He then fled in panic as Der Makellos came with eagerness to greet him. The sight of our brother Hund frightened the overstimulated Maximillian. He took off on a run through Leo's apartment down his hallway with his hands over his ears, screaming wildly.

The flesh crashed into the walls and sobbed loudly, speaking in gibberish. The pain of that inner turmoil made any thinking of value useless. Leo and Der Makellos chased after that disturbed creature as it desperately sought a place of asylum within his apartment.

I could hear Leo screaming out in panic, "Christian, honey, what is wrong? Please speak to me. What has happened?"

Maximillian freaked out even more when he turned his head and saw that black hound and Leo in pursuit of him. He let out a scream of terror and kicked in the spare room door. Without looking back, he headed right for the closet in that room. The flesh slipped inside and slammed the door behind him. The boy crawled into the dark corner, rolled into a ball and trembled completely despondent.

Leo didn't attempt to retrieve the frightened Maxx from his place of hiding. I could hear him outside that door telling Der Makellos that the boy needed "quiet time" when the unhappy hound tried scratching at the door. He must have thought we were playing the game of hide and seek with him. Leo had to pull Der Makellos away from his making that disappointed bid for attention with us, by saying that Christian Axel would come out when he was calmed and ready.

After getting the flesh to a place of safety, Maximillian let go of the wheel and fled to the farthest end of the wheel room. He did as me and Mad Max, falling to the floor covering his head for protection.

By that point Max and Christian were getting wilder in their battling. Both were bloody, torn and showed signs of wearing out. All three of us Max boys held our breath hoping that they would soon end their combat in stalemate. We were aware neither could outright beat the other. They could, however, injure themselves in a scuffle. We could only hang on and wait for the outcome of this long overdue skirmish.

At least an hour passed before the grunts and wails of the conflicting shards began to weaken. Other than the sounds of those two clashing there had been complete silence. To my terror a sound was beginning in the distance. I uncovered my head and stole a look at Mad Max.

He was doing the same thing hazarding to glance back at me. I could see the fear in his eyes. He knew that sound just as I did. The noise was the tapestry cyclone whirling on the horizon. The shattering was coming.

I jumped up despite my respect for Max and Christian and yelled at them, "Stop this nonsense I beg of you. Do you not hear the tapestry? Listen you fools, you are kicking holes in the wheel's defenses. TOP this NONSENSE I BEG OF you. DO you NOT HEAR DAT? LISTEN you

FOOLS. That shattering will get us all if you persist in this fracas."

Christian had become quite tired. He was tattered in many places. At last, he backed away from the equally torn and fatigued Max. The Soul watched him retreating with suspiciousness in his expression but didn't give chase. I noticed the two powerful shards were shrinking in size almost as rapidly as they had become the giants.

The Anger shard grumbled, "Tell that fucker to stay on his side of the wheel room or next time I shatter him for truth."

Max growled back, "You come back, and you will find yourself the one sent to the void motherfucker."

Christian stopped his backing away momentarily appearing to be deciding if he wanted to re-engage with the Soul. I noticed he looked at his cut up hands before he came to the conclusion it was best to let this insult go for now. I grabbed him around the waist and shoulder aiding him to continue his journey back to our side of the wheel.

I saw Mad Max do the same for Max. with our Anger and Soul finally separated from their combat, things calmed down quickly. Even Maximillian had felt safe enough to rise back to his feet, though like me and Mad Max I could tell he was anxious and unsure that all was returning to normal within.

The boy had been completely helpless. He could do nothing thanks to none of us controlling the wheel. That left him locked in a weeping jag, hidden in the back of Leo's apartment room closet that entire time. Mad Max made sure that Max was comfortable then he took his rightful place as the commander of the flesh for our time with Leo.

I felt relieved as the Sadistic shard took the wheel into his hands. He didn't appear injured despite the violence he was dragged through only moments before. I may not always agree completely with my brother Mad Max, but I must admit he is one tough sonofabitch. I watched him shake off that rumble like that sort of thing happened every day. Maximillian and I on the other hand were shaking full of anxiety and feeling sick from the fray.

I opened my eyes and sat up in that darkened closet. The smell of moth balls and cedar swam around my head making my stomach lurch a bit. I reached into my coat pocket and pulled Felicity from her hidden spot. She was scared by all that commotion. I knew she needed a little petting and assurance that everything was alright. The shattering was not upon the boy yet, but it sure as shit was coming.

I stained my eyes and ears in that darkness as I clutched my lamb. The powers were returning rapidly. I could see the colors of the cosmos within that void. All around me the figures danced, and shape shifted in their eternal tango of absurdity.

My ears were picking up the thoughts of everyone in the Haus, and the infernal tapping in the walls. The codes were coming over the wire as they had for nearly two years before. I groaned as I realized we were halfway between this world and the one beyond it. That medication of Doctor Vagner was some useless shit. It wasn't helping at all.

I wasn't ready to leave that spot for a bit. I wanted to see Leo, but I would need time to adjust to the new awareness that had awakened during Max's and Christian's battle. Having superpowers is not the remarkable thing everyone would think them to be, you know.

For starters, I do not have control of them. They never shut off day or night. Sometimes, I think that is why everyone thinks me mad. I suppose it would appear that way to the normal. Constantly hearing everyone's thoughts and seeing the frightening sights of the hidden world can cause a great deal of confusion. It is hard to know which is the situation to pay attention to and which to ignore.

I heard Cora moving her furniture above me. I frowned at that insanity. The woman was still doing that after all this time. If anyone was the nut, it had to be that fucking woman. Who the hell needs to re-arrange there Haus so much? Well, if I ever get the chance I sure as hell am going to ask her what her problem is, that you can be assured.

I could hear the residents discussing their shock that Roland the thug was so artistically inclined. That made me smile. The gossiping in the Haus was usually negative. This was a positive change to hear them saying something nice about someone. Then I heard something that caught my attention.

"They hold Geraldine the captive Maxx. You better go check on her. They are committing slave labor," I heard this man say through the wall.

That made me shiver and my mouth went dry as I responded, "I suspect you are right. I cannot get out there to see her though. Peter has the doors guarded."

That stranger laughed so loud I had to cover my ears as he said, "You go get one of the Voters. They will take you without question. Go now or be damned for your neglect of one you love."

I nodded as my heart began racing with fear at his words. "I do as you say brother. Please mercy, I will go tomorrow without fail."

That man hissed causing me to near piss my pants in full terror. "You are the bastard. You ignore the source. Lucus is the key to all this. Get that manual he writes in. He holds the secrets in his hands. You hit him when you should seduce him. You are a fool, an idiot, a useless monster. You do as you are told or find yourself my dinner."

I whimpered, "As you wish. I beg you leave me be. I swear I didn't know. Forgive me."

He laughed at my terror of him. The fear rolled down my spine, freezing my blood in my veins. I had to get out of there. He was alone with me in that dark space. I had no idea what he may do thinking there were no witnesses, you know. I tried to stand and nearly face planted. I didn't bother trying to get to my feet twice. I took off in a wild crawl on my hands and knees.

I let out a terrified scream when Leo gasped loudly as he saw me rushing from the closet into the dimly lit spare bedroom. The Elder had been sitting next to the bed on the floor, quietly reading a novel while waiting for me to calm down, or so he told me later. His appearance there startled me to near dumbass status.

I cowered covering my head like a fool. He didn't move as I did my best to make sense of his being there and that overwhelming noise all around my head. The sounds were deafening. I covered my ears groaning.

Leo softly called out, "Do you need your headset, Christian Axel? Honey, please answer me. If you say ja, I will go get them for you. I must move to leave for another room. I will do it slowly, I swear it."

I nodded then wailed out, "It hurts, Leo. Help me please. The noise, make it stop."

The Elder whispered, "I wish I could, my bunny. You be still. I go get the headset. It will dampen the sounds a bit, but you must endure this nightmare. You need rest and quiet, my Liebling. You have sanctuary here until these symptoms calm, honey. You are safe with Leo, you know I speak the truth."

I whimpered in agony as I tightened the grip on my ears and writhed a bit trying to find comfort where none can ever be. "Please Leo I beg of you, kill me. I don't wish to do this anymore. I need the silence of the grave. They are going to get me. I don't want to be taken back to Heslach. Leo, I am lost."

He nodded and calmly said, "You are not lost, my lamb. I want you to stay still. I have something that will take away the edge if you trust me?"

I moaned, "Help me, Leo. I do anything. Make it stop."

Leo stood up slowly. "Okay, if you want my aid you must mind whatever I tell you. I will return in a moment. Do not move, my bunny." He left the room in stealth as I continued to sob and thrash in pure agony in that floor.

He did as he told me he would. within only minutes he returned as quietly as he had left. Leo approached my twisting flesh holding the earphones in one hand and a glass of that horrible orange drink in the other.

Leo knelt down and said in a monotone, near whisper, "Take them. put them on, my bunny. This will help quiet the voices you hear." I moaned but reached out and took them covering my ears with gratitude.

The noise was immediately quieted to a dull roar. I shuddered and sniffled but didn't rise from the floor. He sat there watching me panting, sweating and doing my best to calm the boy down.

He then pushed the glass at me. "Drink this Christian Axel. This will grant you the rest you need. I am willing to bet you are not sleeping. This will buy you a little more time. I will speak with the Haus doctor in the morning and see if there is anything more that can be done to dampen this oncoming cycle. Trust me and drink all this without argument, my bunny."

I reached out and took the orange drink from his outstretched hand. I sat up and glared at it as if in trance. I hated that stuff, but I wondered if Leo had a point. I had not slept a full night in several days. Nor have I had any naps.

I thought maybe that fatigue would explain the hallucinations, confusion and weird emotional outbursts. Being sleep deprived can cause psychotic like symptoms. Even this dumb man knows that. I still didn't want to drink that crap though.

I frowned as I looked at it. "I can sleep without this, Leo. I go to bed right this minute if it makes you happy."

Leo shook his head. "There is medication in that drink that will calm your excitement. If you want to see me pleased you will drink all of it. I cannot make you do it Christian Axel. I can only ask you as the one that loves you to do this for me."

I nodded. "If that will bring you peace than I will do as you ask Leo. Can I see Der Makellos?" I turned up that nasty stuff and drank it down.

Leo smiled. "Ah, you bet my bunny, if you think you can handled his thrilled energy. Thank you for the mercy of doing this for me." He reached out and stroked my cheek causing me to flinch in a startle.

He frowned as I pulled away from his painful touching. "I apologize my bunny. I forgot that bothers you during stress. I will keep my hands to myself unless you ask me otherwise."

I handed him back the glass and began wringing my hands with anxiety. "It is okay Leo. I just didn't expect your caress. I thank you for the headset. It is helping. I am ready to see my buddy Der Makellos. I wonder if he is not angered that you had them remove his manhood though."

Leo chuckled with humor at that. "Well, I am sure he is a little pissed but let's face it my bunny. There was no chance he would use it. The dogs are not like the humans. Their couple always results in the puppies. There is no pleasure in it either."

I glanced at him with confusion. "Thank goodness no one allows such a thing on the humans. Otherwise, I would be fixed too. I get no thrill from the couple, and I can never have the baby either."

Leo's smile melted to a look of concern. "Christian, did something happen tonight to set off this fit? Did Jakob upset you during your date or coupling?"

That made me looked to the floor in shame. "Nein. The date with Jakob went well, Leo. I didn't sleep with him either. I swear it no matter what he tells you."

Leo gasped. "Oh? then I am to assume Jakob was upset that you refused to bed him? Did he get ugly with you about it?"

I shook my head. "Nein, he was interested in someone else's couple. I escaping his lustful intent while his eyes were caste in another direction."

The Elder raised an eyebrow. "He was wanting to be with someone else. Who the hell could have drawn his interests from you, my bunny? Did a God fall to earth?"

That made me chuckle despite the sorry state I was in. "You are funny Leo. For you information, I hired a handsome man to play the role of wanton lover. I couldn't betray you with Jakob, my Liebling, and Jakob is the bottom. There was not a chance in hell I could penetrate the man. I feared he would feel jilted, so I fixed the issue. I offered him another option. To his credit, he didn't fight the switch too much. Turns out he was worried about injuring you heart by tasting what he knows is eternally yours exclusive. This solved the issue. He saved face and I saved myself from yet another nightmare I don't need."

Leo grabbed his chest and covered his mouth tearing up. "Ah, my love. You honor me. I cannot find the words to thank you for being the honest lover to your Leo. I am the luckiest man in the world."

I smiled bitterly. "Nein Leo, I am. You put up with far more than you should with this worthless lover of yours. I am sorry to have frightened you, and I ruined our night together. We get so few anymore."

He smiled with adoration in his eyes. "My love, you are too hard on yourself. You are here with me. I don't care if all can do is look at you. Having you near me is all I ever need. Now if you feel up to it, we can go to the bedroom. I need you to lay down before that medication begins to work. You are a big man, and I am not strong enough to pick you up to carry around like I used to. Der Makellos can visit you after you are safely under the covers." I took the hand he offered to aid me to stand.

I followed Leo out of the room to take to his bed. He watched in silence as I undressed. I was already feeling the heavy fatigue of his sedative taking effect before I got my boots off. I yawned repeatedly barely able to keep my eyes open.

I decided to keep the headset on, Leo later removed it when I feel into a deep sleep, and motioned to him I was ready to visit my Hund. The eager pup rushed into the room and leapt on the bed. Der Makellos bathed me in kisses causing me to giggle despite my feeling quite drunk and slow.

I barely remember him laying down next to me. I petted his soft fur and was claimed by the medication induced slumber almost immediately. I don't recall anything for the rest of that night. Leo had allowed Der

Makellos to stay with us, and he apparently crawled into the bed next to me taking the Hund's place during the night.

I awoke wrapped in his cuddle with Der Makellos asleep too at the foot of the bed. I was confused as to my location for a bit. That caused a mild panic. It didn't help that the thoughts of the residents were coming in loud and clear. I saw the headset on the nightstand next to me. I reached out in desperation to snatch them up and put them back over my sensitive ears.

My wild movements woke up both my bed mates. Leo stretched with a thrilled grin as Der Makellos come rushing forward to continue the game of "kiss chase" that we had begun the night before. I laughed as I pushed the over adoring Hund off my face. The Elder watched me losing my battle to remain dog spit free with much humor.

Then he decided that Der Makellos shouldn't get to have all the fun. He joined me in my struggle against the happy Hund. When we managed to back our offender into retreat Leo turned on me and began an attack of kissing of his own.

That made me laugh as the silly man planted his lips all over my face, neck and chest. Within only a few moments I realized that his adoration was not like that of Der Makellos. He wasn't playing. I felt his interest in more than kissing pushing into my stomach as he rolled on top of me still playfully forcing his kisses.

I gasped in surprise at his aggression as he forced himself between my legs with a huge smile on his face. "I believe I have won this battle. To the victor goes the spoils?" He leaned down and engaged me in a kiss of passion.

I breathed into his mouth, "That is what they say, Leo. You have vanquished me. I bow to your superior strength."

He moaned out in thrill, "Don't I wish I were stronger than you, my bunny. You make me go weak every time we touch. If you are not ready than I can wait, but if you would allow my couple with you, I am most grateful for it."

I nodded without saying a word. To be honest, I was feeling a bit pensive about this sexual act after the night I'd had. That said, I rarely tell Leo nein. He is good to me, and if allowing his penetration makes him happy, then who am I to deny him?

Leo smiled and re-engaged his kissing with intense vigor. I braced myself as I saw him reach to the nightstand and grab the lube. I knew that in only moments he would unite with me in a physical expression of our spiritual love.

Let me make this clear if I have not already, Meine Liebe. I don't enjoy the penetration sex in any capacity, not even with Leo. I merely endure it with the understanding for my sacrifice he will give me the mercy of my own release. If I had my way I would never put up with that horror ever again.

Be assured the second you are matured enough to manage sex the proper way with your Mann, you will never have to endure it yourself from me. I not only hate having it done, but I also don't care for engaging in it myself with you. It is the only way that you can be with me carnally at the moment so I tolerate it like you must.

I growled out interrupting him. "Well, if you don't like it then why not just wait till I can do it the right way, Master." He popped me with his cane.

Master Maxx snarled back, "Debbie isn't going to stop using you to line her pockets, now is she? You expect your legal Mann to go without the pleasure of his rights with his Frau when no one else is keeping their hands off? You will get used to this type of penetration just like I am. In fact, I noticed you already are handling it far better than I ever have. I must endure such a horror to this day to keep you safe from the worst things Debbie could do to you. So, I suggest you stop your bitching. I don't ask you to do anything more for me than I do for you."

I hung my head in shame when he said that. "You're right Master. I apologize for my stupid outburst."

He put down the cane and hugged me tightly letting out a loud sigh. "It was not stupid, Meine Liebe. I know this disgrace of your youthful age and horrors of enforced sex get to you. I have been there, and still do go there more often than I would like to admit. This whole situation has been fucked up from the start. So, let me try to offer you a bit of peace, or maybe it will not help at all. Think of sex with your Mann and Master as being a special thing. It is not like that nasty shit Debbie pulls despite the unnatural spot that I am forced to penetrate you. It is more like what Leo, and I have. I told you I don't like that kind of sex, but I love Leo and that brings him pleasure. You bring me pleasure the same way. Like Leo does for me, I give you equal return. I do that because I return the love you give to me. No matter what you believe nor what anyone says, physical expression of love through sex anyway possible is honorable when the love is real. There is no shame in it. Not between Mann and Frau, nor between me and my lover Leo."

I turned and cast a curious glance at him. "What about the Vampire, Master? He is your Mann. Is sex with him honorable for you?"

Master Maxx groaned. "Nein, I do not love Jonas, Meine Liebe. I am his hostage. He had no right to blood bond me without my approval."

I narrowed my eyes. "What if he blood bonds me, Master. Am I supposed to love him?"

That made Master Maxx lower his head appearing hurt. "If you love him there is nothing your Mann Maxx can do about it. I can collar you and make you mind my orders, but no matter what I do I can never be Master of your heart. Maybe you will fall for his charms, Meine Liebe. After all he is not the rapist that attacks you as the little girl. You will not be ignorant of his offer to bond with you as you were with me or me with him. He likely will be like a hero compared to the criminal that will beat you into submission and enforce his lust on you all the coming years."

I nodded. "You might be right, Master. I doubt it though. Seems to me he is a pussy coward. He sends you to be the bad guy while he sits at home waiting till the hard work is done. Besides, I don't see him here beating up Russell and giving me happy meals. I think he is wrong to expect that I will forget that even though he didn't rape or beat me like you have, he also didn't help me. I don't like everything that you do Master, but I love you despite it. If you say I must get over the anal sex stuff, then I will do what you say and shut up about it. You are worth it."

Master Maxx looked up with a startle. "You mean that Meine Liebe?"

I nodded. "Yes I do, Master. You take care of me, and I will take care of you back."

He pulled me around and hugged tightly then kissed me deeply nearly breaking out in tears as he said, "Equal for equal my Frau. I will always be here for you until death takes me for her own. I thank you for the mercy."

I frowned. "Mercy? I don't know what that is Master, isn't that what you told me? I think that being in love is the worst prison in the world. Debbie and Russell cannot hurt me like caring for you does. Now I have to be worried all the time that someone at the Haus will get you or that one of them is making you cry like they do to me. I bet you feel the same way. I don't see how being in love is such a wonderful thing. In fact, I am fairly sure I hate it."

He stroked my cheek. "Damn, you are a wise little girl. Well like it or not, you and I are trapped in the nightmare of affection for the other. Love if real, it is usually a terrible sacrifice. More than once I wish I had never fallen for Leo and you."

I nodded. "Yeah Master. I agree. It was probably the dumbest thing you have ever done, and certainly is one of the stupidest I ever have. Except maybe getting into the car with Chenoweth."

Master Maxx laughed loudly. "Nein, that was the most boneheaded move ever made by Chenoweth. Did he not notice your horns, Demonseed? Well, he got what he deserved messing with my frau. He should have stuck to innocent little girls and left the jaded, cold hearted Priceless female alone. That asshole learned the hard way you haven't survived as long as you have being the helpless victim that will lay there and take it. Meine Liebe has fangs and a thirst for revenge. No one was looking and that man underestimated your fury, ja?"

I turned around in his lap and snuggled in. "I don't have any idea what you are talking about Master. I told you Chenoweth hung himself. Can we get back to the story please?"

Master Maxx snickered. "Hung himself with a knife. Interesting way to kill yourself. Okay, where was I? Oh yeah, Leo was having me prove that I love him for truth."

I suppose it was the sedative from the night before, or maybe the deteriorating state of mind I was in. Whatever the reason, I found his intercourse that morning difficult to fake my way through. Worse, I found no sexual interest in his attempts to give me an equal return for enduring his penetration.

He never said a word when after several minutes of his skillful oral adoration I was not showing any signs of thrill. I know that hurt his feelings, but I think, like me, he blamed the sedative medication. Leo gave up his quest and pulled me into a spooning appearing to have decided I needed affection more the release for that moment. I went along with him saying nothing. I knew deep inside had it been Karsten or some other pretty frau doing that blow job that morning she would not have found me as disinterested as Leo had.

At that time, I could only assume that my unpredictable ability to find an erection with Leo was because he is male. I really am not turned on by a man in any way. I had to assume there can be no other reason, since I do honestly love him.

When I met you I finally was able to prove once and for all that I am indeed as straight as I always assumed I was. I notice I never have any problem showing interest in you like I have with Leo many times.

That is despite your being far too young jet to thrill me as the mature female. In the beginning I admit it was pretty tough to get over the immature little girl looks. Thank goodness you grew up fast or I would still have to close my eyes and pretend you are older.

Turns out, the correct parts are all that matters to the non-schwuler male. Though, I would have much preferred you to be at least sixteen or even better, over eighteen. Yikes!

It took a bit to convince Leo to let me out of his cuddle. I needed to get up and get a shower. The sex with a man always makes me feel disgusting. Nothing will calm that sensation of filth but a hot shower and scrubbing. It keeps me from going mad from it. Leo finally relented with much groaning that I had barely arrived and already I was preparing to leave him.

I felt bad that he was being slighted by my irrational behavior earlier. I invited him to the shower and gave him bath service hoping that was at least a little of a makeup. He seemed to enjoy that a great deal, which in turn made me less anxious that I was going to lose his interest in me. I knew that he was the only one that really cared a damned thing for me. If he grew out of love with the boy, I had no one left in the world to turn to. If Leo had asked to cut a hole in my chest to fuck, I likely would have let him, that is how desperate I was to keep his affections.

When we got out, I dressed him, then myself. He told me that he was sure Geraldine had sent my breakfast. He went to check the door to see if the plate had been left as I went to his kitchenette to make him some coffee. I recalled that man told me I had to go check on that lamb. I made up my mind I would ask Rolf, not that dreadful Byron nor Friedrick, if he would take me to the stables after my lesson with Peter.

I came into the living area to find Jakob standing there with Leo. The Queen was already smiling and dramatically speaking with his hands to the Elder. His smile turned into a huge grin when he saw me come out with Leo's coffee in my hands.

"Ah, there is my baby Maxx. Come to you auntie you clever devil and give me a kiss." He come flying at me nearly sending me into a freak out.

Leo tried to grab him and hold him off his misinformed eagerness but missed. I held still trembling as Jakob lavished my face with kisses and squeezed me in a tight hug making much racket.

He suddenly stopped his insane adoration and pulled back with a frown. "Uh oh, you wear the headset. Oh, my Gott, Leo. You didn't say anything. I apologize Maxx. I didn't know."

I shrugged. "Know what? That I like music? That is why I am wearing the headgear, Jakob."

Jakob's eyes went wide. "Okay, then you say you are listening to it with a headset that is not attached to the record player?"

That startled me. "Huh? Well, it must be a special pair that plays without the records. I can hear the music in them."

Leo cleared his throat. "I think we need to drop this conversation, Jakob. You heard Maxx. He likes the music. That should be enough said, ja?"

Jakob shot me a baleful glance then resumed his smiling. "Ja. That is fine. I was merely here to thank you for that glorious date Maxx. Leif is quite the artist. I swear I never got to bed last night. He took all those hours to finish."

I frowned. "Well, I hope that portrait was worth the lost slumber. He was quite slow in his art?"

That made the Queen cover his mouth feigning shame. "Oh, you misunderstand Maxx. That painting isn't done. Leif has to come back tonight to finish, if I let him ever be finished that is."

I giggled. "Ah, okay, so I understand now. I suppose that more than his brush got wet, ja?"

Jakob slapped my shoulder playfully. "Oh Maxx. You are so bad and so fucking right. That man made me into the artist myself. I swear I could sing last night."

Leo laughed. "Well Jakob, it is so good to see you happy again my sister. You been in the slumps far too long. This Leif a serious interest or just a little fun?"

Jakob clicked his tongue, flounced and snapped. "Leif wishes that Jakob does more than play with his brushes. This morning when my gorgeous artist lover went to leave the apartment for home, you know to get a little rest for later, he called to me in shock. I thought he must have tripped and fallen. I rushed from my uhm boudoir to find him standing in front of the door staring in disbelief at something on the hallway floor. I joined him and you are never going to believe this Leo, but there were at least ten baskets of flowers, candies and other romantic things. All of them had invites from many Dominants of the Haus looking to go out stepping with Jakob." He reached into his jacket and pulled out a handful of small envelopes that had various men's names on them.

Leo let out a yelp as he reached out to take a few from Jakob that was grinning with thrill. "Oh, let me see. There are so many."

Jakob nodded then shot me a look and kissed the air at me. "Ja. Every eligible schwuler in the fucking Haus has put in his bid for my affection Leo. It is all thanks to our little Maxx here too. His taking me out last night and making such a grand entrance, made me the hot tamale of the month."

I scoffed. "Jakob, need I remind you that it is your beauty, grace and poise that did that, not Mad Maxx. Give yourself credit where credit is due. Everyone wants to be in love with the Queen. Darling you are that girl."

He grinned and petted his hair still gazing at me. "You are too much honey. Leo, you lucky bastard. You hold on to him tight, I mean it. If you ever turn your back I am stealing this gorgeous man from you. Once I have him I will never let him go."

Leo threw one of Jakob's invitation envelopes at him with a growl. "You keep your puss claws out of my lover. I ever catch you fooling with him I will break your whiskers off, Jakob."

That made Jakob laugh loudly. "Ah, you are such a joy, Leo. I swear I am the happiest girl on earth. I have my Leo and Maxx looking out for this old Queen. Plus, the love of the most beautiful artist, Leif. Ah that man reminded me how much I love sex. I swear to God I won't be able to sit for a month. That man was the beast." He pretended to wipe sweat from his brow.

Leo nodded. "You do glow, sister. I would be jealous, but you notice I have the same satisfied smile on my face." He caste a wanton glance at me.

Jakob chuckled as he shot me a look. "So, that is why you rushed off?"

I shrugged and looked at the floor while sighing. "Had to do something, Jakob. You set off that desire in me, and the way you looked at Leif I knew that I was the third wheel. Thank God I had my Leo rocked and ready to keep me sated. It was the gentlemanly thing to do, stepping out of the way of that great love affair I saw in you two's eyes."

Jakob slapped my shoulder playfully again. "You are not even going to stand there funning me, Maxx. You know damned well a third wheel with us schwulers is always a glory. The more cocks the better. You left me for Leo, but I am not angered or jealous for it. You gave me my confidence back and got me laid for the first time since Kilian fucked me over. I thank you for being the romantic gentleman to this silly girl. I will never forget your kindness and true expression of friendship. Be assured I will love you for all my days. You ever need anything, then Auntie Jakob is here for you." He leaned in and kissed my cheek softly.

I smiled. "I love you too Jakob and always will, my friend."

Leo sniffed. "Aw, that is so beautiful. Now get your filthy paws off my Maxx, sister, before I break your fingers. So? What I want to know is which offer you going to accept?" He looked at one of the envelopes in his hand he had taken from Jakob.

Jakob flounced as he snapped. "All of them silly. Jakob is shopping for the best of the best in this pony show. The second she finds herself the right horse she intends to ride that man right to the finish line." He popped his tongue and put his hand on his hip dramatically making me giggle at the most overly feminine move.

Leo frowned as he read a few of the names. "Shit, Jakob. Half the schwulers from the club are on these invites. Why the hell have they never asked you before this morning? We see them in two days for Maxx's outing into the ranks. You'd think day could wait that long and ask you in person."

Jakob grinned as he sashayed to the door grabbing his envelopes from Leo. "Well, they all knew that Jakob is about to be off the market, Leo. They are eager to get in line, that is all. They all fell for Kilian's lies about me. Then last night they saw that man of yours treating me like the Queen I am and suddenly they understood what they all should have known. Kilian is a lying piece of scat. Ugg, I still cannot believe I let that man beat me down for a decade. What a stupid young girl I was. Oh well, I am the woman now. I lived and learned. Now this Haus will too. Oh, Maxx honey, I nearly forgot why I came up here in the first place."

Leo sputtered in surprise, "What? You mean you didn't come here to brag? Shit, if it were me enjoying such newfound popularity I would have been visiting every apartment on every floor."

Jakob snapped and flounced. "Oh no, you did not just say that, Leo. You keep this gorgeous man a secret I seem to recall. If I were as lucky as you I would indeed knock on every door, call the new stands, and even print them on the billboards. That said, I came up because Matz came banging on my door early this morning right after Leif left in a tizzy."

I dropped my head and groaned as I backed up toward the hallway.

Leo saw that and shot me a look of fear. "What did he want Jakob?"

Jakob petted his hair. "He was looking for Maxx. I told him that Maxx was not with me. I asked him what he wanted, and that idiot wouldn't say. Though he seemed pretty upset over something. When I said I thought you were with Jonas he said that the Vampire should be sent over the banister. Can you believe that? Anyway, you better go see what that fool wants before he messes around and gets Jonas gunning for him Maxx. He told me to tell you if I saw you before him is important that you come home and speak with him quickly as possible."

I groaned out, "Okay, thank you Jakob. That will be enough of this conversation."

Leo appeared suspicious. "Wait, is something going on with you and Matz, Maxx? Is that what set you off last night like that? You boys fighting?"

Jakob gasped. "Oh hell. This is all my fault isn't it? Leo, Matz said a few ugly things to Maxx over my date with him last night and Maxx lost his temper. Honey I didn't mean to upset your untroubled home. Tell me baby, how can I make this right?"

Leo snorted. "Is what Jakob says true, Maxx? Did Matz get upset over that date with him?"

I shrugged. "How the fuck would I know? Matz is a crazy motherfucker. I am not a psychiatrist. I wouldn't even dare to guess his problems. I will go find out what is bothering him this time. Jakob you need not get involved in this stupidity of his. I can handled that dumbass, I swear it."

Leo frowned. "That is exactly what worries me. Maxx, my bunny, listen to your Leo. If Matz is becoming a problem for you, ask him to move out. Do not go throwing him over the railing, okay? Promise me you will not resort to violence over whatever is going on between you two."

Jakob gasped as he grabbed his chest. "Holy hell. You think it is that serious, Leo? Oh, please honey, promise Leo and your Auntie no killing. That fucking Kilian would be thrilled if you mess up so badly. He and Reece would make sure you never get out of Heslach. That father of my would be most happy to aid those demons in keeping you their hostage for the rest of your life. Trust me love, I know all three of them better than I ever wished to."

I nodded but kept my eyes to the floor. "I swear to you both I will not kill Matz. There is not that big a problem between us. He is merely the whiny bitch is all. The man gets on my nerves. I will ask him to leave before it gets to that point."

That seemed to satisfy Leo and Jakob. I spent a bit longer petting Der Makellos and visiting with Leo and Jakob. Before I knew it, the time had grown late. I needed to head down to face the music with Matz. I secretly knew that he likely had visited with an angered Lucus, I had beat the man up, and wanted to warn me he was going to Gretta over it.

I sighed as I left my Leo's loving arms that morning. I assumed there was a chance that I wouldn't see him again. Jakob's warning about Kilian and Heslach rang in my ears as I went down the steps, my overnight bag in tow, to the fourth floor.

I went through the apartment door expecting to see Matz sitting on the couch in a pout. I nearly passed out when instead of my flat mate, I found Lucus on my sofa with a huge smile on his face. I felt frozen in the spot unable to speak. Then Matz came out of his bedroom with a frown. He sat next to Lucus and pointed at the love seat. "We have a serious problem Maxx. Come sit down." The look on Matz face told me this was not going to be a good day for Mad Maxx. That fact became even clearer when I noticed on the coffee table was that notebook Lucus keeps on me.

Chapter 19:   More Dirty Deals

I stared at that notebook marked Mad Maxx Der Brutle sitting on the coffee table feeling the fear filling my knees to weakness. I shot a look of concern at Matz trying to read in his eyes the meaning of this odd early morning meeting with that creepy Lucus. He glared at me without any expression that could indicate the nature of this situation.

Lucus cleared his throat. "Please Maxx. Take a seat like Matz asked you to. Do not offer quarrel in this. You surely realize you have no choice."

I growled out at him in irritation. "You come into my apartment and dare to tell me what to do and add that I am without option. Fuck you, Lucus. You have no power here. Just who the fuck do you think you are? I can tell you right this minute, you leave now or call yourself worm food."

Matz gasped, "Maxx, sit down. You are trying to kill yourself I assume? Well not on my clock you don't. I demand you cease threatening the honorable Lucus. If not for your own life then do it for Geraldine, me, or hell Jakob."

That caught my attention. "Jakob? What the hell does he have to do with anything? You dare to bring up his name in front of this rude bastard? Well, I can see I have a busy morning ahead. I need to send two cocksuckers to their graves instead of one." I shot a look of hatred at Matz.

Lucus blew out his breath. "You have always been a hardheaded bastard Maxx. Sit the fuck down. I refuse to threaten you despite the fact you have no problem doing such ungentlemanly actions yourself. I wish to remind you I didn't go and report you for striking me last night. That ought to be worth you granting a few moments of you time if nothing else."

I scoffed. "Go ahead and report me. I get a few lashes and the beautiful memory of your laying their at my feet bleeding. Not too bad a trade I would think."

That made Matz nearly come unglued. "Okay, that is enough. Sit down Maxx or I will go tell Gretta what you did. Lucus may be the gentleman, but Matz is not. You have done enough damage already. Like it or not, you have to work out this issue with the honorable Lucus to make up for beating him up like he is the common criminal." He pointed at the loveseat nearly ready to have a fit.

I chuckled bitterly as I shot a look of humor at Lucus. "Well, he had that coming Matz. The man called me a whore, insulted Jakob and threw money at me in public demanding I service him. He should have gone the fuck home and thanked his lucky stars he is the great and powerful King Lucus. Had he been anyone else, I would have killed him on the spot."

Matz groaned and covered his eyes with his hands. "You are the fucking whore, Maxx. You would kill this Dominant for stating the truth of it?"

I gasped. "Matz, you sonofabitch, shut your mouth. What is wrong with you, agreeing with his lies."

Lucus laughed out loud. "Give it up Maxx. I told you last night I figured out your game with Matz. He is your pimp, and you are in fact a whore. The only lies being spewed are coming from your mouth. Be still. You have nothing to worry about. I am not going to tell a soul. In fact, I signed Matz's silly confidentiality agreement in my own blood this morning. You boys secret is safe with me."

I snorted as I nodded and crossed my arms. "Is that so? Ah, okay I get it. This meeting is about your interest in becoming the client. I should have guessed that. You need not bother with Gretta. Not when you can get your taste of the Priceless for a discount, ja? Pervert."

Lucus nearly fell off the couch in shock as he stammered out. "Nein, you misunderstand Maxx. I would never dare such a low practice such as blackmail. If I desired to purchase your services, I pay like anyone else does. I will tolerate your threats, but I cannot allow you to question my honor without just cause. I do have to demand an apology for that insult."

I smiled with demons rising within. "You want me to be sorry for judging you the pervert and low criminal do you. Well, tell you what. I apologize to you the second you return the service for acting like the ass last night, and all the years you have stalked. I will be happy to say such a thing is accepted then ask you kindly to fuck off and leave me alone for good."

Lucus groaned but stood up and bowed to me. "I apologize to you most honorable Mad Maxx for my foul behaviors and conversation while inebriated. It was not only uncalled for but beneath me and you to act the asshole like that. I beg your mercy and forgiveness with the promise it will never happen again. I swear it." He lifted from his bow appearing to be awaiting my own statement of remorse.

I glared at him. "Very nice. That ugly mother of yours certainly taught you proper manners. When you are sober enough to recall her lessons, that is. However, you apparently weren't listening. I said I wanted you to say you are sorry for stalking me and promise to stop it. Go head. I am waiting for that oath motherfucker. Then I am happy to grant you the mercy of forgiveness and bid you a nice life."

Lucus sat back down. "Nein, you will never get that promise from me Maxx."

I shrugged. "Then your apology is empty and not accepted. I assure you that when I get the chance I will end your following me the way you insist I do it." I sat down causing Matz, that had been about to freak out at my rudely denying Lucus mercy, to appear to calm immediately.

Matz cleared his throat as he stole a nervous glance at Lucus. "Maxx, I am going to ignore that you are obviously suicidal to deny Lucus his honest apology. Instead, I wish to focus on the makeup that Lucus has worked out with me over your unjustified attack on him last night. What the hell is with the headset? Why are you wearing that? It looks stupid."

I made the sound of the raspberry. "I already said he had that coming. You make me repeat myself, both of you. Seems you fellows need to get hearing aids instead of headphones like I have."

Matz glared. "What the fuck does that even mean? Shit. You are not making any fucking sense. Be that as it may, Maxx, you have no choice but to offer a service makeup for striking him. You should have gone to Gretta if you had an issue with him. There are rules in this Haus for a reason."

That made me laugh wildly. "Oh? Well, there is also a rule against prostitution isn't there? And gambling? Yet, I dare say neither of us bother to mind them. Gretta would have done nothing to stop that man from following me but maybe a fucking fine. He is the rich man. Money means nothing to him. So, exactly why do I need to adhere to any of rules? Peter told me that the Dominant need not mind the rules if he is willing to take the punishment. Well, I take the punishment. Go tell Gretta motherfucker. I am not afraid of you, Lucus, nor that snotty FemDom."

Matz scoffed. "You may not fear any of us, but I bet you do not feel the same about that Mann of yours named Jonas. What do you think he is going to do to you when the Honorable Gretta tells him you are the prostitute to keep enough money to avoid living in his home? You think he will only give you a few lashings? I think you better consider the consequences before you go running that ignorant mouth, Maxx."

I glared at Matz with indignation but inside I realized he had a fucking point. "Ah, okay, so let's assume I do care about such fantasy. I am listening, but you better hurry up. I have a lot to do today including murdering both of you without getting caught."

Lucus gasped. "There is no reason to be so damned hateful, Maxx. What I desire from you as the makeup will not be a hardship."

I snarled. "You speaking like you know what I think is disgusting. Please do tell me all about what I find bothersome and don't. I am all ears."

He nodded. "Alright I will just get down to it then. I desire you visit with me daily, that's all."

I laughed sarcastically. "Ah, okay so putting up with sucking your cock or being fucked by you daily is not a hardship for me you say? Wow, you know me so well, Lucus. To think I assumed you would be asking for something unreasonable. I only hit you once, fool. You think I owe you daily for it? Fuck you, Lucus. No way am I going to agree to this bullshit. Go ahead and tell Gretta. Fucking tell Jonas, see if I care. I would rather be sent to Heslach."

Matz glowered. "Be still, Maxx. Let him explain. He has not asked for your sexual services, but he is willing to pay for this meeting with him each time you come and speak to him. Don't be stupid and turn him down."

Lucus cleared his throat and smiled nervously. "Matz is right, Maxx. I am not interested in forcing your couple with me not paid or otherwise. I merely want you to share information with me about your daily dealings with the power of this Haus. I already told you I am never going to report your attack on me to Gretta. This offer is not a blackmail. I am asking to be a client but not one of your common men. I will pay you for your words only. Not your sexual artistry. I am not one that needs to stoop to such a low level to obtain a lover. I must ask you to stop insulting me by assuming that is my interest in you."

I snorted. "Well, sure sounded like you were interested in a base love affair with me last night Lucus."

Lucus sighed. "I was drunk Maxx. I admit that freely and I have apologized. Now, are you willing to take my offer or nein? I will pay you good money. Matz has given me a price and I have agreed to pay it up front with no quarrel."

I glanced over at Matz that wore an expression of pleading on his face. "Does he speak the truth, Matz? He will pay me to be his spy and the money is worthy of the risk I take to give his nosey urges pleasure?"

Matz nodded. "Ja, I would say so. Lucus is being most fair in his offer. The money is easy Maxx. This is a great offer, take it. It would help you with our, uhm, situations."

I groaned. "I hate you Lucus and do not desire to see your face even once a lifetime much less every fucking day. That said, if Matz says you pay a good some for it, I will do as you request. When do you want me to start doing this service and what time of day can I expect to provide for your interests?"

Matz blew out his breath appearing relieved as Lucus smiled then said, "I wish to start this very day. You meet with me every night before you leave for the client or your Mann or come home to your own bed. Whenever that happen."

I nodded. "So, eight-thirty?"

He smiled even brighter. "Ah, ja, that works for me. I think it would be best to meet with you in this apartment at eight-thirty every night to get your report. I don't want anyone to know what is going on. We need to be discreet."

I glared at him feeling most nauseous. "What the fuck do you plan to do with what I tell you happened during my discussions with the Elders and Voters, Lucus? I don't like this, any of it."

Lucus frowned. "You told me that I am an evil man for not stepping up to stop the injustices I see going on in the Haus. Well, I have decided you were right. If I am to aid to change the ways things work here then I need to know what is going on. I need to know the thoughts of the ones in charge. Only you have access to such information. Jonas and others tell you things that I could use to influence and cause more positive outcomes."

Matz crossed his arms. "He means that he wants to help the submissives of this Haus have a better life Maxx. Is this not what you wish to see yourself? Lucus can help the silvers and blacks with our help."

I snorted at that. "Our? Humm, exactly how are you involved Matz? It is Mad Maxx's ass that will be put to the yard if I get caught telling tales out of school to Lucus, not you. The risk is all mine. Besides that, you already are the eyes and ears of another fool. Did you disclose that to Lucus? How can I be sure you won't betray him and me by proxy with that big mouth of yours."

Lucus started chuckling, which startled me after what I had just said to Matz. "You're speaking about Matz being Malfred man, ja? Maxx, I know that he is to report to that Elder. Well, no more. I pay him to switch teams."

I nearly fell off the loveseat at that information as I shot a look of shock at Matz. "Is this true, Matz? You now work for Lucus and leave Malfred in the cold?"

Matz nodded as he looked at the floor appearing mildly shamed. "He offers to pay me. Malfred only could assure the Wolfpack was brought in. We served him well but without a fortune, that Elder has left us to swing. Lucus can keep all of us from the streets and you in your apartment. I hate to betray our buddy Malfred but when it comes down to it, friendship won't pay the bills."

I nodded with a cat smile of bitterness. "Ah, you are the Judas I assumed you to be. For the right price you can be bought. Mad Maxx may be the whore selling his ass to the highest bidder, but Matz is far worse. He sells his soul."

Matz scoffed. "Say whatever you wish, Maxx. I will not respond to your attempts to upset me. I look out for Matz, and my brothers. Malfred works only for his own selfish interests. Lucus has a plan to fix the horrors in this place. I am most happy to join his army. I would think you of all people would be happy to pony up with anyone willing to step in and do something about the horrible waste of lives and torments seen daily within these walls."

I giggled again full of the sarcasm. "I never thought you the humanitarian, Matz. I suppose it was difficult for me to notice such an exceptional quality when you are forcing yourself on me. Funny how your nasty cock in my face blinds me to the truthful caring soul you truly are."

Matz looked at me with his eyes wide, then shot an anxious glance at Lucus. "Ah, don't mind what Maxx spouts honorable Lucus. He is being rude as usual. I would never do such a thing."

I laughed even harder, full of bitterness as Lucus glared at Matz with an expression of disgust. "You don't? I guess I was hallucinating all that foul intercourse with you that you paid for. Thank God you set me straight. Oh wait, speaking of that you said you tire of the long suffering straight Mad Maxx. You reminded me that I have to service you to keep you from fighting with me all the time. Your lusts drive your jealousy over me doing my fucking job. So, you don't want to hear another word about my dislike of sex with a man. I am insane to recall such a discussion with you, ja? Well, you have nothing to worry about Matz. I suck your dick and let you fuck me without further quarrel. Lucus here is happy to fund your foul interest in being my regular client. Looks like I will not have to endure a daily dose of Lucus, but sure as shit going to have to be on my knees for my pimp each time the sunrises. I thank you Lucus for arranging that I can finally come home, and after attending Matz's urges, I get peace and quiet at long last."

Matz dropped his head with a gasp and Lucus cleared his throat nervously. "Uhm, I don't think I wish to be present for this personal situation between you two. This is not my business."

I scoffed loudly as I yelled at Lucus with anger, "It isn't? I thought you wanted me to report my daily dealings with you for the fee you pay. This is merely one of the issues I tolerate. I think you better define what exactly you desire I tell you and what I can keep for my personal use. You don't desire I discuss Matz's sexual interest in me, but you want to hear the dirty details of the Vampire's lusting? How about Peter? Want me to rush to you over the Honorable Claus perhaps? Did Matz give you a list of my clients? Do you want to know if Osvin or Justus like the rim job or their hodensack tickled? Hum?"

Lucus gasped. "Oh, my Gott, nein. I don't want to know of the sexual habits of anyone you endure Maxx. I am interested in the pillow talk only."

I giggled at that. "Oh, I see. You like to hear the insults, threats, and gross things they say before and after the sex. Got it. Matz here, well he likes to call me a whore and make me believe he does me a favor cuming in my mouth instead of my…" Lucus yelled out in interruption.

"Enough, okay, I understand you anger Maxx but please use some decorum here. I mean I want to know of any relationship's they have with others, plans for the future, or laws they hope to push through Gretta. I don't want to hear any of that carnal stuff." He was nearly panting in horror at my crass discussions.

I smiled at him with wickedness. "Well, your wish is my command your majesty. Now if you are through bothering me, I have shit to do. Are you ready to follow or can I expect you will merely wait for the report of how many times I took a piss later today?"

Lucus squirmed a bit then said, "We don't need to be enemies, Maxx. I swear to you we are on the same side in this war to change the Haus."

I stood up with a chuckle. "If you hope to beat the Vampire, Kilian or Malfred you better be smarter than you are appearing to me this moment. I am your enemy, Lucus. Not only do you force yourself into my nightmares as the thrilled spectator but now you intend to become a power within the very thing I hate the most. I don't care about changing this place unless it is to turn it from a solid to gas. Just in case you misunderstand me; I want to see the Haus burned to the ground and every Dominant within it too.

Matz, I will see you later for your God damned service I know you expect and Lucus, I suppose you for yours after that. Yuck! I am out of here." I picked up my overnight bag and fled out the door before either of those assholes could stop me.

It was nearly nine in the morning, and I needed to get down to see the Voter Rolf. I promised that man in the closet that I would go check on Geraldine. I knew that to breaking my promise to him would result in terrible punishment, but to be honest I had been missing that lamb a great deal.

I was more than happy to go see her and the other lamb babies. It seemed ages since last we had visited. Plus, I wanted to introduce them to Felicity you know.

I turned around with a gas. "But Master, Malfred made you let them go back to the flock. Geraldine couldn't be in the stables." He reached out and popped me extra hard making me writhe in agony.

Master Maxx growled out in irritation. "Nein, that nightmare was a stupid stress filled hallucination. I was a little confused back then. I only imagined Malfred made me do that nonsense. Geraldine was there and I knew it. How else could she be cooking for me silly?"

I sniffed back tears from that stinging swat. "Even if you imagined letting them go to the flock Master, Geraldine would be an old sheep, not a lamb anymore." He popped me even harder, really making me squeal that time.

He snorted in increasing anger. "Geraldine, Ryker, Annette, Milo and Abelard are lambs, Meine Liebe, not sheep. They are always lambs. Dogs don't become lions and lambs don't become nasty sheep."

I started to argue that insanity, but my leg was really burning so I dropped it. He cleared his throat and went back to his story.

NOTE: Master Maxx/Christian Axel is incredibly smart, but in this case his fantastical delusion about the lambs Leo had bought him in his youth make him sound intellectually disabled. Even I knew at age nine, lambs grow into sheep and sure as shit cannot cook meals. You are about to see the seriousness of a fixed delusion such as this one.

Despite being shown evidence, several times over the years, and the memory of letting the lambs go, Mad Maxx holds tight to this belief with childlike and magical excuses. A strong delusion often develops when the great lie is preferable to the painful truth within the schizophrenic. These kinds of delusions are often difficult if not impossible to break thanks to these maladaptive psychological responses to attempts to force a sense of reality about them.

To this day, he still believes Geraldine and the others live as eternal lambs in a pen out in the stables, but like Annette waiting in the green fields, it is all in his head. It exists only behind the shattered looking glass.

I made it to Rolf's apartment in record time. The whole way I grumbled to myself about the bullshit Lucus and Matz had pulled on me. That idiot Lucus really thought he was going to be capable of wrestling the power out of the hands of Jonas, Kilian, Malfred, Peter and Gretta. What a self-important moron was all I could think. I decided to plan to send Lucus to the bottom of the silver well the second I got the chance. His interference with my attempts to escaping the Haus had finally gotten on my last nerve.

Besides, that fucker had all the dirt on me he needed for several lifetimes to send me to the yard. I damned myself for not killing him the night before when I had a clean shot at him. Oh well. I realized one good thing about being stuck in his employment was it granted me a second chance to send him to hell. All I needed to do is be patient.

I knocked on Rolf's door doing my best to calm the boy. The Voter answered rather quickly with a huge grin on his face.

I smiled back at him. "If you are not too busy Rolf I wonder can I borrow you for a favor?"

Rolf chuckled. "You have another list and wad of cash? Where the hell are you getting all that money? You can tell your buddy Rolf. Some FemDom is the sugar momma for my main man Maxx, ja?"

I chuckled at that. "Shit, don't I wish. Nein, I managed to snag some cash from Matz's win fall on his tables is all. What I ask today is you take a walk with me."

Rolf frowned. "Huh? Okay, is someone bothering you that you cannot handle alone?"

I shook my head still chuckling. "You always assume the worst, Rolf. Nein, I can handle myself these days. I wish to go to the stables and Peter prevents my leaving without a Dominant of worth on my arm. Are you free to escort me?"

He nodded. "Sure, anything for you Maxx. I could use a stretch before breakfast. What is in the stables? A honey that has caught your eye maybe. One that enjoys the violins of Barber, I bet." He grinned with mischief in his eyes.

I shrugged. "Well, you could call the girl I wish to visit a honey. I think she would indeed enjoy Samuel Barber as well. I can ask her when we get there. Thanks for that amazing idea. I do owe her for all she has done for me."

Rolf yipped. "Oh, my goodness. Let me grab my coat. I desire to see this girl of ours. Has she a single sister?"

I laughed. "She does, but I don't think Annette would be interested in you, brother. That lady already has three fellows fighting constantly for her affections."

Rolf whistled. "Damn, she must be a looker then. Well, I will take my chances and add a fourth man to her mix, ja?"

I shrugged. "Then good luck to you Rolf, though I find it a little disturbing to think of it. I know Annette. She will refuse you."

He rushed off and returned quickly with his coat ready to go. "Don't be so damned sure, Maxx. I can be quite persuasive you know. The girls love Rolf and God knows I love them."

I rolled my eyes. "This one will be immune to your charms lover boy, but as you say, maybe you're that persuasive. I pray she sees you as the player you are. If not I will have to knock you the fuck out for messing with my family."

He chuckled. "Family? Ah. You intend to marry her sister then? Well, good for you Maxx. I myself am not the marrying type, you know. I like to keep the options open, but I am not against it. You should settle down and make some children with the honeys, like Egon. He and his lady are expecting a baby soon. Have you heard?"

I shook my head. "Nein, I had not, but that is great news. I have not had a chance to speak to him since I got back. The one time I saw him I was, uhm, busy with other business. I supposed he married that beautiful girl Monika?"

He nodded. "Sure did, that lucky bastard. A happier man never lived. Shit, I hate to see him, when I still do. That glory is all he speaking of anymore. You'd think he was the one about to give birth rather than that gorgeous Frau of his."

I laughed as I walked alongside Rolf down the steps for the front door. "Egon is a good man, Rolf. I think many children from him would enhance this hell hole. Surely they will all be the great heart like their mother and father, ja?"

Rolf snorted. "Nein, those two will spoil their children to demon status no doubt. I, however, am proud to see the man finally getting the happiness he most honestly deserves. Now, to get you married off to this beauty you take me to see." I interrupted him with a gasp.

"Nein, Rolf. You shut that perverted stuff up. You maybe don't have boundaries, but I would like to think Mad Maxx does. I would never even consider such a nasty thing with Geraldine. Yikes! You will give me nightmares with such unnatural talk." I glared at him in disgust at his suggesting I marry and sleep with a lamb. What the hell?

Rolf put up his hands insinuating surrender. "Okay. Damn, don't bite my head off Maxx. I am with you. Play the field before settling down. I was merely saying having a sturdy frau and little ones would likely do you much good."

I nodded. "I agree with you Rolf and I do intend to marry as quickly as possible. But not Geraldine, not ever."

We discussed Byron's pouting over my continued refusal of his advances. Then he told me that Friedrick was dating a lovely frau and that had further isolated his love starved brother Voter. I chuckled as Rolf compared Byron to the horny hound looking to mount anything that held still long enough or was unlucky and couldn't outrun him.

The door guards let us out without quarrel. Rolf reminded me to stay close. I peered into the distance and saw that a couple of Russians with rifles had stepped out of a small building in the distance. They were watching Rolf and me with suspiciousness. I felt a shiver go down my spine realizing they were making sure that if I attempted to run they could quickly end my flight.

Rolf saw me keeping a baleful eye on the snipers. "Let it go, Maxx. You stay close and they can piss in the wind. Fucking Peter is a bit overzealous in his fears you will try escaping. I know you better than that."

I nodded but didn't let the shooters out of my sights. "Where exactly are we Rolf? This Haus is located in East Germany I have figured out, but what town?"

Rolf shot me a look of caution. "Stop that Maxx. You know better. I cannot tell you that."

I scoffed. "I knew you were not really my friend."

Rolf stopped his march to the stable and glared at me with irritation. "Cut it out Maxx. I won't be guilted or tricked into giving you information that will get you killed. I am your friend. In fact, I love you like a brother. You know where you are, then you will fuck up and try to get the authorities involved. That my dear Maxx will get you murdered."

I snorted. "You are full of shit. The police will come and put everyone away that could dare to kill me for telling on the evil they do here."

Rolf looked into the sky as he said, "You are wrong there, Maxx. If you figured out that the Haus is in occupied territory than surely a smart boy like you realizes the police belong to the Haus. You go to them, and the Guard won't need to waste a bullet on you. The cops will blow your head off for them. Maxx, you are a hostage here unless someone with a lot of power helps you escape it. It would take a lot of money, and so many favors only the very top have such a rolodex. If the Guard don't get you then the Russian authorities of this country will. You cannot just walk across the border Maxx. They would shoot you on sight, both the Eastern and the Western border guards. Your best bet would be to find a FemDom that makes you smile and find the pleasure where you can take it. Otherwise, you will be in misery living here for all your life. This is your home. Like it or not."

I glared at him. "Nein, I will not accept that. I am not of this country Rolf. I never agreed to any of this. I want to go home, m real home."

Rolf shot me a look of caution,. "You do? Okay, exactly where is that Maxx? You have lived here since you were a little boy. I see the scars that you had before the Guard dragged you here. What kind of home did you have before? Not one of worth apparently. You intend to return to the one that did that to you?" He pointed at the scar on the left side of my face.

I smiled with evil. "Nein, Rolf. I cannot return there. The one that did such a thing is long burned up in a terrible arson related fire. Someone burned him up. Him and his home. The ones that keep me hostage here would do well to remember that. Mad Maxx will not put up with much more of this bullshit. Sooner or later, I am going to tire of these games you all play with me. When that happens, you can tell Gerard I said hello."

Rolf scoffed. "I cannot believe you dare to stand here and threaten me Maxx. I had nothing to do with your abduction nor the torment you suffer still."

I nodded still smiling with demons in my eyes. "That is true Rolf, but you also do nothing to stop the ones that do. You could smuggle me out of here, but you don't. Don't think I won't take that into account when and if I carry out the justice you all surely deserve."

Rolf looked at me closely then blew out his breath. "Holy hell. You are going buggy again aren't you? Fuck. The headset, I saw it so often in the past I guess I got used to seeing you in it. I forgot what that shit means. Damn me. You know, I just saw Leo and Jonas the other day and Peter. Not a fucking one of them said a word about this."

I glared at him. "What do you mean buggy? Because I state the truth of it that makes me crazy does it? Well, fuck you Rolf."

He snorted. "I am not going to get into this with you Maxx. I learned my lesson when you still wore that blasted metal. You are my friend even if you are fast forgetting it. Come on with me. I take you where you asked to go. We will drop this before it gets any further. I will have a few words to say to the correct ears when next I see them. Fucking assholes let me walk right into a trap." He took off towards the stables cursing several of the Elders and Peter under his breath.

I followed him feeling extreme aggression filling the boy. I looked over at Mad Maxx standing there holding Christian back best as he could. I couldn't figure out how the fuck that Anger shard was managing to project his interest from that far away. I looked back at Max at the end of my chain. He was glaring at Christian struggling against Mad Maxx with an expression of concern. I then shot a nervous glance at Maximillian.

The Seducer stood there smiling back at me as he said, "Better keep your eyes on the wheel brother. My time is coming. Soon enough your old buddy Rolf and all the others will taste my blade. Maybe I get Leo too and that silly Jakob you care about so much. Mad Max the sadist, what a joke. You couldn't harm the fly with your stupid adoration for these idiots. Not a one of them helps you. They help themselves at the boy's expense. Well, they don't fool Maximillian. I can see what they are. Users, scum, liars, all of them."

I wiped the sweat starting to beat up on my brow. "Mad Maxx, you keep Christian back, hear me? I am having trouble here remembering who the Anger is and who is Mad Max."

Mad Maxx groaned. "Sorry brother Mad Max. I was so busy focusing on holding back this beastly shard I lost my focus for a moment there. Make the boy calm down. It is under control. We wouldn't want Geraldine seeing us in discord with each other. She gets nervous easily. Plus, they overwork her, ja?"

I groaned. "That they do. Maximillian, you shut your damned mouth before I cane you motherfucker. Your only job is to lay there and take it. Stick to your function and open that mouth only when the clients or bosses tell you too otherwise. I am sick and tired of hearing your voice."

Maximillian scoffed. "The feeling is mutual, cocksucker. You come near me, and I will show you how to lay there and take it."

I snorted. "Good luck with that. Come any closer and the last thing you hear from me is my singing your funeral dirge, you sonofabitch."

Max bellowed out, "Stop. Maximillian shut up. Mad Max, do your job or I will not allow the Seducer to relieve you when Peter comes for his services."

That got my attention. "Shit. Okay, your wish is my command Max. There is no need for threats so foul. I give you no problem."

That was a close one. I was well aware I couldn't beat Max no matter how tough I am. Having to endure that sex with Peter was exactly why I split off to create Maximillian in the first fucking place. Max knew I could handle anything but that horror.

I stole a glance at Maximillian and saw that fucker grinning in victory at my being put in my place. I wanted to beat that schwuler shard to death for such arrogance, but I dared not infuriate the powerful Max any further. I knew he wasn't bluffing.

Rolf led me thru the stable door. I looked into the pen where my babies lived and found it empty. That immediately sent me into a wild panic. Someone had moved my lamb family. I looked all around at the other pens and found only the swine and horses. Rolf stood there appearing confused as I ran from pen to pen growing more upset by the second.

I finally ran back to where he stood. Sweat had begun to pour down the boy's face from the growing anxiety even though it was below zero outside. I was feeling the burn of fear within. All around the sounds of the animals seemed to amplify even through the protection of Leo's magic headset.

I yelled out to the weirded out Rolf. "They stole my family, Rolf. Help me. I fear they are going to kill them for supper. That is why the man told me to check on them. He knew my lambs were in trouble. Oh Gott, where have they taken them? I need to hurry before it is too late. Find Rudolph. He knows where the cocksuckers take the lambs for the slaughter. I have to save them."

Rolf seemed as panicked as I felt. "Calm down Maxx. What are you speaking about? Your Lambs? You mean the ones that Leo bought you? Is that what we came here for?"

I nodded wildly. "Ja, ja. Where are they, Rolf. Someone stole them."

He groaned loudly. "Oh, shit. You don't remember do you poor boy?"

I whined out feeling that I may explode. "I don't understand your language, Rolf. Where are my babies? That Kilian said the wolves killed them. That DJ told him. Please nein, I cannot let this happen. I have to find them."

Rolf put up his arms in a gesture that I needed to calm. "Hush, Maxx. That Kilian is lying. Your lambs are fine. I saw them only yesterday. The attendant took them out for a bath is all. They were filthy and needed to be groomed. I promise, all of them are fine. We can come back later when they are returned, dried and white once more."

I wrung my hands while pacing. "They are at the bath service. Are you sure? Can you find Rudolf? I want to hear him say this."

Rolf sighed. "Maxx, you have to listen to me brother. Rudolf is still healing in the hospital from that accident he was in. The substitute attendants didn't realize that you may come for the visit. Come back to the Haus with me and then this afternoon we return. You will see I tell the truth. The lambs will be finished with their baths by then."

I sped up my pacing and shook my head. "Nein, I go nowhere until I see my lambs. I can wait for them. You tell Rudolf I am here. He will speak to me Rolf. He knows me, ask him to come and verify the lambs are safe."

Rolf stood there a moment appearing unsure what to do then he said, "Okay, you stay right here. I mean it. Go nowhere else and I go find someone that knows where they are drying the lambs. Give me your word, Maxx. Listen to me, I want your vow."

I nodded. "I swear I go nowhere till I see them and Rudolf. Go find my lambs Rolf." I grew even more agitated and wrung my hands faster.

He took off into the deep core of the stable to ask after my babies. I could hear the laughter of Kilian through the walls. He was thinking I had been fooled into believing the lambs safe when in fact he had them killed. I felt the tears stinging the boy's eyes. I couldn't handle this. I needed my babies, or all was lost. My chest felt like it would cave in from the sorrow at the idea that the Dominants had eaten them for dinner.

Rolf retuned with a young black collar male.

The boy stared at me appearing in awe and frightened. The Voter pointed at the empty pen, "Where did they put the lambs from this pen? Tell the Priceless what you told me a moment ago Dieter."

Dieter cleared his throat. "Uhm, they were, uhm, in the bath? We put all the wet lambs near the heaters, so they don't get cold till they are dry. If you follow me I take you to see the ones that live in that pen."

That caused me to look up from my agitated pacing. "You say you know where my lambs are?"

Dieter nodded but backed away with his eyes ide in fright. "Ja, if you come with me I take you to them."

I smiled with sudden joy. "Ja, I come with you. Lead the way." I came at him, and he backed up so fast he nearly fell from his panicked retreat.

Rolf come rushing after the two of us as Dieter hurried along and I followed. I saw all kinds of animals along the way. I wondered if Ghazi, Marc, Kloe and Aara had ever met my lambs. I didn't see my black collared children around, but I was aware they tended Cora's horses. That Head of the Haus Elder kept her animals in a special barn off in the distance. This stable was for the commonly owned livestock.

Dieter stopped in front of a small pen in the center of the stable. A huge heater was blowing out thru a fan in the wall.

He pointed into it with a nervous smile. "These five. They are the Elder Leo's lambs."

I looked into the pen and saw my lambs standing there shivering. A rush of relief came over me as I pulled hard on the pen door trying to get inside with them. Rolf come up and grabbed my arms causing me to cry out in shock.

"Nein, Maxx. You let these lambs be. They are stressed from that bath they got. You want to visit them in person we have to come back later as I told you. You look and see they are safe. Now I must insist we return to the Haus." He pulled me back despite my struggle and whimpering to get inside with my babies.

I dropped my head and wrung my hands when he let me go. "But Rolf, I need to pet them. I can wait till they are dried. I am patient."

Rolf snorted,. "You may be, but Rolf is not. It is fucking cold out here and I have things to do. I will bring you back later if you insist but I am not standing around for hours in this fucking stable waiting till they dry, and neither are you."

I started to argue but Rolf put up his hand for silence. "You say another word Maxx and I won't come back with you later. You can ask Byron or Friedrick, but Rolf will refuse your request."

I moaned out as if in pain. "Alright. I come with you, but I want to see them later."

He nodded with a bitter smile. "Ja, I got that. What time are you free to come back?"

I really dropped my head at that. "I am not free to return, Rolf. I am busy all the rest of the day and night."

Rolf looked sad all at once. "Ah, okay, now I understand better you're not desiring to leave. Tell you what we can come back first thing in the morning."

I shook my head. "I am busy tomorrow too, Rolf. I don't have another chance to see my babies for another four days."

He blew out his breath appearing as frustrated as I felt. "Four days? Well, that could work. How about this. You hang in there until Tuesday, and I bring you out to see them, then take you to town after."

I looked up at him in a startle. "You can do that? Take me off the grounds, I mean."

Rolf grinned as he nodded. "You damned right I can. You be patient and in four days you see the lambs and then you and I go chase the village girls at the local pub. Do we have a deal? Do recall I promised you that when you broke the collar I would take you out for a night on the town."

I smiled with glee. "Ja, you did say that. Okay, I am happy to agree to this Rolf. Do you need it in writing?"

That made Rolf laugh loudly. "You are something else Maxx. Nein, I trust your word without such bullshit as the contract. You say goodbye to your lambs, and we need to get going. Thank you Dieter for your help. You take particular care of Leo's lambs, or you will be sorry for it."

Dieter nodded with that look of worry in his expression. "I sure will Master Rolf. I thank you for the mercy of it."

I blew kisses to my lamb family and with some difficulty managed to pull myself away to follow Rolf back to the Haus. I was grateful that the man in the closet was wrong. Geraldine looked healthy and was even getting the bath service for her hard work. That makes me feel more secure to know.

I furrowed my brow. "Rolf, I wonder since the lambs looked smaller than I recalled them to be. Are you sure those were the right ones?" I thought maybe Deiter got them mixed up with another family, you know.

Rolf chuckled. "Ah, that is what happens with the bathing you know. Shrinks the wool. Surely you know that. Didn't you used to do your Master's laundry?"

I nodded. "Ah, okay that makes sense. No wonder they never grow too large. The regular bathing keeps them little like that, not lack of feed."

He reached over and ruffled my hair causing me to flinch and near run away. "Oh, sorry Maxx. I forgot. Uhm, ja it is the water that keeps them small. They are well loved and cared for. You need to stop worrying about it. In four days, you can see for yourself they are all enjoying good treatment." He frowned at my anxious keeping a distance due to his unwarranted touching like that.

I stole a nervous glance at him. "Ja, I will do that. Then we go to town, and I find a Frau. Once I have one I make the children and Peter lets me leave for good."

Rolf stopped his walking as he did earlier seeming suddenly surprised. "hat? Is that what he told you? Is Jonas okay with this?"

I shrugged. "I don't care what Jonas is alright with, Rolf. I make the children, then Peter and me are through. That is the contract. I am eager to find my mate anyway. Then I can have the natural relationship that is my truest desire."

Rolf looked at the ground. "Wait a moment. You uhm, don't have a girlfriend then?"

I shook my head. "Nein. I am not allowed one. Only the man I told you that."

He nodded. "Ja, you did but I assumed you would merely keep your affairs with the females secret. What the hell was all the romantic stuff you got me to pick up for the other day if not a lover?"

I sighed. "It was for Jakob. He needed a little romance in his life that is all. Maxx made sure he got it."

That made Rolf gasp. "You and Jakob? No way. Maxx, that is not right."

I chuckled. "You misunderstand Rolf. I am not with Jakob. I am with Matz. I told you this already."

Rolf shook his head. "Nein. You are pulling bullshit with Rolf. I assumed you took on that thug to help with expenses. You surely do not sleep with that fool. Maxx, you are straight."

I looked at my boots. "Doesn't matter that I am. Peter and Jonas will not let me be. I need that Frau. I tell them both that I am the schwuler hoping they lose interest, but I seeking the female to marry."

Rolf blew out his breath. "Nothing changed when you broke that metal did it? They lied to you and still you believe in Peter's worthless contract?"

I glanced at him feeling a bit panicked. "You think they will try to fuck me over again?"

He nodded. "I am surprised you don't consider that yourself, Maxx. After all that has happened I find it odd that you would trust those snakes in the grass."

That made me more than a little nervous. "Maybe you are right, Rolf. I will need to get extra protection no doubt. I thank you for the wise advice."

Rolf smiled. "Anytime brother. You watch your back and Rolf will help, ja?" We took off on our journey back inside once more.

I bid him a good day and rushed down to see Peter for my lesson. I barely made it before becoming late. My father was sitting on a table asleep as he had been the day before. I winced but walked up and cleared my throat loudly.

When he didn't respond to that I shook him gently. "Peter, I am here for the lesson."

He come up out of his slumber and backhanded me with suddenness. That backed me up in fear. He stood there glaring at me appearing furious.

Then he grabbed the tawse sitting next to him and shook it at me. "How dare you awaken me or touch me without permission, worm."

I dropped my gaze and wrung my hands with nervousness. "I beg your forgiveness Peter. I thought you

211

said to wake you if you slept when I arrived for the lesson. I suppose I misunderstood."

He laughed at me most cruelly. "You are a stupid sonofabitch. You didn't misunderstand. I did say that."

I looked up at him feeling confused. "Then why did you hit me for following your orders?"

Peter glared. "Because you did exactly that. You followed my command, submissive."

I gasped then felt faint. "I don't understand, Peter. What is the right fucking answer. You hit me if I do it and you hit me if I don't."

My father took another step toward me, and I stepped back in fear while keeping an eye on his tawse. "You fear my striking you? Why? You have taken many beatings. What is one more? You can surely handle one for standing up for yourself."

I shook my head. "Nein, I don't want a beating Peter. I want you to be pleased and stop hitting me."

He stopped and groaned. "There it is. You desire to please me? Only my submissive would care about such a thing."

I could hardly breath. "Or someone that doesn't want to be hit anymore. I am not your submissive, Peter. I just want to live in peace. No more pain. Please, I beg your mercy. Tell me what I am supposed to do to finish this damned Dominance training and I do it willingly. I do not wish to battle you every fucking day. I cannot in such a war with you."

Peter rolled his eyes. "Oh boy. I really did a number on that egg head of yours, didn't I? Well? What are you waiting for? On your knees. I desire that pleasure submissive service of from my sexual artist. Maybe I will demand a violin serenade tomorrow to go with the blow job."

I gasped. "Huh? Whatever do you mean?"

He chuckled bitterly. "You think I didn't see that little stunt in the Great Hall last night, Maxx? Jakob was thrilled and I admit you still can dance like the champion despite that bum leg of yours. I think tomorrow you had better bring that Roland with you. He can play while you suck my cock since you seem so eager to woo another cock or two along with my own."

I shook my head in confusion. "Seriously Peter? You are expecting me to believe you are jealous of Jakob?

Peter began to undo his trousers. "Shut up, Maxx. I am aware you play a fucking game with me and Jonas. Well, you are wasting your art on the likes of Matz and Jakob, little Maximillian. I know you are not the schwuler. So, you soil yourself for nothing. I am not buying the lies. You forget that I trained you to look like the seducer boy. I must admit I am enjoying watching you struggle like a dumbass accepting the offers of any cock that comes your way in such a useless attempt to fool the wise. Tell me something Maxx, how many showers do you take a day now that you have no metal as the excuse for enduring sex you never wanted?" He chuckled hard as he hand motioned me to kneel.

I stood there fuming at his taunts. "I don't care what you believe, Peter. I am with Matz and Jakob willingly."

Peter really laughed hard at that. "Are you? Well then you are a bigger idiot then I ever realized then. You are straight Maxx. If you are fucking around with the schwulers trying to convince yourself you are not, then you will fail as miserably as you are the Dominance training."

I felt the tears rising to the surface. "Shut up Peter."

He paused his laughter and put his hand up to his ear. "What did you say, Maximillian? I couldn't hear you. Maybe it is the all that cock you suck finally damaged your vocal cords or did it just rot your teeth?"

Suddenly Christian broke loose of Mad Maxx's hold and flung me from the wheel with vigor. The boy led out a loud wail of fury and came at Peter fists flying. The Voter saw too late that he had gone too far in his hateful words. The flesh led go a right then left hook right into his sternum. Peter immediately backed up and threw a punch himself.

Christian caught that blow in the stomach but despite his lack of air he kept coming. I laid there on the floor nearly ready to shatter from fear as Max came rushing past me grabbing Christian and dragging me by my chain behind him. The two struggled as Maximillian took the wheel to keep the boy from hitting the floor in a catatonic fit.

Peter's second punch sent the Seductive shard right to his knees. He stayed there covering the boy's head unwilling to do battle with our ex-Master. Peter stood there over us for a moment panting and startled at our quick withdrawal from the fight.

He caught his breath as Max managed to subdue Christian and pin him to the wheel room wall. Maximillian didn't move a muscle, nor did any of the rest of us, unsure what to do to keep Peter placated and the flesh free from pain.

The Voter finally stammered out, "You almost did it Maxx, but I see you have returned to what you know the second you find your attacker fights back. Get up. You want to stop me, then do it."

Maximillian shook his head then whimpered out. "Nein, you will beat me then I go to the dungeons or Heslach for it."

Peter growled. "Take that chance, Maximillian. You stay on your knees, and I will treat you like my sex doll. I will not go gentle either. I intend to hurt you bad today for failing jet a third time."

Maximillian nodded. "Better to endure your interests then lose my bid for freedom. I give you whatever you want Peter. I will not fight you. I know you are trying to trick me. It won't work. In the end you will merely beat me down and take whatever you wanted anyway. Blow jobs with a busted mouth are worse than just sucking the damned cock in the first place."

Peter approached the boy still kneeling with his head covered. "Have you no pride left at all Maxx?"

I shook my head. "Pride does nothing for the corpse, nor does it mend a broken bone."

Peter scoffed. "You are weak, worthless, useless, a failure."

I nodded. "As you say Peter. If you desire to say abusive things then be my guest. Nothing I haven't heard before and likely the truth. Do you think that bothers me? Nein, I am nothing at all Peter. You can be assured that will never change. If that makes me the failure then so be it. If being a Dominant means I live in the dungeon I would rather never be one. However, you still have to adhere to that contract you have with me. I go to medical school and gain the Frau. I produce the child and you let me go on my way."

Peter leaned down into the boy's cowering face. "You fail the Dominance training then they recollar you, fool."

I looked up at him in a startle. "I have till I am twenty-three to finish that fucking training. I will be long married and long gone by then Peter."

He chuckled then grabbed the back of my head holding me tightly by my hair as he finished undoing his pants. "Did you think I didn't see the headset? You schizophrenic motherfucker. You are a fucking fool despite your intelligence. No woman in her right mind would married your crazy, overused ass much less submit to children with you. Tell you what Maximillian. I will just sit back and enjoy my thrill with you. One day soon maybe even your daft brain will realize you live in the world of fantasy. Now get to it, submissive."

I have to say as usual, Peter kept his promise. He did use me as the sex doll. He enforced the oral services for a bit. Then he stopped me, left the room and returned with a stranger I never saw before. To my horror he had invited in a buddy of his and the two of them took turns making me wish for death. They both made fun of my weeping and begging them to be less rough with me. It was not a good start to the day with Claus and Jonas still on the agenda.

This other fellow he called Hermann appeared to have been waiting around for Peter to call him in. That motherfucker was not even a Haus member. The guy was visiting someone on the third floor. I was beyond humiliated at that whole terrible scene but with Peter you have to be ready for any dishonor. The man is a fucking trainer of the highest caliber. If anyone can break a spirit in half it would be him.

When the two finished there fun with me, I was released with a quick thudding in the chains for not finishing my studies the night before. I actually was more than happy to take that beating. It allowed me to leave the wheel and hand it over to Mad Maxx the masochist. I was ready to get the fuck to the back of the wheel room for a good cry over that nightmare scene.

I took the wheel to protect Maximillian as Der Hund had previously ordered. I must say that no one can wield the tawse like Peter can. Of course, you already know that don't you, Meine Liebe? That day was no different. His funning with Maximillian didn't knock any of the vigor from his swing. I was striped worse than the zebra by the time he finished thudding the back of the boy's thighs. I agree with my brother Maximillian. It was not a good day at all.

I decided to allow Maximillian a bit longer of a break before heading up to visit Claus. He was beyond grateful I volunteered to run the wheel till we got there. Peter finally released me from his chains and stated my lesson was over for the morning.

I didn't hesitate. I grabbed my books and wiped the boy's eyes. That Hermann and Peter continued to gloat and make crude statements. The shame didn't come like it usually did after such horrible abuses of the flesh. It seemed that something was blocking the expression of our normal guilt mechanisms. That did make me wonder but believe me when I say I couldn't get out of there fast enough. I could pontificate on the reasons for this odd disconnect while running far away from those two brutes.

I began the long trip up the steps to visit with Claus. I damned myself for making that deal with him for every Thursday at one to get my metal busted so long before. The only consolation I had was that Bladrick was long the corpse. At least there would be no more London Bridges with the bloody piss blow jobs with him anymore.

I was deep in thought about ways to finish that contract with Peter by sending his ass to the grave. The voice of Lucus called out to me twice before I recognized not only the sound of it, but that he was hailing me by name. I stopped dead on the steps groaning at this motherfucker always appearing at all the worst times in my life.

I yelled out without looking back at him, "What the fuck do you want now, Lucus. Shit, do you not see I am busy."

Lucus responded from just behind me, "I was only desiring to make sure you were alright."

I turned around with fire blazing in my eyes. "You see me standing here? Do I not look fine to you? Why would you assume me to be less than healthy?"

Lucus stood there on the step below with a look of pity in his eyes. "Oh, uhm, well. Peter. I know he can be rather abusive. I was worried that fiend had gotten to you today."

I scoffed. "Sonofabitch, Lucus. Do you have cameras in all the rooms of the Haus? How the fuck do you know what Peter is or isn't to me?"

Lucus looked at his shoes. "I, uhm, saw him get Hermann and heard things. Christian, do you maybe want to come to my apartment for a bit. To calm down before you attend to Claus. It is only twelve thirty. You need maybe to have a little quiet time or at least a shower?"

I glared at him. "Oh, is that the plan now? You invite me to your apartment then when no one is looking, do far worse than I already endured and will endure today. I suppose you think yourself clever. If I needed a rest or shower I have a fucking apartment of my own, Lucus. I need not get naked and helpless in one that belongs to the predator like you."

Lucus frowned. "Matz is in your apartment, Christian. I heard what you said this morning. There is safety from such unwanted touching in my home, but not your own. You go there and maybe Matz will demand his paid service. I know you are aware of that. Now you know I am too. That is why you don't go there first for that sanctuary you surely require. Please Christian. I offer you asylum. I swear on my honor I won't bother you nor make you do anything against you will. If I had desired to do that I could have forced it through blackmail or even paid. You must realize I do neither. I also have followed you for years and never once did I take your service through rape. Why would I do such a crime now? Think, you know I am being honest with you."

I narrowed my eyes. "If you are, so what? Why do you fucking care if I need the shower or a place to fucking regroup my nerves? I am merely your spy, Lucus. As you pointed out, you have followed me for years. Surely, you know it will take much more than Peter's cruelty to take me to the breaking point."

He nodded still appearing to hold that strange expression of pity. "Ja, I know it will. That said, I don't think it right that no one has cared enough to offer even the basic human kindness. Let me do this mercy for you Christian. I beg of you."

I chuckled bitterly. "What is in it for you? No one does anything without expectation of payment. I am not the naive fool you take me for."

Lucus nodded. "I do this for the sole payment of your relief of pain, Christian. Nothing more and nothing less. It cleans my soul of a bit of the filth I have acquired by aiding you in cleansing your own."

I began to feel the world shaking slightly under my feet. I shot a frightened look at the floor. Then I looked up to see the swirling vortex opening up in the ceiling. The fucking shattering was threatening to tear a hole in the tapestry. I had to get out of there fast.

I felt the drool start to pour out of as my mouth started to malfunction. "Sing a song of six pence. A sperm pocket can cry. Three and twenty years, before I'm baked in a pie." I felt my muscles tighten causing me to stomp and push out the boy's arms trying to stop the coming catatonic state.

Lucus gasped and grabbed me by the upper arm dragging me up the steps as I began to repeat myself and twitch uncontrollably. He didn't fool around. The Dominant rushed me (nearly carrying the boy) to his apartment making much racket about me not learning better than to drink so much.

Even in my deteriorating state, I realized that Lucus was speaking like that so all the residents around us would think me drunk and not realize I was having a fit. I wish I could say I wondered why he was going out of his way to aid me like this, but at that moment I was kind of busy.

In the wheel room the wheel had malfunctioned. No matter how hard I pulled it wouldn't budge. Mad Max came forward to aid with his strength. When the two of us were unable to break it from the stalling, Maximillian joined us in the attempts.

Eventually it was evident it would take all five us shards to pull the flesh from the fast coming slumber of catatonic stupor. For a moment, Max and Christian called a truce. All five brothers gripped the wheel, dug in our boots and began to work together to free the boy.

In the meantime, Lucus got the trancing flesh through his door. He hauled him right to his bathroom and turned on his cold water faucets full blast in the tub. It took him some work, but he finally was able to bend the boy down far enough to get his head under that frigid stream.

Like so many times before this, Peter had managed to stress the boy out enough to require the freezing water shock treatment. It was the only known way, at that time, to keep the flesh from the living death.

This time, for a change, we were lucky. With all five shards sharing the load and Lucus's quick action, the boy began to recover almost the second that horrid sensation went ripping thru his head. With a sudden jerk, the wheel broke free sending all the shards sprawling but Mad Max. That tough shard managed to keep control while the rest of us recovered from the traumatic spill and fucking cold ass bath.

I led out a miserable wail. "Please, Lucus, I cannot breathe. You are drowning me. Mercy, I beg of you."

The Dominant immediately pulled me back out of that stream and put a towel over my head. "Okay, calm down, Christian. Take deep breaths. Matz told me you missed your medication by two doses. If you don't keep that heart rate down a seizure will onset shortly. You cannot stop that Thorazine like you have done. The Grand Mal can kill you or even cause a coma to onset. You stay still. Keep this towel over your eyes, rest. I go get your meds. No arguments. If you move and set off another fit before I can aid you, then Kilian may catch wind of it. Nod if you understand what I tell you and are willing to trust me to help you escape detection."

I wasn't sure I could trust what Lucus told me, but I was so frightened and confused I decided to chance it. I nodded and I heard the Dominant haul ass out of that room. I reached into my pocket and felt around till I found Felicity. I snuggled that lamb to my chest and rolled into a ball, never removing that towel just as Lucus insisted.

I turned around to check on the other shards and was relieved to see my brothers Mad Maxx, Christian, and Max had regained their feet. Then I shuddered in full on horror when I noticed one of us was missing.

My sadistic eyes searched the room. I saw him, the missing Max boy. Laying in a near lifeless pile was Maximillian. All around him his essence was leaking out. He trembled and shuddered, the shard was severely injured. I shot a look of terror at Mad Maxx and saw Christian standing behind him smiling at me with wickedness. In his hand was knife covered in Maximillian's essence. He had fatally stabbed our Seductive shard. The shattering was coming for our fallen hardest working, and second most important shard for survival. Oh Gott, my creation was dying before my eyes and there wasn't shit I could do about it.

Chapter 20: Crazy Lies

I rushed over to the dying Maximillian. "Brother, speak to me. Oh Gott, Max, he is going to shatter."

Christian laughed with a sound like a hammer hitting metal. "Good, I killed that schwuler pig. I am tired of him allowing the flesh to be passed around like the whore. Someone had to put a stop to it."

Mad Maxx glared at the Anger shard. "Christian, you fool, do you ever think? If not Maximillian then who is going to handle the disgusting schwuler sex? You? I think not. Holy hell, we are in big trouble."

I wailed as I rushed for Maximillian. "Call Der Hund, Max. This is an emergency."

Max shook his head appearing full of sorrow. "Der Hund cannot aid us brother Mad Max. He didn't create Maximillian. There is nothing he can do to save him."

I reached his side and gently rolled him to his back. I saw that his eyes were closed, and essence poured from his many stab wounds and the mouth. I gasped in horror as I knelt there trembling. I always said that I don't even like Maximillian but seeing him there on the wheel room floor expiring, well it brought a strange kind of sadness over me.

I shot a pleading look at Max. "Please Max, call Der Hund anyway. We cannot just sit here doing nothing while he dies. Don't you even care?"

Max nodded. "More than you can know, Mad Max. You gave birth to him and me. This is my brother I watch in pain. I think it is a good thing we will perish with him. I don't desire to continue without him with us. It was hard enough to lose Taube but to lose Maximillian, that I cannot survive. None of us can."

My eyes went wide in shock. "What do you mean none of us can?"

Max glared at the smiling Christian. "Maximillian keeps the boy alive with his seductive skills and ability to tolerate the most humiliating of abuses. He protects all of us from the worst of it. with him gone, the Dominants of this place will rip the boy's mind apart with their brutal torments."

Christian's grin melted into one of angered disbelief. "Max lies. We don't need that prissy. He dies and is the end of it. Good riddance. Then, no more laying there and taking it for the Mad Maximillian. We kill anyone that dares to try touching the flesh."

Mad Maxx scoffed. "You are stupid, aren't you? Do you see the guards at the Haus doors? They carry guns. You been shot before Christian. Did you forget that even you cannot withstand a bullet. The second you raise the boy's hands to Peter or Jonas, they will call those fellows with the weapons. Then bye-bye all of us."

Christian suddenly looked worried. "Lies, you are trying to scare me. It won't work. I am not falling for it, cocksuckers."

226

"They tell the truth of it, Christian. Kneel to your Master, you dogs. What has happened to our Maximillian," the voice of Der Hund boomed thru the wheel room sending all of us to our knees, except Maximillian. He laid there fading fast.

He was speaking to us from outside the boy. Our core couldn't get into the flesh yet. The shattering was coming on but for the moment his Max shards and Christian were still too densely packed together to allow him entry into the wheel room.

Meine brother Mad Maxx, who usually can speak to Der Hund without getting him too angry, usually, spoke up, "Honorable Hund. The Anger got out of control during a stick in the wheel. He has attacked our brother and felled him. Maximillian is not going to survive."

We all fell to our faces covering our ears in agony as Der Hund let out an otherworldly wailing sound. "You motherfucker, Christian. You killed me. Why have you betrayed your best friend so foully?"

Christian whimpered, ja you heard me. I couldn't believe that either, but I heard it with my own sadistic ears. "Brother Hund. Forgive me. I didn't know. I would never do such evil on purpose."

Der Hund bellowed out with fury, "Purposeful or not, you disobeyed my wise orders. Mad Maxx, you were supposed to block Christian unless it was too much. You didn't do your job. You betray me as well."

Mad Maxx moaned out in fear. "Nein, Master Hund. Christian did this horror while I was distracted by the stuck wheel. I beg mercy. Please forgive me."

Der Hund scoffed. "There is no mercy for any of us without Maximillian. He is the shard that holds such a luxury for all of you. I cannot grant what you all allowed to be shattered."

I couldn't handle the agony of knowing not only was Maximillian dying but Der Hund was beyond despaired over it. "Master Hund. I created the Seducer. Allow me to attempt to repair him."

Der Hund suddenly gasped. "Mad Max? You understand that such a thing is not possible? Once a shard is shattering there is no fixing it."

I nodded feeling tears beginning to well into my eyes as I stood up to stand my ground against the Master shard. "Ja, I know Master Hund. That said, I must try even if you will not grant permission. Maximillian is my own son. A father can heal the son. Defense is found in the lies he tells."

Max stood up from his kneeling with suddenness. "Allow the father to heal the son, Der Hund. I will give him some of my own strength to aid him. Mad Max is my father and Maximillian is my true brother. A brother will aid to heal a brother. A soul can provide the mercy his taking the pain brings to us all."

Mad Maxx stood up keeping his eyes to the floor. "I will give Mad Max some of my as well. Maximillian is my father. The son will aid to heal the father. It requires intelligence to seduce perfectly."

Christian stood up too. "I offer my own aid in this endeavor to heal the fallen Maxx. Mad Max is my own brother, and Maximillian his son. An uncle can heal the nephew. Anger can protect the humiliated from giving into despair."

Der Hund called out sounding full of gentleness. "The unite brother, father, son and uncle. Become one and heal the blessing you all took for granted."

The wheel room shook and trembled as each of us began to glow. I stood still as death while the glow came over me blurring the borders of where I begin and end. Christian walked into me first causing me to grow in size. Next came Max and then Mad Maxx last. I had become a single powerful shard with all the powers and weaknesses of all us combined.

I approached the quivering, fading Maximillian and dropped to my knees. Without hesitation I laid my huge hands on his wounds closing my eyes. Each of the Max brothers and Christian pushed a portion of his own strength into the seducers leaking holes.

Maximillian shuddered and opened his eyes. "Ah, help me Mad Max. I cannot hold on much longer."

I nodded as I pushed in the combined essence of the shards faster. "Be still Maximillian, we are here. Allow us to heal you."

The schwuler shard groaned from his pain. "It is too late. I have been poisoned with Christian's anger."

I gasped as I watched all the combined essence of his brother shards poured out of his knife wounds as fast as I pushed it into him. That made me realize that in order to save him we had to close his injuries or there was no hope to prevent his shatter.

I reached into my chest and pulled the struggling Christian free throwing him into the wheel room wall. "I command you to purge this foul reality from Maximillian. That blade was never meant to be tasted by him. Let it go back to where it came."

Christian's eyes were open with in fear. "Why did you break me free Mad Max? I want to aid you to heal Maximillian."

I growled out so loud the room trembled from the sound. "Then you come forward and take back the burden you tried to unload on one that didn't deserve your vengeance. Do it now or be lost from all of us for all time." I pulled back the Max boy's healing hands to allow the Anger to do as he was commanded.

Christian nodded then knelt next to the dying shard. Without hesitation nor disgust he put his mouth to Maximillian's. This was not a kiss of lusting. He knew the only way to remove what he had forced into the schwuler shard was to take it back through the opening of his mouth.

Christian began sucking the air out Maximillian. With each breath that Maximillian let out, Christian pulled it in, taking all his poisonous fury with it. Almost immediately the wound holes in the seducer shard closed as a foul black substance that resembled glowing tar flew out of Maximillian's body into the Anger shard.

The second I witnessed Maximillian's breathing come into Christian clear of that black shit, I reached out and laid my hands on his bare chest. He let out a loud gasp and Christian backed away. I closed my eyes and focused harder than I ever had in all my days. I let loose the excess strength I had within as did Mad Maxx and Max. I began to shimmer red to Maximillian's clear veneer.

He wailed in agony as the red glowing filled him from the tip of his head down to his toes. I didn't relent though he had begun to beg for mercy. I understood that there is no birth without blood nor life without pain. Maximillian was on death's door. The only way to retrieve him was to recreate what had been destroyed. This was assured to be a most unpleasant experience for him by the nature of the act itself.

I admit it was hard to listen to his pleas, crying and break down as the three of us burned away his borders. I had always said I hated Maximillian. That is a damned lie. I created him to take what I could not when Peter forced his special services request upon me.

The honest truth is I not only am proud of him for being the perfect seducer he is, but (and if you ever tell anyone I will beat you Miene Liebe, I mean it) I love my son Maximillian. More than my cane, or even Annette. He is the son any father would be so lucky to call his own.

I teared up as Maximillian melted in my hands to a blob of goo that glowed with crimson. It trembled with a weak heartbeat at my feet. I could still hear his pleas for mercy echoing in my ears.

I stole a look at Christian. He was leaned into the wheel room wall wiping his eyes. I shot a look of disgust at him. I hoped he felt the shame he deserved for doing this dishonor to the one of us that should be treated with the most respect.

I got back to my feet as Max and Mad Maxx broke free returning me to Mad Max the lone shard once more. They came and stood next to me staring down at that gelatin mass with frowns on their faces.

Mad Maxx shook his head "Then it is over. Maximillian didn't make it."

Max sniffed loudly. "Looks like it brother. We tried all we could. There simply is no way to save a shard."

Christian dropped down to his backside staring off into space. "I am so fucking sorry brothers. I didn't know I would beg forgiveness, but I suppose it doesn't matter now. We are finished."

I scoffed. "You are all the idiots. You give up when we have won our brother back. Look."

They all let out a collective gasp as that glob moved and shifted. The glowing became blinding as it formed into a torso. Two legs and two arms sprouted just as the neck and head popped out between the shoulders. Within only mere moments a new Maximillian lay on the wheel room floor appearing asleep as he dried out in the air.

Mad Maxx could barely whisper. "Is this the same Maximillian? Did we create a duplicate like you did Max?"

Max shot a nasty look at his brother Mad Maxx. "I am no damned duplicate. I am the only Max."

I chuckled as I backed away to give Maximillian room to stand when he regained his alertness. "Better step over here with me, brothers. This fellow is going to be pissed in a few moments. I wouldn't want to be anywhere near those fists of his."

They shot me looks of surprise. "Then it is the same shard?"

I nodded. "Damned right it is. He is going to be looking to kick ass, seriously. If you don't move it then, well, be ready for a fucking black eye." They rushed to my side as Christian also moved far away from him as possible.

Suddenly Maximillian opened his eyes and mouth letting out a blood curdling scream. "You sonofabitches. That fucking hurt, dammit, cocksuckers, motherfuckers. I am going to kill you for that." He sat up struggling to get to his feet, glaring at all of us in fury.

I put up my hands with a cat smile. I couldn't help it, I was just so happy to see him healed, alive and well, you know. "Now, settle down prissy boy. Couldn't be helped I swear it. You needed to be reborn, or you were going to shatter. You surely wouldn't take vengeance on your brothers for saving your life."

He managed to stand. "Ja, I would. Come here and fight me like a man, asshole."

Christian came forward. "Calm down brother. I am the one that did this, not them. If anyone deserves your vengeance it would be me. I take your blows without quarrel. I have it coming."

Maximillian glowered at him as he snarled out, "Fucking right you do, motherfucker. Give me that blade of yours. I will cut your balls off for that bullshit you pulled."

Der Hund's voice boomed out like thunder, causing all of us to drop to our knees including Maximillian. "Enough, there will be no more attacks on each other. That was a close one. I would punish Christian for this horror, but I suspect he has realized the hard way that my orders must be followed, or we find ourselves worm food. I ask you, Christian, are you ready to dare to attack any of my creations again?"

Christian shook his head while casting his eyes downward in shame. "Nein, my old friend. I apologize to you and the honorable Maximillian for my stupidity. It will never happen again. You have my word."

Maximillian scoffed. "Your word means nothing. I don't even know why we need your violent ass around here. I can kill anyone that needs it. You serve no function. I vote Christian be deemed worthless and shattered immediately."

Der Hund roared out, "Maximillian, be still. All of you are equally important to the survival of this boy. No one is to be shattered by anyone's vote or word but my own. The time is coming for my shards to rest for a season. You show wear and tear already and there is still a bit of a journey till the shattering arrives. You have your orders, get to it and cut out the bullshit." His voice went silent as death as each of us shot the others looks of surprise.

Mad Maxx threw his leash at Christian. "You are off leash, brother. Take your place and mind. You heard Der Hund. All back to work. The break is over."

I groaned as I accepted the wheel allowing Maximillian a moment more to rest before that damned Claus, you know. This gave Mad Maxx a moment to re-leash with the free Christian. I hated this Lucus fellow, but I was the only one ready at that moment to get the flesh back to its function. I took a deep breath bracing for whatever horror that damned nosey bastard had left to collect.

Lucus returned to find the boy still rolled up tightly into a ball holding Felicity to his chest. I had not bothered

235

to remove the towel from my face. Though we had recovered Maximillian and the wheel I thought it better to remain still as long as possible. That bad scene had been a close one. I was in no hurry to get back to the noise that we called life. It seemed to me any break the boy could get should be held on to long as possible.

I heard him re-enter his bathroom. I perked up my ears and put all the Max boys on full alert. There was no telling what this cocksucker was up to. I could only guess at why he had aided the boy when the sure signs of a fit began to onset.

It was of a wonder to me how this bastard knew about that icy water shocking business. I began to suspect that he had spoken to Leo, Jonas or even that fucker Malfred. It made no sense that he knew about that secret tip to end the living death behaviors without having discussed it with one of my old Masters.

He stood at the door breathing heavy but not saying anything for several minutes. I trembled slightly waiting for him to try attacking me. Lucus was apparently aware of my weakened state. If he didn't intend to force himself on the boy, then why the hell had he pulled me to his apartment and not my own. No one does something for nothing. I was sure that had to be his reasons for getting involved in that horror.

Lucus cleared his throat then said softly, "Christian, can you hear me?"

I wanted to pretend I didn't, but I was due at Claus's place in short order and didn't have time for games. "Ja, I do. Why do you keep me here Lucus? I have to be somewhere. State your price for your help then let me be on my way."

That made the man gasp. "You are lucid? That is a pleasant surprise. Come, sit up and take your medication that Matz gave to me. Hurry up or you will be late to fulfil your promise to the Honorable Claus."

I pulled off the towel and sat up still holding my lamb to my chest. "You told Matz of this humiliation? Damn Lucus, why don't you go announce it to that DJ so everyone can know my business."

My sudden movement caused Lucus to take a step back in fear. "Nein, I didn't tell him of this fit. I merely stated you sent me for your missed dose of medication. Please do not give me trouble Christian. I don't desire an argument and you have no time for one. I leave the pills here on the sink counter. There is a cup in the cabinet for the water. You can refuse to take them, but I assure you a Grand Mal will follow shortly if you don't. This little catatonic fit is the only warning you're going to get. Next time, maybe I won't be there to sneak you out of the public view. I am sure Kilian, and his dogs, watch and wait for the chance to snatch you up."

I shuddered. "If I don't take this I will have the Grand Mal? How do you know this Lucus? You are not the Haus doctor."

He frowned and shrugged. "That its truth. I have followed you a long time Christian. I have seen this behavior in you before, some time ago just before the time of Malfred. I also took it upon myself to read up on your brain disease. This medication you take cannot be stopped abruptly like you tend to do. The chemical imbalance it causes will disrupt your system. You need not taking my word for it. Skip the medication and learn it the hard way. I cannot make you do it, nor do I desire to. You are the free man. Do as you please. I warned you, that is all I can truthfully do."

I narrowed my eyes. "Okay, you have given me the warning, Lucus. What I wish to know is why do you bother in the first place? I am as you say the free man. What is in it for you?"

Lucus chuckled and crossed his arms. "You are smart enough to know the answer to that Christian. However, if you desire to hear it I will tell you. I enjoy watching your struggle. You die of a cataclysmic seizure or get taken away to Heslach, then my Priceless watching days are over."

I glared at him feeling resentment fill the boy's chest. "Ah, ja I suppose I did suspect as much. I am a little surprised you would admit to it so readily though. Tell me something Lucus. Is your life so fucking boring you need such low distraction? Oh, wait a minute. Silly me, I know. You are the sadist at heart like most in this Haus. My disgrace brings you the hard on. You listened outside the thudding room door stroking your cock to the sounds of my cries of pain. Am I right?"

Lucus snorted with observable irritation in his tone. "You need not insult me, Christian. I admit that I do find thrill in your struggle, but not of the perverted sexual kind. It is quite rude to accuse me of such foul interests as you have. You know nothing about me at all, but you judge me with such harshness. I thought better of you than that."

I raised an eyebrow. "Did you really? Well, seems to me you know all there is to know about Christian Axel, but as you say I know nothing about Lucus. You follow me around like the blood hound and interfere with my business. I ask you politely, threaten, and even attack you, and still, you persist in this nosey endeavor. What the fuck is your problem? I would think a Dominant of your status, wealth and lineage shouldn't have to stoop so low as to enjoy watching the trainwreck that I call my existence."

Lucus scoffed. "Well, shows what you know which is nothing. I was born into the class of royalty, Christian. From the moment I could walk all I needed to do is point and whatever I asked for, it was mine. All my childhood, teens, and young adulthood there was not a thing not within my grasp. I have never known a time when everyone around me didn't bow or scrap before me. I never even had to prove my worth or talents. Even my name carries the evidence of my lot in life. Lucus Victor, named after the famous Queen of my kinship herself. Without any boundaries on what I could acquire there was no struggle of any kind to enjoy the best that civilization has to offer to the human race. Travel, money, lodgings, the taboo, and even relationships were of only the finest and highest caliber for Lucus Victor. This resulted in a lack of leaving anything for me to desire. Without desire there can be no dreams. Dreaming of things that are just beyond your reach, which is what makes getting up in the morning worth the effort. When everything comes too easy, life loses its luster, and the gold never glitters. I tried everything to find that lust for life that I see in everyone around me. Yet not even the activities that draw adrenaline, such as dangerous sports or drugs, quickened my heartbeat. A deep numbness overcame me at an early age. No matter what I did boredom and apathy was the result of it."

I sneered. "Aw, poor baby. It sounds like you have endured a very hard life, my brother. I must beg your forgiveness that I feel no pity for you though King Lucus. So, you are the idle rich man. What the fuck does any of that have to do with your following me around like the stalker?"

He chuckled bitterly. "It has everything to do with it, Christian. I came to the Haus fifteen years ago when I turned twenty. I thought maybe the vices and game of life and death would quicken my pulse. Much to my despair I discovered rather quickly that the truthful risk within these walls is shouldered by the kidnapped children, and the wealthy benefactors who take perverted thrill from it. As I said, I am not the pervert. I found it disgusting and disgraceful the things I saw going on in this place.

Yet, even with my powerful ties I realized quickly that there was nothing I could do to end the cruel practices nor even slow them down. I spent many a night in the first year trying to figure out a way to halt the horrors I was witnessing executed against the lowest rungs of society. I did make phone calls and tried to get my powerful connections involved. To my ultimate shock, the only thing I managed to do is recruit several part time members as each came, investigated, then rented apartments on the seasonal third floor.

My mind numbing boredom quickly dissolved to depression and hopelessness. I stayed in my apartment for the next five years unable to talk myself into rejoining the world outside or inside the Haus. I believed if I couldn't even wield enough influence to shut down this abomination called Das Kaiser Haus what good was my birthright?

During my half decade of self-imposed isolation, I found solace within the study of sociology and small group dynamics. On the sixth year that I called this apartment my home I decided to venture out into the halls once more.

At first, I was unsure why. Over time I realized I was testing the ideas and theories that I had learned thru the books I read on the subject. I wandered watching, recording and in time made predictions based on my knowledge of future life, death and rises in power.

Seven years passed and the numbness returned. I grew so accustomed to witnessing the brutality and lack of empathy in this Haus, this stupid game I played with

241

myself of prediction lost its ability to thrill me just as everything else ever did in my life. I was becoming despondent and depressed once again. I had started to think it was time to end my own life. I felt guilty for leaving this horrific place in my wake, but to be honest I had waited long enough that I lost my vigor to try to aid these woeful souls that find themselves wearing the black or silver collar.

Then everything changed in a single morning eight years ago. I had managed to get the poison that would end my torment without a lot of pain. I had not managed to talk myself into taking the vile stuff yet, but I was sure working on it. I was on my way to the kitchen to get my breakfast tray. I was deep in thought of reasons to finish the endless monotony of the boredom I called my life when a small, blond boy with a signature scar rushed past me in the hall. He was screaming at the top of his lungs begging for aid to define "bath service." I noticed this young kid wore no collar and yet was no Dominant.

I had never seen such a thing before in all my time in the Haus. I was immediately intrigued by this rare sight. I followed the boy for the next few weeks and was enthralled as I witnessed you become the Priceless of legend, Maximillian the unwitting collar of Peter. I forgot all about that plan to kill myself, over the weeks, then months as I followed you around watching you struggle to maintain your life and sanity.

Over time, I finally realized that I was living through you Christian. The more I witnessed, the more I wanted to see. You have all the lust for living that I never possessed. Your need to survive against all odds woke up the sleeping spirit within me. I am hooked to your bid to gain your dreams of freedom the way a junkie craves their fix."

I sat there staring at him unsure what to say to this most unexpected admission. "You study me like I am nothing more than a rare beast in the wild? Your life holds no meaning for you, therefore you feel entitled to eavesdrop on another less fortunate soul? You claim to be desirous of ending the terror within the walls. So much so that at one time you thought of ending your life when you couldn't do it easily. Yet, you thrill at being the voyeur of one of the most atrocious abuses of a human life possible. Lucus, do you hear yourself? I think those pills sitting on your sink countertop would do you more mercy than they ever could for me. That is fucking insane man." I got to my feet clutching Felicity even tighter with fear starting to grip my spine. I told you crazy people really make me nervous. You never know what the fuck they may do.

Lucus looked up at me with a startle. "Nein, oh you misunderstand, Christian. I mean, ja that is what I said. I admit until the other day when you finally caught me following you around, I believed I was enamored with your struggle as you said. The abuses you survived and still do seemed to quicken my pulse with excitement. I assumed it was some kind of perversion I had never heard of before. I didn't realize that what I mistook for living through you to gain an adrenaline rush was actually, uhm." He stopped and dropped his eyes to the floor.

I glared at him. "Actually what, Lucus? Say it. You think you love me? Is that what you think you have discovered after I told you to stop your cruel watching my failures?"

He nodded slowly as he took a deep breath. "Ja, I realized the reason my heart sped up each time you survived a terrible situation was because, well, I was grateful that you would still be, uhm, with me. I went home after your abruptly calling me out and thought about how willing I was to accept your anger over what I had done all these years. I think, I had always hoped you would notice me, desire to speaking to me even."

I rolled my eyes. "You want me to believe you have suffered an unrequited crush on me for eight years, Lucus? You must be funning me. I was a God damned twelve year old boy. I am still only sixteen. You are what, thirty-five? Are there not millions of schwulers of your age out there dying to share your bed? You need not follow around the Priceless like the eager schoolboy seeking the Frau far above his level. I don't believe a fucking word of your story except that you are the bored aristocrat. That is more than a little obvious if you live in this hell hole voluntarily. How many collars have you owned and killed or sold off to circuit once you were bored of them? How many lovers of worth have you tossed or taken for granted in your effort to curb your jaded voyage thru life?"

Lucus snorted. "You speaking like I am the playboy that would use another person like the napkin for a runny nose. That is unfair and untruthful. I have had a few lovers in my youth, but they were of the same listless curse. I found them as droll and weary of everything as me. They were not the hopeless romantics nor even the lukewarm affectionate. Partners among those of my class are stiff and proper to a fault. Nothing, not even sex, is without protocol and boundaries."

I snorted then said with sarcasm dripping from my tone, "Once again you have my pity, Lucus. To think I thought I had it bad. You had to endure the intercourse without the lusting for it. How have you survived such hell?"

Lucus glowered. "You make fun of my pain because you never have felt the emptiness of such a life. There is such a thing as having too much luxury."

I nodded with anger breaking out in my expression. "I will trade with you any day of the week, Lucus. I would happily engulf the ashes of abundance while you can endure the brutality of the truthful nothing. Then you will be able to find your thill and dreams in abundance. That will be because you will never acquire a fucking thing, not even your right to say nein when someone desires to fuck you or follow you around enjoying your humiliation of it."

Lucus once again looked to the floor as if embarrassed. "I understand your anger, Christian, and I accept that I have earned it. I have used you to meet my own selfish needs just as everyone else you have ever known has. I can see that now. Please hear me when I offer to make up for my short comings."

I reached into my coat pocket to put Felicity back into her hiding spot. "I am listening, motherfucker. Hurry it up. I have an appointment to get to. You see, unlike you I have no choice. If I am not at Claus's in ten more minutes then I break the oath I swore to him. You already know about that though, don't you? It is one of many I was forced to make, or I would still be in my metal, not that this so-called Dominance is that much different to me. I think you would be happy to see me keep it. If I do not go soon, then how shall I be of future entertainment to the bored boy King Lucus?"

Lucus shook his head. "Claus had no right to demand such a price for that which you earned a thousand times with your blood and tears."

I shrugged then with irritation in my tone, "I will be sure to let him know you say that. I am certain he will fall on his knees immediately and grant me the mercy of freedom from his foul lusting for the rest of his days. I thank you so much for the mercy of it."

Lucus glared at me. "There is no need to be sarcastic nor unpolite Christian. I am not interested in becoming your enemy."

I laughed with bitterness. "Well, there is a truth. Nein, you are about to offer to become my lover. That is what this bullshit of helping hide me out from Kilian and his dogs is all about, ja?"

Lucus looked up at the ceiling blowing out his breath. "And what is so wrong about offering such a thing? I can look out for you, support you financially, and with me at your side, bastards like that Kilian will not be so quick to fool with you. Not many in this Haus are brave enough to get into a pissing match with the blue blooded Lucus you know."

I began walking towards him with an evil smile spreading across my face. "Oh? Well, what a deal you offer to Mad Maxx. I should drop to my knees right this minute and show my gratitude that the great and powerful King Lucus bothers to caste his favorable eye at this lowly, overused, whore, ja?" He backed away with fear entering his gaze.

Lucus stammered, "You need not whore any longer, Christian. I am willing to pay all your bills and give you a life of ease. If you would say ja, then I can assure you luxury, protection, and a kind hand with a loving heart all the rest of your days."

I nodded smiling even larger, the demons rising within. "Oh? And what do you want in return for all the treasure you are swearing to heap upon my worthless head, Lucus? I have nothing but this scar covered flesh and my silver tongue that can tell the most beautiful lies to trade for this most generous offer you are making."

He backed up further watching as I stopped and picked up the pills popping them in the boy's mouth. "What you have to offer is exactly what I want. I have never desired anything in my life that could not be mine with a snap of these fingers. Until you that is. I refuse to flex my powerful connections to have your against your will nor do I want to rent your false interests in me by the hour. Please, will you at least consider my offer to be your truthful lover and live in partner?"

I snorted with laughter as I swallowed the pills. "Ah, live in you say? What about Matz? You think I should throw him from the apartment? Maybe right over the railing out in front of the door? I thought you were his latest buddy. Here you are trying to steal away his meal ticket. Shame on you Lucus."

That made him angry. "Matz cares nothing about you. He has no idea the value of the treasure he takes for granted. I would never ask you to sell your flesh to support me. That is beyond dishonorable, but to hear he also abuses his privileges with forced intercourse and foul words. That is unbelievable." He stopped backing away and stood his ground.

I approached him getting close enough to intimidate. "You are incredibly arrogant Lucus to assume you know anything about desperation. Matz doesn't rape me fool. He pays me like everyone else. He gains no special privileges just because he aids me in my survival. Him and the wolfpack are High Born Dominants but they are not so unlike this nothing Priceless. Matz and the other wolves have no fortune, no future, no choice either. The five of us do what we must while the wealthy like yourself feed on our failures like the swine at a trough. Well, tell you what Mister Aristrocrap, oh I apologize, aristocrat pig. You desire to taste my favor you will purchase that pleasure like any other rich motherfucker in this Haus. If you intend to make a meal out of me or the wolfpack, you will pay for it like anyone else. Your lineage doesn't mean shit to Mad Maxx. I see no difference in you than any other bag of bones in a fancy suit that is as common in this place as the parasites in the intestines of a dog. You go see Matz and choose your perversions. He will collect your money and I will make your fantasies a reality until your dime runs out. Good day, Lucus." I pushed him out of my way, throwing his towel on the floor as I rushed past him out his apartment door.

I headed up the steps for the sixth floor while turning to see Maximillian. I wondered if he had recovered enough to deal with the lustful interests of the ancient Elder Claus. He was sitting against the back of the wheel room wall holding his temples appearing to have the headache.

I hazarded speaking to him. "Brother? You going to be strong enough for this? It has been nearly two years. Claus may be the randy goat by now or the worn out near corpse. There is no assurance that another nineteen months of advancing age slowed down this buzzard to tolerable yet."

Maximillian groaned. "You turned down Lucus's offer Mad Max? Why? He offers one cock versus untold numbers of them as the prostitute. What the hell is wrong with you?"

I groaned at that. "Maximillian, you are a fool. Lucus would desire to take away the tiny freedom we still have. He desires to keep the boy, brother. You know, he pays the bills and therefore we owe him everything. It keeps us from the mercy of saying nein."

Maximillian glowered at me. "As if our denial matters to anyone else, you idiot. Peter, Jonas, and Claus, they will not hear of any refusals. What the fuck do we care to add another one to that mix. No more nasty Osvin, Fritz, the wolfpack and Matz or that cocksucker Justus, to name the ones we know. I think Lucus for them is a fair trade off."

I shook my head. "Maximillian, you are not thinking straight. If we piece meal it then we can still refuse the money. Besides, do you think Lucus will fund the black collars and Karsten's cost of living for them? No way. He intends to fuck the boy for the price of the grocery bill and nothing more. Then if he tires of your seductive techniques, and in time he will, we are back on our asses struggling to work. You dare to isolate Matz and the wolves like that?"

He crossed his arms and rolled his eyes. "You are a bastard Mad Max. Lucus could maybe call in his connections and get Peter off my ass brother. I cannot take much more of that father of ours bringing in the bums from the street to fuck me. That was humiliation beyond what even I can tolerate. That Hermann was gross and perverted to the hilt."

I nodded while dropping my gaze in shame. "I am aware brother. I may not be at the wheel, but I can see and hear what you suffer. I know you do have many good points in your argument for taking that offer of his, but I desire you stop thinking with fear of Peter. If you could see pass that nightmare then you'd realize there is wisdom in what I say to you."

Mad Maxx shook his head. "Brothers, forgive me for sticking in my nose but Mad Max you are wrong. There is a way to keep Matz's aid without rebuking Lucus's offer."

That statement not only made my eyes go wide, but all the other shards gasped as I stared at the Masochistic shard in shock. "Are you funning, Mad Maxx? Do you hear yourself? Shit, maybe we do have the schizophrenia. That is the most insane thing I have ever heard. You actually desire to take Lucus up on his horrific offer? Creepy, stalker, arrogant King Lucus. You may be missed that is who we speaking about?"

Mad Maxx snorted. "Ja, I know whom we discuss Mad Max. I am saying there is some validity to what Maximillian points out. One client versus many. If he were our lover, then even Jonas and the horrid Peter may back off their most vicious assaults. We could get a look in that book of his and see what he has hidden from us. That information could be helpful in figuring out a way out of the Haus even without this Dominance training or medical school. If nothing else it would tell us of the plots we have yet to discover surrounding us."

I turned around and shot Max a baleful look. "What do you say brother? Are you going to side with these two nutballs or with the wise Mad Max?"

Max dropped his head and said nothing.

I nearly fainted at that. "Really? You side with them? Lucus, Max, it is Lucus who we discuss. Am I the only fucking sane one around here? You are all out of your minds."

Christian growled out, "You didn't ask me for my vote brother Mad Max."

I glared at him with fury. "I don't care what side you take motherfucker. You are dumb enough to stab the shard that Der Hund told you to protect. You deserve neither respect nor do I trust any vote you would bother to submit to your brothers."

Christian crossed his arms and pouted as he said, "Well for your information I side with the Maxes. Lucus may be creepy, but he is that way to everyone, not merely the boy. There can be value in commanding the heart of one so loathed and feared as him."

I snorted angrily. "Ficken Dich, Christian. In fact, all of you boys can suck my cock. We already have a lover far wealthier than Lucus. Leo is the richest in all the Haus for all the good it has ever done us. Why the fuck do any of you think this motherfucker can do better than one that loves us as much as that Elder does? The answer is simple, he cannot. You all have gone daft."

Maximillian bellowed back, "Leo may love the boy, but he is viewed as high strung, weak hearted, and romantical. This Lucus is the stuffy, self-important kind of fellow. May I remind you he is of the royal blood. This may mean nothing to us, but to the other residents it means everything. The Dominants of this Haus bow and scrap to him. If we must endure the lusting of the man to survive outside of Jonas's claws we cannot do better than the powerful Lucus."

I rolled my eyes as I approached the Elder Claus's door. "Shut up Maximillian and get up here to taking the wheel. Your job is to play the pincushion not to do any thinking."

He glared at me. "I am not feeling well, Mad Max. You know being melted down and refashioned takes a lot out of a guy. My head is killing me. Looks like you are the man for this job. Oh, I apologize. I said that wrong. I meant to say better get on your knees like the frau for the honorable Claus. I cannot handle him and Jonas in another two hours. Forget that. Besides, I seem to recall you are intimately familiar with the proclivities of this particular Elder. You managed him the very first time we met him, ja?"

I groaned feeling my own head starting to pound as badly as Maximillian claimed his to be. "Maximillian, this is bullshit, and you know it. Mad Maxx, you get over here and manage the wheel for this scene."

Mad Maxx shook his head. "Nein, I almost came apart the last time I managed Claus alone without Maximillian. No way I am doing that shit again."

That really pissed me off. "You sonofabitches are going to sit on your thumbs and force me to manage this old man? You know what? I am beginning to feel remorse that I saved you Maximillian. Motherfuckers, the whole lot of you. When I am done with this old goat I am kicking all your asses, except you Max. I have no quarrel with you brother." I knew better than to threaten that mean cocksucker. I had seen what he could do. Yikes!

I heard Mad Maxx and Maximillian chuckling behind me as I knocked on Claus's door. I did my best to stifle the grumbling under my breath about all the Judases that seemed to surround me. The Elder answered after the second bid I made for entry. I almost gasped in surprise at the sight of him.

His bright fierce eyes had grown droopy and foggy. Claus had always been the wrinkled old man since I had been unfortunate to know him, but this fellow that wore his skin apparently couldn't fit it well. It hung on him like the oversized suit with a slight grey color and tons of creases where they didn't appear to belong.

Claus's haggard, sorrowful face suddenly broke into a thrilled smile. "Oh, my Gott. You are here. I pray it is not a dream. Is this my little, uhm, big Mad Maxx come to visit his Claus at last?"

I caste my eyes to the floor and forced a smile in return. "It is me Claus, come to keep my word to you with honor. It is Thursday, one o'clock ja? Just as we agreed so long ago. That is if you still desire my adorations. I am not a little boy any longer."

The Elder looked me over from head to toe with an expression of satisfaction. "I confess when I saw you from afar I thought maybe you had lost your attractiveness with your maturity reached. However, I am looking upon the most handsome man I think I have ever been thrilled to have in my apartment. Come in my boy. You are most welcome here and Claus is the blessed for making deals with only the most honorable heart." I followed him into his apartment feeling a bit of fear roll down my spine.

The memories of enforced molestations, the tag team bloody London Bridge (Claus and the deceased Bladrick you may recall), and other traumas filled the wheel room. For a moment I thought I may faint away over the overwhelming despair that had come over me from it. Claus hobbled to his couch, same fucking one as always, and sat down. I stood there trying to maintain my consciousness, breathing shallow breaths and damning my existence all at the same time.

Claus eyed me still smiling but not as widely as before. "You are indeed looking good, Maxx. I confess I have been excited for the last two days waiting for this hour to be upon us. I could think of nothing I desire more than to hold my boy in my arms once more. You bring back the joy into this Haus where there has been only misery and death since you broke that collar and left your old Masters in your rearview mirror."

I caste a quick glance at the door that used to belong to the late Bladrick with a bit of nervousness. "Did he, did Bladrick suffer greatly before the reaper took him?"

Claus nodded as he dropped his eyes appearing to grieve. "Ja, it was terrible. The pain got so bad he screamed day and night no matter what the doctors tried. It went on for weeks like that until at last the Gotts took mercy and ended his agony at last."

I looked away trying to stifle my smile of thrill at that wonderful news. "Ah, I am sorry to hear that Claus. Bladrick was a good man. Surely he didn't deserve such a sad ending to his glorious life."

Claus nodded then sighed. "Funny thing is one of the last things he said to me before the horrible pain took his sanity away was that you would ask me about this very thing. He told me to assure you that he had paid what was owed you. He added he hoped that would bring you a little peace to know it." He shot a look of curiosity at me.

I shrugged as I kept my gaze at my boots. "It must have been the pain speaking, Claus. I have no idea of what Bladrick was speaking. He was like the grandfather to this worthless man. I am glad he no longer suffers and has found his rest at last."

The Elder leaned back and crossed his arms with a small smile on his face. "A grandfather you say. Hmm, you are not as polished as once you were in the art of lying Maxx. I suppose the years without the whip are to blame for the tarnishing of that silver tongue of yours. I am not the fool. You hated Bladrick and I know why you did. He earned it, there is no arguing that, my love. That said I have often wondered if your level of disgust for Claus compares to the contempt you had for my late brother?"

I chuckled with a small grin. "Nein, Claus. I don't hate you if that is what you ask me. I confess you were not my happy choice of the lover, but you were good to me despite it. I can point at no scars on my flesh and name them after you."

He frowned as he suddenly appeared serious. "That I will accept as truth, but I wonder. How many scars are in the fold of your soul that Claus can lay claim to?"

I laughed and glared at him with mischief rising in my eyes. "You are still the dirty girl I remember so well, Claus. As always I see you wish me to stroke your ego before I employ that same skill to your cock. You know damned well I am still terrified of you. I doubt I will ever get over the foul things you and Bladrick did to me, and you intend to continue to do. Long after the buzzards claim your flesh I will be screaming out your name in the darkness from the nightmares you cause. I am traumatized to medication for life over your taking advantage of that little silver I used to be. Claus the monster lives on inside my head until at last I too find the mercy of my grave."

Claus broke out in laughter along with me. "Shit, I retract all I said about that tongue of yours laying idle too long. You still know just how to bring me to thrill. Come here and allow me to adore you as you promised you would. You waste my time with small talk. I have better things for you to do with that magnificent mouth of yours.

And I wish to see the rest of the beauty you have grown into since last I viewed your naked flesh."

I nodded. "As you wish honorable Claus. I do whatever you desire, but don't ask me to call you Master."

He giggled with thrill. "Get on your knees, Maxx. You need not worry I will request such an indignity from you. Besides, I intend to keep your mouth too full to do any speaking and your mind too full of terror to make any sounds than the most guttural ones." I grimaced and shot a look of hate at Maximillian and Mad Maxx.

Without quarrel or qualm, I followed the limping Claus to his bedroom to fulfil my promise to keep his bed warm till the end of his days. I would like to say that old Claus was mostly brag and no true show. That would not be entirely the truth of the matter.

Even at his advanced age that man was lusty, and capable of much humiliation in the intercourse with me. It didn't help that he had not had a single sexual encounter since I had been gone to Heslach.

The only mercy that I received that first time back in his bed was that thanks to his elderly status, once he reached his apex he was good to go for another week. Claus was no longer capable of multiple rapid recoveries that the Vampire, Peter and many other of the younger males could terrorize me with at will.

That made enduring Claus's nasty penetration and sexual interest in me bearable, if only barely so. I made short work of the eager old man and allowed his cuddle for a bit as he lavished me with many kind words regarding my skill at bringing him intense pleasure. I listened to the bullshit flattery for a bit then decided to ask about his crossdressing since I had not seen him much in a long time. Plus, I was worried he would work himself back into a lustful frenzy if I didn't interrupt that dirty speaking of his.

I pointed at his closet. "You still wearing the pretty gowns and hosiery, Claus?"

He frowned as he stroked my cheek, then laid his old head on my chest. "Nein, there is no reason for this old gal to dress up anymore. The music has stopped, and the party is over for Claus. I am the oldest resident of the Haus now Maxx. The joke of Das Kaise Haus. How could I dare to appear among the people that already find me a doddering old fool wearing one of my beautiful dresses?"

I scoffed. "You are no old fool Claus. You are number two in line for the power of this Haus. You may be advanced in age, but you are still the lion. What has happened to the fearsome man that once had me trembling in my own piss that I may have displeased him?"

Claus sighed and kissed my chest appearing sorrowful again. "He went to the coffin with Bladrick, my spatz. Do not hold it against me please. I can take anyone's scorn but that of my ex-collar's. We all have our season Maxx, and my has long passed away. Watching Bladrick's painful exit reminded me of my own demise, I fear. It was a lesson I could have done without but one I cannot forget no matter how hard I have tried. I look in the mirror and all I can see is the coming darkness of oblivion."

I reached out and grabbed his chin staring into his wizened old eyes with sternness. "Forever is a long time and you are correct it is coming to claim you soon. I think that is all the more reason to live like there is no tomorrow, Claus. You would dare to forfeit the last chance you have to dance and laugh? After the reaper comes there will be no more mirth, no sunrise, no second chances. I would think the lionhearted Claus would desire to be remembered for his going out like the atom bomb, not slinking away to the shadows like a mouse."

He grabbed my wrist that held his chin. "Maxx, you don't understand. I never could handle being viewed as the clown. A nearly eighty year old man in a gown would only bring the Haus a belly chuckle at the absurdity of such a sight."

I nodded as I let his head go and he laid it back down on my chest. "Ah, okay I see. Your wrists have gone limp at last. You can no longer wield the whip or thudder to shut up any that dared such rudeness."

He whimpered. "Nein, they have not. I simply, I don't, fuck, I don't feel the fire for life anymore Maxx. I no longer want to do anything but lay in the bed and await my doom. I don't know what is wrong with me."

I stoked his cheek causing him to shudder. "It is called depression, Claus. You spent nearly two years attending to your dying brother. That forced you to look too close at reality and gain an empathy that most humans can deny. We are all mortal, my Liebling. You cannot beat this disease without aid. You lay here and waste time you no longer have. You may as well be dead already if you decide to continue on that path. Take my advice and put on your gowns. Go to the Great Hall and demand they play the music that moves your soul and feet with it. You will find your assessment of being the clown is false. I dare to bet you will have no problem gaining the eager man to spin you around the dance floor proud to show you off as his own."

Claus nodded and I felt wetness on my chest as the tears fell from his eyes. "I will do as you say Maxx if you can promise to be there when I do it. If you are wrong and the laughter breaks out at my appearance, at least I can be assured your merciful asking me to dance with you."

I chuckled. "Are you fucking kidding? No way I would come anywhere near you if such a fantasy were to become the reality. I am in no mood for a thudding from the mighty Elder Claus. Hell, I would be running for my life begging for mercy the whole way."

That made him laugh hard. "You always knew how to make me feel better Maxx. I have missed you more than you can ever know. I am grateful you are home at last. I think with you around to aid me to overcome my doubts maybe I can find the strength to throw one or two more parties worth going to."

I nodded. "Of that I have no doubt Claus. Now if you are done with me and are well satisfied. I need to shower and get ready for my next appointment."

Claus groaned. "Ah, Jonas, eager to get his fangs into you is he? My poor boy. I wish I had thought to blood bond you when first I enjoyed your favor that night so long ago. If I had, you would belong to me and not that fiend."

I sat up in his bed frowning. "Ja, I never thought of that, but it would have been more merciful had you done exactly that. Yet, you didn't, and here I am. No need to lament what can never be Claus. Am I to assume someday soon I will see you in a glorious gown dancing to the sounds of the classics?"

He sat up as I got out of the bed headed for his bathroom and tub, "You can indeed Maxx. I have a special red number I had been dying to show off before Bladrick found his end. Maybe I will throw a spring fling and don that gorgeous material."

I smiled as I started closing the door, I need some privacy, you know. "Well, make sure to invite Maxx. I will come to witness your finding out I am wiser than you give me credit for." Claus threw a pillow at the door laughing at my statement while I went to work to prepare for the most brutal of all my lovers. That includes the moody Peter. Yikes!

If you recall, a long time ago during the beginning of this story. I told you that Claus would never see me to his door when his clock ran out. I learned during these final years of his life it was not indifference that caused this seemingly rude behavior.

That man was found of me for truth and saying goodbye was something he could never find the strength to do. Even if only for a week. I came out of the bathroom to find him pouting still in the bed at my coming departure. I walked over and allowed him to kiss me, despite the grossness of it.

He teared up as I pulled away and whispered in my ear. "When you leave pick up the gift I left for you by the door. Don't forget to come back next week. I live for it." He let go of me and rolled over to his side trying to keep me from seeing him cry.

I promised to return but he didn't respond. I left the room and headed for the door. There sitting on a table was a modern medical reference book with an envelope attached. I picked it up and found three hundred dollars inside it.

With the money was a note that said, "This little gift is to assure you have enough to eat this week. I know Jonas doesn't give you any cash to survive. Claus swore you would enjoy freedom from the Elders' oppression for keeping him company in his final journey. I know this will aid you in maintaining what was promised you. Love always, Claus."

I scoffed and mumbled under my breath, "You would do better if you left a fucking fake ID and passport Claus. Shit. Freedom he says, that is a bigger joke than an elderly man in a ball gown, which is truth." I left his apartment feeling both miffed and touched at the same time.

While it is true that his money was not very helpful in getting me out of the Haus to real freedom. It was at least a kind gesture that he was not required to make. I was not so ungrateful that the man bothered to care if I could afford a meal during my incarceration within the walls.

I stuffed that money in with Felicity and took off towards Jonas's place smiling with thrill at Maximillian. "I do sure hope that head of yours is better brother. This time you are taking the wheel, dammit. I tolerated that intercourse with Claus, but the Vampire forget it. If you refuse, that is fine, Mad Maxx can take my place. You boy's piss with Mad Max on this I let go of the wheel entirely and we can turn to stone right here close to Kilian's apartment. How would you like that?"

Maximillian scoffed. "Ficken Dich Mad Max. I will take the wheel the second that Bat starts to get touchy feely. Stop being a baby. You never have any problem managing the intercourse with Leo I noticed. You know what I think? You like the sex when the man is someone you desire."

I chuckled. "Uhm, duh. That Leo can give me the orgasm, Maximillian. That Vampire, yuck. Where the hell do I even start? Anyway, you be ready to switch. I am not going to argue with you over the obvious."

I was startled to see Matz standing at the top of the stairs next to the Vampire's apartment with a worried look on his face. I rushed over to see what the hell was so upsetting that he dared to come up to the sixth floor. If anyone caught him he would be punished most brutally for the insult.

He saw me and motioned with vigor to hurry up more. I practically broke into a run feeling a sudden terror rising within my stomach. I knew whatever was bothering him, it had to be the worse of news.

I got within earshot and Matz called out, "You need to see Karsten right away, Maxx. She said it is most important and cannot wait. Do you have time to slip down to see what is wrong?"

That caused the fear to nearly paralyze me to the spot. "What? Karsten? Has something has happened to the black collar children? Matz, she surely told you the nature of this request. Do not leave me in terror like this, damn you. What has happened. I don't like surprises, brother."

Matz frown and shook his head. "She called the apartment but no matter what I said she told me that what she needed to say was for your ears only. I can only verify that the black collars are safe and sound. However, she seemed to indicate there is an issue. Please Maxx, I am as frightened as you are. Go see her and find out if this is something that can be easily fixed or not."

I nodded., "Okay brother, led the way. I am due at the Vampire's apartment in one hour. We have to hurry."

Matz took off down the steps with me hot on his heels. Both of us traveled in silence with speed. I could sense he was nearly coming apart with worry and to be honest he regained a bit of my respect over it. Any man that cared that much for the little helpless lambs of my flock couldn't be all bad. No matter what had transpired between us, it was clear Matz was a good and kind person deep within his soul.

He and I arrived at her apartment in record time. I noticed he was panting and sweating as badly as I was. For me it wasn't from the run. I began knocking on the door and I saw him wince with each sound. It was evident he felt much more than anxiety over this mysterious meeting. I shot him a look of worry when after several minutes Karsten still had not answered.

Matz barely whispered out, "Christ Maxx, something bad has happened. I can just feel it in my bones. Oh Gott, what the devil could be the matter? Do you think Osvin told or maybe the wiry Lucus?"

I shrugged with irritation in my tone. "Stop that guessing game shit, Matz. You stir us up before we have reason to suspect anything of that sort has happened. Shit, if you are trying to scare me, then consider that mission accomplished. There is no need to go any further." I heard Karsten approaching the door at last.

She opened it a crack and stuck out her head. "Matz? I told you I desired to see Mad Maxx alone. Why are you here? What I need to discuss with him is none of your business."

Matz flinched at that. "Uhm, Karsten, Mad Maxx works for me. Anything you discuss with him is my business."

Karsten shook her head with irritation in her face. "Matz, you do not own Mad Maxx. He is entitled to private conversations with another without the insult of having to share it with his fucking pimp."

That made both of us gasp as I put my finger to my lips hushing the FemDom. "Where the fuck did you hear such nonsense. Holy hell, Karsten. You say that to the wrong people, then Matz and I will be in dungeons in seconds."

She nodded. "Ja you would so I suggest you send Matz away and come in here to hear what I have to say."

Matz snorted. "I will be happy to leave the second you tell me where you heard of this prostitution bullshit. I need to know the name of the man's ass I need to kick."

Karsten frowned. "That would be Marc's ass, Matz. He overheard Roland discussing the beautiful night he enjoyed with the Priceless to the other volves. Roland didn't know Marc was within hearing range. The boy is most upset in that he has discovered this dishonor is what the Priceless suffers so that he could be free. Now, leave. I want to speaking to Maxx alone."

I shot a look of pain at Matz. "Do as Karsten says brother. I will speak with Marc, and you can give a warning to Roland about watching what he says in mixed company." I felt as if I may puke realizing my little lamb knew of my shameful actions.

Matz nodded and took off down the hallway as Karsten opened the door and allowed me to enter. I walked inside and was immediately set on guard. She had the curtains drawn and candles lit the darkened living area. Roses were in vases and petals scattered on the couch blanket. Violin music played softly in the background on her stereo. I gasped and turned around to demand the meaning of this strange scene from Karsten.

I nearly hit the floor in a dead faint. The beautiful FemDom had been in a terry cloth robe. When I turned around she let the it fall away revealing skimpy red lingerie under it. There was nothing left to my imagination seeing her in that gorgeous little outfit she wore. The only thing it managed to hide was that she wasn't wearing a damned thing of worth.

I choked on my words. "Karsten? What the hell, uhm, you seem to have lost your robe."

She giggled as she began to approach me with the look of a hungry lioness in her expression. "Ah, seems it fell off Maxx. Oh well, it was getting rather warm in here anyway. Why don't you come and sit with me on the couch. We can discuss what I wanted to see you about."

I shook my head as I began to tremble all over, and my clothing seemed to feel too tight too. I could barely breath from that fucking shirt collar and my breeches, well I was going to bust out of the later without a doubt. "Karsten, where are the lambs? You shouldn't be running around here like that with the little ones likely to wander in and see what they are far too young to know."

Karsten giggled into her palm, the way Jakob does you know. "You are funny Maxx. The black collars are at the stables for another two hours. We are alone. Just you and I." The FemDom rushed me and wrapped her arms around my waist before I could break out of my stun enough to flee her.

Okay, I will admit it. The reason I couldn't get out of the dangerous situation is because Maximillian and Mad Maxx, hell even Max and Christian were all fighting me like demons trying to take the wheel from me. Earlier I couldn't beg any of them to handle the boy. Suddenly, there wasn't a shard not ready to beat his brothers to death to get a taste of that sexy woman that was obviously interested in coupling with the boy.

I swooned as my heart sped up to alarming rates. Damn, that woman felt good hanging on me like that. "Karsten, please I beg mercy. You must stop this right now. I cannot assure you are safe from my desire to take you for the couple if you don't put that robe back on and let me leave right this second."

Karsten nodded as she grabbed handfuls of my hair from the back. I suddenly realized I had forgotten my headset in Lucus's bathroom. "I want you to make love to me, Maxx. I am yours to do with as you please. I will not say nein. I am even willing to pay your price to have you.

Tell me what I must do to get you to treat me like your lover and I will do it no matter the consequences." She pulled my head down and began kissing me with wild passion.

Her tongue forced its way into my mouth. I felt my knees go weak and I melted in her embrace unable to find the strength to pull away. She tugged on my locks of hair with vigor treating me like the puppet on her experienced string. I was helpless to end the sweeping pleasure that filled every molecule of the boy's flesh.

Karsten let go of one side of my head never breaking from the lustful kissing. I felt her reach down my breeches. She gasped and without pulling away began to stroke ma growing interest with a sureness I had never known before.

I moaned and felt my eyes roll back in the boy's head. I was completely her slave by this point. I could not think, nor deny her a thing. If she had wished to cut off my fingers and cover me in honey for hungry ants, I would have let her.

She let go of my head completely and withdrew her hand from my pants. I felt her trembling hands attack my blouse buttons with wild eagerness. I allowed her to fumble the first few trying to get ahold of the ancient drives that had overtaken my good senses.

Then the beauty began to grind her barely covered flesh against the boy's crotch. That was it. I could take no more. I pushed her hands out of the way and began tearing at the buttons with my own lust driven hands. Karsten whimpered and groaned as I ripped off the jacket and blouse, throwing them both to the floor. She moved her lushest lips to my chest sending me into spasms of thrill that flew down my spine and nesting within my painfully engorged manhood. I had to have this woman, or I was sure my dick would blow clean off.

Karsten's kisses linger on the boy's chest for a moment. I reached out and kneaded her perky breasts marveling at the silky skin and the electrifying sensations holding her signs of femininity caused within my groin. I leaned down and kissed them both, lingering on the nipples believing I could die right that moment a very happy man at last.

It would have likely continued like that for hours had the FemDom not demanded I remove my pants immediately. I momentarily found the strength to question this most unexpected seduction. I tried to beg her to let me leave but she ignored me. I gasped in thrill as she reached down and unbutton my breeches. She dropped to her knees taking them down to my ankles with her. I nearly blew the sexual gasket right then and there.

That marvelous woman grabbed my cock and before I could question her again, put her mouth on it sending me right to dumbass status. I couldn't even recall how to speak any language for several moments as Karsten's most skilled tongue blinded me with ecstasy.

I would have been happy to end that most appreciated act of mercy enjoying her oral talents, however Karsten stopped just before I was driven over the edge. I stood there nearly naked and completely within her power unable to say nein as the beauty walked over to the couch and laid down on her back. I could hear the drumbeats of the wild in my ears as she called to me. Mad Maxx come make love to me, let me die a little in your arms, I am ready to set you free.

Chapter 21: The Strange Couples

I stood there staring at the beautiful FemDom laying on her couch with her legs open in full invite for a couple with me. I caste a glance downward. I found my breeches around my ankles and manhood more ready to spread my seed than it had ever been before. There was no doubt I wanted Karsten carnally and obviously the woman felt the same damned way.

I groaned as I closed the boy's eyes trying to regain control of my lustful urges. I had to remind me this was not just any FemDom laying across the room begging my sexual affection. It was the mother of my black collar flock.

If I dared to unite with her in this fashion I was sure to risk the lives of Marc, Kloe, Ghazi and Aara. I doubted the woman would be willing to continue a professional relationship thanks to her anger at me when I refused to become her lover after this act.

That was if I could end it at all. It was far more likely that the second I tasted this gorgeous lady I would be hooked for life. With the easy access to sex with the correct gender for my preference right under my nose. I doubted I would wish to do much else than fuck her eyes out any and every chance I could get. My studies, training, ability to work as the prostitute, and tolerate Jonas would all suffer greatly if that happened.

Not to mention I am not the love them and leave them type of guy. The second I found my apex with her I knew I would never want another female. The way I saw it, if I went through with this intercourse, Karsten could call herself Frau Weiss for truth.

Meine honor demanded that I marry the woman I cared enough for to sleep with. I could never treat a female like the sperm pocket. I know how awful that feels and I will be damned if I will do that to anyone else.

Sadly, Karsten is sterile. That mattered because when she and I could produce no natural children, then I would be forfeit in my agreement with Peter. If I didn't find another female for breeding children, which surely would break Karsten's heart, then all would be lost.

To fail to produce a single child for the Haus carried the punishment of being recollared as Peter's submissive for life. Karsten then would lose her Mann Maxx to the violent Peter for good. My blood bonded Frau and my Mann Jonas will lose all legal rights as part of the punishment included if I failed to fulfill that contract. Just so you know.

All these things were going thru my mind as I gazed at the object of my deepest desires. Karsten was indeed a glory to behold. It seemed to me she was the Goddess dropped to Earth. I couldn't believe there she was laying calling out to me, eager to join me in her heterosexual coupling.

Saying nein to her request, when all I wanted to do was yell hell ja, was going to be the hardest thing I had ever had to do. Yet, I had to turn her away or suffer a fate worse than death for both of us.

I pulled up my breeches. I struggled a bit to get that beast of a disappointed cock of mine covered up. Damn did I want that woman. Yikes! Karsten saw that I was packing up the too she worked hard to obtain and whimpered with dissatisfaction. I took a deep breath and closed my eyes swallowing hard.

She sat up on her couch with a frown. "Mad Maxx, what are you doing? I told you I will pay your fee. I have the money that Roland reported he paid for this intercourse service. Please don't do this to me. I don't think I could bear it if I were to understand that I am not sexy enough to fuck even when paying for the pleasure."

That made me flinch with startle. "Huh? Oh, my Gott. Wait, you think that I am the whore that you can merely pay? Oh Karsten, my beauty, you need not pay for sex. That is an insult to a gorgeous FemDom such as yourself." I had not realized she assumed that because Roland had paid to have sex with me, she could do it too.

Karsten shook her head. "Well maybe you think it is, but not me. I want to be with you Maxx and I don't care if I must pay to do it. Now, I have the money for your fee. Remove your clothing and come lay with me. I have purchased your sexual services, so you have to do whatever I ask without quarrel. That is how it works, ja?"

I sighed loudly and dropped my head. "Nein, Karsten. I mean ja that is how it is done for the males, but not the FemDoms."

That made her gasp in shock. "What? I don't understand. How does it work for the FemDoms? Tell me and I will do it. Hurry Maxx. I need this. I want you to make love to me."

I trembled as I tried uselessly to adjust my swollen manhood to a comfortable position keeping my shamed gaze away from that pretty woman. "It doesn't work for the FemDoms, Karsten. I only sell to the Dominant males. Peter forbids any intercourse with the gender of my truest desire. I only whore to obtain the money to attend to my little ones and you, my Liebling."

Karsten shook her head, and I could hear her panting as if about to cry. "Nein. I won't accept your telling me that you will not break a stupid oath to Peter when no one will ever know. Make an exception for me Maxx. Please I beg of you."

I stole a glance at her unable to tear my eyes from her amazing breasts. "Karsten, we will know. I cannot just use you for my pleasures and forget about it. I am not that kind of man."

She smiled sweetly at me. "That is supposed to be my line, love. Come here and be with me. I understand we cannot be together for truth. I am not asking to be your Frau. I wish to be your honest lover only. You will have to marry one day. I am mature enough to handle the pain when the day comes you must leave me."

I near broke down in tears of frustration when she said that. "You may be Karsten, but Maxx is not. I already am falling in love with you more than I was willing to admit until now. If I go any further with you than I already have, I will be yours for all my life. Then I am doomed. Are you mature enough to handle watching me submitted in a collar at the feet of Peter? That is what is going to happen if I don't leave right this minute."

Karsten's eyes went wide. "You are falling in love with me? That is the most wonderful thing anyone has ever said to me. You surely are only saying that to make me feel better about your refusing my advances."

I shook my head unable to hide my emotional agony. "Nein, I am not. You are everything I would want in a woman Karsten. If this were another world, another place, you wouldn't have to ask me for anything except to get the hell off you. You have no idea how much I want you or how many times you have been in my dreams. That said, please, I beg mercy. I am the marrying kind of guy. Sex is not love I am aware, but when there is already true love, sex is the ultimate expression of it. I can never have intercourse with you or the deep emotions I hold for you will overwhelm me to stupidity. You must believe me Karsten. My turning this offer down is because of my inability to stop my feelings for you, not because of lack of interest."

She looked to the floor then back up with a bitter smile. "I didn't think they made men like you anymore, Maxx. The true gentleman. I suppose I am the unlucky one, or perhaps the luckiest, depending on how you view it. Our years are too far apart for such a travesty as marriage even if I could bear the children you owe to fulfill your oath to that horrible Peter. There would be nothing but pain for us both as I advanced in years and you so far behind me. I am no fool. That said, I will accept that you cannot be with me thanks to your respect for me and not because you don't find me a worthy lover. I apologize for the embarrassment I have caused you and me over this misunderstanding. I hate that I am so desperate to hold you I have shamed myself this way. Can you ever forgive me?"

I frowned and approached the saddened beauty. "You have nothing to be ashamed of Karsten. You are a beautiful sight to behold. I will treasure the memory of this afternoon for all my days. I thank you for the mercy of it. It surely will get me through many a tough night stuck in the loop of enduring sexual lust from those I do not desire. I owe you a debt for it. Allow me to repay you for it right now." I leaned down and re-engaged her in deep passion filled kissing, but I kept my breeches on.

She moaned in her throat as I gently urged her back to the prone position. I dropped to her ears, then nipped and licked her neck. Karsten whimpered and grabbed the hair on my head pushing my face hard into her silky soft skin. I kept lavishing her with kissing as I dropped to her breasts. I was thrilled to linger there for several minutes.

278

That part of a woman's anatomy is of particular interest to me since the males I was accustomed to don't have these remarkable attributes. I cupped, kneaded and licked both with much care and eagerness.

Karsten wailed and ran her nails into the flesh on my back when I fondled her sensitive nipples with my tongue. She had begun to pant loudly, begging once again that I take her without further hesitation.

I continued my tour of her flesh with a brief stop on her flat tummy. As I licked and kissed it I marveled at the lack of hairiness and smoothness of her skin. She had none of the roughness that I hated so badly in the male. Kissing her was like running a silken ribbon or the fur of my Felicity across my lips. It caused me to shudder with wantonness so harsh it was nearly driving me to madness.

Still, I didn't stop my attempt to re-pay her for the oral service she had granted me. I moved down across her patch of soft pubic hair. I pushed my nose into it. I breathed in her sex scent as if enjoying the most sublime perfume of a rare flower. It was truly magnificent to my senses. Kasten trembled and moaned out in ecstasy as I took her beautiful thighs into my hands.

I pulled her closer and spread her legs apart. Without further hesitation I dropped between them and started my oral service return on that gorgeous FemDom. I recalled all the lessons I had learned from Annette and the girls in that bathroom years before.

Within seconds the soft tissues and delicious juices of the female sex organ filled my mouth. Her taste on my tongue had sent me into a frenzy of thrill that Karsten appeared to be appreciating quite a bit. She yipped, yelled, moaned and grabbed handfuls of my hair pushing my face firmly into her swelling clitoris.

It didn't take long for her silky thighs to quiver in my shaking hands. I could tell she was closing in on her orgasm. Her wails of delight pushed me harder to do all I could to please her. A sudden strength I had not expected rushed from her legs. With a loud groan Karsten closed them around my head breaking my hold as if I were a weak kid.

She took hold of handfuls of hair on the back of my head pushing me harder into that incredible vagina of hers. "I am cuming, my love. Don't stop. Oh, my Gott. Holy fuck," she screamed out while bucking into my face like the wild horse.

I was helpless to free myself of her apex, and to be honest I would have happily suffered any injury to stay there forever. Her vaginal secretions flowed into my mouth in a wave that tasted of the pure blue ocean. I was in fucking heaven, I confess it. I had done this act with a woman before (if you can count Heidi, Helga and the teenage girls in the bathroom such a ding) but never had I found it so stimulating as I did that day with Karsten.

The urge to fuck her was threatening my promise to deny such luxury for the good of us both. As she relaxed and the vaginal spasming slowly halted I was overtaken by my baser drives. I pulled free of her grips and topped the woman in a single move. Karsten gasped and opened her eyes to find my face in her own forcing a wanton kiss onto her mouth.

I tore at my breeches trying to undo the buttons. My eager cock was chafing on the material. It's begging to be released to do the job it was designed by nature to do was making me stupid with urgency. Karsten responded to my clumsy attempts to disrobe by wrapping her legs around my waist pulling me in with all the strength she could muster.

She wailed out, "Ja, ja, please Maxx. I need you. Fuck me, I beg of you."

One of the buttons on the breeches was stuck. I ripped and tore at it breaking out in a sweat as Karsten continued to chant out "fuck me." I was beyond hearing anything else. That room could have caught fire and exploded for all I cared. The only thing that matter was getting my cock into the gorgeous woman.

I realized I had to stand up to get that hindrance to my desired action to relent. I pulled back from the eager Mistress and told her I need a moment to get ready. She nodded and released me from her leggy hold. I got off the couch to my feet taking my lust filled eyes off her for a moment to attend the offending button.

It was at that moment I suddenly came to my senses once more. I realized at last, I was about to make the biggest mistake of my life. *Well, one of many big mistakes anyway.* I took a deep breath and rushed for my jacket and blouse laying in a discarded pile on the floor.

Karsten sat up with a loud wail, "Maxx, where are you going? Nein, You need to finish what you started, damn you."

I shook my head while forcing on the blouse and running for the door at the same time. "Karsten, you are repaid for what you granted me. I already told you this cannot be. Forgive me, beauty, but I cannot do this. I must go before I do something we both will live to regret." I tore out into the hallway with my breeches undone, blouse vide open and dragging my jacket in my arms.

I slammed the door shut behind me never looking back. I rushed down the narrow hall knocking over silvers, blacks and even Dominants in my haste to get to a private spot. My hard on was threatening to break my dick in half. I had to get somewhere to release that pent up orgasm or suffer the pain of the blue balls for ignoring it. Or worse, returning to Karsten to finish the job.

There was only one place close enough and for sure to be without witnesses that time of the day. I groaned as I spotted the door of the storage closet from hell. I started to run on past it but the painful erection in my pants demanded I relent my hatred for that space just this once. I opened the door and slipped inside, panting in both left over sexual thrill and unimaginable disgust at the location I found myself in.

I flipped on the light, locked the door and finished undoing the breeches. Without hesitation I took up my own manhood and closed my eyes refusing to acknowledge the scenery. I pulled up the vision of the beauty Karsten, her smell, taste and sounds within the wheel room memories. I stroked with expertise to the sounds of the climaxing FemDom imagining her smooth skin and gorgeous lips.

It didn't take but a few moments for my own cries of ecstasy to ring out as I released my orgasm into that stinking closet floor. It seemed I came forever before at last that pent up lust was satisfied, and I found peace within once more. I leaned into the door doing my best to catch my breath from that most intense climax.

Slowly, I regained my control and opened my eyes. I felt the boy's stomach lurch as I realized what I had just about done. Shit, I had nearly blown everything I had worked so hard to accomplish over a single moment of thrill.

I found it most disgusting that I stood there half dressed, over a wet spot of my spilt seed in that damned place of horrors. This dishonorable and deplorable behavior could not be permitted to occur ever again. I could not have my fucking cock to start calling the shots like almost every perverted Dominant in that stinking Haus appeared to do.

I sheepishly readjusted my breeches and buttoned up my blouse. There was luckily a box of paper goods and cleaning solutions on the shelves. I grumbled and cursed at myself as I used some of it to wipe up that humiliating mess I had made of the floor.

As I finished my chore, then put back on my jacket, I checked on my lamb. Felicity was still safely hidden in her spot. I took a moment to apologize to her for throwing her into the floor at Karten's place like a damned fool (*and for daring to bring her back to the place where she had suffered great injury from Kilian. That was completely uncalled for*).

I slipped back out of that closet without anyone noticing. I checked carefully before exiting, you know. I limped along the hallway headed back to the stairs as I noticed the Haus clock. I had another thirty minutes before I was due at Jonas's apartment. That made me sigh as I realized that knowing what I was missing only made dealing with the Vampire harder. I wanted nothing more than to run back to Karsten, take her in my arm and make love to her till my dick fell off.

I began up the steps with the sad understanding I would never be able to see Karsten again without always having someone with me. I simply couldn't trust myself to play nice. I wanted her too much, and she certainly felt the same way about it. I decided it would be best to come clean with Matz regarding this dangerous situation. I hoped he would understand and not turn into the jealous bitch like he tended to do.

I made it to the apartment rather quickly. When I opened the door I expected to find Matz on the couch pouting but to my surprise he wasn't sitting there. I shrugged at that most unusual scene and headed for the kitchenette assuming he had gone for a snack.

To my surprise, he was not in there either. I started to leave when I hear Matz moan out from his bedroom. That frightened me. I became worried thinking he had gone to confront Roland and found the man more than he could manage. I rushed for his room in silence to check on his state of health.

I opened the door slightly and nearly hit the floor in a dead faint. I couldn't believe my eyes. There on the bed was Matz wailing out in sexual thrill. He was playing stallion to his mare Roland. The two were going at it so fiercely they didn't notice me standing there nor hear me come in. I didn't know what to do or say so I quietly closed the door and left the apartment before either of them realized what I had been witness to.

I stepped out into the hallway still in shock. I mean I was glad that Matz had found someone else to fulfil his lustful urges, but Roland? I had not been aware he was a bottom. That stunning revelation had me reeling in absolute disbelief. He had been a virgin only in penetration, but not in the act of being the one penetrated.

I was leaned up onto the apartment wall when I heard Lucus call out my name. "Christian Hey, Christian. Are you okay?"

I turned to see him standing a few feet away with an expression of concern on his face. "Ja. I, uhm, have had a strange day is all Lucus. I would appreciate it if you wait till later to bother me. I am in no mood for it right this minute."

He nodded. "Ah, okay I will do my best to stay out of your way then. However, I must tell you that you left your overnight bag and headset in my apartment earlier. You surely would want to have those items back? You are attending Jonas tonight, I assume?"

I groaned. "Shit, ja I am. I forgot that will mean I cannot meet with you at eight-thirty Lucus. Jonas is not one to allow me to wander off at will, you know."

Lucus scoffed. "Is he not? I thought you are the Dominant now. Did Jonas forget that? How can he think to treat you like the submissive and say where you can and cannot go and when you can?"

That startled me. "Huh? What is that you say? I am the Dominant, Lucus. However, if I try to leave, Jonas will become angry."

He crossed his arms and snorted. "So what? He may be your Mann, but he is not your Master Christian. Jonas doesn't own you anymore. No man or frau does."

I nodded as I stared at him feeling confused. "That may be true Lucus, but Jonas hits pretty hard. I don't care for it. I leave then when I get back a beating is sure to follow."

The Dominant shook his head. "What the hell is Peter teaching you? Nothing, it would appear. If Jonas beats you

286

for enacting your rights as the Dominant you can take him before Gretta. Beating another freeman is forbidden without just cause. Then only Gretta can grant the right to the lashings. Don't you know that rule of the Haus?"

I looked at my boots. "Ja, I know it Lucus, but I also know Jonas and Gretta. He will beat me, and nothing will be done about it. A fine maybe? Then he will merely beat me harder for it. Same goes with Peter. I don't do as they say I find myself bloody or worse without a ticket out of this fucking Haus in a couple years."

Lucus frowned as he sighed. "Well, you are going to be stuck in this Haus anyway then Christian. If you fail to take your place as the Dominant, then Gretta will see you re-collared soon enough. Not even the powerful Elder Jonas can stop that from happening."

I gasped. "You lie. Jonas can stop Gretta from doing that cruelty. Peter will aid me to pass the Dominance testing anyway so what you say doesn't even matter. Why are you bothering me with things that are fantasy? I told you not to piss with me right this minute and here you are doing what I asked you nicely to forgo. What the hell is wrong with you Lucus? Do you want me to kill you? Is that it? Your suicidal dreams returned to you or something."

He shook his head. "Nein. I am only stating the truth of it. Besides, you started this conversation not I. You owe me a report at eight-thirty and instead you stand here offering excuses that make no sense. I paid for the service you are now trying to deny me. Then to add insult to injury you threaten me yet again. Damn Christian, you are not as honorable as I was lead to believe you to be."

I stood up straight removing the boy from his leaning into the wall with fury in my eyes. "You dare to accuse me of dishonor? I will remember that while the Vampire breaks my face for leaving his bed to meet with you over some bullshit report I could give you right this moment."

Lucus scoffed. "The information I desire is not within your grasp yet. I don't care about Roland sneaking around with Matz, nor do I desire to hear shit about the nonfunctional Claus's sexual perversion with a teenaged boy. It is Jonas's moves I am interested to know about Christian. You will come see me and tell me what he says tonight as you promised. That idiot won't dare to lay a finger on you."

I stared at him in bewilderment that he had somehow known about Matz's affair with Roland, "You are daft, Lucus. Jonas will indeed beat the fuck out of me, but I will be here black eyes and all as I swore to. You are a motherfucking bastard to put me in this dangerous situation yet still claim to be in love with me. I should not be so surprised I suppose. I assumed that royal blood would be a cut above the others I have ever known. I see I was wrong. You are common in everything but name."

Lucus glowered at me. "You need not insult me Christian. I will accept that Jonas will abuse you and you will allow that to occur without punishment. In fact, now that you pointed it out to me I think why would he relent?

288

He doesn't have to fear any reprisals from you, Peter, Gretta, nor Matz your lover. He can control you as his submissive without bothering with the rituals of submission, ja?"

That made me angry as hell. "You cocksucker. I am not Jonas's submissive. Take that back or I will beat you ass and accept the fucking punishment for it."

Lucus smiled at me. "I only repeat what you tell me Christian. I apologize that it pisses you off to hear the truth, but I cannot ignore that it is the honesty of this situation as you explained it to me."

I caste my eyes to the floor. "What the hell do you expect me to do Lucus? I fight him or Peter, then they beat me up, get away with it, and I risk my chances for medical school. You wouldn't stand up to either of them yourself in that same spot. There is nothing I can do about it. I don't appreciate you making sport of me over that sad reality. I am the freeman and I desire to stay that way too no matter what I must endure to keep that status."

Lucus smiled even bigger. "That is the spirit Christian. You have the right attitude indeed. I do not make fun of you. I point out the facts. Now, if you had protection from a strong ally, say for example, me. Well, those two brutes would think twice before daring to beat you up or pass you off to their buddies for their twisted sexual kicks."

That reminder of Hermann made me shudder. "What is this you say? You are offering me protection from Peter and Jonas? How can you do that? Even if you could, how the fuck can I afford such a luxury? I am not royalty nor wealthy like you Lucus."

Lucus chuckled with much humor. "I thought you smarter than that Christian. I have already told you how and the price for it. If your lover were the powerful aristocratic Lucus, Jonas would not be so quick to bust you up. Peter would think twice about using you as the sex doll with his friends too. Neither would be in a hurry to have me go and lodge a complaint with the honorable Gretta, now would day? That FemDom may be able to ignore the new Dominant Mad Maxx, but she sure as hell wouldn't dare to anger the well-connected Lucus. All you have to do is accept my offer. Be mine, Christian. I will take care of you in every way possible. That I swear to you."

I glared at him. "Forget it, Lucus. Never going to happen. I already have one of those and I am happy enough with the choice."

Lucus really laughed at that. "You mean, Matz? Ah, well hate to break it to you, Christian, but I do believe you have been replaced by the violinist Roland. They will be moving in together soon enough and you, my spatz, will be left in the cold without a roommate nor protection of any kind."

I shivered in fear. "Bullshit Lucus. Matz is just sowing wild oats, that is all. Roland doesn't have the means to support him, nor does Matz have enough income to shelter them without me. I don't care if they fuck till the cows come home. That is one less worry off my shoulders if they are the truthful lovers."

Lucus stopped laughing and shot a look of pity at me. "I suppose then you have not heard. Well Christian, Roland can support Matz these days. your little attempt to woo the Queen Jakob with his skillful serenade caught the ears of the Haus orchestra. They gave him the job of first violin in their troupe. Roland is now the wealthy man. He is in there right now celebrating his newfound success with his lover Matz. No doubt they are trying to figure out how to break the news to you that you are history to them."

I felt the world beginning to spin around me. "You lie. That cannot be. Matz wouldn't betray me nor would Roland. They are my friends." I closed my eyes as I remembered how fast Matz turned on Malfred when the offer of cash was waved in front of him by Lucus.

Lucus frowned. "I do not fib to you Christian. You can ask Jonas, he would know since the Elders oversee the accounts of the minstrels. Don't you find it marvelous that Roland has found fame and regained his family fortune. Ah, but apparently you didn't quite do enough for that wolf. To thank you for that kindness, he has taken the heart and protection of your only source of aid in this Haus. I apologize that you had to hear this news from me and not from the one that owes you everything for your mercy."

I did my best to hide the agony that his words caused me. "Well, good for Roland then. I am happy for him. He is the finest musician I have ever heard. It is no wonder that the Haus would snatch him up before anyone else could. Now, if you are quite done crowing thinking you have backed me into a corner, then I would request you give me back my things I accidently left earlier." I was overwhelmed with stress over the idea that without my prostitution money the black collar flock was doomed.

Lucus nodded. "But of course Christian. I left them in the living area of my apartment." He took off with a hand signal to follow him.

I went after him mindlessly with fear driving my steps. I needed to speak with Matz and ask him if he did intend to leave with Roland. I found it almost impossible to acknowledge that the two could walk away and leave the helpless Kloe, Marc, Ghazi and Aara to be devoured by the Dominants.

I had assumed Matz and Roland to be of good heart, but I knew deep down that I most likely saw what I desired to see in them. If Roland has indeed become wealthy, I was more than boned and the black collars finished. I decided that beating or not, I would have to return around eight-thirty to my apartment to confront Matz with Lucus's suspicions.

I went inside the apartment behind Lucus. He pointed at the coffee table where my headset and overnight bag sat waiting for my return. I said nothing as I rushed over to grab the objects. I was ready to be free of this asshole even if it meant dealing with the king of the cocksuckers Jonas.

He stood by the door watching me as I gathered the bag and put my headphones on. I turned and took off with speed to leave but Lucus reached out and grabbed my arm as I was almost out of there. I glared at him, and he stared at me with a smile. Then before I could stop him he pushed me into the wall and put his lips to my mouth forcing a kiss.

I struggled in his grip as he pressed harder pinning me to the wall momentarily. I broke free of his hold and backed away feeling frightened beyond imagination. I wanted to strike him, but I dared not give him cause to seek out Gretta's judgement against me for it. If I dared to hit this man of powerful standing this time I would need to kill him. If I let him live then, I risked serious repercussions that may result in my re-collaring.

He stood there smiling at me but didn't move to come at me again. I couldn't get to the door without putting myself back within his reach. It was a silent stalemate for several minutes.

At last, I couldn't take the pressure any long, "Let me pass Lucus. I will be late for Jonas. He will kick my ass for it. Is that what you want? To see me beaten twice in the same day?"

Lucus grinned. "If you would accept my offer you would never be beaten by that bastard again. I will let you leave when you say ja to be my lover."

I scoffed. "I told you I don't desire a lover. Let me be Lucus. You are deluded. You don't love me, you merely are enamored with what you think you see in me. I am straight, damn it. I don't like sex with the man anyway. That you surely know."

He nodded his head. "That I do. However, you sell your artistry to the secret schwuler, and I dare say that you do not go and play shuffleboard with Claus, Jonas nor Peter. You tolerate the intercourse with them, and you will with me too. You can end your humiliation as the male prostitute and enjoy the freedom, protection, and luxury I can offer you. All it costs you is your allowing my adorations without quarrel."

I looked at his clock and saw I only had five more minutes to get up the stairs to Jonas. "Alright, I will think about it Lucus. Now move aside. I have to go. You are making me late."

Lucus frowned. "Think about it? Nein, I want you to say you will take my offer."

I shook my head. "You dare to not afford me time to consider the consequences of such a union carefully? You are the brute no better than Peter or Jonas. I say I will think about it, and I will. You have my word of honor. Now let me go, damn you."

He sighed but moved away from the door. I fled with speed, not looking back, accepting another word nor halting. I was not only in a hurry to get away from that freak, but I was in no mood to have a barrage of backhands or dry sodomy when the Vampire was slighted by my disobedience to his orders.

The truth was I had no intentions of seriously considering Lucus's offer. The last thing on earth I wanted was a real live-in lover. Leo was capable of attending any romantic needs I had, and Matz, though we had our issues, was capable of providing me with work to allow me at least a bit of freedom. I hated the prostitution business, but at least with it I could control where the money went, and I had some say in who I slept with. I could deny a customer requests or even refuse to do anything with them at my discretion.

What Lucus proposed was a promise to end my ability to say nein and decide how to spend my money. I knew better then to think if the loving Leo wasn't going to fund the purchase and care of my flock, that the selfish Lucus would do it.

I only told him I would consider what he offered to get the fuck away from that creepy guy. That day had not been going well. *Okay, that Karsten business, wow, which was the best thing ever but otherwise the day sucked.* I was certain it was about to get worse as I knocked on Jonas's door.

The Vampire came to answer quickly. "Ah, there is my Christian Axel. Come in my love. I thought I would die waiting to hold you in my arms."

Well, arms weren't the right word for what he couldn't wait for. Claws would have been a more accurate statement. He wasted no time demanding I follow him to his bedroom. I winced as he shut the door behind us and showed me the lancet he held in his hand.

I took a deep breath. "Already? Two weeks have passed. That cannot be right Jonas. I thought you just fed."

He chuckled with mirth. "You always say that. Stop arguing and get yourself prepared for my blood couple. Hurry up Christian Axel. Strip down and get that lustful urge rolling in your veins. I desire to get my transfusion and satisfaction before our dinner at the Great Hall."

I groaned but began doing as he said wishing I had not masturbated only half an hour earlier in that closet. Getting another erection so close to that release with all the stress that had just been laid at my feet was going to be tough to say the least.

The Vampire stood there watching me fumble and fail at finding my sexual interest no matter how much I focused on that beauteous Karsten. Even with my eyes closed and that fresh memory of the experience with her, my manhood was not rising for the occasion. I have to say it didn't help matters that Jonas was clicking that damned lancet open and closed as he stood there impatiently waiting for me to get into the lustful state.

He finally growled out after fifteen minutes of my useless stroking. "Dammit Christian Axel, are you trying to piss me off? What the fuck is wrong with you? I would think at sixteen your dick would get hard if it were rubbed by the wind."

I felt fear rising at his angry words. "I apologize Jonas, but I think it is that fucking medication I take. Sometimes, well, I just cannot get anything to respond. Maybe if we wait a few hours and try again I will have better luck."

Jonas bellowed out, "Fuck that. You do as you are told or pay for it." He flew forward and backhanded me with all his strength.

I whimpered as he pounced on top knocking me to my back on his bed. His eyes were flashing with fury as he gnashed his pointy teeth. I felt my heart speed up as I dropped the wheel and hauled ass to the back of the wheel room. Maximillian rushed past me and grabbed it before the boy could fall into a trance.

I laid there staring into the Vampire's eyes unsure what to do. "Jonas, please mercy. I will try harder. Give me a few more minutes. I am sure I can do this for you."

He struck me again this time with much more force. "You had your chance Christian Axel. You know what I think? I think you are fucking around with a female or masturbating without my approval. I told you no release is permitted except with your Frau. I don't see the bitch here. Do you know what I will do to any woman I catch you with that is not the Priceless?"

I shook my head feeling the panic overwhelming me from within. "Nein Jonas. There is no female, I swear it. I am not spilling my seed either. It is the medication that numbs my abilities, I swear it."

He punched me in the chest causing me to sputter for air "Then why are you taking it? I told you Kilian cannot force you to take the blood testing. You stop those medications you hear me? I will not have that shit interfering with my feedings. In two weeks, you show up here like this I will punish you by crushing your hodensack. There won't be any need for it to make the children if the fucking cock it is attached to doesn't work."

He reached down and grabbed my, uhm, boys. The Vampire applied pressure to them causing me to struggle and gasp in agony. He laughed as I began begging him to stop, swearing I wouldn't take the medications anymore.

This went on for several minutes until he was certain I was beyond terrified that he was going to rip them off. I screamed in horror as he suddenly struck me with the lancet just above my left collar bone and dropped down to feed on the blood that welled from the wound.

It was then I recalled that if he couldn't gain my lust before feeding, he would accept my terror. I closed my eyes and endured the disgusting act of his sucking my blood best as I could. There was nothing that I could find in my head to distract me from hearing his gross feeding noises and repulsive moans of thrill.

As usual, the second he was full he forced himself between my legs and engaged me in his dry, rough, penetration intercourse. I did my best not to vail or cry over the humiliation of this but to be honest, to this very day, I often lose that battle. That day was not any different.

Jonas always enjoys making me weep and cry out like that. It is why he is so brutal in his partaking of his Mann rights. There really is no other reason for it. Lubrication and a little gentleness would make the sex at least tolerable.

You be warned that he may behave the same with you, Meine Liebe. I would like to believe I can protect you from such a cruel couple with him, but I am not the fool I used to be. What Jonas wants, the Vampire gets. My best advice is to act like it hurts even if it doesn't. Never let him think otherwise or he will make damned sure it does.

I nodded but didn't look back at my Master. Stories of the Vampire Jonas's brutal behaviors always scared me when I was little. I had no interest in asking any questions that may spark answers I was simply unprepared to hear. Yikes!

Once he reached his orgasm, he allowed me to leave his bed to shower. I was reminded by him twice to make sure to attend the feeding wound before returning but instructed to stay undressed. I wondered about that but did as he told me to do. I was most unhappy and mildly traumatized over that surprise blood coupling business but since it was over I allowed my mind to return to the truthful troubles at hand.

I needed to figure out a way to gain a leave of absence at eight-thirty. I really didn't care about that meeting with Lucus, but I was interested in visiting with my flat mate Matz. I need to know if he was planning on moving out to allow Roland to keep him. I would require as much time as possible to find another way to attend to my bills and the black collar flock.

I began running down a list of potential first floor low Dominants that may be willing to assume the role of my pimp and protector just in case Lucus was right. I hadn't even finished my shower when I came to the conclusion that things were looking pretty grim if I did lose my pretend lover.

Any candidate I could think of had serious issues with anger, was a loudmouth or likely would make Matz seem like the gentleman in comparison. I began to damn myself for caring more about the feelings of Roland and Jakob then looking out for my own best interests. What a fucking fool I had been. It goes to show that a good deed can be and often is punished.

I got out of the tub and attended that nasty wound Jonas made when suddenly I recalled something that could answer my predicament assuming Matz was leaving me. Jakob was "outing" me to the schwuler club in only two days. I smiled at the boy in the mirror as I remembered that most important event was coming up.

I thought it probable that I could find one among them willing to take the place of the wayward Matz. That happy thought managed to calm my nerves a bit. I needed to completely relax, and I didn't wish to wait all night to find out first thing in the morning that I would need to seduce another Dominant that would be willing to play the role of pimp at that Saturday meeting.

Things were starting to look up. Once I had a plan B, just in case, I convinced myself that most likely Matz was not leaving me and Lucus was full of shit. All I had to do was find an excuse to take a break from the Vampire to speaking with Matz and everything was going to be alright, or so I hoped.

I came out of the bathroom to find Jonas still in the bed. That caused me to raise an eyebrow of curiosity. More so when he demanded I re-join him in it. I mean the man can be lusty but that fast. Not even he could do that. I did as he ordered but felt a bit of fear at this most strange request.

He smiled as I crawled in under the sheets. "What are you doing, Christian Axel? I cannot enjoy the view with it covered up." e pulled them off me.

I gasped and sat up immediately,. "Jonas surely you are satiated for a bit. I just took a shower. You intend to go for seconds already?"

Jonas chuckled. "Give me your wrists, boy. I desire a bit of bondage today. I know it is not your favorite, but you will humor me or be sorry for it."

That really set me into fear. "What? Why are you suddenly interested in such dishonor? I will not give you trouble if you desire something. There is no need to tie me up Jonas."

He frowned. "I said give me your wrists. Stop the arguing. I am your Mann and I say I wish to engage in bondage. Do as you are told. I mean it."

I shook my head. "Jonas you are my Mann but not my master. I don't have to relent to any request you demand. You know better. I am the freeman not the collared."

Before I could react, he punched me in the stomach sending me into a spasm of breathlessness. He snatched up my wrists when I was too overcome by lack of air to fight.

In moments he had cuffed, and chain locked, both arms to his metal headboard. I wheezed and sputtered doing my best to recover from his ambush blow.

He crawled off the bed leaving me there battling against the restraints. "I do apologize Christian Axel but to be honest I knew you would throw a fit about what I am about to say. I thought it best you be kept from doing anything stupid in your anger."

I stopped fighting the chains and glared at him feeling a sickness from within that was not caused by his striking me. "I am angry that you bonded me, Jonas. What the hell are you about to tell me that would make me more so."

He looked at the floor appearing shamed. "Well, that little fit I threw over Kilian's insults the day I threw him out, he threatened to take me before Gretta and report it. You understand if that bitch found in his favor, and she would, it was likely that I would end up in the dungeon for more than a week and whipped to boot. I cannot allow such indignity to be handed over in front of the Haus. It would make me look weak and open me up for further attacks from both Kilian and many other enemies I made on my way to Elder status. That is how he blackmailed me into paying him back for the damage I had done him, the rat bastard."

I scoffed. "Okay, but what the hell does any of that have to do with you bonding me, Jonas? So, you lost a little money to that snake. You think it all right to take out your anger at him on me? That is unfair and you know it. Let me out of these cuffs, damn it."

The Vampire didn't look up as he let out his breath slowly. "I am not taking out my anger on you, Christian Axel. I am holding you still to pay my debt. Kilian didn't want money, my dove. He wants to have sport with you."

I wailed out. "Oh, nein. You didn't. God damn you Jonas. Let me go. You have no right to promise anything of me to pay a debt you fucking owe."

Jonas bellowed out in fury interrupting me. "You will what, Christian Axel? How dare you curse and try to threaten me. You are a nothing. You are merely my Priceless collar, boy. You think breaking that metal changed our relationship? Nein, you still belong to me for all your life. You will allow Kilian his payment and thank me for the mercy of it. That is final."

I began to sob loudly as I watched the Vampire scurry off to answer the knocking at his door. I pulled and twisted in those cuffs, but I was bonded tightly. There was no getting out of this nightmare unless Jonas brought the key to undo the padlocked chains that held me.

Within a few moments I halted my struggling. I whimpered in terror while Kilian and his brother Reece came into the room followed by the Vampire. He wore an expression of irritation on his face as obvious as the one of fear on mine. The vile snake brothers were carrying that stereo, headset, a blindfold, and a spider gag between them.

Jonas growled out, "Kilian you motherfucker I only agreed to you taking a turn with my Mann. You dare to bring a buddy with you? Who the fuck do you think you are?"

Kilian chuckled as Reece came over by the bed and put the stereo and headset on the nightstand. "You know damned well this is my brother and the boy's doctor I brought with me. The way I see it you will back off and let me enjoy my payback or I can leave with Reece and call Gretta. Up to you Jonas."

The Vampire scowled at Reece. "You planning to fuck Maxx too? Fine doctor you turned out to be. No wonder the boy is still crazy as the hatter. Shit, were you taking his favors the whole time he was in your care at Heslach, you dirty cocksucker?"

Reece chuckled as he ran his eyes over my naked flesh with a wanton look in them. "Nein, this will be a first for me. Kilian has bragged so often of the talents of this patient I just couldn't resist getting a chance to see them for myself." He reached out and ruffled my hair and I pulled away violently causing him to giggle.

Jonas scoffed. "I don't believe you Reece. Be that as it may, I believe I have no choice in this matter. All I can say is you better get your thrills while you can. After this, I ever catch either of you fooling around or even looking at my Mann, you will find yourselves growing a tree for it."

I yelled out in fury. "Jonas, you kill them right now. Let me out and I help you do it. Please, mercy, they have the voices machine."

Kilian laughed out loud and motioned Reece to come get his spider gag. "Ah Reece, you hear that? Mad Maxx fears the sounds of people speaking. Too bad for him. Put this on his head so that mouth of his can only function the way it should. I desire to hear nothing but screams without the commentary from him. Also, use the blindfold. No reason for him to be overwhelmed by too much light or knowledge of who is attacking him. Oops, almost forgot. Put this pinwheel where I have ease of access." He held up that fucking torture device making damned sure I saw it.

I immediately went into a wild thrashing attempt to break my arms, wrists or both. I needed out of those restraints before these criminals could torture the boy. Reece had Kilian aid him pin me to the bed as the two worked together to place the spider gag and headphones on my head. The last thing I saw before day put on that blindfold was the Vampire's look of confusion as he watched the wicked pair setting me up for their tortures.

The darkness forced me to rely on my other senses. I could hear the two brothers speaking softly discussing who would start the sexual assault and where. I could no longer close my mouth nor speak with that fucking gag pinning my tongue down to the floor of my mouth. There was nothing I could do but pull and groan loudly as the brothers prepared for their attack.

My hearing was suddenly overtaken by the sounds of many people speaking in many languages. They were loud as hell, but I couldn't cover my ears. I tried leaning my head over and brushing off the headset.

One of the brothers grabbed the harness of the gag and held on tightly. I couldn't see which it was. There interference prevented me from freeing my ears of that noise. I nearly choked when that bastard, which one it was, forced his cock into my restrained mouth with much vigor.

I kicked wildly hoping to make a connection in my blindness but again all attempts to end this rape failed. I felt the pinwheel tear into my right thigh sending me into spasms of agony. The man raping my head refused to back off despite my choking and attempts to scream.

With air becoming sparse, thanks to the fucker forcing the deep throating, my sight gone and hearing overwhelmed, the painful sensation of that pinwheel attack was heightened to excruciating levels. This went on for several minutes. I was quickly becoming confused from the horrific discomfort and that sensory overloading in my ears.

I let go of the wheel unable to take another second of the fast-tanking nightmarish situation. "Mad Max, I cannot do this brother. I apologize but I was not made for this kind of sex. This is torture most foul. Call Mad Maxx in on this. Maximillian is out."

Mad Maxx looked over at me as I yelled that. "Nein, I cannot do this one either Mad Max. I am the masochist, but this is the physical mixed with the psychological torture. I will be damaged by such a foul practice."

Mad Max growled in fury. "Motherfuckers, what good are either of you? Am I to assume you both leave this shit to me yet again? I was not built to handle the schwuler sex. Are you trying to kill me off? Then do it with Christian's knife and be quick. I would rather be shattered than endure this nasty crap."

Max frowned as he pushed Mad Max toward the wheel. "You must handle this Mad Max. You are the only one of us strong enough to do so. I apologize, but there is no other choice. The Max boys are right. Neider of them can manage it. They would shatter."

Mad Max lightly punched at Max. "Get off me, Max. I am going. This is bullshit." He took the wheel still fuming, but not daring to disobey the powerful Soul shard's orders.

I closed my eyes and pulled hard at the restraints. I did my best to calm down the rising panic caused by the sensory overloads and inability to get enough air. My breathing was rhythmically blocked by that fucker's member cramming into the boy's helpless mouth.

It was at this point the pinwheel cutting abruptly stopped and the man assaulting my head halted as well. He removed himself allowing me to gasp and pant for precious oxygen a few moments. I thought they had decided it was enough when after another few moments no one appeared to be touching the flesh.

Then the sounds of those people went silent as well. I laid there unsure what to make of the quiet and stillness around me. I couldn't see or hear a fucking thing. Then all at once that man forced his cock back into my mouth and resumed his brutal assault. I felt the other one grab my legs. I kicked with all I had but that fellow managed to get between them anyway. I realized the two had switched positions during that brief moment.

One of those sonofabitches had used my head to gain the erection. He was on his way to force his intercourse while the other worked on getting a hardon of his own. I was beyond furious at that shit. I twisted and struggled despite the hopelessness of it. I wasn't going to just lay there and take it. I intended to make it as difficult as possible for the Altergott brothers to get their thrills. I briefly wondered if Jonas was going to sit there and allow this horror show to continue.

No matter how hard I rocked the boy and pulled, the brother managed to penetrate me and begin his cruel thrusting. I fought for air and continued to struggle but I admit that I was losing strength fast just as that sound of all the people speaking began again, louder this time.

I tried to turn my head and knock the headset off, but the brother was faster than me. He grabbed the harness and resumed his enforced blow job. I was about to give up the fight and call it a loss when the sounds of lambs calling for their mother began to echo thru the headset. I held my breath as the noise somehow brought me a bit of peace in the middle of that horrid gang raping shit. I closed my eyes, not that I really needed to, and focused on their sweet voices while doing my best to block out the sensations of the foulest of violations of my flesh.

Those people speaking from before were still there too, but they had become the background noises. I marveled at each little lamb crying out and realized there were at least five of them. I felt a rush of fear down my spine as I thought to myself these must be the voices of my lamb family.

Just as that revelation hit me, I heard the sounds of wolves howling in the distance. The lambs calls became frantic as if they too could hear the predators approaching. My heart began to race and sweat poured down my face as the noise of the wolves grew closer and the lambs' calls became frantic.

I began to struggle viciously causing the cuffs to cut into my wrists while I twisted and bucked wildly. This caused my attackers to increase the tempo of their own violent attacks. I tried to scream and was blocked as the bastard grabbed my head and held me tightly to his groin forcing his cock halfway down my throat. He wouldn't relent and allow me to get a breath. The panic at having my airway cut off further stressed out the already overwhelmed senses of the boy.

The wolves in the headset lit on the baby lambs. Tear flowed freely down my cheeks as I was forced to listen to them growling out furiously as the lambs screamed in agony. My mind was filled with the sounds of ripping, cries of pain, and wanton massacre.

While this horror filled my ears, the brothers brutally battered, raided and raped the boy's flesh. Even me, the tough Mad Max, could take no more. I kicked the wheel with all my strength and hit the floor as the lightening filled the wheel room. The flesh immediately went into the spasms of the Grand Mal seizure.

I laid on the floor covering my head with the other Max boys and Christian. I began wailing in pure torment of that nightmare that I could not shut out of my memory. This frightened the other shards that had never seen me become that unsettled before. They joined in with my song of despair. Our calls of distress grew so loud; Der Hund could hear it from wherever he goes. Within moments he came running from the nothing to find out what had happened.

For a moment, he was in that wheel room with us. I assumed the shattering had arrived at last and we were finally going to get a much deserved rest. I got up to my knees and all the shards followed my lead.

Der Hund stood there eying us in disbelief. "Mad Max. What is going on? The boy is resetting, and you are a mess.

All you appear despondent. The shattering isn't here yet, but I see you spread so thin I can enter the boy. Speak to me, damn you."

I sniffed loudly and kept my shamed gaze to the floor. "The Altergott brothers are abusing the boy. They are using techniques so foul neither Maximillian nor Mad Maxx could handle the agony of it. As it turned out, neither could I. Forgive me Der Hund for this dishonor."

Der Hund shot me a look of pity then reached down and stroked my cheek lovingly. "You have no reason to apologize, Mad Max. Kilian and his brother know things that can drive the boy to madness. None of us can handle such a state, not even your Master Hund. I thank you for standing up to protect your brothers when called. I know how hard that was for you. I assume you kicked the wheel to end the pain?"

I nodded. "Again, I beg forgiveness for it. I didn't know what else to do. Kilian recorded the wolves killing our lambs. That DJ was right. They are dead."

Der Hund shook his head. "Nein, Mad Max. Those were other lambs you heard murdered. You saw the lambs healthy and safe only this morning, remember? Besides, Geraldine sent up your supper to Matz. I saw here doing it only moments ago. You calm down, all you boys need to relax. It is horror that someone's family was harmed but it was not our own, of that you can be assured."

I let out my breath in relief, though I was still upset that the wolves had killed the poor stranger's lamb family.

"I thank you for the mercy, Der Hund. The boy will become alert soon. I think I can manage the wheel if that raping is over."

Der Hund nodded. "I think it is. Their apex has been reached. The Vampire will send them away now."

I growled out in fury, "They kept fucking the boy despite his seizure. They are pigs."

Our Master Shard frowned. "They are animals, Mad Max. Neither cared that the boy was in peril. In fact, I believed they intended to kill him. Christian, my old friend. You will need to kill these men. Mad Maxx, you create a plan to get them into a place of disadvantage, then let Christian loose. Mad Max, you and Maximillian aid Mad Maxx in anything required to get this mission completed. I want them dead as soon as possible. They are a danger to our survival."

Each Max shard and Christian nodded in unison as we said together, "Your will is our own."

Der Hund rushed from the boy before he recovered his consciousness. We all shot looks of disgust at each other as the sounds of the dying lambs echoed through the wheel room in repeat. We realized the Altergott brothers had not removed that fucking headset yet. They are assholes.

Several hours passed before the boy finally awoke from his seizure induced slumber. I, Mad Max, took the wheel as promised. I opened my eyes to find my hands free, and the Altergott's gone. I was alone in the bed under the sheets.

Slowly, I sat up and rubbed the burns and cuts on the boys flesh from our struggling and that fucking pinwheel. I was startled as I recalled that stereo and headset. I turned to look at that nightstand and found they too were gone. The agony of their forced sexual assault was the proof that I had not had a wicked nightmare. I was beyond furious at Jonas.

This bullshit of his thinking himself still legally allowed to do with me as he would his submissive had to stop. I got out of that bed, albeit with much groaning from the pain, and hit the shower. I scrubbed off an inch or two of skin trying to wash away the foulness of that tag team rape.

I got out, found my clothing and dressed rapidly. I was buttoning the last button on my blouse when Jonas entered the room with a smile on his face.

He cleared his throat then said, "Well, you look better than ever Christian Axel. I bet you are hungry, ja? I am too. Now with that nasty business finished we can head down to the Great Hall for dinner."

I glared at him full of fury. "Fichen Dich, Jonas. You had no right. I am not your fucking submissive anymore. You cannot just trade me off to pay debts you owe. I am leaving. I don't give a shit if you are my Mann. No Dominant can abuse another like you have done and just get away with it. You fear the dungeons and lashings? Try to come after me and then you will see both. Kilian is not the only motherfucker that can demand judgement against you." I picked up my jacket and pushed past him headed for the front door.

Jonas rushed after me and yelled out, "You leave this apartment Christian Axel, and I will rescind your freedom from Heslach. I am not just your Mann, I am the Guardian too. I am your Master, like it or not. You are free to everyone but me."

I turned around picked up one of his fancy vases and threw it at him making connection with his head. "You cannot have me sent to the nuthouse at will, motherfucker. Did you think me too stupid not to check on your powers over me? You can rob me blind and force me to medical treatment, but you cannot lock me up without proof I need to be." The Vampire hissed with pain as he held his forehead and looked at the shattered ceramic shards at his feet.

He then glared at me angrier than I had ever seen him before. "You are angry, that I can appreciate Christian. That said, I will not tolerate your insolence over it. You think I cannot call Kilian, Reece or even Doctor Vagner and get any of the three to justify sending you away to the hospital? If you didn't consider that then you are more the fool then I ever thought you to be. You go to Gretta over this little scene today and when I get out I will make sure you are back in that cell within moments. Kilian and Reece can have their bit of sport with you on a daily basis then, and I won't have to clean up the piss after they send you into spasms from it. Do you hear me, Christian Axel? You do as you are told and shut up your speaking like you have the choice in this Haus. You are lucky I let you keep that apartment downstairs as it is. Don't dare to push me any further or I can make thing far more difficult than you ever imagined it could be, collar or nein."

I snarled at him, "Is that so, Jonas? Well, we will see about that won't we." I grabbed up my overnight bag and fled for the door with the fear of his words starting to take their effect on my resolve to stand my ground.

Jonas yelled out, "You go think about what I said and be back here in one hour for dinner. If you are one minute late, be ready to take a trip back to hell, boy. Don't piss with me. I mean it."

I snorted and took off out of his apartment slamming the door behind me. I ran for the stairs with fear nipping at my heels. I needed to speaking with Matz. If he could assure me that I was not in danger of losing his partnership then I was certain I could find a way to deal with Jonas without giving into his threats.

However, if I was indeed about to be abandoned to my fate of slow failure to maintain independence, I knew I had better do my best to get over Jonas's infraction against me. Everything was riding on Matz's answer.

I crashed thru the apartment door startling Matz that was sitting on the couch. He was necking with Roland. They both sat there staring at me in pure shock as it was only seven o'clock. They had not expected me home for another hour and a half. Neither said a word as I stood there panting out of breath and beyond livid. I did my best to keep the sound of desperation out of my tone as I asked, "So you and Roland are lovers. This is fine. But I heard a rumor that you are moving in with him Matz. Is this true? Are you leaving me to fend for myself. Matz dropped his gaze to the floor and sighed deeply. I felt like my heart was going to blow up as I awaited his answer.

Chapter 22: The Gay Men's Group

Matz took a deep breath, then shook his head. "Nein, Mad Maxx, I am not going anywhere. I am ashamed that you found out about this affair with Roland like this, but sooner or later I would have to address it. It will change some superficial things between us but that fear you have that this means I will leave you to fend for yourself is unwarranted."

I led out my breath and wiped my brow with relief. "Oh, thank Gott. I thought for sure that with Roland at your side the two of you would abandon me and the black collars."

Matz frowned then looked at Roland. "You see how my Maxx treats me, my love? Where is the trust?"

Roland chuckled. "Don't be so hard on Maxx, my sparrow. I would have thought the same damned thing in his situation and so would you."

Matz shrugged. "Well, you and he are wrong about Matz, that is for sure. I don't betray those that are true brothers. You, the wolfpack and Maxx are the only real family I have. I dare not do such evil to the ones I love."

I nodded. "I can see that you are fully honorable Matz. I apologize for thinking otherwise. I thank you for the mercy of it. Roland I thank you for the mercy of giving Matz someone to adore. I am glad to see you both so happy."

Roland blushed with a smile. "Ah, well we have you to thank for any joy we have today, Maxx. Your serenade request for the services I took from you set me in the sights of my Matz and the Haus orchestra. Without your faith in this silly man, I would never have been given such beautiful opportunities to make all my dreams come true. You are a good friend, brother. I will never forget the mercy you showed or the happiness you helped me to find." He pecked Matz on the cheek with a quick kiss.

Matz smiled at Roland with pure adoration in his expression. "Roland is correct there, Maxx. I saw my gorgeous man for the first time the other night when he played for Jakob and you. I knew he played the violin, but until then I never saw such passion, vigor, or such beauty in him before. I swear to God I fell in love with him the second he ran his bow across that violin and my heart." He took up the wolf's hand into his own.

I grinned at that obvious affection they expressed for each other "Well, that is a relief to hear. So, if you are not stealing my Matz to run away with you to another home, am I to assume you plan to stay on the first floor then? With your newfound popularity, surely you will be seeking a move up a level or two?"

Roland reached into his pocket and pulled out many hundred dollars tossing them on the coffee table. "Nein, I will eventually move up a level but not yet. Matz tells me you are seeking to move Karsten and the black collar children to the third floor. This money is a large chunk of my earnings. You can use it to make that deposit payment for her lofty flat. Next month, when I am paid, I will look into my own place somewhere close to her. That way when I am not practicing or playing I can be around to help Valitin and Magnas continue to guarding them and you while you work."

I nearly fainted at the sight of that money and the words he said. "Are you funning me, Roland? This is magnificent and most unexpected. Thank you. I am of course thrilled to have a larger place to shelter Karsten and the black collar children." I smiled with pure glee, realizing that thanks to the FemDom having more room, I would be capable of saving a few more silvers from death.

Roland dropped his eyes to the floor maintaining his bashful smile. "Aw, it is nothing Maxx. I know you and Matz can keep the rent paid with your artistic talents Maxx. I have been most blessed since tasting your skills. I have found the lover and a future at last. I will be the wealthy man soon. All thanks to your faith in me. It is the least I could do, ja?"

I was finally calming down from that scare of thinking Matz was leaving me. "I am most joyed to hear you are the success Roland. You are of course welcome to stay with Matz in this Haus anytime you like. I am so glad to see the two of you found love. Now maybe Matz and I will have no further quarrels, ja? A man that is well adored is the easy going fellow indeed I am told. Ah, this kindness you are doing is most appreciated Roland. If it is not too much, given all that you already have done for the flock, I would like to ask you or Matz to do me the favor of selecting the apartment. It shouldn't be too much of a hardship. I think that it would be a real honor to inform that glorious mother of our black collars to prepare to move on up the steps. She surely will be most grateful for the mercy of it." I took a place on the loveseat across from the lovers wiping away the heavy sweat from that most comforting discovery that Lucus was wrong about Matz leaving me.

Matz frowned, then sat forward looking at me hard. "Maxx, uhm I don't think Roland is being clear with you. This money is not a gift."

I was startled at that. "Huh? What? Roland said he gives this money for the payment for Karsten's new apartment. I heard him Matz. You trying to tell me I am hallucinating that?" I was a bit more than a little confused by his strange statement.

Matz shot a look at Roland that looked at his lap quickly. "Uhm, my Liebling? Can you go to my room and give me a moment alone to speak with Maxx?"

Roland nodded then kissed his cheek. "I need to get downstairs and grab some fresh clothes my love. I will do that right now and give you two a bit of privacy to discuss business." He got up and without another word left me and Matz alone in the apartment. He didn't take that large wad of cash I noticed. Now I was very confused and more than a little stressed by this odd behavior of my flat mate.

Once Roland was gone Matz sat back and sighed loudly. "I was going to talk to you about all this tomorrow when you got home. Since you are here, then I suppose there is no time better than this moment. This money Roland has given me is a lot of income Maxx. The cost of the startup fee for the third-floor apartment is extraordinary and he has offered enough to do this for Karsten and then a little extra."

I nodded with a bit of nervousness creeping back into my consciousness at his words. "Uh, okay Matz. I told him thank you for the mercy of it. You say this is no gift he offers? Then I am to assume he wishes for a return service. What is it that he desires for his payment?" I felt my breath coming shallow as I already could assume I knew the answer to that question.

Matz stared at me without a waver in his gaze. "You are a prostitute, Maxx. Roland desires to have access to your artistry. He will choose from that menu and take the services as you have the time to grant them. Furthermore, he desires to stay in this apartment with us. He offers to pay for the living expenses as they arise and stay in my room with me."

I sat there staring at him dumbfounded. "I don't understand this Matz. I know he is the bottom, and he has you to adore him. Why the fuck would he desire any further service from a whore. That makes no sense. As for his living here, I said he could stay with you, but I meant overnight for the trysts, not every fucking day. I can barely stand having you around much less another noisy bastard disturbing my peace."

Matz shook his head and crossed his arms. "You are not going to sit there and pretend you don't know why Roland would still desire your services. Come on, Maxx. You are far more advanced in your experience with sex schwuler style than that. You surely realized since you have been with him, Roland is not a true bottom, Maxx. He enjoys both situations. Too bad that I cannot provide for his interest in playing the top. I tried that back in my younger days and that shit is not for Matz. Yuck. He and I made the agreement he can fulfil his needs for the penetration sex only with you. The whore Maxx is the safe solution to our one weakness between us. I can enjoy my lover and he will alleviate any frustrations at my inability to return the favors the way he likes with you. I can be assured my Roland will not be seeking such a thrill in the arms of one that maybe would work to replace me."

I groaned and covered my eyes at that horror. "Okay, fine, I understand that. I want to give this apartment to Karsten and the children. I will agree to provide the service he has paid for. That said, I will not relent my vote of nein in his moving in with us Matz. I will not have him in the next room like a fucking spider waiting to pounce every chance he gets. Forget it. Now that you have someone to attend your baser urges I can finally have my apartment sanctuary back. I intend to keep it free of the demands of sex that I don't desire." It was making me sick that I had ended Matz interest in me but gained Roland's in his place. Damn if I am not the unlucky motherfucker.

Matz scoffed then put his feet up on the coffee table "Once again you are not paying attention, Maxx. I told you

322

that Roland and I agreed to monogamy with each other, with one exception, you. It is only fair that if my lover can enjoy your artistry when he can afford it that his Matz be permitted the same mercy. In fact, we agreed that unless there is a good reason neither of us can be with you without the other allowed to be involved if he chooses to be. You can keep Roland from moving in officially if that is what you really want, but you would be a fool to say nein. He will still be here when I call in my service or him with you. At least with him as the third roommate you and I will have a much easier time affording the needs of the growing family of black collars. That is what you intend to do, ja? Purchase more silvers? Then I would suggest you accept Roland's most generous offer and get the fuck over yourself. Besides, I could use his help keeping up with you. Your illness is a bitch to handle all alone. Roland is calmer in nature. He will keep me from fucking up with you as I have been doing."

I sat there with my mouth open in shock. This was worse than hearing that Matz was moving out to be with Roland. I didn't know what to say to Matz. I wanted badly to help the little silvers, Karsten and the black collar flock, but this arrangement he was proposing was intolerable.

I couldn't fathom having to add both Roland and Matz to an ever growing list of men waiting in line to literally fuck me over. The idea of having them in my own fucking Haus as the paying customers and flat mates was unimaginable. This situation was turning into a fresh kind of nightmare that only the days in the bat collar could dare to compete with.

Matz allowed several minutes to pass before he cleared his throat and said, "Well, then it is decided. Roland moves in tonight. You will see the wisdom in this decision in time Maxx. You have no idea the cost of things. That is what I am here for. With Roland on our side, we cannot lose. Marc and the others will be safe even if your clients grow scarce. This is the perfect answer to all our problems."

I shook my head feeling the tears beginning to well up. "Nein, Matz. There has to be another way to aid the silvers and flock. Please, I need time to come up with a solution we both could agree to."

Matz snorted. "Christ Maxx, you are not in the position to refuse Roland's merciful offer, and neither am I. The tables and prostitution business are hit or miss. He has the steady income that we do not. I already told Roland this idea of his is a done deal. You will get over it. Now, why the hell are you home so early? You look a mess. What has happened with Jonas? Lucus will be here soon for his report. Are you staying till he gets here?"

I covered my face and began openly weeping. "Nein, I have to be back at the Vampire's apartment within the hour. Matz, I cannot. I just need to be going. Tell Lucus he can call me the dishonorable one. If I don't return, then he will not be getting any reports anyway. They don't allow me the pencil to write letters from Heslach, you know." I got up and tore from the apartment rushing down the hallway blinded by my tears of despair.

I didn't know where I was going. I didn't have to be back to Jonas's for another forty-five minutes, but I needed to calm down before the Vampire caught me in my weakened state. I started for the stairs when I suddenly thought of Jakob. I turned tail and ran for his place, hoping that his wise advice could save me from this horror that was closing in all around me.

I arrived at his apartment and began knocking with vigor. Several minutes passed before I realized my rock of advice was out and about. I leaned into his door and slid down onto my backside. I pulled the boy's legs up to my face and allowed the waterworks to flow without even attempting to stop the tears.

I felt so damned alone and hopeless. I feared that Jonas was right. Breaking that collar didn't change anything. I was more the submissive to him, Peter and now Matz (and apparently Roland was joining in the dogpile on Mad Maxx) then I had been to my Elder Masters' collar less than two years before. The knowledge that I was failing to find my freedom was threatening to tear the boy's mind apart.

I was deep in my sorrows when a hand laid on my shoulder sending me into terror overload. I led out a loud scream and tried to run reflexively. I had not seen Lucus slipping up on me while I sat there emptying out my pain in the open of the hallway floor.

He managed to grab my upper arm before I could flee from the scene in that blind panic. "Whoa, Christian. It is okay. It is only me, Lucus. Calm down please. I meant you no harm. I thought maybe you were injured or in need of aid." He held me tightly as I struggled to get away. It took a few moments to recognize his identity in my deeply traumatized fright.

When at last I understood I was not being attacked I said, "Get your fucking hands off me Lucus. What the fuck do you think you are doing? Planning to assault me right here in front of Jakob's door perhaps? Well, take a fucking number, you bastard. I will get to you soon enough without you trying to cut in line, pervert."

Lucus jumped backwards letting me go as if I had struck him rather than merely yelled. "Oh, my Gott. I would never do such a thing. Christian you need to calm down. I am insulted you think I dare such a brutish act against you."

I glared at him with pure anger in my expression. "Then be insulted and see if I give a good God damned. I am sick to death of all the damned sickos in this Haus. That would include you Lucus. You need to be somewhere else? I suggest that you get going to be there immediately if you know what is good for you."

He narrowed his eyes and scoffed. "You know I am a fucking Dominant too, Christian. I don't have to do as you say any more than you must follow my orders. I will leave when I am damned ready to and not because you demand it. As it is, I came by and see you sitting here weeping in despair. I was kind enough to see if you needed aid and I get treated like a criminal. You are most rude. I would think based on the condition you are in, any friend you can get you should be grateful to have him."

I dropped my gaze in a bit of shame that he was correct that I was behaving like the ass. "Well, I told you I am fine. So, if it so suits you, then you should go on about your business and leave me alone. There, is that better King Lucus?" I wasn't ready to be apologetic despite my being wrong in this situation. I admit it. I'd had a dreadful day, you know.

To my surprise he began to chuckle at that. "King Lucus? You are a comical one, Christian. I can simply never stay miffed at you for even a moment. Okay, I will be the bigger man and apologize for startling you like I did. I didn't mean to offend you. I seriously thought something was wrong. Like maybe that rat fuck Jonas had injured you perhaps."

I shook my head. "Nein and ja. It's complicated. I suppose I should apologize for jumping to conclusions with you."

Lucus stopped laughing and stared at me appearing a bit shocked that I said that. "Uhm, I accept your apology. I think that was one. Never mind all that. What do you mean it is complicated? Jonas either injured you or didn't. I don't understand."

I wiped my eyes and sniffed back my remaining tears. "I don't wish to discuss this with you, Lucus."

He snorted. "You must do so or have Matz give me back my money. I paid for the report of Jonas's movements. You either give me what I bought or forfeit the deal. Simple as that."

I sighed and shuddered as I looked at my boots. "I don't think you want to hear about Jonas's behavior this afternoon, Lucus. You said you are not interested in the twisted perversions of the Elders. I have no information otherwise to share."

Lucus gasped. "Oh hell. What could Jonas have done to send you into the crying jag here in front of Jakob's apartment door Christian? Shit, are you alright?" He looked me over from head to toe.

I shrugged. "It wasn't what that bat did. Well not really. Jonas is always going to be Jonas. I am accustomed to his brutality. It was that motherfucker Kilian and his brother Reece that I let get to me. I will be fine as I said. I am being the idiot to act like the novice to such cruelty is all. Sometimes it bothers me more than it should I suppose."

Lucus shook his head appearing more than a little startled at my words. "Kilian and Reece? Wait. What the hell did they do? I thought Jonas threw that sneaky bastard out of his apartment."

I nodded and blew out my breath. "He did and that apparently is what caused the situation that I ended up in. Jonas says he broke some Haus rule in his breakup with that snake. Then Kilian blackmailed him into granting him a favor or he would take the case before Gretta. Jonas was too pussy to take the punishment you know. Anyway, yours truly ended up paying that Bat's debt with his dignity and then some. Kilian took advantage by bringing his brother along for the sport with me."

Lucus covered his mouth in horror as his eye went wide. "Nein. That sonofabitch Jonas used you to pay a debt he owes. That is illegal, Christian. Come with me right now. We are taking this case to Gretta. You cannot allow this to pass without punishment for Jonas or next time it will be worse. He cannot do such abomination to a Dominant and he knows it."

I shook my head and did my best to keep the bitterness out of my tone. "I cannot turn him into Gretta,, Lucus. She will punish him there is no doubt. However, Jonas will retaliate by having me sent away to Heslach. Then Reece and Kilian can have me around bonded all the time for their sick fun and games. There is nothing I can do about this. Jonas is my guardian and the Altergott brother desire to have me locked away for their unchecked thrills." I covered my face with my hands trying to calm my desire to break down weeping again.

Lucus growled out, "Fichen Jonas. Ficken the dirty Altergotts too. You will need to kill those motherfuckers for sure, Christian. If you don't, they will keep coming at you. I see clearly there game. They hope to set you off and force you into Kilian's control. Those rats." He gnashed his teeth as his eyes flashed with anger.

That response surprised the hell out of me. "What? Kill them? Lucus, to murder another Dominant carries a death penalty for the Mad Maxx. You better keep your voice down about such a thing. I don't need a rumor floating around you know." I was starting to think maybe Lucus wasn't all bad after all.

Lucus shot a worried look around to make sure we were alone, then leaned in and said, "Look, I realize such a crime if discovered would get you put to the yard. That said, if you don't do something about these monsters then they will get you. Let me do a little thinking about how to end them without getting caught and I get back to you tomorrow on it."

I nearly fainted when he said that. "Is this a joke? Lucus are you trying to set me up? Who are you working for? I am not falling for this bullshit. I have no intentions of killing anyone. You go tell your boss, Gretta, Cora or whoever I am not a killer, damn you. I am not stupid. I can see right through you cocksucker. You thought yourself so clever. Nein, you are trying to get me recollared or worse, killed. I have to go now. You stay the hell away from me. I will tell Matz to give you the money back. I no longer will report anything to you."

I began to storm off as the stunned Lucus yelled out at me, "Wait a minute Christian. You got me all wrong. I thought you needed that money. Surely you cannot just throw away the cash I pay for your aid in the eavesdropping without risking difficulty maintaining your independence."

I turned around and glared at him with a sarcastic smile breaking out on my face. "Ja, I can deny your most dangerous, I mean generous offer Lucus. Turns out you are as shitty at predicting the future movements of others in this Haus as you are at hiding you true intensions to get me put away. Matz isn't moving out as you accused him of motherfucker. Nein, Roland is moving the fuck in. Good day to you Lucus. I have to go before that Vampire Mann of mine does worse than chain me up for his buddies gang raping. Do not bother me anymore. We are done speaking and that is final." I took off without looking back while heading to return to Jonas before I got into more trouble with him.

I couldn't figure out what was really going on with that creepy fucker Lucus. It was too far-fetched to believe that intelligent, wealthy man was suddenly discovering a fetish for the teenaged lover that far into his maturity.

As it was, Lucus had no history of messing around with the silver children or black collars of the Haus. Nor any man or Frau in all his time there. To think that somehow I brought out the child molester in that man was not logical at all.

I had been trying to figure out what game he was trying to play with me for days. At last, his requesting me to be his live-in lover made sense. I had to assume he was lying about his involvement in plots of the Haus. It now appeared to me that either Gretta or Cora had put the man up to tying up the loose end called Mad Maxx.

Both FemDoms had good reason to wish to see me dead. They rose to their positions thanks to their involvement in Peter's conspiracy to use a fake Priceless to hijack the two positions of ultimate power at Das Kaiser Haus.

Cora had taken the Head of the Haus after I cleared the throne of that pesky Xavier. Gretta was raised to the run the entire population as Head of the Voters thanks to my seduction of Jonas and subsequent submission to the Elders.

You see, she had guaranteed the greedy, lusty old schwulers her acceptance of their petition to own the Priceless collar if they would see her raised instead of Peter that was the one in line for that position. Gretta knew that my truthful identity as Peter's son, if ever discovered, would render her position null. She, Peter and me would all be put to the yard over that lie.

Now the funny thing was that Leo, Jonas, Peter, Gretta, and Malfred all were aware of the truth. So, with so many already in on the secret and nothing happening over it why did the FemDom still fear me?

Well, the answer was simple. Neither Claus nor Cora knew of it. Kilian didn't either nor did the other Voters. As long as those two stayed ignorant of the full plot details, then Gretta's position was safe. If they ever found out she knew, the end would come swiftly for her. Cora and her were no longer allies.

You don't know this, but the females can be quite nasty when their relationships bust up. Cora and Gretta were both the hot-headed types. Over the years they had been off and on again lovers. Gretta is the bisexual while Cora is the truthful Lesbian.

When Gretta left Cora's bed for a handsome Dominant from among the Voters of a sister Haus, the old woman blew a fuse. Then to make matters worse, Rolf and Peter both had a quick love affair with the fickle Gretta that forced Cora to witness her desired Frau rubbing her newfound lovers right into her face. Needless to say, by that time Gretta was no friend of the jilted and angered Cora.

My assuming Lucus was secretly in the employ of the shady FemDom head of the Voters was not such a paranoid thing to think. With so many reasons to see my mouth shut for good, there was no doubt Gretta could send someone after me. It seemed to make perfect sense to suspect him of such foul skullduggery, you know.

However, it would turn out this time, your Master Maxx was wrong. Lucus was not aiding that criminal female at all. The one thing I could never have guessed was that the man was instead looking to knock both Queens off of their thrones. He intended for the Haus Monarchy to be run by the King instead, but we get ahead of ourselves, ja? We will get to the soon enough.

I knocked on the door and the Vampire answered. He kept his furious gaze to the floor while he stood there holding the door open. I flinched when I noticed the large bandage across his forehead. I had cut him rather good with that vase I threw at him.

I trembled as I said, "Am I to come in or are the white coats coming for me?"

He growled out in a pout. "Depends, Christian Axel, is the Guard coming for me?"

I shook my head. "I told no one of your crime."

Jonas looked up with a small smile on his bat face. "I spoke to no one of your own. Come inside and we let this be forgotten. However, you ever throw, strike, bite or accost me in any way again, you can trade in that beautiful black I give to you to wear for the white jacket with only one arm. You hear me?"

I nodded as I dropped my gaze in defeat. "Ja, I understand, Jonas. I give you no further quarrel. I don't desire to fight with you."

He chuckled as he pulled me into his disgusting embrace. "Nor do I want to battle with you, my beauty. I forgive you this time. What do you say to me for showing mercy, Christian Axel?"

I endured his hugging while keeping my eyes on Mad Maxx. He was having to restrain Christian pretty hard. "I thank you for it, Jonas." I nearly choked on the words.

Th Vampire let me out of his arms. "That is my boy. Now, we go to the Great Hall. Claus and Malfred have agreed to join us for dinner."

I looked up with a tiny shard of hope in my heart. "And my honorable Uncle Leo? Is he coming to supper as well?"

Jonas shot me a hateful look. "Huh? Nein, I didn't ask him to go with us. That old biddy is a drag since you went to the hospital. I don't desire his company to ruin my digestion. All he does is mope and pout. I think he is suffering the hardships of the lonely bed that comes with his station."

I glared at him. "You and Claus do not have such difficulties, ja? I thought you told Leo you would share your glory with him for his part in your hijacking my freedom. What happened to that promise?"

Jonas really roared in laugher at that. "Ah, you are the strange boy. You hate the sex with the man but here you are asking about taking on another cock? Damn, Christian Axel. You'd almost believe you are the schwuler with questions like that. For your information Leo can call your services any time he likes. I don't deny him. However, he must ask me for them himself and I refuse him any overnight cuddling. He says out of pure principle he refuses to be beholden to my good favor. Oh well, his loss, ja?" The vampire reached out and swatted my sore backside.

I yelped then dropped my gaze as he continued chuckling in great humor. "Well then, too bad for Leo, I guess. Oh, and Jonas. I am the schwuler. I told you this already. I even joined the Friends, Brothers, Lovers Club of the Haus." They were called the FBL for short, of course.

That made the Vampire nearly choke on his own spit in shock. "What? Nein, you did not. That social group is only for the gay men of Das Kaiser Haus. You are not schwuler, Christian Axel. No way they let you, a straight man, join them."

I smiled as I watched the pure fear start to creep into his expression. "Shows how much you pay attention, Jonas. I keep trying to tell you, but you are not listening. I am the schwuler and I have the live-in Matz and my Mann to prove such. Kay and Eric have invited me to join them with their own prissy hands. You don't have to believe me. In time you will see that I desire nothing but to be in your bed. Even though you seem to have no issue with sharing your lover, I am only interested in you. Last I checked you are a man so that means I am gay after all. You opened my eyes to my mistake of thinking myself straight, don't you know. Did you say we are to be at the Great Hall? I do think we are going to be late, ja?" I was enjoying his fright at the fact that I maybe was telling the truth and no longer interested in finding him that female Priceless he wanted.

Jonas nodded with that stunned look on his face. "Uhm, ja, sure we need to go. You know Christian Axel, I was thinking maybe I should speak with Peter. You know, get him to allow you an experience or two with the Frau. Just for a little practice for the Frau of yours of course. What do you think of that?"

I shrugged. "I wouldn't bother if I were you. Peter could give me complete control of my sexual services and I would still be in your bed ready to serve you and only you. As it is, I am feeling a bit moody over having to endure Peter and his buddies. I come home to my truthful lover expecting a little tenderness over such indignity. Instead, the Mann I love trades me like chattel to that snake and his brother. I must say I am beginning to think you don't care for me the way I do you, Jonas. That is too bad. I would have been the honest partner to you but since you think it okay to have me fucked by others, then next time I choose one myself. The FBL is just the place to find a sturdy young stud to give me all the rough thrill I want. Oh, my goodness. Listen to me rambling on about such things that matter not to you Jonas. I apologize. I am ready to go to the Great Hall if you are." I turned and headed out the door.

I had to cover my mouth the whole way to the Great Hall. It was nearly impossible to hide my smile of wickedness. I was enjoying that I had managed to goad old Jonas into buying that I intended to cuckold him over that Kilian business. He was sullen, somber and silent the whole walk there.

It served him right. I may not have been capable of turning him over for punishment but I sure as shit could teach him a lesson myself. I let Maximillian take the wheel and do his magic to make sure Jonas would think twice before ever trading me off to anyone like his submissive again.

Claus and Malfred were already waiting at the table when we arrived. I smiled with evil as I pulled out Jonas's chair but kept my eyes on my two victims. I intended to seduce Malfred and Claus as if they weren't already puddy in my hands long before that night. The second I sat down, my tongue went silver, and the show began.

I spent the next two hours doing all I could to openly flirt with both Elders. I was without any shame in my candid wanton speaking and eye cuddling. I spent a great deal of time acting as if I was hanging on every word the men said. I directed my seduction behaviors at Malfred in particular because I knew that would really piss Jonas off the most. I was careful not to neglect the grieving Claus. He was acting more like his old self thanks to my obvious attempts at distraction.

Malfred was loving every second of his sudden appearance of having gained my adoration after assuming I hated him for truth. Claus was also more than a little eager to be lavished with my attentions. During this entire staged act as the lusty whore looking for a good time, Jonas sat there fuming, unable to do a thing to stop me.

I realized such a disgusting display should have been beneath me. That said, Jonas had to pay something for allowing the Altergott brothers to rape me in payment for his crime. If I could have seen him whipped or put into the yard it still wouldn't have made up for what he did to me. This minor threat of my finding a thrill in another's bed was the best I could do given the circumstances.

Believe me when I tell you, my little revenge tactic worked wonders. Jonas was without a doubt more than a little worried by the end of that meal that his precious plans for the Female Priceless were in serious peril. His Priceless stallion had convinced him he'd gone schwuler, or at least bisexual for truth.

If my acting job in the Great Hall didn't completely cause him to find my claims credible, the one I did in his bed that night sure as shit did. The moment he got me into his room I came at him like I couldn't wait to have him take me. The Vampire nearly fainted at my feigned, but realistic interest and crude descriptions of what I wished him to do to me. Thanks to Jakob I had learned such things that made a bottom appear eager.

Of course, I was lying thru my teeth, err, nubs. Sex with him, or any man, was the last thing I really desired that night. The boy's flesh burned and ached from that rough abuse at the hands of Peter, Hermann, Jonas, and the Altergott brothers earlier. I ignored the pain and continued my unbridled attempts to appear lustful.

Da Vampire bought the act as fully as he had the flirting bullshit earlier with Malfred and Claus. For the first time in all the years I had been with him, Jonas was the one on the run that night. He was not so interested in the couple with a willing Christian Axel.

Ja, you heard me. He couldn't gain an erection. Hell, if I had known such a thing could have gotten me out of a service to that fool earlier, then shit I would have screamed fuck me to him every time he even looked my direction.

Sadly, this bullshit of appearing the aggressor only worked that once. I have tried it since then, and most of the time it does the reverse. Let me give you a valuable piece of advice my Demonseed Frau. Don't ever flirt with the Vampire or appear thrilled at his touching unless you are ready to carry out every promise and sexual threat you utter to him. The very next morning when he came at me, after a night of enduring his nasty cuddle and dreadful snoring, I pulled it again.

Well, as I said, be prepared for your bluff to be called. This time the Vampire was most happy to make all my fake foul dreams come true. When he was through plowing me like the sailor back for shore leave after five years at sea, that sonofabitch rested and went for seconds.

I was barely able to walk by the time the clock struck nine. I was more than a little grateful to be finally free of his claws. If he had gone for thirds I would have needed a fucking wheelchair to get around the rest of the day, no doubt. Yuck and double yuck! I had to practically claw my way out of his glue like goodbye embrace and nasty lippy kissing.

I rushed down the stair not bothering to attempt to sneak over to say good morning to my lover Leo. I'd had enough of any man holding me in his grip. Poor Leo would have to wait until I could shower and scrub several inches of skin off. I needed to feel fresh before I could tolerate another sexual situation with either gender. I could not be sure about the females since I never got to be with any of them.

I busted thru the apartment door to find Matz and Roland sitting there on the couch. I groaned as I recalled that bullshit arrangement that Matz had approved behind my back with the violinist. I shot them both an angered look as I hurried past them headed for the shower.

I was ready to punch either man that dared to speak a single word to me that morning. To their credit they seemed to read my lack of tolerance for conversation. They sat there in silence and allowed me space to attend to my second shower of that morning without interruption.

When I finished my freshening rituals I hurriedly dressed and returned to my bedroom. I sat down on the floor with Felicity and rushed thru the last few lessons that Peter had assigned me the first day of the Dominance training. I was in no hurry to get another thudding no matter how light it may have been the day before.

I had just finished and was packing up the books to ready myself for the trek down to see Peter when a knocking began at the bedroom door. I growled out that whoever it was could enter. Matz stepped into the room appearing a bit nervous.

I glared at him but kept packing up the books into my bag. "Well? What the fuck do you want Matz. I am heading off to my appointment so make it quick."

He nodded. "Uhm, well you have Fritz tonight at nine to attend. Roland and I discuss it and we will take our services from you around three when you get back from the dentist."

I stopped everything and looked up at him in shock. "Okay Matz, I don't know what bothers me more. That you and Roland are the greedy pigs to be asking for your service so quickly or that you seem to think I am going to see that dentist again. I told you I am not interested in either of those things you speak of. Leave me be and wait till I am done with Fritz to call the favors. I thank you for the mercy of it."

Matz shook his head but kept his eyes out of my gaze. "Nei, you will go to that dentist. The honorable Leo, you uncle has already paid the man. As for me and Roland, we are not going to wait three days in line. We are the customers like Fritz or Osvin. You come home at three and attend your job. Karsten's new apartment is already being procured and as soon as the black collar maids have it ready, she moves in. You owe the service for that service. That is the way it works, and you know it."

I groaned as I put the last book in the bag. "Fuck, fine then. I will be here at three. You are both the bastards for being so cruel."

Matz looked up at me with seriousness. "It is not cruel to get something for the sacrifice he and I both make for you. He could have moved to the third or even fourth floor. I could have left you and moved in with him. We are honorable to you, are helping you keep the children safe, and you will be the honest one back for it. That is final. Stop arguing what you know is our right. That said, I almost forgot to tell you. Geraldine left your breakfast. Come grab it before you leave and take your pills. The Dentist expect you by twelve thirty. Do not be late or I am sure Leo will not be thrilled. Oh, and what the fuck did you say to Lucus? He came by this morning and demanded his money back. The Dominant said he no longer requires our services. Did you attack him again? Can I assume the Guard is coming to punish you for it?"

I shook my head as I pushed past him to head for the kitchenette. "I didn't touch him, Matz. That is why he is pissed off. Glad you did as he told you and gave it back. That is at least one problem solved." Matz followed me as I grabbed Geraldine's plate of food.

He winced as if my words injured him. "Maxx you are the fool. It was easy money Lucus offered us. I guess you would rather earn it the hard way, ja? You forgot your pills."

I took off the plastic and grabbed the pancakes then headed for the door. "Lucus didn't offer easy money, you idiot. I may as well get paid for what I am already forced to do. There is no reason to add that fucking intrigue business to my shitty lot in life, Matz. As for the pills, you can forget them. Jonas ordered me to stop taking them. You have a problem with that take it up with that bat. I don't desire anymore black eyes and I hate that poisoned shit anyway."

Roland gasped as I hurried past him. "Matz, oh shit. You cannot let him go without taking his meds. You know what Malfred said brother."

I stopped and glared at Roland with hate burning in my eyes. "You can shut up about anything fucking Malfred has to say in this Haus, Roland. Your so called brother already betrayed him by becoming Lucus's man anyway. I maybe cannot stop you from staying here. I will have to endure your lustful interest for the sake of my black collar family. I will not however, tolerate your fucking sticking your nose where it does not belong. I am only warning you this once. You cross me again and I show you why they leveled me Priceless."

Roland leaned back on the couch with fear in his expression, "Maxx, buddy, hey calm down. I didn't mean any harm. Take care that you don't get sick that is all. I meant to help you out, not start a fight with you."

Matz snorted. "Now you see what I have to put up with, Roland. Maxx is the aggressive bastard. You would do well to let him go without arguing. He will be sorry for being the dumbass soon enough."

I turned and glared at Matz. "You are getting on my last nerve, Matz. If I were you, then I would take my own advice rather than giving it to Roland. You flush those pills down the toilet. I am not taking them anymore. and that is final, asshole."

I tore out of that apartment grumbling under my breath what evil I wished to do to both those idiots. If only I didn't need their help so fucking bad I would have done it too. I was still more than a little angered by the time I got down to the thudding room. I found Peter standing next to the chains laughing and visiting with that horrid Hermann.

I immediately trembled in fear. I was in no mood to be used as foully as I had been by that man and my father the day before. I decided to stand my ground and damn the consequences. I had finally had enough of this constant using me like the fucking sex toy everywhere I turned. It was starting to get more than unbearable. Let me say, the yard was starting to look like a coveted alternative to the life I found as the so-called Dominant.

Peter saw me coming in. "Ah, there he is. Right on time just like I trained him to do. You can be assured Hermann the boy will do anything to avoid the punishment. I think I will be the gentleman and allow you to go first today. I am feeling generous you know."

That really pissed me off. "Fichen dich. I am not going to let Hermann, or you fuck me, Peter. You try it and I will kill you." I threw down my bag and prepared for the fight.

Hermann flashed a nervous look at Peter as the man broke out in laughter. "Now this is funny. Look at that, will you? He thinks he has a choice. Well, I am glad to break the monotony of gentle sex with this little nothing. Looks like he has come to offer a thrill worth having for a change. Hermann, you take the left and I will take the right." The man smiled and nodded as they both came at me.

I swung my fist with all my might the second they got into my reach. I ended up making contact with Hermann in the chest. The man groaned and staggered but didn't fall. Peter stuck me in the stomach. I sputtered out all my air but stayed on my feet as well.

Hermann threw his fist at me hitting me in the jaw as Peter lit on me with another blow to the sternum. I gasped and backed away but maintained my stance of aggression. The moment Hermann came in for another swipe at me I struck him again. This time I busted his nose.

He groaned and covered his face as the blood began to flow. Peter let out a loud chuckle then flew at me hitting me in the groin. I let out a wail and fell to my knees blinded by the agony.

I gasped out and was barely able to breath. "You sonofabitch. That is cheating. You don't fight fair, you pussy."

Peter jumped onto my head and took me into a choke hold before I could recover and stop him. "Ah, you think I care what you call me? There is no pride in beating down my submissive. I fight to win Maximillian, not for honor. Hermann, you aid me to get him over there. We are going to have our fun with this nothing and make him thank us for the mercy of it, ja?"

Hermann nodded his bloody head then came over and kicked me in the groin nearly sending me unconscious from the pain. There is no reason to go into much more detail on this beating and the tag team rape after it. I couldn't do shit to defend myself as they hauled me to that thudder table.

They took turns keeping me restrained while the other did as he pleased. They made me beg them for more and thank them for their assault by the cruel practice of torturing my hodensack. *You don't have that sensitive part but believe me when I tell you my Frau when enough pressure is put on them. A man will do anything to stop the torment.*

By the time they were both satiated I thought for sure my balls would fall the fuck off. I was sort of hoping they would. Then no one could use them to get me to do as I was told anymore. S*eriously the damned things are a real liability you know. No matter how much or often they torture them it never loses its ability to send you straight to hell. Yikes!*

The sad part of all this is that I really no longer cared when someone used me for the pincushion sex. I was pretty fucking used to it. As long as they used the lube and didn't do anything too violent, I could almost ignore them most of the time after the first few minutes of their entry. The size of the cock does matter though, trust me.

I only fought Peter over it because I didn't think it right that he could bring in the non-members to whom I owed nothing to. This Hermann had no business taking his thrill with me when he never granted me a single service return. I had to stand my ground against Peter using me this way or I feared soon enough he would bring scores of friends each day. That simply had to stop, or I was sure to either find injury in their intercourse or even worse end up with a disease.

You see the Haus made sure that every resident, no matter their status, received free of charge STD testing every three months from the Haus doctor. If anyone dared to miss their testing they would be isolated until caught up or even exiled for refusal.

The Haus's foundation is that of pleasures of the carnal types. To not keep tabs on the residents sexual health would guarantee it would eventually become nothing but a pit of illness. Because of this ridged practice, one could be assured that the sexual partner, willing or not, was not going to give you the fucking clap or worse.

If anyone ever got back a dirty test, they would be exiled if a Dominant, killed if silver or marked if the black collar with a scarification letter on the upper left hand. Peter bringing in the strangers to fuck me opened me up for not only the indignity of truthful rape but threatened my life.

As you may have already guessed I could not leave the Haus. If I received an order for exile it was an automatic death sentence. With that said, you have to understand his bringing this Hermann in was an attempt on my life whether he thought of it that way or not.

The two of them had a good laugh at my panting, whimpering flesh as they finished up their brutality on me. I was already the broken man, and it wasn't even but a minute past noon. It was an hour of tag teaming, torturing shit right on the tail of that rough intercourse with the Vampire. Well, it was enough to send even your well experienced Master right to the edge of fucking madness.

Peter kept that asshole Hermann with him as he retrieved my books from the bag. I did my best to pull myself together and redress as he went over my lessons. When he finished, he handed me another lesson plan and reminded me of my testing that is coming Monday. I stood their trembling with my eyes down caste trying to forget the horrors I had only just endured.

He chuckled at my lack of going against anything else he demanded. I was forced to listen while he bragged to that man of his breaking me in as the small boy. I closed my eyes and tried to ignore the descriptions, which were still far too fresh and painful in my memory, of that horrible collaring ceremony the day I discovered hell on Earth for the first time.

They had quite a bit of sport over my silent tears as they discussed my humiliation openly between them. I didn't think that I was going to survive to make it out of that thudding room without falling apart on the floor as a weeping, insane, useless mess.

As the clock reached twelve fifteen, Peter finally relented his verbal attacks. He then told me that I was not to be attending his training the next day. He had to go to see a sick relative and would not be back in time for the lesson.

That happy news lifted my broken spirits just enough to allow me to limp over to grab my books. My tears stopped and I wiped my eyes before I hit the door. I managed to leave the two monsters with at least a tiny shred of dignity still within me.

I wasn't going to see that dentist, but I didn't want to go back to that apartment for a bit either. That horror of Hermann and Peter made me less than interested in paying up my end of the bargain that had gotten my black collar family to a safer floor.

I knew I would have to endure Roland and Matz's service request but needed a bit of time to settle down. I believed if I had to tolerate even seeing another cock for a bit I would blow a gasket and never recover.

Since I couldn't go hang out at Karsten's thanks to my own lustful interests in that beautiful woman, the only place left to hide was the dentist. I rushed to his office and made that appointment right on time.

The fellow was not an unkind man. He had me sit in his chair while he made molds of what was left of my teeth. The dentist explained he was using them to try to reconstruct what my teeth should have looked like. He stated it was going to be a tough task to do since there was nothing left to use for the pattern of the dentures.

Then he told me that over the years as my mouth grew they would have to keep readjusting the fake teeth. He was pretty confident that by the time I was twenty-one, the final set could be made and replicated as they wore out over my lifespan.

It was kind of cool to watch his working with that mouth clay and seeing the pictures of what the fake teeth would look like, and how they would fit inside the mouth. He was thrilled to be getting to use an innovative technology on me, thanks to the amount Leo was willing to pay him, that would allow my dentures to be difficult to remove. He didn't want me to suffer a slip that was common among the elderly at such a young and sensitive age.

I listened as he gave me the instructions for the upcoming surgery to remove all that was left of my natural teeth. I was surprised to find out the day he removed them, I was to receive a temporary set of teeth that would keep me from being all gums until I had healed enough for the permanent teeth.

The whole exam, molds and instructions took about two hours. He was returning in two weeks to get me "set up with a new perfect mouth." He then gave me antibiotics of a different kind to heal up the numerous abscesses under my broken nubs.

I was warned if I didn't take them all I could get sick or even die if any of that infection got to my heart. This was one time I wasn't going to argue about taking medication. He scared me enough to decide I needed this stuff no matter what the Vampire said about not taking any more pills.

I was just about to leave and was feeling better about the whole dentures thing when he said, "Just think Maxx. In two weeks, you will have a beautiful smile to go with your dashing good looks. The women surely won't be able to resist you. I bet you are already the most popular young man around."

I frowned at that and responded "That is my most unfortunate luck. Perhaps you can make the teeth look like a horse mouth. Then I won't be the item of interest any longer? How much would you ask to do such a thing?"

The Dentist stared at me in shock for a moment then busted out laughing. "Ah, you are the comic. I swear you had me for a minute there, Maxx. You are too funny. Have you ever thought of doing the comedy shows? I bet you would be a natural."

I nodded as I left. "Ja, there is no doubt I am since my whole life is a fucking joke." I wandered down the hallway feeling like the prisoner headed for the firing squad.

It was nearly three and the time to play the whore was arriving. I went up the steps keeping my head down and gaze to the floor. I couldn't have been more miserable had I been heading to my own funeral.

Lucus was leaning against the wall as I topped the fourth floor. "Christian, how pleasant to see you. I do hope you are enjoying a peaceful day." He chirped out sounding happy as the lark.

I glared at him without expression. "Fuck off, Lucus. I don't need any more trouble right this minute. Save the insults for later. I am all used up at the moment."

Lucus's smile melted to concern. "Alright, then I will try to avoid such dishonor. Peter brought Hermann again I noticed. You going to be okay?"

I stopped my march to the apartment and sighed loudly. "You tell me Lucus since you seem to know everything. I stood up like you told me to, you know. I have some rather painful bruises and not sure I will be capable of siring children but hey, I proved I was the Dominant. Peter and Hermann were happy to do everything I demanded they do."

He gasped then smiled., "Ah so you fought and won then. Good for you."

I groaned. "You are an idiot Lucus. I demanded they do what they made me tell them to do. Hard to maintain the façade of control when your balls are in a vise grip, brother. Tell you what. The next time you think to put stupid ideas of standing up for myself in the boy's head, just keep it to yourself, okay. I already told you once, better to suck a cock without the busted lip. Well better to be fucked by one without nearly getting your own broken off. You have a good day and leave me to my hellish one if you don't mind."

Lucus reached out and grabbed my arm holding me a moment as I glared at him angrily. "Christian, I apologize. I didn't realize that they would dare to keep torturing you. I assumed if you threatened them with Gretta they would relent their unfair attacks."

I shook my head in disgust. "You are pretty dumb for the genius everyone thinks you to be Lucus. I told you no one fears the Mad Maxx's words to Gretta. She wouldn't believe me since I am supposed to be insane. They can do whatever they want to me, and I cannot do shit about it. Look, I don't have time to discuss this with you. I am due in the apartment for more unwanted sex. Roland and Matz will maybe pull out the rake or rip off my toenails if I am late. I am tired Lucus. I just want to do my job and be left in peace. Please leave me alone."

Lucus led go of my arm and looked at me with pity in his expression. "Christian, if you will please listen to me. Take my offer to be my lover. I can stop this horror if you will allow me. Once you are seen as mine all of them, even Jonas, will back off their bad behaviors with you. They will fear my reprisals, I can promise you that."

I shot a look at the apartment door and shivered at what I knew was waiting behind it. And what about Matz and Roland? You expect me to abandon them when they have not done such dishonor to me?"

Lucus groaned. "Christian, you better start to think of your own welfare. You don't do something soon, then Peter, Jonas and the stinking Altergotts are going to rip you apart. Is that what you want? You are no good to either of them dead anyway. I dare say that with Roland making the minor fortune with a Haus job, the boys will do fine without living off the artistry of the Priceless. You come with me Christian, and you will never have to endure the lustful interest of some foul bastard for cash again. I will spoil you and grant you a kind hand in all matters. I am the gentleman both in and out of the bedroom." He smiled at me blushing a bit from his mild discussion of his intentions to sleep with me.

I shook my head. "What if you cannot stop Peter and Jonas from abusing me? Then what? I end up in your bed, without my support system of Matz and Roland, and still will suffer the foulest of assaults."

Lucus smiled with sudden realization that I was indeed thinking over his offer seriously at last. "I told you already. Gretta can ignore you, my love, but she won't dare to go against me. Those two will find out the hard and fast way I am not one to piss with. If they injure my lover, they will answer for it to the aristocrat Lucus. I will see they mind their fucking manners or pay dearly for it. Think Christian, what do you really have to lose? Do nothing and nothing gets better. Give Lucus a chance and find your luck changed for the better."

I looked at the clock and saw it was three with a loud groan. I said, "Can I give you my answer tomorrow after the FBL meeting?"

He nodded with a thrilled grin. "Of course you can, Christian. I will be there too. If I could be so bold, may I ask to walk you back to your apartment after the meeting? We can discuss this further then, ja?"

355

I nodded with a grimace. "Fair enough. I will see you tomorrow then." I took off for the apartment to attend my horrible job.

As expected, the sexual services with Roland and Matz was a nightmare come to truth. They were not violent nor crass about it. It was merely the fact that I had to endure them both at the same time. No matter how skilled you may be, such a thing is a lot of work. I was worn from the torture and poor night sleep in the Vampire's clutches. I simply wasn't up to speed enough to handle that situation without finally breaking down into tears the second Matz went to take his turn in the mount.

Roland had already found his orgasm this way and was far more sensitive to my obvious distress. He did manage to get Matz to rush the job, but it was too late. I was already in the crying jag. To their credit, they both stuck around doing their best to try to calm me down. It took over an hour to get myself back together.

Roland insisted I go to my room and take a nap. While I was sleeping the wolf called Fritz and put off his first night of service to the next. He wasn't trying to be the ass. He simply knew that I was at the breaking point. Looking back, Roland was most wise to do that behind my back. Fritz would turn out to be a real challenge. If I had tried to deal with his difficult ass that day after all that trauma, it likely would not have ended well.

I spent the rest of the afternoon sleeping off the terror of that last two days. That night, after I was told there was no job in the first-floor apartment waiting on me, I attended all the studies the horrible Peter sent home.

By the sunrise of Saturday morning, I was starting to feel a bit better. I no longer was desperate enough to throw all I worked for away so I could run to Lucus's arms like a little scared bitch. When Matz came to my room to ask me to eat the breakfast left by Geraldine, he found a much more peaceful less weepy Mad Maxx.

I came out to enjoy the meal left to me by the hard working lamb of mine with a bit of a smile. I was looking forward to seeing Jakob that morning when he came by to pick me up for my "outing." He always made me feel a bit more peaceful and as of late, if you don't count Lucus, he was the only motherfucker around me that I had not been forced to endure the fucking penetration sex with.

I was finishing that delicious meal when Roland came in and sat down on the couch across from me. He smiled as he watched me eat then leaned back to let Matz sit down next to him. I suddenly felt nervous at the way they were looking at me. *You know that look, Meine Liebe. Like day are seeing you without your clothes on, ja that one.*

Roland cleared his throat. "You know having you there with us in the bedroom yesterday was really glorious Maxx. I was thinking if you didn't mind too much of making that a regular thing. I mean I will pay for the pleasure of it of course. Just think of all the money you will make and without the fear of violent clients. You know Matz and I are safe."

I glared at him while I finished chewing, saying nothing. Matz shot him a look of concern then sat forward.

"Maxx, you should take this generous offer. Think of Marc, Kloe, Aara and Ghazi. You can get more of them even. Roland is offering to become the regular customer on your list. That is an assured steady income. You cannot beat that." He sat back and took Roland's hand into his own.

I scoffed. "In my Haus? I will have a fucking client living in the bedroom next to mine. That gives new meaning to taking your work home with you, doesn't it? Have either of you considered how you would feel if the thing you hate most was your flat mate?"

Roland gasped. "Are you saying you hate me, Maxx?"

I shook my head. "Nein, I hate enduring the sex with you Roland and even more with Matz. However, I am not the picky guy. I hate all sex with a fucking man."

Matz growled out. "Well for someone that bitches about it so much you certainly are skilled at it. Enough of this discussion. You will take Roland's offer even if you are ungrateful for the mercy of it."

The knocking began at the door before I could argue any further. Matz rushed and answered it to find my date, the Queen Jakob, standing there with a big silly grin on his face. I wasn't willing to spend another moment with these most ungracious roomies of mine. I tore out of their snatching the thrilled Jakob as I rushed out. He didn't even have time to say good morning before he found himself being dragged by his arm alongside me.

Jakob led out a loud whooping noise the moment he was able to catch his breath from that surprise hijacking. "Damn honey. You sure know how to whisk a girl off her feet. Where is the fire baby? I wish you were in this kind of hurry to head to my place for a nooner."

I snarled back at him. "I apologize, my Liebling. The wolves in my apartment were getting on my last nerve. I didn't wish to spend another minute putting up with the bullshit they spew, nor have you be forced to endure it."

Jakob halted his traveling with vigor. He nearly pulled me to the ground with the force of his refusal to continue our wild run from my apartment. He stood there staring at me appearing a bit miffed, while I recovered from that near fall his sudden stop caused.

He shook my hand off his arm and glared at me with seriousness. "What the hell Maxx? I wasn't going to say anything, but I heard the rumor that Matz and Roland are lovers. I find there is some validity to that gossiping with that violinist in your haus this morning. My spatz, if there is any truth to what the haus is saying about those two you have to throw Matz out immediately. If you don't the other Dominants will suspect you are in the triangle relationship. Such a thing normally is a badge of honor for the schwuler, but not when the players are two criminal thugs and one feared Priceless. You will ruin your reputation."

I crossed my arms and snarled back at him, "What the fuck do I care what anyone says about me Jakob? Since when did wagging tongues mean a fucking thing."

Jakob snapped and then put his hand on his hip. "You better give a shit about this dishonorable situation you got going on, brother. Once it gets out you will be viewed as the low whore and without any respect left to your name. Less than decent Dominants of this Haus will be gunning for your favors. Is that what you want? To not be capable of going to gather a breakfast tray without fear of another mass attempt to rape you in the hallway like when you wore that silver?"

I nearly choked at that. "Seriously? You think that will happen just because Matz and Roland the lovers live in my Haus? I am not with them Jakob. How the fuck can anyone think otherwise? Matz simply cuckolded me with Roland is all."

He nodded as he clicked his tongue. "Ja, I can fucking see that Maxx. So can the rest of the Haus. Your allowing such an insult to continue without tossing Matz to the curb will appear to be granting permission rather than what it really is. The only reason anyone will believe you put up with that betrayal is if you are in on the love affair. You surely understand that."

I dropped my gaze to the floor feeling my mouth go dry. "Oh. Shit. I never thought of it."

Jakob snapped and flounced. "Apparently you didn't. Matz is taking advantage of you, love. You have to throw him out if he has decided to trade you off for Roland and that is that. Tell you what. Today, when I introduce you, we find you a respectable lover to replace that dog with. I know Leo will understand. He holds your heart, but he can do nothing to protect you from that dreadful Jonas or that horrid Peter's attentions. Honey you need to have someone with you that can stand up to those creeps. Even Leo would agree with that."

I shuddered at his words of advice. "I keep hearing about such a necessity as of late Jakob. Why the fuck can I not just throw Matz and Roland out and live alone? I don't desire to replace him with anyone, damn it."

Jakob giggled into his hand dramatically. "Ah, you poor baby. You surely didn't fall in love with Matz did you? I never assumed you cared for him other than sharing the expenses. Broken heart or not you have to get back upon that horse, or the other way around. You cannot survive in this Haus without an extra income. I know Leo would aid you willingly, but without someone playing the roomie to cover his help the rumors that you are sucking cock in the closets to pay the bills will fly faster than the winter snows. Jonas will drag you back to his apartment in seconds if that horror were to be spoken in whispers around the hallways."

I nearly fainted when he said that. "Oh, my Gott. No one would say such evil about me, would they? It is not truth."

Jakob stroked my cheek with a look of pity on his face. "You are so young and unworldly for one so badly used as you have been, my love. The truth is not something that entertains the bored residents of this place. You take your auntie's advice. We find you an honorable "cover" lover and avoid the catastrophe that is setting up in your world before it is too late. You know I would never tell you anything designed to injure you. This is for your own good."

I nodded feeling queasy as Lucus approached the two of us interrupting this most disturbing discussion. He was wearing his finest suit and was fixed up as if going to the opera rather than a silly club meeting. Jakob saw him and nearly swooned when the man offered his greetings. I could tell by the look on Jakob's face he was impressed with this man I viewed as a pain in my ass.

"Good morning beauties. May I be so bold as to request that you honorable gentlemen allow this humble Dominant to escort you to today's meeting of the FBL?"

I thought Jakob was going to pass out as he barely breathed out. "Ah, ja. Such an honor is most appreciated. We thank you for the mercy of it." He grabbed at his chest and fanned his face while blushing.

I narrowed my eyes at Lucus with irritation. "Wait, Jakob. Can I have a moment to say something to Lucus in private?"

Jakob's eyes went wide in shock. "Huh? Uhm, Maxx what are you doing? The Honorable Lucus has been most polite and kind enough to offer his escort. I think you are too new to understand the proper protocol. It is insult to deny him such a request."

I snorted. "You are mistaken, Jakob. I am aware of the correct manners in this situation. What you are unaware of is that I know Lucus well. I need to speak to him for a moment, then we can head downstairs."

Jakob was really startled at my admission that I was not a stranger to this powerful Dominant. He nodded in his shock and backed away to allow me a bit of space to say a few words to the man. The Queen stood over by the wall watching the scene in awe as I leaned in close to the suddenly thrilled Lucus to talk where no one could hear my message.

Lucus smiled brightly as I said, "So, if I were to take your offer Lucus, would I be able to get the details in a contract?"

He nodded then leaned next to my ear and said, "Meine love, if you say ja, then I do anything you ask of me. A contract can be arranged."

I pulled back and nodded while keeping my eyes to the floor. "Okay then. I suppose we should be going. We don't wish to be late to our first meeting, ja?"

Lucus's grin was so large it nearly cut his face in half as he offered his arms for me and Jakob to take. "I agree Maxx. Shall we be off then? Let's go and join our brothers and start the tongues wagging. I wish for everyone to see how blessed Lucus this morning is to have two of the best looking men in the Haus with him." Jakob giggled and swooned as I rolled my eyes at that bullshit.

The three of us took off down the stairs arm in arm as I considered Jakob's warning and Lucus's offer more seriously. I guess Lucus thought I had already decided to say ja to his offer, though he was wrong. I merely wanted to know what protections I could get before making up my mind.

I wanted to look over other potential candidates while I had the opportunity to see all the schwulers of worth in a single place. Only one thing was truthfully clear that morning. Matz and Roland had to go and the Priceless had no choice but to go on the hunt for a new roommate before my nightmare got any worse. As if it weren't already almost as bad as it could get.

Eric and Kay, the longtime lovers and heart of the FBL, met our strange threesome at the entrance of the Great Hall. It was going to prove to be an "outing" unlike anything the FBL or I had ever encountered before. Like everything else about my life in the Haus, the legend of the events that morning would become Priceless.

To be continued in book four of The Collar King Series: The Golden Collar

About Author: Alexandria May Ausman

Alexandria May Ausman in her 16th year was diagnosed with Schizophrenia. She was quickly abandoned by her foster parents. While still only a teen, she was forced to battle this devastating illness alone.

Alexandria has struggled with lack of a support system, numerous psychotic episodes, exploitation, homelessness, and an uncaring mental health system.

Alexandria raised two healthy children. After obtaining her bachelor's degree in psychology she worked as a child abuse investigator and became a diagnostic psychologist while acquiring her Master's in psychology. Alexandria never forgot the experience of 'slipping through the cracks.' Her life's goal is to help people suffering abuse and/or mental illness have access to necessary services. By accident, she became a model of 'gothic attire' and the World Goth Queen.

She began writing a fictionalized account of her life experiences after a catastrophic return of psychotic symptoms. Today, Alexandria is retired, and homebound due to crippling symptoms of Schizophrenia. She currently lives in Tallahassee, Florida, with her loving husband and a loyal support dog.

www.ingramcontent.com/pod-product-compliance
Lightning Source LLC
Chambersburg PA
CBHW071507260626
47170CB00002B/290